THE INVISIBLE FILES
Classic Monsters Anthology #4

www.YeOldeDragonBooks.com

Ye Olde Dragon Books
6909 Ackley Rd.
Parma, OH 44129

www.YeOldeDragonBooks.com
2OldeDragons@gmail.com

TABLE OF CONTENTS

FOREWORD

We're coming to the end of the fourth year for Ye Olde Dragon Books. What a wild ride! We didn't quite know what we were getting into when we broached the idea of starting our own publishing company over lunch at the Train Wreck Saloon in St. Louis during the 2019 Realm Makers Conference. Over the past four years, we've been blessed with some of the best authors in Christian fiction. They've put up with a couple of novice publishers while we "learned by doing," and they've been very patient as we grappled our way around the contracts, the editing, basically the whole process of putting together a collection of stories that are totally unrelated to one another except for the one underlying theme. The incredible creativity displayed by these authors continually amazes me. You would think that, given one theme, everyone would write similar stories. But NO! Every story is a diamond, different in color, cut, and size. What mind-blowing imaginations!

Fairy Tales were a bit more of Michelle's "thing," while my heart rested with the Classic Monsters of the fall anthologies. Slowly, we began to see them blend over these last four years. You'll always find a little bit of whimsy, a little bit of fantasy, a bit of science fiction, and a touch of horror in all of our collections. That's because we now have such an eclectic band of writers! We've even had a few historical drama pieces in past anthologies. We appreciate our authors, many of whom come back time after time. Their stories just keep getting better with every collection.

In *The Invisible Files*, we celebrate the character long-ago brought to life by the great Claude Rains in Universal Studios' production of *The Invisible Man*. He was a man changed by a science experiment gone wrong. We have a few of those in this collection, though not in the same vein as that age-old book by H.G. Wells. We have illusionists, super-heroes, vigilantes, and even aliens. We have some bad science experiences, and misused medications. We have some writers who are new to our anthologies, and we have many returning contributors who are the backbone of our endeavor. To all of our authors, new and old, we salute you and send our heartfelt gratitude.

To our readers, we do it all for you! Thank you for coming back time and time again to read these wonderful stories. We hope you will enjoy them as much as we have.

Blessings,
Deborah Cullins Smith
September 2024

It's hard to believe we've been doing this four years now. Next spring will start our fifth year doing the anthologies. When we release the as-yet-to-be-titled Three Little Pigs-themed anthology, we're retiring the anthology that launched the whole party, ***When Your Beauty IS The Beast.***

Thanks, to everyone who has ventured out on this journey with us. It's been fun, sometimes frustrating, sometimes nerve-wracking, sometimes mind-blowing, but always an adventure of discovery. Our authors are amazing, just the variety of visions and viewpoints and new ways to twist around a tried-and-true theme or trope, and make it fresh and new, and sometimes truly bizarre.

We couldn't do it without you.

So sit back, and since it's that time of the year, grab your favorite pumpkin-themed refreshment, and settle in for an exploration of what it truly means to be invisible.

Michelle L. Levigne

GHOSTS, PIZZA, AND OTHER COMFORTS
H.L. Burke

Belle sank down in the front passenger seat of her mother's sedan, praying no one from school would see her.

"I'm so proud of you, dear." Her mother beamed. She stared forward through the windshield, seeming to be blissfully unaware of her daughter's face, now almost as red as the caped hood that was part of her humiliating new uniform. "*The Slice of Enchantment* is our family's legacy, you know? Your older cousins, your aunts and uncles, even me! We all did our time serving pies and bringing joy to this dreary old town. Why, your dad and I even met there. I told you that, right?"

"Just fifty gazillion times," Belle muttered.

"Yes, well, it's the only place in Ivywood where dreams come true. The happiest place on Earth!"

"That's Disneyland, Mom."

"Nah, they've got nothing on The Slice."

Belle fell silent. It wasn't like anything she said would make a difference. Her whole family was delusional.

"Besides, this will be good for you," her mother continued, giving her an obvious side-eye. "You'll meet new friends, get out of your shell a little."

Belle liked her shell just fine, but there was no point in telling her mother that. It was hard enough going through her sophomore year as the daughter of that weird, fairy tale-obsessed family that ran the kitschy pizza place. Working there? What little remained of her social life was doomed.

Probably sensing Belle didn't want to talk, Mom turned on the radio. No music, just a news report about a recent supervillain attack in Yakima. The Department of Super-Abled's (aka DOSA's) superheroes had caught the guy, but only after he'd trashed a local convenience store. Belle indulged in a fantasy about a supervillain knocking down The Slice so she could get out of this awful first job. Not going to happen in their sleepy small town, though.

They turned into the parking lot of a dilapidated strip mall. Half the storefronts were empty, either with "For Lease" signs or plywood over the windows. In the center of it all, like a garish beacon, stood the fiberglass castle exterior of A Slice of Enchantment Family Fun Center, a long name for a glorified pizza parlor with a handful of arcade machines and an overly complicated theme.

Her mother pulled to a stop next to the side door.

Well, might as well get this over with.

Belle checked her apron pocket for her cell phone before springing out of the car.

"Wait! It's your first day." Her mother scrambled out of the driver's seat. "Can I come in and get a picture?"

Belle's chest tightened. Knowing her mother, that would be all over social media, probably with captions about the family legacy and how proud she was and how cute she looked in this stupid, stupid Little Red Riding Hood get-up. What if someone from school saw?

She thought fast. "Uh, I don't think that's very professional. Like, it's my first day at work, not kindergarten."

Her mother's shoulders slumped. "I guess you're right. You've just grown up so fast. Okay, then. Best of luck, Belle, and watch out for the Big Bad Wolf."

"Yeahhh," Belle drew the word out. Her family's weird, multi-generation obsession with fairy tales had been cute when she was six and she and her likewise "named on the theme" cousins had gotten together for princess tea parties and movie nights. Now? She couldn't wait to do her time at the Slice of Enchantment and be free to get a normal job.

She turned to the employee entrance and rang the bell. A moment later a lanky teen wearing a hairnet over his brown hair opened the door and eyed her skeptically. When his gaze fell on her red hood, white shirt, and black vest, he clicked his tongue.

"Ah, the fresh meat. Come on in. I'll get Phil."

Belle slipped into the backroom and the smell of cooking pizza, buckets of cleaner, and aging upholstery washed over her. Of course, she'd eaten at The Slice innumerable times. The family discount was too good to pass up. That said, she'd been actively avoiding it for the last two years. It wasn't surprising this guy, who was only a couple years older than her and probably hadn't been working there long, didn't recognize her as the boss's niece. Not that she'd been able to escape the place, even without dining there. Her family tended to use the building to host holiday parties, so she'd spent every Christmas there for as long as she could remember. She'd even been allowed to use the kitchen facilities for as long as she was old enough to help with holiday meals.

They walked past the area where a couple of women in hairnets and disposable gloves portioned out side salads, adding exactly two slices of cucumber and two tomatoes to each in turn. Ahead were the conveyor-style pizza ovens and the prep station with every possible pizza topping imaginable.

They emerged through this area, past the window with the heat lamps, to the section behind the counters.

A middle-aged, balding man was putting in the till trays. He looked up as they approached and grinned. "Ah, Dylan. I see you've met my niece."

"Uh, I guess I did." Belle's guide glanced at her, a single eyebrow arched. "I didn't realize she was one of them, though. Which princess are you?"

Belle's cheeks burned. "I'm Belle."

"We've got about an hour until we open," Uncle Phil continued, typically oblivious to her embarrassment. "I've got some tax paperwork I need you to fill out, but when that's done, Dylan, could you take her on a mini tour? She knows the basics, but you can give her the inside scoop."

"Sure." Dylan smirked.

About fifteen minutes later, Belle looked up from the last tax form and set her pen aside. She hoped she'd gotten her social security number right. She'd been too embarrassed to text her mom to verify it, like a little kid. Even if this was a lame first job, it was still a job. Time to start acting like an adult about it.

Leaving the papers on the breakroom table, she stuck her head through the door, peering out at the cashier counters. A couple of other employees had joined Dylan: a teen girl with olive skin and a bob of black hair and an older woman who was setting up the drink station.

"Uh, hey, I'm done with the forms," she called out.

"Great. Give them to me." Dylan held his hand out. "We can drop them in the office before I start your 'tour.'"

The teen girl snickered.

Belle's lips pursed. Sure, maybe this was a little lame, but they worked here too. Did being the boss's niece immediately make her less cool, though?

As soon as he had her paperwork, Dylan quick walked out into the lobby. The restaurant's garish decor continued throughout the building. The main dining area had a huge gas fireplace that was meant to look like a campfire, around which sat life-size statues of the Three Little Pigs. There were fairytale murals painted on every wall and chalked on every window. On one wall, a mannequin with ridiculously long hair leaned out of a fake window about halfway to the vaulted ceiling.

There were two dining rooms and a game room branching off the main dining area. Each was themed to a different fairytale. The room to the left had fake marble floors, a glittering chandelier, and elaborate "palace" details to represent Cinderella. The room to the right had walls painted with a forest scene and in one corner a large children's playhouse made up to look like Little Red Riding Hood's grandmother's cottage, complete with another mannequin asleep on a twin bed within.

Dylan jerked his thumb at the cottage playset as they made their way through the lobby toward the back office. "Cleaning that thing is a nightmare. Especially after children's parties."

"I bet," Belle said, hoping she sounded sympathetic.

The arcade/game room in the back was Pinocchio/Pleasure Island themed. Kind of ironic, considering what happened to the kids in that story. To the right of this was an atypically mundane, undecorated door marked, "Employees Only." Dylan tapped on this.

Uncle Phil opened it and took the papers from him. "Excellent. You showing her the ropes?"

"Yeah. What station do you want her on?" Dylan shot her another smirk. "She going in the wolf costume?"

Belle winced. She'd seen the "characters" who would roam about the dining area in costume, blowing up balloons or doing silly dances for the kids. The costumes ranged from the aforementioned Big Bad Wolf in a full-on fur suit to an aged princess dress with plastic tiara. None of them looked particularly comfortable, and all inevitably humiliating.

"Nah, just bussing to start. Unless you really want to do some entertaining, Belle?" Uncle Phil eyed her.

"No, bussing tables is fine, sir," she said quickly.

He laughed quietly. "I've got payroll to do, but I'll see you in a bit. Don't have too much fun without me."

As the door shut behind her uncle, Belle glanced around. "We're opening soon, aren't we? We can skip the tour—"

"Nah, wouldn't want you to miss out. Come on." He jerked his thumb toward the game room. "Let's start here."

A dozen arcade cabinets were crammed into the circus-themed room. A fake stage jutted over it with stringed marionettes suspended midair, unmoving and dead-eyed.

"We give refunds if the machines eat tokens, but only if the kids didn't ignore an out-of-order sign." Dylan motioned toward one of the machines. A piece of paper had been taped over its screen warning people not to use it. "Some kids'll just pull off the signs and try to play anyway."

"I mean, they're little. Maybe they can't—"

A burst of electronic music and flashing lights caused Belle to jump. She inhaled sharply and spun to face a retro-looking game cabinet that had randomly come alive.

"It does that sometimes," Dylan said blandly.

Belle steadied herself. "Do they all just … go off like that?"

"Specifically that one. Phil says it's a quirk in its programming, to draw people in by catching their attention. Me?" Dylan glanced at her. "I think it's haunted. Half the junk in this place is."

A shiver cut through her as the adrenaline from the jump scare faded, but then she pulled herself together and glared at him. "Nice try. I'm not six, you know?"

"Hey, if you don't believe in ghosts, that's great. Just letting you know, weird things happen around this creepy old place. Come on. I'll show you the costume room next."

He turned away and walked out of the arcade room. Belle moved to follow.

Something flew across the room and landed at her feet. Lukewarm liquid splashed over her sneakers, and she shrieked.

Dylan glanced back. "You okay?"

Belle stared down at the paper soda cup that had burst open at her feet. "Where ... where did that come from?"

Dylan looked around. "Some kid must've left it in here last night and the cleanup crew missed it. Looks like your first cleanup job. Congratulations."

"But ... but it flew ... or fell ..." She took in the room. Maybe it had been balanced on top of one of the games and toppled off due to ... a small, unfelt earthquake? The breeze of her and Dylan's passing? Something ... not ghosts.

"Yeah, that's weird." Dylan shrugged, then his eyes glinted. "But you don't believe in ghosts, so it's okay, right?"

She squared her shoulders. "Right."

Heart still beating a little too quickly, Belle followed Dylan across the dining area to another "Employees Only" door. This one, however, was not painted to blend in. Instead, a rose trellis framed it and there was a funhouse mirror attached to the door itself. Belle's grandfather, the founder of The Slice, had meant it to look like a magic portal, a "Through the Looking Glass" thing, though she wasn't even sure that counted as a fairytale. It didn't quite live up to his intentions, though seeing her own wavering figure next to Dylan's as he opened it did have an uncanny valley vibe.

Dylan flipped a switch and weak lights hummed to life on the ceiling, casting eerie shadows over the small storeroom.

This was one room of The Slice Belle had never been allowed to enter. Uncle Phil worried that the younger family members would dirty or ruin his "props" playing with them. Now she took it all in.

On the back wall were two doors marked "Princes" and "Princesses." Bathrooms or changing rooms for the performers, she guessed. Along the walls were shelves and racks of every fairytale themed costume imaginable. Pointed wizard hats, several plastic crowns, scepters, robes, dresses ... most impressively a full on "fur suit" of an anthropomorphized wolf slumped in the corner, its head lolled forward against its furry chest.

"Normally only the long-time employees pull character duty," Dylan said. "Though you're family, so maybe you'll get lucky? Think you'd like to be the wolf?" He pointed to it. "Check it out. You can even put the mask on if you want to."

She wrinkled her nose. "No thanks."

"Oh, don't be a killjoy. We sanitize it after every use." He prodded her shoulder. "At least take a closer look. It's cool, right?"

Belle stepped forward, examining the suit. Its glassy eyes had a dead look to them. The fur was bare in patches and matted in others. How many people had worn this thing? How many snotty kids had wiped their boogers—

The wolf's head shot up and grinned at her. It lurched forward, grabbing her by both arms with big furry mittens. Belle's heart tried to jump out of her body. She screamed.

Stumbling back a step, she tripped and sat down hard.

The wolf loomed over her, head tilted to one side.

"Ha! Gotcha!" Dylan stepped forward, pumping his fist.

"Wh … what?" Belle's eyes darted desperately from the teen to the wolf. As she did, the wolf pulled off its mask, revealing the girl she'd seen earlier, now grinning.

"Great job, Em!" Dylan offered the girl/wolf a high five. "You played that perfectly. I almost wondered if you'd changed your mind and weren't in the suit, it was so still."

"Pretty much held my breath after you came in." Em focused on Belle. "You okay, kid? It's just a little hazing. No hard feelings, right?"

Belle felt like crying, but breaking down in front of the two slightly older teens would only make this worse. "Right," she forced the word out, hoping it was convincing.

"Dylan?" Uncle Phil called out from across the restaurant. "Is Hazel here yet?"

Dylan stepped out into the dining area. "No. I think her shift starts at one. Why?"

"When she gets here, I want to go over the books with her. Something's not adding up again…"

Dylan cringed back, and he cussed under his breath. He quick-stepped it out of the costume room, headed toward her uncle's office.

"Thanks for being a good sport. I need to get this thing off. It's almost time to open and no way I'm cashiering dressed like a mangy German Shepherd." Em turned away and entered the room marked "Princesses."

Alone for a moment, Belle drew a deep breath. That had sucked. That had really sucked …

Something rustled among the racks of princess dresses, and she flinched. Was someone else waiting there to jump out at her? She narrowed her eyes at the clothes. Yeah, they were swaying slightly, almost like there was a breeze coming from somewhere. She reached forward and pushed them out of the way.

Nothing. Well, there was a small pile of candy wrappers. Kind of random, considering how clean Uncle Phil liked to keep the place.

"Eleven o'clock!" the older woman from the drink station called out. "I'm unlocking the door. Stations, everyone!"

Shaking her head, Belle let the dresses fall back in place. There was no such thing as ghosts, just lousy coworkers, but dang … this place gave her the willies.

~~~~~

It didn't take long for Belle to settle into a routine. As the youngest current employee, she was relegated to bussing tables, using the carpet sweeper to try to get up crumbs, and running pizzas, burgers, and other "kid-safe" foods to the customer's tables.

One of the few family dining establishments in her small town, there wasn't a day when The Slice wasn't busy. During peak hours, some of the employees would dress up in the costumes and go out to entertain the kids. It wasn't like Disneyland levels or even quite up to party entertainer levels. Mostly they handed out balloons and did TikTok dances … full on cringe. Belle prayed no one ever asked her to do that. She'd want to disappear completely.

Thankfully, after their first prank, Dylan and Em left Belle alone. None of the other employees took much notice of her either, though a lot of that was Belle. Making friends had never been easy for her. The few times someone tried to make friendly conversation, she froze or blurted out lame, one-word answers.

Mostly, Belle kept to herself, not hanging out for long in the breakroom before or after shifts, keeping her head down when she worked for fear someone from school would come in and see her in her embarrassing "uniform."

Uncle Phil checked in on her every so often, but he seemed distracted. The tills just weren't adding up, and a few times when she'd had to fetch him over something requiring a manager she found him in his office, watching and rewatching the security tapes from the cameras aimed at the tills.

After about a week, she decided that even if she didn't really love working here, it was … okay. The extra spending money was nice, and the work was mindless but not tedious. Sometimes there was free pizza and she refilled her water bottle with soda without anyone saying anything, leaving her on a constant sugar buzz.

Not that the place wasn't creepy. In fact, the longer she worked there,
~~~~~

the more things just seemed … off. Things would go missing then turn up in weird places. Sometimes she'd get a feeling she was being watched, even in sections of the restaurant that were empty and lacked security cameras.

On her two-week work anniversary, her mom drove her in for her noon to four shift in a thunderstorm. Rain hammered against the roof of the sedan, and the windshield wipers worked double time just to keep the road visible.

Her mom gave a low whistle. "Man, I haven't seen it come down this hard in a long time. I'll try to pull right up to the door so you don't get soaked."

"Thanks."

Jumping out when her mom parked, Belle rang the buzzer. A moment later Em let her in. Behind her, the break room was dark.

"The power's out," Em said.

"Oh, dang." Belle stepped out of the rain. "Uh, what do we do then?"

"Hang out and wait for it to come back on, I guess?" Em led her into the eerie restaurant where Dylan, Rodrigo the line cook, and Felicity who usually worked the pizza line were leaning against the counters.

"Okay, next question," Felicity was saying. "Favorite soda?"

"Mountain Dew," Dylan said.

"Coke," Rodrigo added.

"Interesting." Felicity turned to Em and Belle. "You, Em?"

"I usually just drink diet whatever," Em said.

"Not really an answer, but okay. New girl?" Felicity eyed her.

"Uh, Sprite, I guess. Why?" Belle asked.

"Ice breaker. We never really talk as co-workers, you know? Like I'm always busy making pizza while Rodrigo's doing the burgers, but who are we really?" Felicity held up her smartphone. "I found this 'get to know someone in twenty questions' list. I've already gotten through the first half with these guys, and I'm finding out a lot."

"Oh, okay."

"What's the next question?" Rodrigo pushed, clearly more into this than Em or Dylan.

"Uh, if you could have a superpower, what would it be?" Felicity read.

"Money creation," Dylan said.

Felicity furrowed her brow at him. "That's not a superpower."

"It should be," Dylan said. "Think about it, just snap my fingers and a twenty appears? I'd never have to work again, be able to buy whatever I want—"

"Wouldn't that be counterfeiting?" Em asked.

"So I'd be a super*villain*." Dylan shrugged. "Worth it to be rich. I just wouldn't use my powers where anyone could see."

"I still don't think it counts," Felicity said. "Like, I follow the Super Spotter Blog. I know all the big named super-abled people—we in the fan community call them sables—on both sides of the law. There is no sable power that would be 'money creation.' I think you need to pick a superpower that actually exists like flying or superspeed or pre-cognition or something."

"That's no fun." Dylan scowled.

"I mean, it's got to be flying, right?" Em hopped up to sit on the counter between the cash registers. "It's the coolest power for sure."

Rodrigo shook his head. "Nah, man, you seen that Wildfyre guy on the news? He can shoot fire out of his hands! Way cooler—"

"You mean 'hotter'," Belle broke in.

"I mean, if you're into older guys," Felicity shrugged. "I'll admit, Glint's also kind of a zaddy, and he's like my dad's age—"

Belle's face heated. She'd been going for a fire pun, not remarking on the attractiveness of the sable. Why did she always make things awkward? "Uh, yeah—"

"What power would you like? Remember, has to be an *actual* power?" Felicity cut Dylan a meaningful glance.

Belle's mind went blank, suddenly unable to remember a single superpower.

"I don't know. I guess I don't know a lot of superheroes. It's not like there are any in this boring old town." She forced herself to think, trying to remember everything she'd ever read about sables in the news or seen on social media. Only the most basic powers, like flying and superspeed, came to mind. That seemed awfully boring. Her coworkers probably already thought she was lame without adding her dumb answers to their game. "Is there anyone who can, I don't know, speed up time?"

"I've never heard of that," Felicity said. "What would you do with that power, though? Just make things happen faster?"

"I was thinking like if I was bored at work I could get to the end of my shift faster."

"That's not very heroic, though," Felicity pointed out.

"I mean, not all sables are heroes," Dylan said. "Some are villains."

"Do you have to be a hero or a villain just because you have powers?" Belle asked. "Maybe you'd just want something to make your life a little better without having all the danger and excitement of superhero-ing. Like if you had a power like that, you might not even let people know you had it so DOSA wouldn't recruit you. You'd just use it and keep it a secret."

"I don't know. If I had a superpower, I'd tell *everybody* about it," Felicity said. "Wouldn't you *want* to be a hero?"

Belle bit her bottom lip. Not really. She spent most of her life trying to stay out of the spotlight. Heroes had to talk to people, make speeches, be out there in bright, colorful costumes designed to draw attention. It sounded horrifying to her. She'd rather just … disappear. That was an answer, though, wasn't it?

"Is invisibility a superpower?" she asked.

Something crashed in the kitchen. Felicity and Em jumped, Belle flinched, and Rodrigo swore in Spanish.

"It's the ghost again," Dylan snickered. "Maybe you should go talk to him, Princess. Or would you rather go hang out with the Big Bad Wolf again?"

Em practically cackled.

Belle's skin crawled. Her heart still hammered in her chest, though. "Shouldn't we see what that was, though? Something fell down."

"I told you, it's a ghost," Dylan persisted. "You know all about—"

"It's not a ghost!" Belle snapped, the ferocity in her own voice surprising her. Dylan shied back.

"Dang, a little touchy about the ghost thing, are we?" He clicked his tongue. "If you're so worried about it, go check it out. I'm sure it's nothing scary."

Belle's jaw clenched. "Okay. I will."

She pushed past her co-workers and stepped through the swinging doors into the kitchen. Her skin immediately went cold. There were no windows in this part of the building, just darkness. She put out her hand and found the metal countertops on one side of the narrow "standing space." She knew the flat top and deep fryers were on the other, so she leaned away from them. They might still be hot even with the power off.

Dang, I can't see anything, though. She fished out her phone and turned on the flashlight. A good dozen to-go containers that had been stacked on the counter, waiting for orders, were now strewn across the floor. *Well, those are wasted.*

She took a step toward them, intending to pick them up and toss them in the trash, when the rubber mat squeaked.

She froze. Was someone there? Was this another of Dylan and Em's pranks? Trick her into going into the dark kitchen where someone would jump out at her? Did they really think they could get her again like that? Dang, she hated people—but if they weren't doing that, if it were just her imagination, and she acted like they were, they'd also think she was stupid. Like she'd pranked herself.

"Is anyone there?" she whispered, hopefully not loud enough that the people back by the registers would hear.

Nothing. Just silence. She held her breath, listening. Nothing. Maybe she really had—

The world exploded with snaps, whirs, the roar of fans, and so many beeps and clicks. Lights flashed on. She gasped and jumped, dropping her phone.

"Power's back!" Rodrigo shouted.

"Gee, thanks, Captain Obvious," Dylan said dryly.

Belle sucked in a steadying breath. What was with this restaurant and things trying to jump scare her? Now even the power was at it. Muttering to herself, she retrieved her phone, bent down, and scooped up the to-go containers for the trash. As she straightened, her eyes fell on something... On the counter, next to the to-go containers that hadn't fallen, was a hamburger bun, open, with a slice of cheese and some of the ham from the sandwich-making supplies on it. Beside this was a knife, covered in mayo. Someone was making a sandwich?

"Hey, did you figure out what made the noise? Oh, hey, um —"

She spun and found Rodrigo had entered the kitchen.

He cleared his throat and motioned to the half-made sandwich. "I know you're his niece and all, but Phil really doesn't like the staff to just make food in here."

"I wasn't ... That wasn't me," Belle stammered. "The lights just came on. Do you think I'd make a sandwich in the dark?"

"Uh, I guess not." He looked around. "You're saying there was just a half-finished sandwich sitting in here? That's... weird. It wasn't there when the power went off —" He looked around the room, cleared his throat again, and laughed. "Maybe one of the others did it?"

"I guess." Goosebumps broke out over Belle's arms. This was weird. Something was going on.

As she left the kitchen, she heard Em call from out of the Little Red Riding Hood room, "Dylan, you lazy butt, you didn't clean up the playhouse last night!"

Dylan looked up from pouring himself a soda. "Did too!"

"Well, it's messed up somehow. Looks like someone was sleeping in the bed or something."

"I guess it was just right." Dylan chuckled.

"That's Goldilocks, not Red Riding Hood," Belle said. Dylan shot her a dirty look. The desire to disappear overcame her again and she hurried out into the dining area, hoping to find something she could clean. She did a slow turn, looking around. A chair in the Red Riding Hood room toppled backward and crashed to the floor. She cringed. Great, more creepy stuff. She stepped closer, but before she could move, the chair *righted* itself, returning to its original placement.

Belle's knees knocked together. What. The. Heck?

A chair falling over, sure, that could be a draft or a small earthquake or maybe the rumbling of a passing truck. Picking itself back up? No way.

That wasn't possible.

Her jaw hardened. Something was going on in here, and she was going to find out what.

~~~~~

At first Belle's plan seemed impossible, but almost immediately things fell into place.

When she got the schedule for the next week, she had several closing shifts.

Then she'd asked her mother if she could spend the night with a friend from school after work. Her mom had been so overjoyed that Belle actually had friends she hadn't even asked who they were; she just told Belle to make sure she took her phone charger and texted before bed.

The sleepover excuse also allowed her to take a backpack with her to work without her mom questioning it. Now to put her plan into action.

The manager on duty that night would be Peggy, an older woman who worked there part-time to supplement her retirement. She'd be in charge of balancing the tills and making sure the building was locked up for the night.

On weeknights, the restaurant closed at 9 p.m. With the doors locked, Belle began her closing duties, making sure the floors were clean, the dishes washed, and everything spotless for the prep people who would be there early in the morning.

Peggy disappeared into the office to do the accounting for the night, leaving Belle to her work.

Belle took her time. The later she stayed for legitimate reasons, the less time she'd have to spend hiding afterward. Finally, though, everything was done. She went back to the office and knocked on the door.

"I'm all done," she said.

"Oh, good." Peggy glanced at the live feeds from the various security cameras around the business. "Do you need me to walk you out?"

"No, my ride's already on the way."

"Okay, have a good night." Peggy returned to her work.

Belle left the office and glanced around. There was a chance Peggy would watch the cameras to make sure she'd actually left, so she made a point of crossing the lobby where she knew she'd be fully visible.

There weren't a lot of cameras in the building. Some on the exits and entrances, one over the cash registers, and one in the arcade. The large number of blind spots gave her a variety of hiding places. The bathrooms, for instance, or under a booth table somewhere. After some thought, she'd settled on the prop and costume room. It had the most places to hide if Peggy actually did look in there.

Belle slipped behind a row of princess dresses, leaned against the wall, and waited. Time dragged on. How long did Peggy usually stay after
~~~~~

the last employee left? Making sure her phone was on silent, she Googled ghost-hunting tips. A lot involved equipment she didn't have. EVP recorders, EMF Meters, laser grids, and thermal sensors. Man, some people put serious change into this hobby.

She didn't think she needed anything this complicated. Just her phone camera to capture anything that moved in a way that it shouldn't.

When it had been about an hour, she finally dared to peek out of the prop room.

Eerie silence cloaked the restaurant. The arcade machines still blinked with colored lights and she could see the faint glow of the exit signs and some of the neon signs advertising the various beverage options. Streetlights also glowed outside, the light pooling on the floors of the Little Red Riding Hood Room. She stood and took it in for a moment.

Should she call out? Attempt to contact the spirit? See what it wanted?

"Come on down to Stevens Motors, where your new used car awaits!" an enthusiastic voice screamed into the silence.

Belle's breath left her body, freezing her in place, nostrils flared, eyes wide, heart hammering.

"Come down to Stevens Motors!" a woman's voice sang from the same direction. Wait. A commercial?

Somehow managing to pry her feet from the floor, she turned and peered into the Cinderella room. Light now flickered across the tables, but it wasn't some sort of other-worldly glow. No, it was the familiar light from the large screen TV the restaurant had in that room so parents could watch the game while their kids played.

Okay, nothing scary, just the TV ... but who turned it on?

She crept forward, eyelids peeled back for fear that if she blinked something would suddenly be right in front of her.

She reached the wall and pressed herself against it, hoping she'd blend in with the tacky decorations. The remote, which should've been behind the counter for the managers to watch over, floated in mid-air. Someone, or something, was holding it. Someone she couldn't see.

The TV flicked through multiple channels before settling on a station playing retro cartoons. A faint giggle rose from the room, then a chair pulled away from one of the tables.

For a long while, nothing else happened. The television continued to play clips of a cat chasing a mouse around. Occasionally there would be another giggle, but nothing else moved.

Belle's heart rate slowed.

Ghosts ... watch cartoons?

The cartoon ended and another commercial began. The chair pushed back.

Belle flattened herself against the wall, praying whatever it was didn't look in her direction. A minute later the fridge behind the counter where they kept the canned and bottled drinks opened up and a bottle of artisan root beer floated out, silhouetted in the light from the fridge.

This ... isn't really that scary. Maybe it's a friendly ghost?

Gathering her courage, Belle pried herself from the wall and approached the counter.

The root beer tipped back in a clear drinking motion.

Huh. Ghosts drink?

The bottle lowered and someone belched.

Ghosts ... burp? This makes no sense. Okay, Belle, time to be brave. Let's find out what's going on.

"Hey, can we talk?" She'd been so determined to be absolutely silent that instead of a shout, the words came out as a squeak.

A shriek, clearly feminine, answered her. The bottle crashed to the floor.

"It's okay!" Belle rushed forward. "It's just ... me."

Nothing.

Belle swallowed. Had she scared it off? Was it possible this was a dream?

She walked around the counter. The rubber floor mats had prevented the bottle from breaking, but soda had spilled all over. Belle picked up the bottle and grabbed some towels to sop up the mess.

"It's okay. I'm not going to ... I don't know. Hurt you? Heck, I don't even know if you can hurt a ghost. You are a ghost, right?"

"Y ... yes?" The voice came from less than a yard away. A shiver cut through Belle, knowing whatever it was was so close. The ghost sounded uncertain, though, and ... young.

"You don't sound too sure?" Belle pressed.

"Uh, of course, I'm a ghost. Boo!"

Belle crossed her arms over her chest. "That really only works if you lead with it." This did not feel ghostly at all. Something else was going on here.

"Oh, I guess that makes ..."

Before Belle could talk herself out of it, she lunged forward and grabbed at the air where the voice was coming from.

The "ghost" yelped and slipped from her grasp, but not before Belle's fingers had brushed against what felt like a knit sweater with a definite arm in it.

"Ah ha! You're not a ghost. You're a person!" Belle announced triumphantly. "How are you invisible? Are you a sable? A superhero?"

"Settle down!" the not-ghost hissed. "We can't talk here. There's a camera over the cash registers. Come on." An unseen hand grabbed Belle's wrist, and in spite of her newfound confidence that this being was just a person with powers instead of a malevolent spiritual force, Belle still flinched. A sudden twinge of fear went through her, and she pulled away. Should she be trusting this invisible person to lead her out of the safety of the cameras? After all, tills had been coming up short lately. The invisible person hanging out after hours had to be the reason, right?

"You coming?" the disembodied voice asked.

Belle shook herself. If the stranger wanted to hurt her, she probably could've already. Plus, she really wanted to know what was going on.

The not-ghost led her around the corner to the dishwashing station. Now that they were out of the camera's vision, Belle flipped on a light. Still no sign of the person she was with, not even a shadow like in that old fantasy book.

"Okay, now we can talk," the not-ghost said. "What do you want to know?

"You know where all the cameras are?" Belle asked. "Why does it matter? You're invisible."

"You kind of have to," the not-ghost replied. "I can't always keep my power up. It tires me out, and while I can cloak what I'm wearing, it takes a lot of energy to project it into objects. If the cameras catch me moving stuff or carrying them around, people will catch on. I can get away with small things because it's not like they watch the full feed every night. Probably only if something goes missing or gets broken and I'm careful — but you? You're right out there, you know?"

"There's no cameras here," she pointed out. "Can I see you?"

"I guess. It's not like I'm anything to write home about." The air in front of Belle shimmered and a teen girl with curly brown hair wearing an oversized black hoodie and ripped jeans appeared.

"You're just a kid!" Belle burst out.

The girl scowled. "I'm not that much younger than you. Not a baby, anyway."

Belle went over the first time she'd interacted with something "ghostly" at The Slice. It had literally been weeks. "How long have you been hiding in here?"

"I don't know... couple of months?" The girl shrugged. "There's food, bathrooms, I can sleep in the Riding Hood playhouse almost like it's a real bedroom. Better than my last couple of hideouts."

"Why though?" Belle stammered. "Like ... where's your family? Do you go to school?"

"Family — not really. Dad's in prison. Mom — she can't even take care of herself. Haven't seen her since I was thirteen." The girl hopped up to sit on the counter, her feet dangling above the floor. "They tried to shove me into foster care, but when I realized I had powers like my dad — he's a supervillain, not a very big one, but that's why he's in jail—I decided just to take off."

"Wow." Belle examined the girl's face. She wasn't very good at guessing ages, but she didn't think the girl looked much younger than her. Definitely not as young as fourteen, which meant she had to have been on the run for over a year. "How long have you been living like this?

"Three years, maybe?" She swung her feet, kicking the counters.

Belle's jaw dropped. "You've been living in pizza parlors for three years?"

"Not just pizza places. I move around a lot." A grin crossed the girl's face. "When you were little, did you ever look at a toy store and think how cool it would be to stay at one overnight and play with *everything*?"

"Well, sure."

"Or what about being in a furniture store and seeing those displays with beds and couches and wanting to actually sleep in one?"

"Yeah, I guess."

The girl stuck her chest out. "I've done both."

"That's cool." Belle looked around. "My name's Belle, by the way. What's yours?"

"Zelda—hey, we're both princesses. Our parents are so dumb." Zelda slid down. "It's great if you want to talk, but I need to get something to eat. I only have a few hours a night to do my chores before the morning crew comes in and I have to hide." She started down the narrow aisle between the dishwashing station and the storage shelves and prep tables, heading toward the pizza area.

Belle followed her.

"What do you mean by chores?"

"Oh, you know, things I have to do but can't do while people are here." Zelda grabbed a clean dish off the drying rack and approached the pizza prep area. She started lifting the lids off the various topping containers and selecting things from them. "Eating, stashing aside some snacks for later, cleaning up in the bathroom." After a moment, she seemed satisfied with her selection of toppings, so she moved on to the hot line. "Things that people would notice me doing even when I'm invisible."

"Like making a sandwich?" Belle settled her hands on her hips.

Zelda's cheeks reddened. "I got cocky with the power out, since I knew the cameras wouldn't be working. Sometimes I get hungry in the middle of the day and it's *hard* to wait for everyone to leave. With the power out and the kitchen dark, I thought I could grab a snack without anyone noticing—would've worked too if I hadn't knocked over the dumb boxes." Zelda opened the little fridge beneath the prep counter and pulled out a jar of pickles. She twisted it open and plucked out two for her snack tray. "That's how you figured out I was in here, wasn't it?"

"I mean, there have been a lot of little things," Belle said. "You're not as sneaky as you think you are."

"Dang it." Zelda grimaced. "You aren't going to tell on me, are you?"

"No, but … how long can you keep living here?" Belle asked.

Zelda took a bite of a pickle. "As long as I can get away with it. Sooner or later people catch on no matter where I am, but most don't immediately jump to 'invisible teenager living in my restaurant,' so that buys me some time."

"I mean, it's a weird thing for a supervillain to do." Belle chuckled.

Zelda's eyes flashed. "I'm not a supervillain. My *dad's* a supervillain. He hurts people, steals stuff, is … just a jerk. I'm not like that."

"Sorry, I … I didn't mean …" Belle stuttered. Dang it. She was even messing up this interaction. How come she could never make anyone like her? "I'm sorry."

Zelda's expression softened. "It's okay. I guess I do kind of steal stuff, but I only take what I absolutely need. Mostly food. Maybe clothes or something … never money or anything people will really miss. It doesn't hurt anyone, me living here, you know?"

"I guess."

"If you want a villain, you should look at that one guy — the skinny guy with an attitude." Zelda snorted.

Belle arched an eyebrow. "Dylan?"

"Yep. Guy doesn't do it when anybody is looking, but he doesn't know when I'm there. I've seen him pocket money from the registers more than once."

Belle swallowed. Should she tell her uncle? It wasn't like she had proof. What could she say? An invisible girl had told her? Nah.

"So we're cool?" Zelda asked. "You aren't going to tattle on me?"

"I guess but —" Belle hesitated.

Why should she believe that it was Dylan, not Zelda, stealing? Someone sneaking around like this had to be stealing to survive, didn't they? Living like this … it wasn't normal.

She'd already ticked Zelda off once already. Maybe asking prying questions wasn't a good idea.

"But what?" Zelda pushed.

Belle cleared her throat. She did kind of need to know.

"Are you really … happy? Living like this?"

"Yeah, sure," Zelda said, then her flippant tone grew somber. "I mean, there are some things I miss. It's hard to wash your hair in bathroom sinks and, you know, hot meals are hard to come by."

"You're living in a pizza place," Belle said. "There's hot meals here all the time."

"Yeah, but when the ovens are on there are too many people around for me to risk going out. I might bump into someone or someone might see me snatching up a piece of pizza or a burger or whatever." She sighed. "Don't get me wrong, I can get enough out of the fridge to survive. Do you know how hard it is to smell pizza all day, every day, and not get to eat any?"

"Oh, yeah, that sucks." Belle chewed on her bottom lip. "Do you want… I could make you something?"

Zelda's eyes widened. "What? Really?"

"Why not? There's no camera on the pizza line. Plus, I know how to operate pretty much all the equipment and I know where everything is," Belle explained. "Like, I don't usually make pizzas, but I've seen the guys make them enough. If we clean up enough so that no one realizes we were here, it shouldn't be a problem."

Zelda's lower lip quivered. "But why … why would you do that for me?"

"It doesn't cost me anything, and it's … nice, I guess? People sometimes do things just to be nice."

"Not in my experience." Zelda let out a breath. "Yeah, I'd really love a piece of pizza."

The pizza ovens had completely cooled down for the night, and it took a while for them to reheat. While they waited, Belle got a pre-prepared crust and ladled on the sauce.

"Okay, so there's a lot of options for toppings. What do you want?" She motioned toward the little refrigerated compartments where the toppings were kept.

"What … what can I have?" Zelda stammered.

"Uh, well, we've got just about everything." Belle tried to remember the whole list. "For meats there's pepperoni, sausage, ham, shrimp, ground beef, salami, bacon, BBQ chicken, and even anchovies, but nobody likes those. Veggies we have onions, green peppers, olives, mushrooms, tomatoes, jalapenos—Are … are you okay?"

Zelda's eyes were oddly … watery.

"Yeah, it's just … too good to be true. My own pizza with whatever … Oh, boy. I need a minute." She turned away, rubbing her eyes with the sleeve of her hoody.

Belle shifted from foot to foot.

Finally Zelda turned back. "What's your favorite pizza?"

"Um, probably pepperoni, olives, and white onion," Belle said. "You should pick what *you* want, though. I get pizza all the time."

"It's too hard to decide and that sounds really good to me too," Zelda said.

"Okay, I'll make that then."

Zelda loomed over Belle for each step of the pizza-making process. When the pizza slid into the oven, she positioned herself at the end of the conveyor belt, watching as it slowly made its way through the oven toward her. When it reached the end, her hand crept forward.

Belle gently slapped her hand back. "Careful, that's going to be super-hot." She grabbed a paddle and swept the pizza off the wire rack onto a metal pan. "You need to let it cool for a minute before you cut it or all the cheese will just fall off."

"Oh, okay." Zelda stood back, her toe tapping on the rubber mats.

Maybe it was just the privilege of having a pizza place in the family, but Belle couldn't imagine being that excited about just normal pizza.

Finally, the pizza was ready to slice. The cutter rolled through the greasy toppings, stretchy cheese, and crisp crust. Zelda snatched up a slice. She took a huge bite and her eyes rolled back in her head.

"Oh, man, it tastes just as good as it smells." She devoured slice after slice, not even bothering to sit down.

Belle turned off the oven then started cleaning up the prep area. Every so often she'd glance at Zelda. It was weird, but in less than an hour, it felt like she'd forged the first real friendship she had in … practically ever. Since middle school at least, when all her old friends had suddenly got cool and she'd found herself eating lunch alone most days. Maybe it was a friendship bought by pizza rather than anything real, but … it was good not to be lonely.

It couldn't last, though. Even Zelda said she moved around a lot.

"You think you'll stay at The Slice much longer?" she asked.

"As long as I can get away with it," Zelda said between bites.

"Maybe we can visit again sometime, then," Belle said, hoping that wouldn't be lame.

"I think … I mean, I can't risk getting caught, but it is nice to have someone to talk to," Zelda said. "Do you think you could maybe bring me some toothpaste next time? I ran out of my last tube weeks ago, and it's hard to sneak into drugstores. They have a lot of cameras."

"Oh, sure. We have boxes of the stuff at home. My mom gets the Costco packs."

"Thank you." Zelda glanced down at her half-finished pizza. "Do you want some of this?"

"Sure." Belle picked up a slice.

~~~~~

Over the next month, Belle figured out how to sneak little visits with Zelda. Not frequently, but once or twice a week. While faking a sleepover every night wasn't plausible, if she got a closing shift, it was easy enough to pretend she had to work a little late. She'd just draw out her closing duties until just before the manager left. She also found ways to leave little
~~~~~

gifts hidden in places that Zelda knew to check. Bars of soap, toothpaste, and food like noodle cups Zelda could just reheat in the microwave and get an approximation of a hot meal. Candy bars, which were Zelda's favorite. It was like having an imaginary friend — except she was real.

Just knowing that Zelda was around The Slice made it worth going into work.

She tried to keep an eye on Dylan, to see if she could spot any signs he was stealing, but if he was the thief, he was careful. Even Zelda admitted she couldn't prove it, though she promised to keep an eye out for Belle.

About five weeks after she'd met Zelda, Belle arrived for a morning shift, her apron pockets packed with Milky Ways.

She rang the doorbell, and the door immediately popped open.

"Where have you — oh, it's you." Em scowled down at her before looking past her into the parking lot. "I don't suppose you saw Dylan's car in the parking lot?"

"Uh, no." Belle stepped past the older girl. "Why?"

"He's a half hour late, and he's the only one we have on the schedule for the pizza line today," Em explained, walking quickly back toward the front. "Plus he had the closing shift last night and didn't do any prep work. We open in a half hour and nothing's done."

"That's weird." Belle frowned. Yeah, Dylan could be a pain in the butt, but he was normally a pretty good worker, at least from what she'd seen.

"He's not answering his phone either."

They emerged into the front where Uncle Phil, for once not hiding in the office, was pouring himself a cup of coffee.

"Still no word from Dylan?" he asked.

"Nope." Em huffed out an irritated breath.

Uncle Phil sighed. "Maybe it's for the best. Can you call up Felicity and see if she can cover?"

"Sure, but she's a twenty-minute drive away," Em pointed out. "Even if she can come in right away, we'll need prep done before she can get here."

"That's true." He glanced at Belle. "You think you could help on prep for the pizza line? I've never trained you on it, but you've seen it done enough, I'd think."

"Yeah, I know the basics," Belle said. Pizza line sounded way more fun than clearing tables and doing dishes.

"Good." Uncle Phil checked his phone before addressing Em again. "If he does come in, send him to my office. We need to have a talk."

Something within Belle tightened at her uncle's tone. Something was going on. Did it have to do with the stealing? Should she have said something about what Zelda had told her?

Phil headed back to the office while Em got on the phone, probably to call Felicity.

Belle's hand strayed toward her apron pocket. With Em busy, maybe she had time to stash the candy somewhere before work started. She slipped away and hid them in the prop room, knowing that was one of Zelda's favorite hideouts.

That done, she returned to the kitchen. After washing her hands, she slipped on disposable gloves before starting to set up the pizza toppings, making sure everything was in place for the lunch rush.

Em got off the phone, glanced over at Belle, nodded, then started toward the office. Alone in the kitchen, Belle started humming to herself.

"Ugh, what tune is that? It's going to be bugging me all day," a voice whispered a few feet from her.

Belle glanced at the empty space. "What are you doing out here? We're opening in a few minutes."

"It's safe. I'm invisible and the other two are over by the office." A slice of pepperoni rose from the prep station then disappeared with the slight sound of chewing. "I didn't have a chance to get much to eat last night. That idiot co-worker of yours? The thieving one? He was here way late. I actually fell asleep waiting for him to leave."

Belle arched an eyebrow. "Dylan? I wonder if that's why he's late today. What was he doing here that late?"

"Drinking." Zelda scoffed. "He was getting into the tap beers since no one was around to stop him. Must've had three of those big mugs you keep in the freezer before I gave up watching."

"Well, if you're hungry, I put three candy bars on the top shelf in the prop room."

"You're a lifesaver. I wasn't sure how I was going to get through today without starving to death." The mats squeaked as Zelda exited the kitchen.

A moment later, Em returned.

"Felicity's going to try to make it in, but she's babysitting her little brother for another hour or so. Congratulations. You just got promoted to pizza line," she said.

Belle let out a breath. "Really? I mean, I kind of know how, but I've never been trained—"

"It's easy. Most people just order cheese and pepperoni, but there's a few specialty pizzas I want to walk you through. Do you know what's on the Bad Wolf Special?"

Belle nodded. "Ham, bacon, and pork sausage."

"Good, what about the Little Mermaid?"

Belle wrinkled her nose. "Shrimp and anchovies, but no one orders that thing."

"True. Just wanted to test you." Em smiled at her for once. "Um … the Rose Red?"

"Roasted red peppers, tomatoes, and pepperoni," Belle answered.

"You do know your stuff. Must run in the blood, Pizza Princess." Em laughed.

To Belle's surprise, she didn't mind the teasing for once.

"You probably shouldn't make pizza in that." Em motioned toward the red cape part of Belle's ridiculous uniform. "Go hang it up and grab a prep apron and a hairnet. I'll turn on the oven. I want you to demonstrate your technique before the customers start rolling in."

Changed into her new, much less embarrassing uniform, Belle got out the dough for a pizza and began coating it with tomato sauce. As she did, something banged in the back. Em, who had been supervising her, looked up. Her mouth immediately pinched.

"I'll be right back." She hurried toward the sound.

Belle's ears twitched.

"Dylan, you idiot. You're almost an hour—Wait, are you drunk?" Em's hiss carried from the back.

"Ugh, don't yell. No … I'm … maybe a little hungover. It doesn't matter. I can do this job in my sleep."

Slipping off her gloves, Belle risked peeking around the walk-in fridge past the drink station. A red-eyed, disheveled-looking Dylan tried to push past Em toward the time clock, but she put up her arm to block him.

"Yeah, well, you may not be doing this job at all. Phil wants to talk to you. He's in his office."

Dylan's jaw tensed. "What about?"

"Figure it out, genius." Em threw her hands up. "He's waiting."

Dylan swallowed. Catching sight of Belle, he glared daggers at her then staggered past Em toward the office. He swayed a little as he went.

"Idiot," Em breathed before turning back to Belle. "So, where were we with that—"

"You can't prove any of that!" a voice screamed across the restaurant.

Belle jumped. She and Em exchanged a glance before moving out of the kitchen to listen.

"I've seen it on the cameras, Dylan. You've been skimming off the registers every time you've worked a closing shift for the last three months." While not as frantic as Dylan's, Uncle Phil's voice was still raised. "Your father and I are old friends, so I'm doing him a favor by not reporting this to the police, but you can't work here anymore—"

"I only took what I deserve! Working here for years! No raise! Barely any tips. I could make so much more literally anywhere else—"

"Well, then you should've gone somewhere else or, heck, even asked me if you—" There was a crack and a thud and Uncle Phil cried out, then another crash.

Belle's heart dropped into her stomach. "Are they fighting?"

Em's eyes widened. "I'm calling the cops." She rushed back behind the counter and grabbed the restaurant's phone off the charger.

Belle's knees knocked together, but somehow she couldn't move. Another loud bang. Was Uncle Phil okay? Was Dylan really desperate enough to hurt him?

The restaurant fell silent.

"Belle!" Em waved desperately from behind the counter. "Get back here. They say they've got a patrol car in the area. They'll be here in five minutes. Don't be dumb. Hide with me!"

Belle glanced back at the office door. It was open, and she could vaguely see shadows moving within. It was so quiet. She wished she had Zelda's powers, to sneak in and see if Uncle Phil was okay. Where *was* Zelda?

As if in answer, the door to the prop room creaked open about halfway and stayed propped open.

Okay there she is, but she's just watching. Probably smart. After all, invisible or not, she's just a kid like me.

"Em, you out there?" Dylan roared from the office.

Em dropped down behind the counters and out of sight.

Dylan stormed out of the office. In one hand he now clutched the baseball bat Uncle Phil ironically kept in the office for "protection." With the other, he dragged a limp Uncle Phil by the shirt collar.

"I know you're there, Em!" Dylan screamed. Then his gaze fell on Belle. His lips curled into a sneer. "You, Pizza Princess. I'm gonna need you to put everything in the cash registers into a to-go bag and bring it to me, right now."

Belle's shoulders hunched. "I ... I don't know how to open them—"

"You better figure it out." Dylan swung the bat wildly. "I'll bash your uncle's brains in if you—"

Something thudded in the prop room.

Dylan spun around and stared. "Who's in there?"

Nothing happened. Belle's ears strained for any sound that might be police sirens. How long had Em said? Five minutes? Would it be soon enough?

"I know I heard someone!" Dylan dropped Uncle Phil and took a menacing step toward the prop room. "Come out or I go in swinging."

Something moved in the shadows, something big and ... furry?

The Big Bad Wolf costume shambled out, glass eyes glinting.

Dylan's eyebrows shot up. "Em, you idiot. You aren't going to fool me that way." He shouldered the bat and stalked forward.

The wolf tilted its head to one side, like a confused dog.

"Don't be smart with me! Take off the mask, Em!" Dylan screamed.

Belle glanced back toward the counter. Em peered over it, eyes wide. The wolf extended a hand, pointed at Dylan, then toward Em.

"Stop playing stupid—" Dylan froze as his gaze followed the wolf's paw. Em ducked down, but he'd already seen her. His jaw went slack before his gaze darted from Uncle Phil, who still hadn't moved, to Belle, likewise frozen, to Em's hiding place. "Okay, so ... who are you?"

Sirens blared in the distance, but Dylan's focus remained on the wolf.

"Take it off! Take off the mask or I swear I'll beat you bloody!"

The Wolf's hands rose to either side of its head.

Belle inhaled sharply.

Dylan tensed, both hands now gripping the bat.

The mask popped off, revealing nothing. Just empty air where the head should've been. Dylan squealed like a little girl.

Relief flooded through Belle, followed swiftly by terror. Dylan lunged for the Wolf suit.

"No!" Belle sprang. She crashed into Dylan's back. Her blow wasn't enough to knock him over, but his swing went wide. It grazed the Wolf in the shoulder instead. The Wolf crashed to the floor.

"Get off me!" Dylan pushed Belle away, but she tightened her hold about his waist, holding on with all her might. The Wolf surged forward, swinging with furry paws. Dylan screamed and threw wild punches, trying to fend the beast off. One blow crashed into something solid. The Wolf sat down, hard, and Zelda's face flickered into view. Blood trickled from her nose, and her eyes looked dazed.

With a crash, two armed officers burst through the front doors.

Dylan fell to the floor, hands over his head, "Don't shoot!"

"Police, freeze! What the—?"

Zelda's eyes widened, then she flickered out of sight. The wolf costume blurred a little, as if trying to disappear with her but not quite making it. One of the cops rushed forward and grabbed her by the arm.

"It's a sable ... Do you think she's a supervillain?"

"No!" Belle gasped. "She's helping us."

"She's just a kid." The other cop shook his head. He pulled Dylan up and cuffed him. "From what the dispatcher said, this is our guy. Dan, can you check on the man over there? He doesn't look great."

"I'll call an ambulance," Dan said before releasing Zelda and hurrying to see to Uncle Phil.

Zelda flickered in and out of visibility. Belle drew closer to her.

"She's my friend. She's not a villain, I promise."

"Looks like you took a nasty hit." The officer indicated her nose.

"We'll need to get you looked at. What about your parents? Can we call them—"

"I ... I don't ... There's no one." Zelda's expression hardened.

"A teen sable with no one, huh?" He looked thoughtful. "Well, let's get you patched up for now. Later ... I know someone I can call."

~~~~~

The ambulance took both Uncle Phil and Zelda to the hospital, and a few minutes later, Mom came to pick up Belle. She managed to explain about Zelda—well, most of it. She somehow convinced her mom to head to the hospital. Mom wanted to check on her brother anyway.

They had to wait a while before anyone would talk to them, but after about an hour, the doctor came out and gave Mom and the other waiting family members who had assembled an update on Uncle Phil.

Apparently, he was stable though he'd been scheduled for a CT scan for his head injury. While they were busy, Belle went looking for Zelda. It was easy to find her, partly because the police officer from the pizza parlor stood outside her room. He nodded to Belle.

"You can go in if you want to."

"Thanks."

Belle slipped into the room where Zelda now sat, her nose a little swollen, but looking otherwise fine.

"You okay?" Belle whispered.

Zelda shrugged and shifted on her hospital bed.

Belle pulled up a chair next to her. "I'm kind of surprised you're still here," she said. "I thought you would've run by now." She dropped her voice. "I mean, with your powers, how are they going to stop you?"

Zelda glanced at the door to see if anyone was listening. The police officer seemed to be focused on his phone. "I was going to, but I thought you might come to see me, and I wanted to say goodbye first. I ... I can't really go back to The Slice after this. I'll need to find a new hideout."

"Oh." Belle's heart sank. "Where, though?"

"Don't know yet. Wherever I can find." Zelda touched her nose. "I shouldn't have tried to go after that guy. I don't know why I thought I could scare him with the dumb wolf costume."

"I mean, it probably saved my uncle's life," Belle pointed out. "Thanks for that."

"It almost got me killed. He would've hit me a lot harder if you hadn't helped. Thanks for tackling him for me."

"No problem."

Someone tapped on the door, and both girls looked up. A woman with blond hair, tipped with blue highlights, stepped in. She looked to be about the same age as Belle's mom.

"Hello, my name's Prism, and I'm with DOSA," she said.
~~~~~

Zelda cringed.

Belle hopped out of her chair. "She's not a supervillain."

"I'm aware of that." A slight smile played across Prism's face. "You are a sable, though, aren't you?"

"I guess," Zelda mumbled.

Prism stepped further into the room. "From what Officer Bennett tells me, you've been living on your own for a while now. I ran your name and found your parents. Looks like neither are exactly in a state to take care of you right now."

"I don't want to go back into foster care," Zelda whimpered. "I can look after myself. I've been doing that for years."

Prism's lips pursed. "Zelda, hiding in restaurants isn't taking care of yourself. You need to go to school, to have people looking after you. That said, I'm not here to take you to a foster home. DOSA has learned that having sable kids in the system leads to more supervillains to deal with later, so we have a program." She pulled out her phone and turned it around, showing a photo of a large cabin on a wooded property. "This is Camp Sable. It's a place for sable kids who don't have anywhere else to go. You'll have everything you need, a chance to make other sable friends, and even learn to use your powers more effectively."

Belle's stomach twisted. Sable friends. Not normies like her. Of course, she couldn't exactly leave to go to some camp, anyway. Her parents weren't just going to send her off like that, and it wasn't that she wanted to leave home. She just didn't want to lose the only friend she'd had in so long.

Zelda stared at the picture. "For sable kids? So if I was a normie, you'd just throw me back, but since I'm a sable, I get special treatment?"

Wrinkles deepened around Prism's eyes. "I know it's not fair. I wish every kid got a chance at something like what we offer — but I can't help every kid. I can only help the ones DOSA allows, and that's kids like you."

Zelda's lower lip quivered. "Can I … Can I talk to my friend?"

"Of course." Prism put her phone away. "I'll be right outside. Let me know when you want to talk."

With Prism gone, Belle leaned forward. "What are you going to do?"

"Do … do you think if I ran … if I found a new hiding place maybe I could tell you where it is and … I don't want to go with her, but I don't want to be alone anymore." Tears flooded Zelda's eyes. "You don't know how lonely it's been, living with no one seeing me, no one caring if I even exist, no one to talk to. Until you found me, I was always … so lonely."

"I … maybe know a little," Belle murmured. "You're my first real friend in a long time too, but … Zelda, you can't live like this forever, and it's not like I can go with you. I can't be invisible. Believe me, I've tried sometimes." They both fell silent. Belle tried to think of something nice to say, but it all just sucked. "The camp sounds kind of nice. Plus it's DOSA. Maybe they can teach you to be a superhero or something."

"That could be pretty cool." Zelda wiped at her eyes.

"And you won't have to hide, so you can make new friends," Belle continued, trying to think of how good this was for her friend instead of how much she'd miss her. "Plus we can still keep in touch, right? If Prism got here in less than an hour, that means the camp must be somewhere in Oregon. Even DOSA wouldn't have been able to get someone out here from the East Coast that fast. Maybe we can visit and we can talk on the phone—"

"I've always wanted a phone." Zelda glanced longingly at her hand, as if a device might appear there. "They make you too easy to track so I never even bothered to steal one."

"I bet they can get you one," Belle said. "Plus, today proved you have what it takes to be a superhero. You belong there."

With the other sables. With super-powered friends.

"I'll miss you, though," Zelda said.

"I'll miss you too." The girls hugged for a long moment. "Think about it, though," Belle said as she released her. "Hot food, real showers … you need this."

"Yeah, I can give it a try, I guess." Zelda dropped her voice again. "If I don't like it, though, don't be surprised if you find me lurking around The Slice again in a few months."

Belle laughed, but somehow, she knew that wouldn't happen. Zelda would fit right in at the camp. She'd be a superhero someday. She just had to be.

Goodbyes said, Belle stepped out into the hallway with a sigh. Prism took her contact information and promised she'd help the girls stay in touch. She didn't seem like the type of adult who would lie, so Belle felt a little better about it.

She made her way back toward her uncle's hospital room, where she expected her mother to be. Before she could get there, though, another person in a dorky, Little Red Riding Hood cape uniform stepped out of an elevator in front of her, carrying a small bunch of three red balloons.

"Oh, hey, Pizza Princess!" Em said. "I was going to give these to Phil, just to let him know I'm happy he's not dead."

"I'm sure he's happy not to be dead," Belle deadpanned.

Em laughed. "You know, you're funnier than I thought you were— and braver. Man, when you jumped on Dylan with that… weird invisible kid, I couldn't believe it."

"I mean, I didn't really think about it. I just sort of did it." Belle shuffled her feet. "We've both seen I'm not that brave. Remember my first day?"

Em flinched. "Sorry about that. It was Dylan's idea, and you saw what an idiot he turned out to be. Promise, I won't ever do that again." She cleared her throat. "In fact, since The Slice is going to be closed for a few days, what with the crime scene and Phil down for the count, me and a few of the other employees—Felicity, Rodrigio, maybe even Maggie and James—we're talking about doing something tonight. Maybe a movie? You want in? I was going to invite you, but no one had your number."

"Oh." Belle blinked. "You want me to?"

"Sure. I mean, we can't have the pizza gang without the Pizza Princess, right?" Em grinned.

Belle laughed. "I'll see if I can get my fairy godmother to whip me up a pumpkin coach."

"Great. Here." Em passed her the phone. "Add your number to the group text and we'll get you the details."

Belle swallowed as she took the phone. Maybe getting out of her shell to hang out with her coworkers wouldn't be so bad. At the very least, it would give her a story to tell Zelda later.

With a smile on her face, Belle added herself to Em's contact list.

THE END

THE INVISIBLE BOY
Jessica A. Tanner

The house at the top of the hill is haunted—at least that's what Grandma May tells me.

And sometimes, like right now when a curtain seems to move without the help of a breeze and there's the smell of French fries, I wonder if she might be right. I tighten my grip on the straps of my backpack and run for home.

Along the way, I pass by an old streetlamp with a faded poster featuring a boy a bit older than me with wild hair and large glasses—the missing son of the Rogers family who live a street over. A body has never been found and there has been no sign of kidnapping. Did he run away? No one knows.

Grandma May calls from her old blue rocker on the front porch as I draw close. "See a ghost, Lizzie dear?"

"No." I'm nearly out of breath and my answer doesn't have the confidence behind it that it should.

She chuckles. "You're not meetin' my gaze, so I think the answer's yes."

And there's that.

The screen door slams shut behind me.

Pa, his glasses perched on the tip of his nose, looks up from his paperwork littering the kitchen table. "Hello, honey. Have a good day?"

"Sure." I drop my pack on a stool by the counter and hide my head in the fridge. Pa doesn't need to see my tears caused by Kendall Rogers' and her friends' taunts. Those girls are the worst.

I let the cold air kiss my hot cheeks until I sense a presence behind me. I close the fridge and turn around.

Pa's towering over me, his eyes kind. "What happened today?"

My day's troubles pour across my lips and fresh tears drip from my cheeks to the floor.

Pa wraps me in his arms.

I hold on tight for a long while. Once my crying and hiccups subside, I step back. Movement near one of the windows draws my attention, but when I look, nothing and no one is there. Yet I can faintly smell French fries.

Pa brushes hair that had escaped my braid away from my face.

"Always remember, Lizzie, you can bring me whatever troubles you."

"Yes, Pa."

He pulls a handkerchief from his trouser pocket and hands it to me. "Why don't you go and clean up? Maybe try your hand at your homework? Supper'll be ready in an hour."

"Sure." I blow my nose and head for the bathroom at the back of our little bungalow. Along the way, I glance again at the window where I'd seen motion. Still nothing. Hmmm.

~~~~~

Days later, while enjoying an autumn day free of Kendall Rogers and her friends—they'd come down with the flu—I collect leaves. I used to always do that with my mother ... until she passed away.

The leaves beside my feet move—not like a stirring of the wind, but more like someone is picking them up. A moment later they are spread on the sidewalk beside me in a single word: *Hello.*

I drop my handful of brightly colored foliage and back away.

The leaves spell *Wait.*

I pause. I'm not sure why I linger rather than running home at full speed. Maybe it's because of that smell—French fries.

More leaves move than before, all in an organized fashion and definitely spelling out more than a single word. *My name is Fred. What's yours?*

"Lizzie," I say before I can think through that I'm talking to something I can't see. Is he a ghost?

The leaves rearrange. *Nice to meet you. Will you be my friend?*

A breeze scatters the foliage and wraps me in that fry scent.

"Uh ... sure."

I've never had a friend before.

I've not had one in a while. Not since Ma passed and Pa and I moved in with Grandma May. But I don't tell Fred this. Instead, I say, "I'm honored to be your first."

The leaves shuffle into a smiley face.

~~~~~

Every day for a week—even on Sunday—I meet up with Fred. We fish, play cards, collect leaves, talk (me with my voice and Fred with paper and pencil) about whatever comes to mind, and do anything else we can think up. My heart feels lighter than it has in ages.

But then Kendall Rogers and her friends are well again.

And my new friend can't keep the tears away.

Fred tries to get me to talk about what happened.

The words refuse to come coherently. Hiccups and snot make things worse.

Fred gently guides me home and past Grandma May sleeping in her rocker on the porch. I don't feel him release me until I'm standing at the kitchen table where Pa is working on a mountain of papers for another client.

Pa sets down his papers and hands me a handkerchief. "Honey, when you're ready, tell me what happened."

A pencil lifts and scratches a short note on a notepad: *Meet you tomorrow.*

I bob my head before I blow my nose and wipe at my wet face. I hate crying, but it seems all I'm capable of anymore.

~~~~~

The next day I meet with Fred, he gives me a note and a vial full of a clear liquid that smells like fries and seems thicker than water when I shake it. I read: *Would you like to never be picked on again?*

"Yes."

He tugs the note away and writes: *Drink.*

I feel my forehead furrow and my eyes narrow. "Drink what? What's in the vial?"

Yes.

I tip my head. "What's in the vial, Fred?"

A formula. The one that turned me invisible.

I frown. "Did you become invisible to escape your bullies?"

There's a long pause before he finally writes: *Yes and no.*

I sit on the sidewalk, feet in the street, and pat the cement next to me. "Tell me more."

And for the first time ever, Fred speaks — not with leaves or pencil and paper — but with his own voice. "I'm the middle kid of thirteen."

"Wow," I say, and then fall quiet. I'm pretty sure if I talk too much, Fred'll clam up.

"Yeah. Six kids younger than me and six older. I wasn't good at sports or debate team and I wasn't needing to be potty trained ... so sometimes .... I got a bit lost in the shuffle."

I pull my feet from the street and cross them, resting my elbows on my bent knees and chin in my raised hands. "Tell me more."

"More?" There's a snort mixed with his words — like he doesn't believe my request.

"Yes. I've never had siblings and I hardly see my cousins. What's it like having so many people under the same roof?"

And he tells me about the sharing of clothes and space. The harassment from older siblings and sometimes younger. He hardly ever felt seen unless he was being tormented — and he didn't like that.

But as he talks, I think I see a bit of an outline of a boy a bit older than me with wild hair come into view.

Occasionally he mentions an incident where someone showed up late
~~~~~

for a clarinet recital or a soccer game. He even talks about having competed in a science fair and winning ... but his parents had needed to change a younger sibling's diapers right when the announcement was made.

Just as Fred is getting better at talking, I hear snickering. My back stiffens as Fred goes silent. Kendall Rogers and her cronies have found us.

The outline I'd seen of Fred vanishes.

Slowly, I stand. Kendall getting detention and not being able to corner me on my way home had been wonderful, but I should have remembered that since she only lived a street over from me, she could find me and pick on me later.

A couple of leaves stir. Fred must be going.

I glance at the vial still in my hand. I waver. Escaping the coming torment would be great, but how would Pa and Grandma May know I'm still around if they can't see me? Sure I could talk and move stuff around ... I slide the vial in my pocket. I can't disappear on them. Especially since Ma died.

I face my tormenters.

Kendall grins.

My heart pounds against my ribs. What does she have up her sleeve today?

She and her friends come closer. She leans toward me. "Having fun talking to your imaginary friend?"

I blurt, "He's not imaginary."

Her grin turns into a smirk and her eyes gleam. "He? So, you aren't talking with ... your mama?"

My fingers twitch. I want to slug Kendall Rogers.

One of her cronies, Natalie, sidles over. "Cat suddenly got your tongue, Lizzie?"

The other two chuckle.

Pa has never promoted violence. Ma never did either. But Grandma May is an ornery woman—and she did tell me one time about slugging a girl in class to get her to quit calling her sister a hussy. If I lash out, I won't be defending anyone but myself—and since they're not physically attacking, I'd just be taking their bait and getting in a heap of trouble.

I shove my hands in my pockets while tears of frustration prick the corners of my eyes.

Just as I'm ready to spin around and walk away, sprinklers turn on. The sprinklers for the park never turn on this late in the day.

The girls squeal and run away.

As soon as they're around the corner, the sprinklers shut off.

"Are you okay?"

Fred.

I smile. "Yeah. Thanks."

"What'd my sister mean about you talking to your mama?"

My jaw drops to the ground. "Your sister?"

"Yeah. Kendall's my sister. I didn't realize she was the girl who's been harassing you." His voice is tinged with guilt.

"You're a Rogers?" My mind flashes to the poster I pass almost every day and the outline I saw before Kendall and her friends showed up. Wild hair, boy a bit older than me. I wonder if he's wearing those same oversized glasses...?

"Uh huh."

"How long have you been invisible?"

"I don't know, a while. Maybe a couple of months?"

"Your family has been looking for you. There are posters all over town." I reach out, feel an arm, grab hold, and drag him down the street.

He's tripping and trying to get me to let go.

I don't stop until we reach the light post with the poster that I pass on my way home. "See!" I smack it with the back of my free hand, not letting go of him with the other. "People have been looking all over for you. Your parents must be going out of their minds with worry."

Fred finally escapes my grasp.

But I never get a reply. Instead, that familiar scent fades and I hear the slap of sneakers on the sidewalk. The sneakers aren't headed a street over—they're going in the direction of the old house thought abandoned and haunted.

He knows, but doesn't want to go home ... why?

~~~~~

Pa is a great listener, but I've done some of my best thinking going over to Ma's grave and talking things out with her. And I admit, when I really get yammering on a topic I care about, my hands go every which way. Unfortunately, my private moments with her are often used by Kendall and her cronies to humiliate me.

An hour after talking to Ma's grave, I've got a plan.

First, though, I need to talk with Grandma May and Pa.

I kiss Ma's headstone like she used to kiss me before bed, then I run home.

"Pa! Grandma May!" The screen door slams shut behind me

"Lizzie, what's the problem?" Pa pushes his chair back from the kitchen table and stands.

Grandma May looks up from the paper she was reading. "Yeah, where's the fire, girl?"

And I tell them everything—not necessarily in order—but they get all of it. A reminder of me talking to Ma most days after school and Kendall picking on me. A confession about my new friend being a boy,
~~~~~

but then revealing he's invisible and he's the missing son of the Rogers family. I even tell them about Fred turning on the sprinklers and admitting Kendall is his sister.

Both are silent for a long minute after I finish my spiel.

Then, Grandma smiles. "Lizzie's got her first crush."

I wrinkle my nose. "I don't have a crush on Fred Rogers. I just don't get why even after seeing the poster, he won't go home."

Pa scratches his chin. "You mentioned you could see an outline of him after he started talking to you about how he felt and the times folks did show up for him."

I nod. "Yeah."

Pa heads for the door. Grandma and I scramble to keep up with Pa's long strides.

"Whatchya thinking, Pa?" I ask as we head in the direction of the Rogers' home. Is that where we're going?

"Yeah, Ralph, what's cookin' in that noggin of yours?" Grandma May sounds a bit winded.

Pa simply says, "You'll see."

Grandma May and I share a look. *What does that mean?*

~~~~~

After school the next day, I approach the old house at the top of the hill, intending to knock on the front door. I doubt Fred will be hanging out in the park where we normally meet up. The talk last night with the Rogers family revealed that this place used to belong to Fred's grandparents. The two had died in a car accident right around the time school was ending in May. They'd been the ones who usually showed for Fred, and his grandpa liked science—just like he does.

Fred is grieving.

Kendall is too. No wonder she's been so mean. She doesn't know what to do with her hurt.

I've not really known what to do with mine either. Guess that's why her words bring tears so easy.

I reach the small porch by the front step of the house, lift my hand to knock, and pause. What if Fred isn't here? What if he won't listen to me? What if he does ... and still doesn't want to go home?

I shift my weight from foot to foot until I draw up the courage to knock. "Fred ... it's me ... Lizzie. Can we talk? I—I'm sorry I made you uncomfortable yesterday."

Silence.

But then I smell French fries and a curtain stirs in the window near the door.

My heart leaps in my chest. "Fred?"

The door opens.
~~~~~

"I guess this means I can come in?"

The door stays open, but Fred keeps quiet.

I ease my way across the threshold. "You asked me about talking to my ma. Most days after school I visit her grave in the cemetery. I tell her about my teachers, my classes, Kendall … and you. I used to tell her all of that stuff when she was alive."

Silence.

"I miss her more than the stars miss the moon some nights. Pa's a great listener too, but there was something about sitting down with Ma …" I shrug, not sure how to put my feelings into words.

Fred speaks. "I get it. I used to tell my grandparents everything — especially my grandpa. He's the one behind the formula for invisibility."

"Why'd he create it — really?"

"Grand liked to play pranks. He thought if he could turn invisible for a bit, he could pull off some real whoppers."

I smile. "Sounds like a fun person."

"He was. And Meemaw, she baked the best chocolate chip cookies. Never knew how to be on time anywhere, but she always brought something tasty to share."

I can see a glimmer of his outline.

"Cool."

"Yeah."

I see dust smear like he's sliding the toe of his shoe back and forth in thought.

"I miss them," he says. "They died a few days before school let out. A car accident."

"I'm sorry for your loss."

"I'm sorry about yours."

"You've already told me that once before." A corner of my mouth tugs up. During our talks when we fished or gathered leaves or whatever while Kendall was sick with the flu, I did tell him about my mother passing away.

He shrugs, and I catch it as more of him comes into view. I spy his glasses too.

"How does the invisibility formula work?" I pull the vial he gave me yesterday from my pocket and hold it out.

"Grand knew how to explain it best."

I nod. "How would you explain it?"

He pushes his glasses up on his nose. "It causes your cells to absorb light differently … or was it refract the light? But you needed more than that."

"Oh?"

"You had to believe it would work. Believe no one could see you."

"Do you feel that way now?" I smile wider than before.

"I—I don't know." His wild blonde hair to his worn, red converse sneakers are in view. "I guess I feel seen."

I wrap him in a hug.

He stiffens before tentatively hugging me back. "Grand never could stay invisible for more than a few minutes. I usually had to set up his pranks for him."

"Uh huh." I let go and step back. Heat floods my face. I'm thankful Kendall wasn't allowed to come with me.

He runs a hand through his hair, but that doesn't tame any of it. "I'm sorry I freaked when you showed me the poster."

"Your parents do miss you …." I bite my lip to keep from telling him about the plan to get him to go home and because I'm suddenly afraid I've pushed too hard or overstepped.

"I bet they do." He sighs. "Would you like to meet them?"

"I'd be honored to." I nearly drop the vial in my surprise. Do I need to tell him I spoke with them last night? Maybe not. After all, Pa did most of the talking and introducing me might get sidelined by everyone welcoming Fred home. Fingers cross that we really do go there.

Fred gently takes the vial from me and slides it in his pocket. "Why didn't you try the formula?"

My turn to push the dust on the floor with the toe of my shoe. "I may not like getting picked on, but the idea of my pa and Grandma May not being able to see me scared me."

He bobs his head once. "I can get that, sort of." He takes the lead.

We leave the house and head for the sidewalk. I can't just walk beside him, though. "Tag, you're it!" I tap his arm and race ahead.

"Hey!" His sneakers slap the sidewalk behind me.

I giggle and run faster, my fears about the old house fading with each step.

THE END

ERWIN
Samantha Seidel

How close can I get?

The ballroom glittered under the glass chandeliers while the world outside slept. Biologists in cocktail dresses and strapped heels marveled at the potted palms and live orchestra. Roboticists in pressed suits showcased their mechanized wonders to small crowds. Waiters wove through the mass of scientists, economists, and technologists, offering champagne to whomever they passed.

My stomach grumbled when I approached one of the tables piled with hors d'oeuvres. If only I could snag a bite of that mini cheesecake or the chocolate ball. Saliva coated my mouth.

I turned away. No time for a snack.

Without warning, a waitress ran into me. Steadying her tray, her eyes scanned the area. Her brow tensed.

I froze. Sweat slid down the neck of my suit.

Someone called for a drink. She rushed off, still looking for whoever she'd walked into.

I exhaled quietly, warmth returning to my muscles. Another successful test. After years of experimentation and ridicule, I'd finally achieved invisibility. My excitement from a few hours ago bubbled again, making it impossible to stand still. I had to show Bracken. Weaving through the crowd, careful not to touch anyone, I sought his tall stature and blond locks.

A burst of laughter drew me in. George Bracken picked at his finger sandwich while waiting for his companions to calm down.

I slipped between a few party guests, each step increasing my nervous energy. Should I sneak up behind him or just remove the mask?

"Don't be ridiculous, George. Erwin is chasing a 21st century childhood fantasy. I mean, what possible use could invisibility be?"

I stopped between his colleagues. Lucille DeWain had spoken, flicking her black curls with a haughty scoff.

Peter Langford gestured to her with his champagne glass. "More use than your novels." After a coughing fit that shook his beer belly, the roboticist cleared his throat and continued, "But truly, the proof you need is in this room. We've awarded the best scientific discoveries of the 25th century. Every guest has changed the world. And where is Erwin?"

My enthusiasm sank to the expensive carpet. To think Renee wondered why I wanted to be invisible. She was easily impressed when I fixed her father's pocket watch on our first date. But the scientific community required a track record of expensive schools and vague awards. None of which I possessed.

Bracken set his mangled sandwich on the table behind him. "Invisibility has many world-changing possibilities."

Lucille rolled her eyes. "Certainly. For criminals."

"Is that what you wrote in your novel?" Langford swirled his glass dismissively.

"It's actually more about you," she twittered. Her arm came toward me.

I ducked.

She grabbed a small cheesecake off a passing tray. After a quick bite, she continued, "Specifically, the failure of your machines and the police to rid Manhattan of the mob."

Langford's jolly expression morphed into a scowl, provoking a chuckle from the best-selling novelist.

"I don't believe it's your fault, darling," Lucille cooed, olive complexion glittering in the light. "The recent trial proved that cameras are too easily destroyed and witnesses too scared to testify. At this point, the commissioner's trying to find hard proof of criminal activity, like a money trail or ledger. Which you'd know if you read the advance copy I sent you."

Bracken smirked, shaking his head. "We're a little busy trying to solve the mob crisis. Along with world hunger and whatever else you writers can complain about."

Langford laughed obnoxiously at Lucille's straight-backed silence.

Bracken excused himself for the night, collected his award and headed for the door.

Following him outside, I tried to rekindle my sense of triumph. No one had sensed my presence. But the criticisms swirled in my mind.

Streetlamps highlighted the empty road, lights in skyscrapers twinkling in place of stars. The stench of week-old garbage wafted from alleyways. Few people walked the streets. The valet ran to get Bracken's car while he stood patiently by the front door of the hotel.

The moon sat high in the blackened sky, light dimmed by the city's ambience. Yet my childhood wish seemed just as alive here as it had been in the mountains of Colorado.

"I wish I could do something right," I said aloud, without thinking.

"Erwin?" Bracken tensed, looking around with wide eyes. His bewilderment ceased when his car pulled to the curb. Perhaps he thought the valet had spoken. Either way, he wasted no time taking his keys and driving away.

What time was it? I turned down the alley where I'd hidden my bike and coat. Unfastening the hood of my suit, I let the mask hang around my neck like a scarf. After scanning my face, my phone revealed seven missed messages.

All labeled "wife."

I bit my lip. Renee never liked when I stayed in the lab overnight. Of course, I hadn't planned on sudden success and the spontaneous desire to crash the symposium. Maybe the news of my achievement would dull her aggravation.

A quick stop at the lab to store the suit and then I would be home for supper and a scowl. I slipped into the coat to prevent suspicion. Not that anyone out this late would report a disembodied head riding a bicycle. Still, better to not tempt fate. I climbed onto the bike, shifting my position until I found the resistance of the pedals and seat. Muscle memory took over, my gaze taking in the nocturnal life of Manhattan.

I knew the path to the lab well enough to allow my mind to wander to Lucille's cackling about invisibility only helping criminals. There were other, worthy applications. I just needed some time to figure out the implementation.

Shouts stopped my progress. Broken streetlamps threw sparks onto an abandoned police car. One of Langford's police scanner drones sat on the sidewalk, wires cut and camera head shattered.

It could be nothing; people dismantled these robots all the time.

A haunting moan echoed from the blackened alley. I put my feet on the pedals. A loud bang held me still.

Here was my chance to prove her wrong. I could hide my bike, check out what was going on, and leave without being noticed. Same as I had at the symposium. Only this was more dangerous.

Uncertainty prickled my skin. This was why I maintained a strict routine, to avoid crazy schemes with unknown outcomes. One spontaneous idea to sneak into an event now spurred the thought of playing hero. But I'd be doing something right. A little evidence could prevent another trial from ending with "not guilty."

Sweat beading on my brow, my thoughts bounced back and forth, weighing my options. At some point, one side won.

I sucked in a breath. And followed the sounds of terror.

When I seemed close to the source of the noise, I rested my bike behind a dumpster and peered around the corner. Two large men held down a cop. Uniform torn, blood caked in his hair. He whimpered for mercy while glancing at a limp form in the darkness.

My blood chilled. *Get some evidence, be a hero.* I removed my phone from my jacket pocket. Oh, the jacket! I pulled it off, heart thudding loudly at my close call. Fortunately, no one had seen it. With shaky fingers, I started filming.

A flickering light highlighted a silhouette. A woman, hair bathed in red, spoke. Her sneer revealed a snaggle tooth, her piercing eyes focused on her victim.

My phone brightened. The ringer blared. Renee.

I shut it off, trying not to scream. Clutching the device, I dared to look up.

My heart stopped. The trio stared at me.

Directly at me.

My fingers grasped the hood still draped around my neck. I had forgotten to put it back on.

I bolted.

Heavy boots smacked the pavement. I pulled on the hood, fumbling with the fastener. Wait, where was my phone? The slam of dumpsters pushed me onward, leaving the evidence behind.

I ducked into a doorway. Held my breath.

The burly men ran into the street, searching both sides. I melted against the wall. Heart hammering, I was sure they heard me.

But they moved on.

I sank to the ground, gasping for breath. But I didn't dare pull off the mask, fearing they'd come back. After tonight, I'd never be spontaneous again.

Squinting in the dark, I searched for my bike. The gray frame remained hidden against the wall. The same couldn't be said for my phone. I didn't even remember dropping it. But there it lay, shattered glass littering the alley. Checking the back of my head and neck to ensure the suit was fastened properly, I turned the corner. The woman was gone.

The bodies remained.

I shuddered. This was real. Only no one would believe me without the video. And the killers had seen my face. What if they came after me? Could they?

Glaring at the remains of my phone, I whispered an apology to Renee. I couldn't go home, not with so many unknowns. My jacket lay scrunched in the corner, but I refused to put it on. Instead, I took my keycard from the pocket. The spandex suit hugged my body, providing no pockets or bulges to clip onto. I'd need to make a pouch of some kind.

Hooking the card to the cupholder on my bike, I swung into the seat and raced toward the lab. My mind spun with curses directed at my spontaneity. Bracken had suggested I loosen up, Renee that I surprise her occasionally. I should've thought it through. This night would've remained perfect if I'd only done what I always did.

But the suit. After years of being told I was crazy and that my efforts would lead to nothing, I'd succeeded. Renee and Bracken's faith in me hadn't been misplaced. My life wasn't a waste. Yet despite going unnoticed for most of my life, I'd somehow failed at being invisible.

Reaching the squat structure of the lab, I coasted to the backdoor. With a swipe of my keycard, I got in. It took a few minutes traversing the halls to reach the main laboratory, cluttered desks filling the room.

I dropped into the chair at my workstation. Lungs gasping for air, my body curled in pain. There was a reason the symposium coordinators didn't invite me. Sparks of jealousy had clouded my work throughout the day, each moment an attempt to prove them wrong. That I could make a difference with my research. I'd proven my concept by weaving through the elites of the community unnoticed. If only I'd programmed a time machine instead.

Pulling myself together, I rolled to my desk and flicked on the lamp. Scraps of the reflective material still lay there, along with chips, tweezers, and thread. How this epiphany had felt like a blessing. Threading the fabric together into the form of a pouch, I intermittently attached computer chips on the outer layer. I connected each with thin wire and tweezers, following the chart I'd drawn.

After ignoring an itch for a few hours, the sensation became unbearable. I unsnapped the hood, pulling it away from my face and folding it around my neck. Carefully, I scratched my nose. Every now and then, one of the metal chips on my fingers would dig into my skin, relieving and causing pain.

Finally satisfied, I glared at the silvery material on my desk. My life's work.

Gaze shifting, I stared at my only photo. Renee's heart-shaped face smiled back, white veil wrapped around her arms. In the picture I gripped her waist, auburn hair slicked back and smile wide. That man had dreams of publishing his first grand discovery, of crediting his wife for her support.

The man in the picture hadn't realized how many sleepless nights he'd have to endure to achieve his goal. How many people would turn their backs on him. And thanks to my mistake tonight, the publication of my work would cause more harm than good.

Unhampered by adrenaline, the scenarios played in my mind. Once published, my picture would be everywhere. The killers could've gotten a good enough look to recognize me, putting both Renee and me in danger. Even if they didn't recognize me, the possibility of an invisibility suit would entice them, and others with ill intent, to get their hands on one. Lucille's concerns would become reality, criminals ransacking Manhattan without visual evidence.

Staring at my hands, I saw the desk. I'd grown accustomed to only having the gloves, my arms completely transparent when I worked. Now I had an entire suit. Kyle Erwin and his research could disappear from existence. Renee would be alone, but safe.

I glanced at the photo again. No one could know what I'd accomplished. I had to disappear. Grabbing the frame, I removed the photo and stuffed it inside my suit beside my heart. I continued to work on the pouch as well as a strap.

Once done, I felt the suit for its wiring. Removing a few connections caused the suit to flicker until I was opaque. I stood before the mirror I'd used a few hours ago, slipping the satchel over my shoulder. I dismissed the silver spandex as much as I could, focusing on connecting each wire to a corresponding sensor.

My stomach grumbled while my eyes drifted out of focus. A tingle shot through my fingers, causing me to drop the tweezers. Shaking the numbness from my hand, I put the tweezers away. Perhaps I should take a five-minute break.

I grabbed my wallet and shuffled to the vending machine. After buying a bag of chips, I lumbered to Bracken's office. He always said his futon was mine, though I think that was advice from his two failed marriages. Dropping onto the lumpy material, I crunched on stale chips. The world darkened while I thought over my goodbye to Renee.

~~~~~

"Erwin."

I started. Blinded by fluorescent lights, the office blurred.

"What are you wearing?" Bracken's silhouette solidified, tux replaced with a simple polo shirt and lab coat.

I patted myself, feeling my suit, as the evening's events played again in my mind. "What time is it?"

"5:30. I thought I'd start early."

Rising on shaky legs, I checked the wiring. "I have to finish."

Bracken smirked, setting his case on the desk. "You need to go home."

"No." I ambled out the door, checking for other employees. No one walked the halls.

"Erwin, I know you wanted to be invited to the symposium..."

"I was there."

Bracken's thick eyebrows scrunched, slight wrinkles tightening.

I had a plan. I would disappear with my work and the world would go on believing invisibility was impossible. But I couldn't lie to a friend.

Motioning for him to follow, I led him to the full-length mirror I'd been working with. Rather than activate the whole suit, I connected the wiring around my hand to an external battery.

A gasp followed the disappearance of my arm. "You solved it."
~~~~~

I nodded. "When connected to the internal power relay, I'm completely invisible. I clapped when you received the best programmer award and heard when you defended me to Lucille and Langford."

Bracken drew near, inching his finger toward my hand. Or rather, where he guessed it was. Combing his fingers through gelled curls, his deep blue eyes grew wide. "We need to notify the collective."

Disconnecting the battery, I worked on completing the circuits of the suit. "I was stupid to try creating this. The technology is too dangerous to become mainstream knowledge."

"But this is a scientific marvel."

"And it brought me face to face with the mob. My hood wasn't on. They saw me." My heart stuttered at the thought of what would happen to my wife if they found her. But she wasn't in danger. Only me. "I have only my word, and that might not be enough. And given what they've done to witnesses and their families, it's not worth the risk."

Bracken paced. After years of working together, I knew how he problem solved. His thoughts were unable to process without his body in constant motion. "There's a way to fix this."

I forced the words out. "Two officers are dead in an alley. I've seen the news. If I talk or they find me, I'm a dead man. And Renee..." My throat clenched. I wouldn't think that. Focusing on the suit, I finished the last few connections. The silver material flickered, and my body became transparent. I shuddered at the sight of my head floating in midair, even though I knew the rest of me was still attached.

"Erwin." Bracken stared at me through the mirror, still awed by my accomplishment. "There might be another way."

"I doubt that."

"Lucille mentioned a ledger."

A cold sweat suctioned the suit to my skin. Facing my friend, I shook my head.

Before I could protest, he reached out carefully for my shoulders. Finding a grip, he gave a little shake. "With the suit, you could slip into the office of whatever mob boss you saw and steal their ledger. Then you drop it at the police station and you're free."

"I'm invisible, not intangible."

"You got through the symposium last night."

"That's different."

Bracken tilted his head, eyebrows raised. "You can put criminals away without any bloodshed." Not satisfied by my expression, he continued, "It's your best chance of returning to Renee."

Jaw clenched, I thought of her. The life we wanted to build. I could have it all again. I just needed the ledger.

Shaking, I nodded.

Bracken's lip curled with glee. "All right. Put on your mask and we'll look for their base."

Breathless and sick to my stomach, I fastened the mask in the back and followed.

Vibrating with excitement, Bracken got into his car. I traced my hand along the red exterior until I caught the handle, loathing my foreseeable future.

Driving into downtown, the cleanliness of the business parks declined. A barber cleaned the façade of his shop while a troop of women in tight shorts chattered on their phones. The air reeked of excrement and weed. A couple kids played basketball at a broken hoop while the club across the street blasted music.

Head swiveling, Bracken mumbled about the outlook and people.

"You sound like the true crime podcasts Renee obsesses over."

Bracken started, the car jolting slightly. "I forgot you were there. Why are you wearing a seatbelt? Someone could see and assume an invisible man is in the car."

Glancing at the tattooed patrons gripping their pants while they walked, I folded into myself in an attempt to become smaller. "Seatbelts are the law, even for invisible people."

"I think we can make an exception."

"Absolutely not. Living on the edge is what got me in this situation."

Bracken rolled his eyes. "Believe me, you have yet to *'live on the edge.'*" He slowed when a group of people marched into traffic. "What about there?"

I peered through the window and shook my head.

Silence filled the car while he scanned the passenger seat.

I cleared my throat, remembering he couldn't see my movements. "No, not there."

He nodded, shoulders hunching in anticipation. We continued through the narrow streets, observing the variety of downtown Manhattan. We'd stop by large groups of people while I scanned the crowd, Bracken becoming more and more energetic. Each was the wrong sort of gang, yet all terrifying. Burly motorcyclists, gun-toting pimps, sly drug dealers.

To imagine I lived only a few blocks away.

"What about her?"

I glanced out Bracken's window. A woman with red highlights and murderous eyes argued with a couple large men in front of a bar. I leaned over, feeling a sense of familiarity.

She glanced in our direction, beauty venomous.

Ducking, I hissed, "Go. That's her. Go."

Bracken hit the gas, then collected himself and slowed to a normal speed. Head whipping between her and the road, he whispered, "I don't think she saw us. Well, she didn't see you. Probably not me. Orwell's Paddi Wack, that's the establishment. Now we just go in and get the ledger. Well, you go in."

My blood ran cold. The car seemed to cave in, air tightening.

The silence agitated Bracken. "Don't worry, you're invisible. In and out, no trouble."

Body rigid, I repeated the sentiment. The thought continued to circle when we returned to the lab. I slipped in when he swiped his card and listened to our colleagues speculate as to why I wasn't there. Entering Bracken's office unhampered, I curled on the futon, nerves chipping away at my resolve.

Bracken swept in with an eerie ecstasy, shutting the door. "Erwin? You here?"

"Yes."

With a clap of his hands, he marched to his desk. "All right, I say we keep this simple. I drop you off, you go in. I pick you up same place."

My shoulders tightened. "You can't be involved."

"How do you expect to get away? Not on your bike."

I fell silent, looking for a response.

The brightness in his eyes never wavered, even as his body quivered with nervous energy. "You can do this. And I'll be there for you."

Taking my silence as agreement, Bracken chattered about taking down the mob. Doubts continued to haunt me, but one thought held strong. Renee. If not for myself, I had to do this for her.

The hours slipped by, the lab clearing out after a day's work. With the moon high and night life teeming, Bracken drove me to a secluded parking lot a few blocks from Orwell's Paddi Wack.

Inhaling deeply, I traced the door with my hand, caught the handle, and exited the car. Adrenaline surged, but I staved off hysteria by studying the street. People sat in parallel parked cars, wisps of smoke trailing from cracked windows. Gritty lampposts bathed the cracked asphalt in golden orange. The thumping of music from the club and the jingle of a cash register in a drugstore balanced the hushed conversations in alleys.

I walked. Undeterred and unseen.

A man got tossed from Orwell's Paddi Wack, old-fashioned rock music streaming into the street. Quickening my step, I pushed inside before the entry shut.

My body numbed at the sight of the inhabitants. Skull tattoos on thick biceps, grizzled beards speckled red. And knives. So many knives.

The door opened. I plastered myself to the wall before the new occupants stepped into me. I shut my eyes, feeling the panic race through me. Inhaling the stench of tobacco and whiskey, I scanned the space. The establishment had three zones from left to right. The booths held private conversations and flirting, women in tight tops caressing broad-shouldered men. The central pool tables hosted hardened glares that studied their opponents more than billiards. The bar on the far right, bathed in purple light, harbored the most laughter and drinking.

Charting a path, I slowly wove between the patrons. Wisps of smoke lingered in the air, but not enough to reveal my silhouette. Every step brought me closer to the back of the bar. Where to hide a ledger? Maybe in the office?

A man was thrown onto the billiard table. The woman with red highlights pressed a knife to his wrist. Lips curled in a sneer, her snaggle tooth glistened in the low light. "You some kind of snitch? Oh, no. You're just a cheater. We can fix that." A blood-curdling scream echoed in my head as she sawed at the man's wrist.

Bile lodged in my throat. But I stared at the psychotic woman and her victim, making sure she didn't witness when I slipped into the office. Surrounded by darkness, I turned.

A squeak left my lips. Shadows marked the silhouette of a mounted bear. Swallowing my fear, I felt my way to the desk. It had six drawers, not including the shelf with four cabinets and the safe mounted under the taxidermy. Praying it wasn't in the safe, I searched the drawers for a thumb drive.

Nothing.

The door slammed, light blinding. "At least one of you is competent." After shouting to someone beyond the threshold, the woman marched around the desk. Shifting out of her way, I watched when she opened the safe. Never realizing I was there, she removed a red book. After making a note near the back, she returned it and locked the safe. I covered my ears when she screamed, "So who's gonna pick up Freddy when the judge lets him off tomorrow?" Laughter consumed the bar as she stormed out, turning off the light and slamming the door.

Re-entering her code, I opened the safe and retrieved the book. Names, dates, prices, codes. Tons of symbols. Joy bubbled in my chest, but I swallowed it. I still had to get out.

I slipped the book into my pouch, making it disappear. I closed the safe and headed for the door. Everything seemed quiet outside. Inching it open, I peeked at the riffraff. Distracted by booze and billiards, no one glanced toward the office.

I snuck out, holding the book against my hip. Sweat stuck the suit to my body. I drew close to women in clouds of perfume, hoping they'd mask the stench of my anxiety.

A flash of smoke smacked my face. I froze. The cigar-wielding man blinked at me. He sucked in a breath and huffed.

I ducked. The puff trailed through the air unhindered. Heckling by his mates forced him to return to the game. I held my breath when I continued toward the door.

Once out of Orwell's Paddi Wack, adrenaline kicked in. I ran down the street and to Bracken's car. He slept behind the wheel.

I rapped the window vigorously until he stirred and unlocked the car.

I fumbled for the handle, nearly ripping the door off its hinges. Dropping into the seat, I hissed, "I've got it. Drive."

Without hesitation, he pulled out and sped down the street. We reached the police station within minutes. Removing the book from my pouch made it reappear.

Bracken took it and entered the station. He left as quickly, returning to the driver's seat. "It's done."

Relief flooded my body, nerves growing numb at the lack of tension.

He drove toward upper Manhattan, a giddy smile on his face. "You can stay with me until the news breaks, though you should call Renee."

"Why?"

"She's been calling me all night." Opening the glove compartment, he produced his slim phone. The little device vibrated incessantly, Renee's number plastered across the screen.

The panic of the last twenty-eight hours subsided. Tears filled my eyes when I answered. Before she could speak, a stream of words fell out of my mouth. The invisibility suit, the mob hit, my plan to run, Bracken's idea. I told her all and finished with my deepest regrets for worrying her. By the time we reached Bracken's home, I'd removed the hood, letting the world see my tears.

Inside the condo, Bracken prepared spaghetti. I ate ravenously, not sure how I'd gone a day without food.

He smirked while cleaning the electric stovetop. "I guess we're heroes now. Taking down criminals without a punch."

Slurping a collection of noodles, I shook my head. "No, this was a one-time thing."

Bracken rinsed the sponge, brow tightening. "But you could do so much good. Sneak into places law enforcement can't."

"The inspiration for my work was my ability to disappear in a crowd. No one cares what I do."

The twinkle in his eye grew brighter, sincerity softening his features. "All of us change the world whether we want to or not. The difference you make is up to you." He lumbered to the family room, dropped into his overstuffed chair and turned on the news. Nothing mentioned about the mob or the ledger yet.

The rich basil and sleep-inducing gluten suddenly seemed less appetizing. But I finished the bowl, rinsed my dish, and lay on the sofa. I fastened the hood like I'd promised Renee I would. Being invisible amongst friends seemed unnecessary. However, the lack of logic didn't prevent me from drifting to sleep.

~~~~~

Bracken's ringing phone jerked me from slumber and echoed through the whole of the condo. Groggy and numb, I fumbled for the device. Renee. Did that time say 6am? After a quick yawn, I answered. "Hey, raindrop."

"Are you watching the news?"

I glanced at the TV. Live coverage of Orwell's Paddi Wack being raided by the police. The woman with red highlights appeared on the screen as she was led away in handcuffs. According to the reporters, we were an hour into the coverage.

"You forget I was here, Bracken?" I sat up, rubbing my eyes through the mask. "Bracken?" Glancing at his chair, my heart dropped.

Blood covered his shirt. His arms lay limp over the armrests. Skin white as paper, his glazed eyes stared through me.

"Kyle? Honey, you there?"

I stared at my friend, wondering how I couldn't have known. Shocked I hadn't awakened.

Wishing I had.

"Kyle Samson Erwin III, you answer me right now. What's going on?"

I lifted the phone, swallowing a thousand emotions. "I need you to go to my lab and remove everything. Files, materials, my tablet."

"What?"

"Destroy everything. Don't tell anyone why, just say I'm moving to another lab."

A quiver in her voice tensed my shoulders. "Honey, you're coming home. Right?"

Two feet from a corpse I'd once called a friend, I wanted to cower. But I'd been spared yet again, thanks to an ability no one else possessed. An opportunity I couldn't squander. For Bracken's sake.

"Not yet. I have more work to do."

THE END
~~~~~

THE FIRST
Rosemarie DiCristo and Pam Halter

Earth Date One-One-24
My Calita begged me to stay, but I must protect my family. It will kill me to leave her and our daughter, but my whereabouts have been discovered and the Veilian Council has dispatched a Hunter.

I don't understand their mindset. Our planet is dying and our population dwindling. We've kept to ourselves for far too long. I thought when I returned from searching out compatible planets that I would be a hero, but the anger and hatred hurled at me left me in fear for my life. I dared not tell anyone that I unveiled myself to other beings, or that I met and fell in love with an Earthling woman. I had no choice but to return in secret to Earth. Now I have been discovered.

I will return when it's safe. It shouldn't take too long to shake the Hunter they've sent.

~~~~~

We could yell at the top of our lungs, and no one would hear us.

We were that alone.

The never-ending erosion mitigation project at Rockaway blocked boardwalk access to huge swaths of the beach, which discouraged people from strolling along the surf and meant swimming was absolutely forbidden.

But then, we wouldn't be swimming.

"Ready," Oran cried.

"Set," I answered.

"Go!" we shouted together, then took off running down the hard-packed sand.

Each time we came to a jetty, we clambered over it, *not* crossing at the small, flat, safe parts where the jetty met the sand, *certainly not* going around it, but springing onto the rocks and propelling ourselves forward into the creamy surf on the other side.

After all, what was better than the sheer joy of galloping down a beach absolutely free of anyone, even lifeguards? Okay, we passed those two random homeless guys who were there almost every day. But other than them? Despite Rockaway Beach being a part of New York City, it was just me and Oran and our boogie boards, as the incoming waves crashed so hard, they soaked us from the waist down.

"It's summer vacation!" Oran, my-brother-from-another-mother,
~~~~~

yelled as he loped onto and over the first jetty.

"Whoo hoo!" I yelled back.

He was a foot ahead of me, as always. In things like running and jumping, I couldn't keep up; I got too winded. But I didn't let it bother me (much) because in water sports? Man, I was an aquatic machine.

We sped toward the next jetty, maybe three blocks away.

"Rockaway, we love you!" Oran hollered, as he vaulted it.

"Whoo hoo!" I hollered back.

Was fifteen too old to be whoo-hooing your way down beach? Not when your classmates already called you Too-Weird Tirra and Oddball Oran, because "behaving" wouldn't make a whit of a difference.

As Oran leapt onto the third jetty, he thumbed his nose at the sign informing us that boogie boarding was forbidden, too. "We don't care because we're rebels, afraid of nothing and no one! Whoo hoo!"

And I shouted, "Whoo hunnhhh!" as I slammed full force into something that knocked me onto my butt.

~~~~

Earth Date One-Three-37

It's been thirteen years. How I've missed my family. I hope my Calita, my Callie, hasn't forgotten me. I know my daughter has. My Tirra. She was so young when I left.

The Hunter, Hoba Jett, pursued me long and hard, but I've been able to elude him for the last decade. It was fortunate I found that small, unnamed asteroid. The magnetic signature shielded me and my ship from detection, and I had enough supplies to last. But they are almost depleted, and I'm sure Hoba has given up.

I'm coming, my darlings, Callie and Tirra. It won't be long now.

~~~~~~

Oran stopped short. "Clumsy, Tirra." He cartwheeled back over the jetty to prove how clumsy he wasn't.

"I ran into something."

"Yeah. The jetty."

"No!"

"Your feet, then. May I help you rise, milady?" He bent low over me, his dark brown eyes brimming with laughter, his right hand extended.

I shoved it away. "Rejoin the twenty-first century, huh, Oran?" I scrambled up, wiping sand from my backside. We were mid-jetty in the wet sand left behind when the tide went out. I walked forward, hands extended before me, probing...

"Tirra." Oran's voice was merry. "You tripped over—"

I gasped, which made him gasp. "Something's here."

He stared at me.

My fingertips hit resistance. I could see nothing, but I couldn't push my hands past the *something* no matter how hard I tried.

"Oh, look, I can pretend to be a mime, too." Oran mimicked my movements.

"I'm not kidding!" And I grabbed his hands and shoved them against the *something*.

Every bit of color drained from his face, then he yanked back as if he'd been burned, but the surface I'd touched was warm, not hot, as well as cool, not cold.

I kept probing. "It's not metal, glass or plastic…"

"Stop touching it!" he cried.

"It's like some weird combination of all three." I tapped it with my right fist, and the stone ring I always wore, a gift from my dad, made a clunk.

We both jumped.

"Did you hear me, Tirra?" Oran's voice was shrill. He grabbed my arm to pull me back.

I shrugged away. "Stop. It's nothing to be afraid of."

"Some invisible *thing* on the beach? Get away!"

"You get away!" I slapped both palms into his shoulders, but that moved him back as much as if I'd slapped him with a dead fish. I growled, "I want to see what this is."

"I know what it is: some crazy-alien thing, and —"

Whatever it was, it was something good, I knew that somehow, and I had to explore it, if he'd just shut up.

I ran both hands over the surface then gasped again.

"What?" Oran shrieked.

~~~~~

Earth Date four-seven-39

I was a fool to think Hoba Jett had given up. I underestimated him. Now my ship is damaged. I must get to the escape pod and use the Earth's atmosphere to cover the launch. I'll have to time it exactly, when my ship is burning during reentry.

~~~~~

I don't know how long I sat unconscious in the pod, but I've escaped. I'm injured, although not severely, thank the stars. Just a fractured ankle.

The main computer is down as well as my suit-jet, but my suit-com still works. I must get out of the pod before Hoba realizes I wasn't in the ship. Where can I go to prevent him from knowing about my wife and daughter?

First, I need food and water and something to wrap my ankle. I'll see where I've landed and assess the situation. I can't use our technology, or I'll definitely give away my position. I don't think recording my journal entries will, so I'll keep a record this way.

~~~~~

"There's a place that feels like a rim… or an edge… to an open door."
I slowly traced where it curved above me. "About three feet high. Three
feet around." I stuck a hand into a suddenly empty space.

Oran screamed.

I whirled to face him. "What now?"

"Your-your-your…" Oran swallowed hard and tried again. "Your
arm—wrist—hand and wrist—" He gulped again. "It totally
disappeared."

"What're you talking about? It didn't disappear." To prove that I
stuck it into the space again.

And he screamed again. "Your arm from the elbow down totally—"

"You're crazy. I can *see* it." And as if that would prove he was
hallucinating, I dove through the space.

What I saw caused my eyes to bug out, but before I could process it,
I heard Oran yelling behind me, "Oh shoot, oh man, oh my friggin—!
Tirra! Where are you? Why can't I see you? Tirra! Answer me! Tirra!!"

~~~~~

Earth Date four-eight-39
*I had forgotten how difficult it could be getting off the Rockaway
peninsula. I didn't want to take a chance of getting hit by a vehicle while
walking over the bridge, so I ended up slogging my way through the
marsh. My spacesuit protected me, for the most part, and I thanked the
stars it was low tide. The worst part was the smell of dead things all
around me. If only my suit-jet was operational, I would have simply
flown over it.*

*My first priority has been taken care of; my ankle is bandaged, and I
have medication for pain. I felt bad taking things from the medical
facility, but my need was great.*

*It proved more difficult to procure food and water. I used a water
hose from a house and rinsed off the muck from the marsh, but I know I
still carried the stench of it. Nothing I could do about that. It will fade as
it dries.*

*I finally found a convenience store with premade sandwiches in an
open refrigerated case and hid two in my spacesuit along with a bottle of
water. It is not winter now, but I didn't want to take a chance of being
tripped over if I slept outside, so I found an empty house. There were other
humans there, but they didn't seem to hear me come in. I'm still too close
to the escape pod. I'm hoping I can go farther tomorrow now that I have
pain killers.*

I've seen no sign of Hoba Jett, but I know he's out there.

~~~~~

I was in what had to be a spaceship. An alien spaceship, unless NASA
had one so top-secret it was invisible.
~~~~~

"Tirra! Where are you? Tirra!"

It was small, and exactly like the capsule the Apollo astronauts splashed down in, totally round but tapered up top, tall enough for me to stand upright. And I wasn't hallucinating because I touched walls that were solid, brushed my fingertips along consoles with hundreds of dials and panels and instruments way more futuristic than any sci-fi movie I'd ever seen.

"Our Father, Who art in Heaven… Tirra!!! Answer me!"

The walls were lustrous like gold, copper, and bronze all at the same time, but glittery, like diamonds. But the consoles were dotted with dead, unblinking lights.

"Holy cripes, Holy Christmas, Holy Cow, Holy Holy." From the way Oran's voice sounded, he was madly hopping around. "TIRRA!!!"

"Stop screeching!" I screeched. "I'm safe, and I've discovered something wonderful."

There was a slight pause, then Oran started screaming, "Holy Moley Cannoli, I can hear you but not see you." Then he added a couple of loud and frantic "bleep" words.

I snorted. "I told you, I'm *inside* —"

"You're making this up!" His voice sounded panicked.

"I'm *what*?"

Still panicked. "It's gotta be a trick."

Trick? No way. This was real. But… then why did I feel so calm? "Answer me this, Oran; you really can't see me?"

"No. Yes. Oh, crud, I don't know how to answer that—"

"Then how can I be making this up? I'm *in* something: a space capsule."

"Oh crud, oh crud, oh crud, oh crud…"

Just when I thought he'd be muttering that forever, he ordered, "Get out now!"

I leaned out enough to scowl at him. "No way I'm—"

Oran yelped, then seemed to curse his fear. With gritted teeth and not looking at me, he said, "All that's not invisible is your head and shoulders."

Quickly, I glanced down. "I can see all of me."

"Well, so will I!" And he grabbed my shoulders and yanked me forward.

We tumbled to the sand.

"Now you're visible." Triumph laced his voice.

I instantly tried to scramble back to the capsule.

"No, Tirra!" He flopped onto me, pinning me beneath his lanky six-foot-tall frame until I head-butted him away and rolled to my feet.

He rolled to his feet and blocked me, his eyes dark pools. "Try to get back in and I head-butt *you* halfway to Europe."

Furious, I spat out, "Oran. Listen to me. There's something magical in there."

"Yeah. *Black* magic." Now his eyes nearly popped out of his head. "Why aren't you freaking out?"

"Because it's such a calm place…"

"That's them putting a spell on you, so they can lure you in and take you to their home planet! Don't you read the newspapers?"

"You mean the *National Enquirer*? No." I clutched both his hands. "Try to understand, it's *safe* in there." No. Not safe; something awful happened in there; somehow, I sensed that. But there was good, too, or… I didn't know anymore. Whatever calm I'd felt in the capsule was gone, and the feeling of knowing… something was gone, too.

Sighing, I stared at the jetty as if that would make the capsule visible. "I wonder how long it's been here."

"Does that matter? We gotta leave. Now!"

"The tide's out. Have we ever been this far down the jetty before? Maybe that's why we never…"

"Tirra! Get away from it!"

Instead, I turned to him. "I need to know if you can see what I saw." Somehow, I knew he wouldn't.

He chewed his lip, then nodded quickly, so I gently took his hand and guided it to where the ship should be. I felt him flinch when his palm touched the surface then, still gently, I slid his hand and mine to the edge of the space. "See? Here."

His voice quavered. "You mean, 'Feel. Here.' But I feel nothing." He shook his head, sharply. "I mean, something. No space. Just that…" he swallowed hard. "…thing."

"But there *is* a space. Here." And I stuck my hand through.

"Criminy! Sorry… but… it disappeared again."

I could still see my entire hand, and past it, the inside of the capsule. Why couldn't Oran?

~~~~~

Earth Date five-zero-39

It's been two days and still no sign of Hoba Jett. I must be vigilant. He's too good a Hunter for me to think I've lost him.

As much as I want a glimpse of Callie and Tirra, I dare not go in the direction of where we last lived. I don't even know if they're still there.

I'm exhausted and still in pain, even though I've been taking pain medication on a regular basis. It's made me clumsy. And since I'm still veiled, I scared a man earlier this morning while grabbing a breakfast sandwich. He ran right into me.

On the upside, he made such a commotion, I was able to get a cup of
~~~~~

coffee and slip out the door. I have missed coffee for the last thirteen years. There's nothing like it on Veilio or anywhere else I've found.

I heard on the news in the store that a sonic boom was heard and what they're calling a Great White Light was seen. Humans can be so dramatic. That light was just my ship's signature. It's being blamed on a meteor, which they say crashed into the Atlantic Ocean. They've not recovered the asteroid, so it's believed it landed in an ocean trench.

The humans in the house were talking about it last night. I couldn't hear them clearly, but they didn't seem worried. I thought that strange, but I've never spent time with homeless humans.

There's no indication anyone thinks it was my ship, which is good for me. Still, it will draw Hoba's attention. He knows well what veiled Veilian ships look like entering an oxygen atmosphere. I must keep moving.

~~~~~

I ducked and started forward, but Oran pulled back on my arm. "I forbid you to go in there."

"You *forbid* me? *You* forbid me?"

"You can say it the only way left: you forbid *me*?" he used a squeaky-girl voice, "and it still wouldn't change anything."

I got right in his face because, yeah, Too-Weird Tirra was six feet tall just like Oddball Oran. "You're not my brother, unless I have a colossal surprise awaiting me. And you're not my father. I don't have a father. My father died—"

"Don't you dare pull the dead-father card on me now. Too much is at stake."

"Too right! Like trying to figure out why an alien space capsule..."

Where he felt fear, I felt anticipation, longing, peace. Something Too-Weird me didn't often feel, not even charging down Rockaway Beach with my best friend. A long sharp hiss escaped Oran. "By going *in*? Try calling NASA. Or is it NORAD?"

I started wheedling. "Please, Oran; with you right outside, you could..."

"What? Jump aboard as it takes off for Neptune? And what would your overprotective crazy mom say if I let you get kidnapped by aliens?" He must have seen something in my face. "And don't you dare come back by yourself. I mean it. Promise me, Tirra: you will not come back today, or any other day."

I hung my head so I looked chastened and promised.

I'd just come back at night.

~~~~~

Earth Date five-one-39
I've caught sight of the signature of Hoba's suit-jet. I know it well.

It leaves a barely visible shimmering trail of yellow. Thank the stars, I saw it. He's closer than I realized.

My ankle is feeling better, but I still must be careful. I must stay alert. I can't get caught like I did on Cradius. If it wasn't for the rock giant who crossed between us, I would have been killed. I almost was killed when I jumped onto the massive ankle and rode that thing for miles. But at least I escaped Hoba.

I think I'll double back tonight. I usually don't do that so soon, so I'm hoping Hoba will be fooled. And I'm more and more uncomfortable in the house. The homeless humans now seem obsessed with the "asteroid." I know they can't see me, but something in my gut is telling me to get out.

~~~~~

It was after midnight when I reached the jetty with my flashlight and fresh batteries.

It should've been impossible to find, but it was like the capsule called to me. I staggered around the calf-deep surf for maybe fifteen seconds, then found it and made my way inside.

Once in, I got a flash of me sitting on the wooden deck of our home, late at night, gazing at the white-capped breakers as they rolled to shore, hearing the waves, feeling the cool ocean breeze and the strong, glorious sensation of someone cradling me in his arms.

All that in less than a flash, but it left me with the same feeling of absolute peace I'd felt when I'd first entered the capsule.

Immediately I thought, *What if Oran's right? What if it's alien-induced peace, trying to lull me into... what?*

No. Nothing bad. I felt like I was... home.

Shaking that thought away, I bent closer to the nearest console. Everything was labeled with symbols that looked like our punctuation — commas, apostrophes, periods, wavery back-slashes — which had to be their language. Squinting hard, as if that would help, I slid my hand here and there over the consoles, buttons, screens. I stopped at one glowing coppery panel about the size of a Pop Tart, gently placed my right palm on it, then grunted sharply and pulled back. The panel was as soft as translucent Play-Doh.

Head cocked, lips tight, I carefully sunk my palm back in and immediately my ring — the one that had clunked against the outside of the ship — began heating up. Which wasn't as crazy as it sounded, because often, late at night as I tried to sleep, it glowed, giving off pale light and warmth. I always thought that meant something but couldn't figure out what.

It was made of some kind of polished pale brown stone and, according to Mom, Dad gave it to me right before he died. As if he knew he'd die.
~~~~~

It perfectly fit my right ring finger then, when I was two.

It still fit perfectly now.

I pressed tighter into the Play-Doh and suddenly heard a burst of weird bloopy static… Rasping a terrified gurgle, I pulled back.

Silence.

Tentatively, I touched the Play-Doh again. Another burst of static, then: a man's voice.

My Calita begged me to stay, but I must protect…

This time when I gasped, I didn't pull away enough to break contact.

He was speaking English. Or was he? I thought back to those nights when my ring glowed warm, to a soft lullaby I heard in my head, in English and some other language that I could totally understand, at least in my heart.

….but I must protect my family. It will kill me to leave her and our daughter, but my whereabouts have been discovered and the Veilian Council has dispatched a Hunter.

I don't understand their mindset. Our planet is dying and our population dwindling…

I lifted my palm and put it down to the left, then did the same, but to the right, which seemed to work like "fast-forward" and "reverse."

I was a fool to think Hoba Jett had given up. I underestimated him. Now my ship is damaged. I must get to the escape pod and use the Earth's atmosphere to cover the launch. I'll have to time it exactly, when my ship is burning during reentry…

Then…

I heard on the news in the store that a sonic boom was heard and what they're calling a Great White Light was seen…

And then…

It's being blamed on a meteor…

The Great White Flash of Light?! The media went nuts about it, with stupid-wild theories that until this second no one could explain.

Cool. Wait till I tell…

Oh. I guess I couldn't tell Oran.

Anyway, what could I explain?

Fast-forward.

My first priority has been taken care of; my ankle is bandaged, and I have medication for pain…

Static. Fast-forward.

I'm hoping I can go farther tomorrow now that I have pain killers. I've seen no sign of Hoba Jett, but I know he's out there…

Fast-forward through more static.

I'm exhausted and still in pain, even though I've been taking pain medication on a regular basis. It's made me clumsy…

Oh, that poor man.

I fast-forwarded more.

I've caught sight of the signature of Hoba's suit-jet. I know it well. It leaves a barely visible shimmering trail of yellow. Thank the stars, I saw it. He's closer than I realized...

Oh, creepy-scary. What if that Hoba Jett dude came here, now? Who was he, and who was the man making these entries?

I rewound to nearly the beginning.

It's been thirteen years. How I've missed my family. I hope Calita, my Callie, hasn't forgotten me. I know my daughter has. My Tirra. She was so young when I left.

I jerked back, breaking contact, then slowly reached out and touched the Play-Doh again, rewinding.

...know my daughter has. My Tirra. She was so young when I left...

Rewind again.

...my daughter has. My Tirra...

...My Tirra...

...Tirra...

I yanked back so hard I banged the wall of the ship. Holding my right hand with the left, as if to stop myself from touching the panel again, I cried, "Please tell me you're talking about another Tirra. That can't possibly be me." Then I instantly caught sight of my face in the glittery gold-copper-bronze-diamond wall. Only it wasn't my face. It was translucent, as if I had another face beneath the surface that was mine, too, and yet wasn't... and both glowed with that weird gold-copper-bronze.

With a hoarse cry, I scrambled for the door. The Tirra in those journals had to be some random alien. But even if she was, why could *I* enter the capsule? Why could *I* see things? Understand things?

I burst onto the sand.

Oran was there, sweeping a ginormous flashlight along the jetty. When I hit the sand, he whirled and spat out, "I knew you'd—"

But Mom was in the flashlight beam, too. Not furious, like Oran. Her eyes glistened with tears. "You found him, Tirra. I knew you would."

~~~~~

Earth Date five-two-39

I stole earth clothes and a baseball cap from one of the homeless humans in the house while they were out and put them over my spacesuit. I can't completely unveil myself because of my ankle injury. I didn't realize this would happen, but I'm glad to know it. Still, it was enough to get a ride with humans across the Rockaway bridge.

I walked the beach like other humans, although I noticed they were not as covered with clothing as I. But I had no choice. I need to keep my spacesuit on.

There were footprints in the sand around the pod. Hoba must have found it. I dare not go closer. I will walk back down the beach and find
~~~~~

some food. Then I'll come back after sunset.

~~~~~

"Him?" My voice shook.

"Your father, of course." Mom said it like it was the only answer possible. But her voice was impatient. No, frantic.

"My father is dead!" My voice rose hysterically.

Mom gripped my hands. "Is he injured? He must be, if he can't come out. Badly? Tirra! Tell me."

"My father is *dead*. He's been dead since he crashed his private plane when I was two." She knew this as well as I did. I was only saying it now so she could confirm it.

But she said hurriedly, "I didn't know if he was dead or alive. But the Great White Flash! I prayed that was him. Was it? His ship, returning home? Tell me!"

How could she expect me to tell her anything, process anything, with the news she'd just given me? "My dad..." I swallowed hard. "...was a NASA astronaut?"

Oran, silent this entire time, just looked baffled. But Mom's expression radiated her disappointment in me. "Does NASA have invisible spaceships and astronauts?"

"Maybe top-secret ones?" Except, I *knew* they didn't.

She took a deep breath. "Your dad, and you, are Veilians."

"You're telling me we're *aliens*." Not a question but a slightly hysterical statement.

"Veilian," she stressed, as if I'd simply mispronounced it.

"Hoo boy." Oran swayed on his feet.

My eyes filled with tears of anger and fear. "Mom!! You're telling me that for, what, thirteen years you've lied to me about everything—"

"Is he *inside*, Tirra?"

"No. It's empty," I said, with regret for both her and for me.

~~~~~

Earth Date five-two-39

I tried to get back to the pod, but I saw Hoba's suit-jet trail heading right to its location. I must wait. Perhaps he will not notice me hiding behind this rock.

There are a few humans sitting around a bonfire, so I will blend in and hope he will not harm any of them in order to get to the pod.

~~~~~

We sat on the jetty, where the surf tickled our feet, our flashlights illuminating us, but not enough to attract attention. Attention? Heck, Rockaway was part of New York City. We could be sitting plum naked and no New Yorker would look twice.

Quietly, Mom explained. "He was here on a mission."
~~~~~

My voice was shrill. "I know about the mission. I heard about it, or part of it, on the tapes or whatever they were."

"You could hear...?" Oran cried. "Never mind. Go on, Mrs. Anzo."

"We fell in love. So, we married." As if it were that simple.

Was it that simple? Could falling in love with an alien lead to marriage? I glanced at wacky, wonderful Oran, still pale and bug-eyed, and dipped my head. "But..." I couldn't look at anyone anymore. "That means I'm half alien."

"Veilian, Tirra. At least get the terms right."

"Don't scold me, Mom," I shot back. "At least not until I'm ready to deal with this."

Mom sighed. "Anyway, you are *the first* half Veilian. We didn't know what might happen to you if the Veilian Council discovered you. I'm sorry, babe. All these years, I didn't know if your dad was safe, or if he'd been killed. And yes, you're part him and part me. I can't explain how it works. *I'm* not the super alien being. But your body is a shell—"

"A *shell?*"

"Maybe 'shell' is the wrong word. It's like skin—"

"*Like* skin?"

"—because it grows as you do—"

"Grows?"

"Tirra, will you stop repeating everything I say?"

"What do you want me to do? Everything I've ever known is a lie."

She frowned at me. "Not a lie, just... not the entire story."

I looked at her and released a harsh laugh. "You were saying something about my shell? Or was it my skin?" And, shuddering, I remembered that weird face-within-a-face I'd just seen while in the capsule. Which was the real me? The top me? The underneath me? Both?

"No wonder you lied to me all these years," I said, my voice thick with scorn.

She sounded frustrated. "It was for your safety, Tirra. That's all I can tell you."

"Can? Or won't?"

She shrugged. "A bit of both."

I touched at my "shell," then, tentatively, I touched Mom's arm. Mine felt like birch bark, compared to hers. It had always felt different from other girls. Stupid me, I assumed I had dry skin.

"It cloaks—veils—the real you," Mom said.

"The real me whose father is from a place called—what?"

"Veilio," she said.

"Veilio is an alien planet?" But even as I spoke the words, I thought, *No. Home.* And that scared me and thrilled me, all at once. "Mom, about his mission..."

"I do *not* know all the inner workings of Veilian politics. Just that your dad got in trouble—"

I waved a hand to stop her. "He's hurt, Mommy." Reverting to little-girl fear. "I listened to lots of his tapes. My… dad… is hurt."

~~~~~

Earth Date five-two-39
I listen to the young humans talking and laughing and I wonder if Tirra likes bonfires on the beach. Does she remember sitting with me while her mother toasted marshmallows, these soft, white, sweet things completely unfamiliar to me. They didn't look appetizing at all. How surprised I was when I tasted one Callie had toasted for me. Delicious! Tirra squealed and clapped when it was her turn. I had to blow on it to cool it down.

It is a physical pain to have been separated from them for so long.

~~~~~

I scurried back into the capsule so that I could find out more about Dad, so that I—we—could help him.

I, half-Veilian, Too-Weird Tirra, was the only one who could.

I touched the Play-Doh.

I stole earth clothes and a baseball cap from one of the homeless humans in the house while they were out and put them over my travel-suit. I can't completely unveil myself because of my ankle injury. I didn't realize this would happen…

So, what? Dad looks human? Sort of human? Was he too-weird, too—like father, like daughter?

My life was starting to make an awful lot of sense.

Like, I'd always dreamed that people could see through me, just like I've had dreams where I could swim like a fish, or where I could fly. But didn't everyone?

Well, did "everyone" have my other traits?

My hair couldn't grow past my chin.

It was frizzy and couldn't be straightened.

I never felt cold. Never.

Yet I sunburned way too easily.

My eyesight and hearing were fantastic.

I was crazy-good at science and math.

I'd already said that, aside from swimming, I had no stamina for sports.

Too Weird Tirra.

They were right after all.

I moved my hand to fast-forward Dad's words.

There were footprints in the sand around the pod. Hoba must have…

A loud crackle of static, then silence.

"Must have what? Come on!" I pressed my hand harder.

Another crackle, then: *There were footprints in the sand around the pod. Hoba must have...*

"Arrrgh! I already know that!" I practically slapped the console.

Another crackle, then a ginormous "bloop," then no matter how frantically I slid my hand around the Play-Doh, the console, or all the walls of that freaking capsule, murmuring, "Please-please-please. Don't stop now. Please!" ... silence. Only silence.

I think I tried regaining contact like forever. Finally, I left the capsule.

Whatever Mom was going to ask died when she saw my tears. "No... luck?"

I shook my head anyway, stammering, "I don't know anything more. Where he is, what we can do..."

Oran grabbed me in a bear hug and sobbed into my neck.

"Thanks," I said, trying to be flippant. "But he's not *your* dad."

And then I sobbed, too.

~~~~~

Earth Date five-two-39

I saw Hoba hovering above the pod location. The humans I saw, oh, my stars and planets! It's Callie and Tirra—it must be Tirra—and a human boy. I have to lead Hoba away from them, but how? There are no weapons on the pod, and I only have my suit-com.

I wanted to reveal myself. Their weeping broke my heart! But Hoba. He was right there! I couldn't risk it, so I kept my hiding place until they were out of sight, then I watched Hoba land and go inside the pod. In just a few minutes, he emerged, his face ablaze with triumph. I have no idea what he thinks he found. Nothing works on the pod's main panel.

I'm going to follow him at a distance to see where he goes next.

~~~~~

I couldn't sleep. After nearly two excruciating hours, Mom's raspy snores echoed from her bedroom, and I returned to the capsule.

I'd tied my flashlight around my neck, but unlike Oran's super-duper one, it gave off little light. Plus, it kept swinging wildly as I thrashed around, because nothing was there.

Not the invisible "nothing." Literally nothing I could feel, or slide into, no matter how furiously I slapped the rocks.

I climbed onto them, kneeling, scabbering, pawing, clawing... nothing.

Waves washed over me, threatening to tumble me into the surf. I fell once, twice, three times, tearing gashes in my knees, scraping my knuckles, but either the capsule was gone—with Dad in it?—or I'd lost the ability to sense it.

I curled, fetal position, on the jetty, even if it meant the incoming surf choked me as it sloshed into my nose and throat. I was crying for a father I couldn't remember, who'd left us without a word. But no, there were those lullabies in my head, and my ring glowing warm.

"Girlie, are you okay?" cried one of those two random homeless guys who were always around. *He* had a giant lantern whose beam swept over me.

I raised my head. "Get away; can't you see I want to be alone?"

He started forward anyway, but his friend tugged his arm and reluctantly, he backed off.

When I was alone again, a yellowish fog, glimmery like the air when it was super-hot out, rolled in and began settling around me when—

"Tirra!" Oran flashed his Super-Light on me and charged onto the jetty to drag me away. "Mrs. Anzo, help!"

Together they lugged me, flashlights bumping us, arcing wildly, my arms and legs flailing just as wildly, to the dry sand where we collapsed in a heap. "I lost the capsule. I lost contact," I wailed. "How can we find him if the capsule's gone and I've lost contact?"

~~~~~

We were back in our kitchen in dry clothes with my tea untouched. Mom huffed and said, "I came to your room to give you this, Tirra, but found you gone."

"Only one place you'd be," Oran said in a scathing, scolding voice.

My voice was equally scathing and scolding. "Well, bravo; you found me."

"Kids." Mom's voice was so sharp, we both shut up. "No. No reprimands. We're too torn apart over this."

I looked at my knuckles and knees and nearly giggled.

Mom's face looked grave. "I hoped I'd never have to give it to you."

That sobered me, fast. "You never wanted me to know?"

"*We* wanted to keep you safe."

Something in her voice made my spine prickle.

She handed me a necklace, a dainty gold chain with a long rectangular stone hanging from it, brown striped, highly polished. Exactly like the stone that made up my ring.

I peered at her. "What do I do with it?"

"Aside from putting it on? I don't know. Your dad said you'd know. When it was time."

I put it on. The chain was long enough so that the Veilian rock—if that was what it was—touched my heart. I pressed the stone to my chest. Nothing. I pressed the ring *and* stone to my chest.

Nothing.

"Maybe it would work in the capsule," I said.

"What capsule?" Oran's voice was doleful.
~~~~~

"I don't know, Oran! Maybe it's back. At least, we gotta try."

~~~~~

It wasn't back.

Nothing had changed.

The horrible yellow fog still hovered around me, and all I felt when I ran my hands along the jetty was —

"Oh!"

"The capsule?" Mom cried.

"No, it's tiny. One second, I was touching jetty, and then I felt *this*, as if, somehow, it just dropped into my hands..." I grabbed it tight, then carefully ran one hand along its smooth, curving, circular...

"Cripes, she's doing the mime thing again," Oran groaned.

Not circular like my ring. U-shaped. "A cuff!"

"Cuff? What's that?" Oran asked.

"A bracelet thing."

"Then why not say...?"

"Because bracelets are bracelets and cuffs are... forget it." I put it on my wrist.

Oran made a choking sound. "Now your wrist is invisible where the cuff-thing is."

I hardly listened, waiting for something to happen.

Slowly, as if my body heat triggered it, the cuff turned solid.

It was also made of that brown striped Veilian stone, exactly like the ring and pendant.

My breath came out in a harsh rasp, and I rubbed the cuff as if it were Aladdin's lamp. My ring made a slight scraping noise as it skimmed the cuff's surface. Then I heard the familiar, static-y sizzle like I'd heard on the capsule, and my dad's voice sounded in my ears.

I hollered, "The cuff... it's a communicator. I can hear him!"

"What?" cried Oran.

"Oh, thank God," cried Mom.

"Shh! I need to hear!"

~~~~~

Earth Date five-three-39

I followed —

Cripes! Bloopy static spit out of the cuff.

— to an abandoned restaurant. He broke the lock on the rear door next to the —

Static!

— and slipped inside. What is he up to?

I waited for half an hour, and he came back out and flew off. I feel like it's a trap. Did he know I was watching him?

Another burst of static.

I need to know what he's doing. I won't go inside. I'll just look through the door.

Then, silence.

They could tell from my frustrated expression that it wasn't much of a message. I repeated it, anyway, best I could.

"But what does it mean?" Oran asked.

Mom shrugged.

"Even the weather's against us." I kicked at a broken clam shell, bright white in the glow of my flashlight. "When will that fog burn off?"

"What fog?" Oran said.

"That ugly shimmering yellow fog that won't..." I stopped so fast, I nearly choked. Yellow fog? Shimmering smoke? Where had I heard that before...?

With a sharp cry of, "Hoba Jett!" I spun around, glancing in all directions, but now, suddenly, the fog vanished.

"Hoba...?" Mom squeezed her eyes shut and pressed both fists to her throat.

"Mom, what? You're scaring me."

"Hoba Jett is a tracker—a bounty hunter—the Veilian Council sends after someone who's done something wrong, when they feel that person should be..."

"Arrested?" Oran supplied.

"Killed."

I put my lips against the cuff, shouting, "Dad, can you hear me? It's urgent that I tell you something!" Although if Hoba Jett was still hovering... no. I couldn't see... what had Dad called it? Not fog. Whatever it was, I couldn't *see* it. "Dad!"

Bloops and static. I shouted profanity, then I heard:

It's okay, my darling daughter. All is clear. Meet me behind the abandoned restaurant, Franca's Pizza, just past Fort Tilden. Bring your mother. I want to see you both. It's been such a long time.

~~~~~

Rockaway was a fairly long peninsula and *Franca's Pizza*, in Breezy Point, was at least three miles away, so we drove.

We'd barely gone a block when I saw those two homeless guys, this time panhandling in the middle of Rockaway Beach Boulevard.

I grunted. "Even at five a.m.?"

"Maybe they're like Patsy Cline and go walking after midnight." Oran was a huge fan, and a bigger fan of the conspiracy theory that carbon-monoxide poisoning, not pilot error, was what caused the plane crash that killed her.

Mom rolled down the window and gave a buck to the one who'd called to me when I was bawling on the jetty.
~~~~~

"Really, Mom? Now?"

"The homeless always need help, babe."

The word 'help' reminded me of something. "So that's why Dad left us? He was on a mission?"

"To save his people, but he got in trouble."

"My people, too." I continued, "What was he like? I barely remember him. Was he tall?"

"Very."

"Handsome?"

"Eh."

"Mom!"

"It's true. But..." Her merry expression was tinged with nostalgia. "...he was — is — the kindest man you'll ever meet. And, I don't know, dazzling. It was like I couldn't breathe without him in my air."

"Oooh, poetry!" Oran cried. But I sensed the tension in all of us. We'd see Dad again, soon. But then what?

"Hmmm," I said.

"Hmmm, what?" Oran said.

"Well, if the cuff's a communicator, what does the pendant —?" I grabbed the rectangular stone.

"Holy Toledo, what did you do?" Oran's voice shook.

"I don't know!" I cried. "I only squeezed it a little..." But I could see what he saw: the me under the me that was human — about ninety percent *invisible*, my translucent shell glowing coppery, human-ish... and yet, not.

I squeezed the stone twice.

"Great balls of fire, you're totally gone again." Oran took a deep breath. "Mrs. A. Why aren't *you* freaking out?"

"Because Justern could do it, too, obviously."

Oran snorted. "Like anything about this is obvious."

I cut him off. "With a pendant?"

Mom shook her head. "I don't think so."

I squeezed the pendant three times, and in a weird, wavery way, I came back.

Oran chewed his lip but said nothing.

I peered at the Veilian stone. "I wonder what else it does?" I squeezed it twice with my left hand. Nothing. I squeezed twice with my right hand again.

"Ho!" cried Oran.

Invisible again. "I think it's the ring touching the..."

"Don't start experimenting, Tirra." Mom sounded cross. "If you somehow rocketed to Veilio, I don't know what I'd do."

"I'd faint," Oran said.

I squeezed the stone three times and came back. "Mom..."

"Now what?"

We were almost to the pizza place. "Dad never spoke to me before through his journal. Isn't it odd that he did now? And did *Franca's* even exist thirteen years ago?"

"No…"

"And, like…" I licked my lips. "Now that I'm thinking about it, the voice didn't sound like Dad's."

No one dared say "Hoba Jett." But Oran swallowed and said, "I think we gotta go anyway. It's your dad!"

I could've hugged him for that.

~~~~~

I wasn't sure if my rock ring had to be touching the cuff for us to hear any other communications, but I kept my fingers wrapped around it anyway.

Tirra…

I started. It was a whisper, no, a murmur.

Come find me, Tirra. Because only you can see where I am…

A murmur so soft, I wasn't sure if it was "that voice" or Dad's voice, or if "that voice" *was* Dad's voice.

Tirra…

But it was hypnotic…

Come find me…

…and compelling, in a bad way.

Tirrrrrrrrrra…

With a low cry, I jerked my hand away from the cuff.

Oran's body jerked, too. "What?"

I shook my head, unable to form words.

"C'mon, T; I'm spooked enough as it is."

"It's n-nothing; I'm sure it's nothing, just Dad, calling me…"

"Your dad? Or…?"

Before he could say anything else, Mom said grimly, "We'll know in a second."

We'd arrived at *Franca's*.

~~~~~

Breezy Point was so anal about outsiders wandering around, even if they lived farther down the peninsula, that they literally had guard booths on the streets coming off Rockaway Point Boulevard. Dad probably snuck in, veiled. We were okay because Mom waitressed at *Kennedy's*, a couple of blocks away, and everyone knew us. But the morning guard, Claudia, wasn't in the tiny wooden guard booth where Beach 229th Street angled toward Palmer Drive.

No one was.

Oran let out a deep breath. "It's your dad; let's roll."

A fire had destroyed three of the stores in what was once a tiny strip mall on Palmer Drive. Recently, because they still reeked of stale smoke. The only other business—former business—was the pizza place. Empty lots were on both sides of us, and we were closer to the inlet than the ocean. Orangey streetlamps did little to light our way.

Dad... or whoever... couldn't have picked a more desolate spot.

We approached warily, going around to the back because the front door was totally boarded up. As we did, a stranger stepped out of the back door and into the dim light that hung over the dumpsters. Was he Veilian? Well, who else would be wearing some kind of spacesuit and holding... Great Caesar's Ghost! What looked like a sci-fi movie laser.

Er... that couldn't be Dad...

I checked Mom's face. Heck, no, it was not my father, or anyone she knew.

The Veilian raised the laser as if he intended to use it.

Veilian? No, it had to be one specific Veilian: Hoba Jett. Unless there were dozens of space guys running around Rockaway.

"Holey Moley," Oran whispered. But I demanded, "Where's my father? And what did you do to Claudia?"

A blank stare, then, "Oh, the she-guard?" He patted his laser. "Sleeping. Veilians don't kill. Unless we have to."

"Then where's my dad?"

Hoba—if that was who he was—gave us a malicious smile. "I was hoping you could tell me."

I took a breath so I wouldn't stammer. "You're the tracker they sent after Dad. Hoba Jett."

"At your service." He gave a slight bow, never taking his eyes or his laser gun off us.

"We don't want your service," Mom broke in. "We want Justern. *Where is he?*"

We stood silent while Oran pointed his flashlight at Hoba, his eyes wide and glued to the laser gun.

Hoba took a step closer and levelled the gun right at Mom's chest. The only sounds were the crickets and frogs in the marsh and the far-off crash of the surf. We were utterly alone with an evil, despicable alien tracker. I wondered how in the world we'd get out of this. If only there was a way to contact Dad. I didn't dare lift the cuff to my mouth. Hoba would probably shoot us dead.

But Dad was a super-alien; couldn't he hear me without the cuff? And did Hoba even have to know I was using it? Hands behind my back so I could discreetly touch ring-to-cuff, I thought, *Help us, Dad. Please. Help.*

"You are in communication with that traitor?" Hoba was saying, almost as if he'd read my mind. "Call him *now*. Or I'll start with killing this human woman, who I'm guessing is Justern's ... wife?"

Oran made an inarticulate gagging sound. Hoba swung the laser at him. "And *you* are next, boy."

"But we're not in communication with Dad," I protested. "We— I read his journals..."

His eyes narrowed. "Liar! Only *you* can completely sense him, because you are of him. Now once more: where is he?"

"Oh, right; you want us to 'come find him' for you. But I've *never* seen him!"

"Then use the cuff I gave you." His impatience was so fierce, I expected him to stamp his foot. "It's a Veilian link-com."

Did he know something about the cuff that I didn't? "But that never contacted Dad, only let me hear his..."

Hoba neither confirmed nor denied that. "Enough!" He turned the gun on me, but before he could do anything else, I clutched my pendant and squeezed it twice. Suddenly, Hoba gave a roar of anger. "Whaaaaaaaaaaaat??? Where are you, girl?"

Mom gasped. "Tirra!"

Oran gagged again, his fear stuck in his throat, trying to force itself out.

"Tirra, is it?" Hoba sneered. "Well, *Tirra*, unveil yourself or your mother dies. You have three seconds. One."

He can't see me? A Veilian *can't see me? What the —*

"Two—"

Maybe I could spook him by charging him. In active shooter training in school, they said if all else failed, charge the guy. Plus, if the charger was invisible...

So, I clutched the Veilian stone and charged Hoba, screeching like crazy, but before I could squeeze it, I slipped on something and yanked at the golden chain. It stretched but didn't break, and simultaneously I shot upward.

"Holy Christmas!" I shrieked, and would've zoomed to Mars — or Veilio! — if I hadn't let go of the stone.

Hoba shot a laser blast at where I'd been.

"Missed me!" I shouted, and pulled the chain and shot, just as jerkily, a few feet to the left.

Hoba aimed and shot where my voice had been.

"Missed again!" I cried merrily and flew, still jerkily, up and over his head.

He sent out two laser blasts, but they only blasted off a couple branches from the sycamore trees on Palmer Drive.

"Maybe this will help," I chanted, and squeezed my stone three times, and wavered back into visibility.

With a sound like "Harrrrrrrr!" Hoba fired at me, but I squeezed the stone twice and yanked it at the same time, then disappeared and rocketed at a crazy angle onto the tattered awning of *Franca's Pizza*, sliding down the canvas, and hitting the asphalt.

"Unnnhhh," I said, sounding even to myself like a stereotypical comic book character.

Hoba cackled. "I can turn invisible too, girl." And suddenly he vanished.

Or most of him did.

I could see that weird, shimmery, yellow fog, so I picked up a loose, broken brick that had tumbled from the pizza parlor's outer wall and hurled it at his head.

I'm not a thrower. It didn't hit him. But it came close.

"I can still see you!" I exclaimed and picked up a bigger brick.

Hoba snarled with fury, then unveiled and turned to face Mom, pointing the laser at her chest. "One more disappearance or brick and she's dead."

"*No!*" The words tore from my throat, and I became visible where I'd sprawled on my butt, to the right of the restaurant door.

Hoba grinned. "That's better. Now, bring your traitor of a father here. And give me whatever he gave you to veil yourself. I could use it in my line of work."

With shaking hands, I took off the pendant. As much as I hated to give it to Hoba, I knew it would buy time to figure something out. And Hoba had no way of knowing he needed the ring, as well. Or that I *had* a ring. I hoped, anyway.

Carefully, I covered the ring with my thumb. Then I stretched out the other hand holding the necklace. It swung from my fingertips, catching the beam of Oran's flashlight and throwing golden sparkles on the wall of the restaurant. And even though every hero in every movie I'd ever seen said the dumbest line ever, I couldn't help myself. "You'll never get away with this."

Hoba guffawed loudly. "And just who do you think is going to stop me?"

We all held our breaths, waiting for someone — anyone — to swoop in and save the day. But there was no sound. Nothing.

No one was coming. Tears slipped down my cheeks as Hoba snatched the pendant from my hand. Then he motioned with the laser. "Let's go."

"Go where?" Mom asked.

"Inside the building," Hoba said. "You and the girl. The boy? I don't need him." And without any warning, he fired the laser at Oran, who collapsed to the ground.

"Noooooooooooo!" I shrieked.

Mom was next to him, and she dropped to her knees. "It's okay, sweetie. He's breathing."

"But for how long?"

"The boy will be fine," Hoba said in a bored voice. "If you cooperate."

I raged at him, "What was that, then? A warning? You're a monster!" Screwing my face into what I hoped was a *Zap me, I dare you!* look, I rushed to Oran and also knelt beside him.

His face was still and pale, his eyes shut tight. Shakily, gently, I brushed the damp, black curls from his forehead, whispering, "Oh, Oran. Dear, sweet Oran."

He flopped sideways with a gurgle and his shoulders shook.

This time, I didn't let out a shriek but a wail of sorrow. "You've killed him!"

"Honey, *he's breathing*," Mom assured me.

I grabbed his wrist.

He shuddered once more, and although he'd managed to turn his head away from me, I could tell his coloring looked okay and his breathing sounded normal, and his pulse...

But what did I know about pulses?

I came to my feet. "*You're* the traitor; wanting to kill my dad; trying to kill an innocent boy..."

His eyes grew icy. "Careful, girl, I'm not a patient man, and I have a job to do. Now *get inside!* I want this done before it's too light."

I stood my ground. If I could stall Hoba until sunrise, maybe we would be seen by someone. Anyone! Except, those stupid lasers looked and sounded like lightning and thunder, so who would come out to investigate that? Probably not even all those other guards who tried to stop outsiders from roaming around Breezy Point's residential streets, although I was suddenly certain they were "sleeping" like Claudia. And all the yelling? This was New York City. Everyone yelled all the time.

"I can see I was too lenient with the Earth boy." And Hoba raised the laser gun.

I screamed a wild, wordless cry, and threw myself between Hoba and Oran.

"Hoba Jett!" a voice called from the darkness.

A tall man in old clothes and a baseball cap stepped into the light.

"Justern?" Mom asked uncertainly.

"Let my family go, Hoba," he said. "They aren't listed on your manifest. You only have permission for me."

Dad? He sorta looked like me, in his unveiled form. Or I sorta looked like him. And I didn't know what Mom meant. Dad looked very handsome to —

Hoba gave a short laugh. "You and any of your twisted science experiments." He nodded toward me. "That includes *her*."

"But not my wife," Justern ground out.

"She's your accomplice!" Hoba bellowed. "She's as guilty as you!"

"She goes free!"

"She does not!"

I took advantage of Hoba's attention being fully on my father and slowly bent my knees far enough to pick up another broken brick. Just as Hoba turned his head to look in my direction, I flung the jagged chunk at him.

Thunk!

It landed smartly on Hoba's hand, causing him to drop the laser. In a millisecond, Dad leaped at Hoba. The two rolled and grappled on the ground.

At first, it was hard to tell who was winning. What with them disappearing and reappearing, veiling and unveiling, then wriggling out of each other's grasp, then leaping back onto each other, again and again, I couldn't predict where they were until suddenly, they were right in front of me. I know Dad got in a couple of quick jabs and one wicked uppercut, but Hoba was hitting him hard, too.

Mom and I pulled an unconscious, and still breathing, Oran to the side. Even in my fear and desperation, I thought, *Oran, when we're safe, you've got to stop chowing down those Meat Up Grill burgers and fries.*

"C'mon, Dad!" I called. "You can take him. He's only a wimpy bounty hunter!"

"Tirra," Mom said. "Don't distract them. Or anger *him*."

"Yeah, but," I started to argue, then I remembered that Hoba dropped his laser when I hit him with the brick. Where did it land? I scanned the area, hoping to catch sight of it, but the sun was only beginning to rise, and there wasn't enough light yet to see past the street light ring.

Just then, Dad cried out in pain. I looked and saw Hoba standing with one foot on Dad's ankle, the laser back in his hand.

"Bully! Coward!" I shrieked. "Fighting a wounded man. Are you that weak?"

Hoba slammed the butt of the laser on Dad's head, and he fell over. Then Hoba started toward me. Mom stepped in between us. "No one touches my husband. *Or* my daughter. Besides, 'the wife' is getting tired of your—"

"Get out of the way!" Hoba slapped her across the face, and she fell to the ground with a cry.

I screamed and rushed at him, but that only made it easier for his hand to close around my wrist like a vise grip, until I cried out, too.

"Now," Hoba snarled. "Get into the restaurant. I'm tired of this playing around."

"What are you going to do?" I asked as he practically dragged me to the door.

"I'm going to send you to Veilio. The transport is all set up inside and ready to go."

I struggled against him, but it was futile. I couldn't win against a man who was so much bigger than I was. We were three feet from the door when I heard a sound like something hitting wet rubber. In that second, Hoba's feet flew out and he landed on his backside, the laser skidding into the shadows as he cracked his head on the cement.

"Oh no. Not my best friend," Oran said. He wavered a bit as he stood, still pale and a little shaky.

"Nicely done, O," I said. *I* was shaky, too, from fear, relief... and who knows what else.

Then, like the villain in every horror movie, Hoba Jett rose to his feet, roaring, and charged me and Oran.

Zzzzzap!

He grunted and fell again, face-down this time.

"The laser gun!" I exclaimed, looking around.

Mom stood holding the laser. She winked and blew across the barrel.

"But Mrs. A!" Oran cried. "That dude only stunned me. What if —"

Hoba groaned and started to get up *again*.

"Callie!" Dad shouted. He'd risen to his knees. "The laser! Now!"

Mom flung it at him. Dad made two quick twists to the handle and *Zzzzzzzap!* Hoba slammed flat on his back, and this time, he didn't rise.

"Er..." Oran looked down at Hoba but backed away a few steps as he did so. "You didn't kill him, did you?"

"Nope." Dad shot him a cockeyed smile. "Veilians don't kill Veilians. Or we shouldn't. However, Mr. Jett most likely won't wake up for one or two days." He gingerly stood and threw my words back at me. "Nicely done, all of you." But his eyes were on Mom.

She stepped to him, put out a hand, touched him like she thought he'd disappear again. "Oh, Justern... so many years..." She blinked but her tears fell anyway. "You left so abruptly. You know I wasn't nearly through loving you."

Dad pulled Mom into a hug. "But now we have eternity, my sweet." And then they kissed. I mean, *really* kissed.

"What, literally?" Oran had come up behind them. "Can you guys live forever? Can you do something to your spouses so *they* can live forever? Cool."

Dad turned a quizzical grin on him.

"That's Oran, by the way," I told Dad. "You'll get used to him." Then

I nestled into my Daddy's arms with Mom completing a three-way hug.

Oran waited a beat, then said, "But about the forever…"

I pulled away from Mom and Dad. "I thought you were unconscious, Oran." My voice was sour. "I thought he'd killed you."

He shot me a big, loopy grin. "Naw. I was playing possum."

"The grunts? The gurgles?"

"Acting."

"Acting? *I thought you were dead!*" I could feel my eyes bulging with fury, but before I could spit out furious words, I heard Dad murmur to Mom, "Uh-oh, I see Tirra's got your temper."

"Acting and laughing." Oran was laughing *now* as he put on a high-pitched voice. "Oh, sweet Oran, I've loved you forever…!"

"I *never* said that!"

"…and I always will!"

If looks could kill, Oran would be stone-cold dead.

I charged him, grabbing him by his shoulders, but he just grabbed mine. We went around in circles for a bit, then Oran said, "Shall we dance, milady?" and attempted to spin and dip me.

I tried head-butting him but missed as he jerked away.

Dad was saying to Mom, "I think I'll need to get used to Tirra, too," when the two homeless guys I kept seeing everywhere strolled toward us from around the building. The sun had broken the horizon and there was plenty of light now.

"Let me guess," I said as I yanked away from a still-giggling Oran. "You're not homeless. Um… police?"

They shook their heads. The taller one stepped forward. "Greetings, Justern."

"Greetings," Dad said, warily.

"I am Ashtin, and this is Xavis," the tall Veilian said. "We're not here to arrest you. We've been looking for you."

"And watching over your family," the other Veilian, Xavis, said.

"I don't understand," Dad said.

Ashtin laughed. "It's a long story."

Oran groaned. "A long story? I'm starving. Can we hear it over breakfast?"

We all laughed then.

Dad put an arm around Oran. "Sure, buddy. I'm hungry, too, and I want to get to know my daughter's best friend."

"How about your daughter?" I half-joked. "And, yeah, Oran's my *best friend*. Nothing else."

Dad's chuckle gave me delighted shivers. "Of course, my love. Of course. To the getting to know you. And to the belief that he's your friend. Nothing else."

As we headed for our car and Rockaway Point Boulevard, I said, "Wait. What about Claudia?"

Now Ashtin and Xavis looked blank.

"The she-guard," Oran said. "I mean — heck, you know what I mean."

We found her lying quietly in the ruins of *Franca's*. Dad and the Veilians carried her to her wooden guard booth, assuring us she'd wake up and not remember a thing.

"There may be other guards, um, sleeping," I told them.

"We'll scout around for them once we park Jett in the pizza place," Xavis said.

"Now can we eat?" Oran asked.

Dad answered. "Does *Last Stop* still have the best breakfasts on Rockaway?"

"Rockaway and the entire tri-state region," I said.

"Beach 116th Street," Dad told the Veilians, and Xavis smiled, promising, "Be there soon."

Once we were in the car, Oran called back to Ashtin and Xavis, "You guys rock, you know that, right? But can I ask you one thing?"

They nodded solemnly.

"What the heck took you so long?"

~~~~~

Earth Date six-five-39

I've spent twelve glorious days with my Calita and my Tirra. In that time, I've caught up on the thirteen years I lost with them.

I am more in love with Callie than ever. What a resilient, strong woman I married.

Tirra is a delight. Such a quick and humorous personality. Reminds me of myself when I was young.

Oran feels more like a son to me every day. He seems happy to have me, as well. Tirra told me his father abandoned him and his mother when he was just a little older than she the year I left.

It will take me a long time to feel safe here. I've been on the run for so long. But Ashtin and Xavis told me that my fellow scientists realized the truth two years after I left Earth, running from Hoba. They convinced our Council, who authorized several scientists and a few soldiers from the Veil-Corps be dispatched to Earth to find me and to protect Callie and Tirra.

They were also looking for Hoba, but he eluded them as well as I did.

There are now a few hundred Veilians on Earth. Some of our small population traveled to other planets. They should be able to come to Earth now. Those who were convinced Veilio was not dying stayed. I'm sorry to say our own government encouraged them in this belief until they discovered my findings were correct. But by then, it was too late for them to leave. They are surely dead by now.
~~~~~

Hoba Jett has been put in stasis and sent to the Moon in a veiled ship. As there is no Veilian Council to judge him, I assume he'll be there forever.

Soon, the first Veilian cartel will contact the President of the United States before approaching other countries. It is our hope we will be received graciously.

THE END

TO UNSEE THE SEEN
An Enchanted Castle Archives Story
Michelle L. Levigne

"I think we're in trouble," Zella said. "You need to come home right away."

Framed in the small hand mirror named Hazel, the enchanted castle's librarian glanced over her shoulder, responding to a muffled male voice.

'Na in turn looked over the mirror in her hand to Ambrose, who was chatting and laughing and doing one of those complicated, multi-gesture farewell salutes with Rolf, the newly crowned chieftain of the werewolf tribe in the enchanted forest. 'Na found the whole silly clap, fist-bump, spread-fingers, slap, wiggle sequence, with several other hand movements she couldn't recall, both amusing and comforting. This was yet more proof that Ambrose was respected by the various tribes that had taken shelter in the forest. While Prince Ruprick had always appreciated him and considered him his best friend, not just the one who kept him out of trouble, Ambrose had never been given the respect and acceptance he deserved from the royal family of Rathelshiffen. 'Na was pleased by this proof that others in her world recognized his worth.

"What happened?" 'Na asked, pitching her voice soft. The last thing she needed was to alert the werewolves, who were always ready and eager to jump into a fight and prove they were worthy allies to the enchanted castle. They had been doing that since her christening, when their determination to prove themselves to her parents had turned into an argument with the vampire tribe, then a vow to adopt her into their tribe, and then both tribes attempting to kidnap her from the castle nursery.

"Well, Friar Ipswich arrived early," Zella said, turning back to look into the mirror she was using to communicate with 'Na.

"Is he all right?" 'Na fought down a sense of "Oh, no, what's happened *now*?"

Friar Ipswich was a friend from her mother's childhood. He had taught Ashlyn to read and encouraged her to dream of adventures. He also gave her quite a lot of useful advice regarding the enchanted castle, back when she had been sent out on that ridiculous quest to prove she was innocent of blatantly false charges. Thanks to an old house full of magic books inside a time pocket, the book-loving old man had been able to spend years doing research without suffering the ravages of time. Every few years, he came out of the time pocket with useful bits of information, to have a long visit with Ashlyn and Zared. He wasn't supposed to emerge for two more months. When he did come out early, it was for special occasions, such as 'Na's christening, or drastic problems, such as when he uncovered a prophecy that boded badly for the world in general. 'Na had enjoyed several fascinating visits inside the time pocket with Friar Ipswich when she was a child and her parents needed to get her out of harm's reach. The enchanted castle could sometimes be a dangerous place to live, with all the wonky magic stored there, to safeguard the rest of the world. She considered him her adopted grandfather.

"Well, that's just it. He's brought some people with him who are asking for help. They managed to contact him through one of the books he repaired, thanks to a companion volume they have in their library. He seems to believe they're truly in need of help. The problem is ..." Zella gnawed on her bottom lip for a moment. That was always a bad sign, when she was trying to find the right words to reveal some tricky or uncomfortable news.

"Hello. Sorry." The wizard Zerocs peered over Zella's shoulder into the mirror.

Zella's sweetheart had come for an extended visit. He was why 'Na and Ambrose had gone on a goodwill visit to the werewolf tribe, to give the two of them some privacy. The enchanted castle had a distressing tendency to make it nearly impossible for courting couples to be alone at crucial times in their courtships. Ashlyn and Zared were off for the day, attending the christening for the new grandchild of Ashlyn's childhood friend, Lord Dunstan. 'Na and Ambrose had vacated the castle entirely, to keep from being constantly guided into Zella and Zerocs' company by doors and corridors that led to places they normally didn't. General consensus was that the castle was trying to give Zella and Zerocs some nudges in the right direction, when it came to romance. Both couples agreed that the castle's notions of courtship were very clearly old-fashioned and it didn't understand that privacy encouraged affection. Besides, they didn't need any help. Zerocs and Zella could make each other blush or go starry-eyed while exchanging all the fascinating research they had done when they were apart. Their styles of expressing affection were completely different from 'Na and Ambrose, or Ashlyn and Zared, but the castle couldn't seem to understand that. The best tactic was for the other inhabitants to leave the castle until the courting couple had said enough sweet words to satisfy its romantic side. Then 'Na and Ambrose and her parents could safely return.

"This is my fault," Zerocs continued. "I'm sorry. I'm probably over-reacting, but my inimicurse alarms are going off, and I can't figure out where the nasty spells are focused. It's probably a false alarm. I still need to do some fine tuning on the spell's parameters."

"The housekeeping breezes put them in the sage parlor," Zella said. "So it's not a false alarm."

"Oh." That feeling of dread turned into a chill that dropped a lead-centered ice ball into 'Na's belly.

"Is that a bad thing?" Ambrose asked, moving over to join her.

"Have you ever seen the sage parlor?" She managed a smile when he shook his head. "If I had let you and Ruprick into the castle that day we met, the housekeeping breezes would have put him in the sage parlor. And probably taken you to the kitchen to load you with treats."

"Oh. That's ... encouraging." He grinned. "So I take it the sage parlor is a bad sign when it comes to visitors?"

"We're on our way back," 'Na said. "Thank you. Hazel, you can close the window now."

Zella nodded, her expression even more somber, and her face and Zerocs' vanished from the mirror in a swirl of blue and green sparkles. 'Na headed for her horse, picketed a good fifty feet away from the entrance to the central werewolf lair. The horses belonging to the enchanted castle were extraordinarily intelligent, discerning, and calm. Still, the smell of werewolves, even in human form, was enough to make even the bravest horse edgy.

She slid Hazel into the special padded pouch on the side of her saddle, mounted, and explained as she and Ambrose headed back to the castle at a fast trot.

The sage parlor was reserved for people who generated a bad initial reaction from the housekeeping breezes the moment they stepped into the castle courtyard. The breezes then refused to take them anywhere else. The refreshments served them were insipid little cakes, almost too dry to eat, which made the guests thirsty. The tea was just on the verge of not hot enough to drink, and in Ashlyn's own words, tasted like wet paper and not proper tea.

Some exceptionally unwanted visitors had been served tea that, according to an infuriated, rather long-in-the-tooth princess, tasted like it was made with old fish-wrappers. Ashlyn had then asked how this woman knew what fish wrappers tasted like. Infuriated and embarrassed, she had lost control of her disguise spell. Unmasked, she was revealed as a woman who had married and buried five kings in the space of twenty years, and each time was deposed and humiliated by her virtuous stepdaughters and stepsons. The mirrors still insisted the woman had come to the castle under false pretenses, intending to kill Ashlyn and marry Zared. No one ever got a clear answer, because the woman was so rattled by the sudden failure of her magic, she inadvertently turned herself into a water dragon. She started to dehydrate before she understood what species she had become, and therefore was in a panic when she fled to the castle moat. The moat monsters were not happy to have an uninvited guest, and she lost the battle. She hadn't been seen or heard from since.

"The sage parlor is down that short wing that your parents never go into, guarded by those iron suits of armor covered with spikes?" Ambrose guessed.

"Eyesallova says that wing wasn't part of the original castle. It got grafted on soon after the forest started drifting. Some of the people who came through during the centuries, trying to anchor the castle in their kingdoms, theorized that wing came from a truly evil-filled castle in Vanyltransia, where they practiced all sorts of warped, insane magic."

'Na shuddered. When she was a child, she had thought Eyesallova had made up the stories about the bizarre inhabitants of Vanyltransia just to frighten her into behaving herself.

"Like what?" Ambrose asked, as they neared the long gravel road that led to the enchanted castle.

"Inventing new varieties of politification." She winced and resisted the urge to spit. Just saying the word put a nasty taste in her mouth.

"That's bad enough without coming up with new varieties. They truly are insane in that kingdom. No wonder Rolf's ancestors left."

"You should hear Uncle Morris and his cousins talk about some of the things their ancestors suffered, before the vampire tribes emigrated." 'Na breathed a sigh of relief as their horses rode through the gates into the courtyard of the castle. She was curious about what kind of troublesome guests could set off Zerocs' newest invention. She wasn't sure what the inimicurse was supposed to do, but she guessed it was another attempt to create warning beacons that would sense the approach of people with evil intent, so innocent villages could have plenty of time to raise defenses or send for help.

Zerocs came out the main doors to meet them just as the housekeeping breezes swept down, whistling an eerie ululation. The breezes usually went about their duties in silence. The most agitation they had ever shown in 'Na's entire life was to clatter a few utensils against plates, or snap draperies or sheets while doing chores. For them to make any sound was enough to give her chills. Zerocs stopped short and stared, his eyes looking like they would start spinning around inside the thick purple frames of his spectacles. What did he hear? One of his newest spell projects, intended as an anniversary present for Ashlyn and Zared, was supposed to translate the language of the breezes.

"Thank you," she said, turning to address the breezes that spun around her and tugged on her clothes like nervous children. "We are on the alert and we will deal with this." She snatched her saddlebag off the horse with one hand, and Hazel out of the bag with the other. "Hazel, please contact my parents."

"Eyesallova already took care of that," the mirror said. "Your father says thank you, your timing is perfect. They were anticipating how soon they could make a run for it before Lord Stockingray attacked, and how soon Lords Antipatras, Dimwall, and Flibus would join in."

"How many times do we have to say no?" 'Na gripped the mirror's handle hard enough that Hazel let out a squeak, and the silver creaked, threatening to bend under the pressure. "Sorry!"

"Who are they?" Ambrose asked. He took the mirror from her hand and slid it into the saddlebag, slung it over his shoulder, and rubbed her hand as they started up the steps.

"More nobles who think no one has the right to say no to them."

"Not even the lord and lady of the enchanted castle, with enough magic at hand to wipe out all their kingdoms without breaking a sweat?" Zerocs offered them a cheerful grin. "Sometimes I agree with the politificos who claim all our problems are caused by nobles. Not that I'd support wiping out those bloodlines, because most of the magic in the world comes from the noble bloodlines, but..." He shook his head. "Sorry. I've been harassed by some people who also don't understand what 'no' means, even when it's been shouted at them for an hour straight."

"What can you tell us about these visitors? Do you think they've cast a spell on Ipswich to get his support?" 'Na asked, and seriously considered hugging Zerocs, grateful he was there to help.

She would never do that, however. First, because Zerocs belonged to Zella, and second, because a hug might make him faint and scramble his thinking for an hour or two. They might need his slightly off-balance brilliance in whatever battle waited to pounce on them.

She had never before seen—although "seen" wasn't quite the proper word—the breezes so agitated.

"I think they've taken advantage of his principles as a devoted follower of A'theosius and stretched his sense of sympathy to the breaking point." Zerocs grinned. "He's been apologizing in whispers to me and Zella ever since they arrived. The most he can say is, 'Sorry,' and then one of them interrupts, asking all sorts of questions about the castle and Lady Ashlyn. It's like they're preparing to lay claim to the castle, and they're deciding what furniture to toss out so they can bring their own in."

"Oh, wonderful," 'Na said on a sigh. Then she grinned, because oddly enough, life had been a touch too calm in the castle lately. Her parents maintained that a quiet castle was a castle preparing some new mischief. Best to have a constant stream of small crises to snag its attention and keep it busy helping others. Or even better, defending itself against interlopers. Such minor skirmishes always reminded the castle who its true friends were.

"The castle is more alert than usual. A handful of suits of armor have awakened already, and if the ripples I'm feeling in the magical field are any indication, more are waking up. Poor Ipswich tried three times to take a drink, and each time a breeze knocked the cup out of his hand. On the positive side," he added with a chuckle, "I think the visitors turned green with the first sip, but they're playing at too well-bred to spit it out."

"Someday, we have to figure out how to do something nice for the breezes," 'Na said. "We owe them so very much."

"Wait." Ambrose caught her by the elbow, partially turning her to face him. "You went white for a few seconds when Hazel mentioned those lords. What exactly are your parents saying no to?"

"What do you think?" Now her face warmed.

"Ah. Them again." A grin caught up one corner of his mouth. "Well, they do have some right to be concerned. Your eighteenth birthday is approaching. The world could disintegrate if you're not properly shackled by then."

'Na laughed and elbowed him in the ribs. He dodged aside, twisting expertly to curl his arm around her waist and draw her up against him for a quick kiss.

Zerocs blushed and looked away. "Um … what are you talking about? And could you tone things down? It'll just get the castle riled up and they'll lock us in a room together for a few hours in hopes of me and Zella learning from your example."

"There are worse lessons to learn," Ambrose said, blushing a little himself. Always a charming look, in 'Na's opinion. Then he kissed the tip of her nose and set her free.

"More idiot nobles who think all magic will vanish from the world if the heir of the enchanted castle isn't married before she turns into an old maid at eighteen," 'Na said with an exaggerated groan. "Specifically, they want to be credited with saving the world by matching me with their despicable sons."

"They're not all entirely despicable," Ambrose offered. "Quite a few have nice, intelligent girls they want to marry, if their fathers would just get out of their way."

"Could we deal with the current crisis and worry about the perfectly fine pace of our courtship later?" Her face warmed even more. "Now, what else can you tell us about these despicable guests in the sage parlor?"

Zerocs choked on a chuckle before replying. "They don't believe I'm a wizard. My clothes aren't sparkly enough, and I don't wear enough magical rings, and I don't have a pointed hat. Then, the moment Zella introduced herself as the castle librarian and archivist, they turned to me and announced they don't talk to 'mere' librarians."

"They need to die," Ambrose whispered, as the three headed down the hall into the little-used wing of the castle.

"If it's any comfort, the breezes brought in fresh pots of tea in a highly suspicious shade of green. Then they held them high enough, when the two guests tried to take them, one spilled down the man's back and the other drenched the woman's hair. They couldn't do a thing about it," Zerocs added with a snort of laughter.

The two spiky suits of armor peered out from behind the banners decorating the wall, where they had retired. 'Na nearly skidded to a halt, positive she saw the nearer suit of armor tremble slightly before it went back into hiding.

"That's not a good sign, is it?" Zerocs muttered, as they passed the armor.

'Na shook her head. The suits of armor that had accompanied her parents on so many book rescue missions had gone quiet once the castle had been anchored. Nowadays they only woke when there was a threat to its safety, or someone was in dire need of magical intervention. Such as when Garnet, the new queen of the werewolves, had come to the castle for help in dealing with the lying schemers who claimed to be her grandmother and stepfather. Before that, the armor hadn't awakened in large numbers since the debacle of her christening. The suits of armor had stayed quiet, sleeping, even when Prince Ruprick broke into the castle on her seventeenth birthday, and she had been temporarily changed into a four-headed beast. That proved what little threat the prince had been. The suit of armor on the third-floor landing hadn't even reacted when Ruprick knocked it over and it fell to pieces.

"A'theosius, guard and guide us," she whispered, and tugged her tunic straight as she approached the parlor door.

Normally, when guests were shown to the sage parlor, she put on a dress and wore just enough jewelry to fool strangers into thinking she was the stereotypical castle maiden, born to be bait to lure heroes into trouble or stand as the prize in a quest. According to the vast majority of fables and tales, that meant she could be easily manipulated. Friar Ipswich and others who studied the legends of magic theorized that those who let old tales dictate the paths they took essentially became props in new tales and abdicated their right to choose their own actions.

'Na loved seeing the dismay and confusion on the faces of those who made such ridiculous assumptions about her.

Today wasn't a day for playing with false assumptions and using them against arrogant, greedy intruders. She was going in as a castle defender, and if these visitors didn't like having their preconceived notions dashed, that was their problem. They had already insulted Zella and Zerocs. They had used up their one chance to escape without being humiliated.

Zella appeared in the parlor doorway, looking down the hallway, her eyes wide and her hair sticking out in all directions. Losing control of her magic-infused hair was a sure sign of strained nerves. 'Na thought her friend's hair had grown at least two feet longer since she and Ambrose left that morning. A very bad sign for all of them.

On the other hand, if Zella's hair started growing at twice its usual rate, she would be forced to retire to her quarters at the top of the garden tower, to have room for that growth and try to calm her hair into compliance. That would give her and Zerocs all the privacy they needed, safe from the castle's romantic interference.

Zella's eyes widened in the standard, *Do something before someone says something we'll all regret later* look.

"Welcome to the enchanted castle," 'Na said, stepping into the doorway.

"There's my favorite student," Friar Ipswich said, his voice a hearty boom. Usually, he was soft-spoken. Was this a warning sign? Had someone taken his place, wearing a false face, or was he warning her about danger? He leaped from the edge of the chair where he had perched, crossed the parlor in three steps, and wrapped his arms around her. "How are you? Have you found any fascinating new books for me to tame?"

Her mind raced, trying to determine what kind of warning he was giving by mentioning books to tame. Ipswich had a calming influence on restive books, but he had never been known to "tame" books that turned rebellious or vindictive. Most books sensed the moment he stepped into the room that he was there to mend their torn pages and mangled bindings, to keep them free of dust, and organize them properly, and they appreciated it.

He pressed his cheek to hers. "I'm sorry, child," he whispered. "I feel as if I've been spelled half-asleep. I didn't sense magic on them until we came through the gates."

"We'll deal with it," she whispered back, and pressed a kiss to his stubbly, wrinkled cheek.

"And just who might you be?" a narrow-faced man said, with just enough sneer in his voice to make 'Na hope he had taken a huge mouthful of the awful tea before he tasted it. And had to swallow it to avoid displaying bad manners.

"This is the Lady Belladonna, daughter of the lord and lady of the enchanted castle." Ambrose used a frosty voice with a pompous core. It was such perfect mimicry of the most oblivious and self-important noble in King Ruprick's court, 'Na was hard-pressed not to burst out laughing.

"Really?" A plump woman dressed all in pale lavender lace raised a lorgnette to her eyes and studied 'Na head to foot and back again. Clearly, she didn't approve of her leather and broadcloth traveling clothes. "And where might your parents be, little girl? One must assume that they are long gone, perhaps long delayed, to leave the castle in the hands of mere servants and a girl-child not yet in her majority."

"Indeed, that is not the case, and you are sadly mistaken in your … assumptions," 'Na said, putting as much chill in her voice as she could manage without actually exhaling frost. She added extra emphasis to the double sibilant and drew it out. The lavender woman stiffened. A touch of unhappy pink marked her cheeks, proving she did catch the implied word and 'Na's opinion of her. "The reverse is true. We are in the hands of the castle. A great many of the stories of the castle are very true. It is alive, and aware, and you would do well not to offend it so far that it acts."

The narrow-faced man snorted. "How can a building act?"

"Would you like to see some of the many statues that fill the garden?" Ambrose said. "After more than a century, some of them have regained the power of speech, and they can tell you the crimes they committed against the castle." He returned the man's skeptical expression with a frosty smile and a shallow bow that barely moved his head and shoulders. "Now, if you would be so kind as to state your business, we will do our best to attend to your needs and send you on your way before the castle wakes from its current slumber."

'Na caught the upward quirking of the woman's lips, the sudden spark of interest in the man's eyes. Why did she get the impression that implying the castle was asleep pleased them? Did they think the castle was unable to defend itself?

Maybe they were acting snooty to irritate her into revealing just how unguarded the castle was? Maybe they were just advance scouts, preparing for an attack? 'Na hooked her arm through Friar Ipswich's, determined to get him out of reach of danger, if these people started causing trouble.

"Let me get the friar settled, and then we can attend to your problem." She didn't wait for a response from those people but led him out of the parlor and far enough away no one could overhear them speaking.

"What do they want?" She guided Ipswich to a bench placed between the third and fourth sets of doors into the library.

"Research." He frowned. "At least … I think so. I'm sorry, but things felt so clear until we came through the gates. Then that tingly thing your father always complains about washed over me, and it was like everything before was a dream. It's a little frightening. Now I quite understand why it irritates him so much."

Zared's sense for magic at work was an aftereffect from multiple layers of badly woven spells wrapped around him and embedded in his flesh and bones when he was young. Coming into the enchanted forest when it was still separated from the normal stream of time had helped to sever many of those spells and loosened the roots of others trying to control him.

'Na caught her breath as understanding crept up on her. Not enough, though, and not fast enough. Nothing was quite clear yet. She asked him to tell her about the visitors. Lord Arris and Lady Josefa and someone Ipswich couldn't recall. He was positive that a third person had accompanied them from the little house that guarded the time pocket library where he lived, but no one had come through the gates of the castle with them. Arris and Josefa claimed they were servants of a great king. Ipswich couldn't remember who, at the moment.

"Strange, how chilly I've been feeling, until we came inside. Now I'm so hot …" He yanked on the collar of his clerical robe.

Then 'Na understood, and she got angry. She caught Ipswich's hands and tugged the collar open even more.

"Where's your talisman?" She touched the bare spot in the dip of his collar bone where a chain and a gold coin, silver coin, and iron coin, melted together, should have been visible. The mirrors in the castle had created the talisman for Ipswich, at the behest of the library, as a token of their affection for the friar and to protect him from a great many unfriendly spells.

"What talisman?" Then he lost even more color, so his normal indoors pallor seemed to be a healthy field worker's bronze by comparison. He slapped both hands against the bare spot at his throat. "Oh … dear … have I caused you trouble?"

"Not you at all. Them," 'Na growled. She thought a moment, then pulled him to his feet. Instead of sending him to his usual room on the family side of the castle, to rest, she needed to take drastic measures. Friar Ipswich had spent so much time with books, breathing in air filled with paper dust and ink and leather and magic, he might someday turn into a magic book. The healthiest place for him to be was among the books.

The central set of library doors opened before 'Na could reach for them. She led Ipswich into the library, down the central aisle between dozens of shoulder-height bookshelves and just as many study tables. Behind her, she heard the library doors groan as they closed. She hadn't heard that sound in years. Not since …

'Na paused long enough to look back, and see the doors swing closed slower than they normally did. Nothing and no one stood in the way, holding them open. That was odd. Then again, *odd* was normal for the inhabitants of the enchanted castle. This was … uneasy. Unfriendly.

She guided Ipswich to the room sometimes referred to as the infirmary, where rescued books, and books that had gotten into fights over precedence and damaged themselves in the brawls, slamming into each other and leaping off shelves, came to be mended. In the intervening years since Ashlyn had come to the castle and started its awakening and return to its proper mental state, a room had budded off the infirmary. It held several cots, a washroom, and a small kitchen that the breezes kept stocked. This was for emergency situations, when there were so many books in such dreadful condition that those performing the repairs couldn't take time to leave to eat and sleep. They took turns resting and eating, with at least two or three working on the books at all times. The last time 'Na could remember the room being needed was when she had helped her parents rescue fifty books from a water sorceress's lair that had sprung a leak while she was away serving in the Enchanters' Court. That emergency had required them to gather up all the water the books had been soaking in for nearly two months, to coax the inked words back onto the pages where they belonged.

This room would serve Ipswich nicely. The books would protect him if Arris and Josefa tried to reinstate their control over him. He would have plenty of quiet to rest, and the breezes would fix all his favorite foods. Being surrounded by books would replenish the part of him that was already more book than man.

Ipswich let out a long, gusting sigh of relief the moment they stepped through the door into the infirmary. His color looked better by the time they stepped into the sleeping quarters.

"Thank you, my dear." He patted her hand and gently freed himself from her support. "This will do very nicely." Then his smile faded. "But I don't like leaving you to fight those two. They've got something entirely nasty up their sleeves, if they'd go to such lengths to use me as a shield to sneak them in here."

A muffled thud came from behind them, and 'Na turned, just in time to see a faint smear of light across the doorway from the library into the infirmary. She shuddered, sensing that some kind of magic had tried to cross that spell-protected threshold. Trying to catch hold of Ipswich again? Or was this what had brought Arris and Josefa to the castle? They wanted to confiscate a damaged book before it was entirely healed, before it could protect itself?

"My parents will be back soon," she said as she backed toward the door. "They'll get this all sorted out in no time. No one can stand up against Lady Ashlyn and Lord Zared. Especially when they've been caught trying something nasty. Don't worry. Rest and get your strength back. You're going to need it. We have all sorts of new treasures to show you, when you're feeling better."

Ipswich chuckled at her words. That encouraged her, but her smile faded as she broke into a trot and hurried out of the infirmary and across the library.

Zella was just coming into the main entryway when 'Na stepped out of the library. She shook her head and waved her hand for 'Na to go back inside.

"Something isn't right here." She glanced around before pressing on the latch to open the library door.

"Did they finally lower themselves to tell a mere librarian what they wanted?" 'Na asked as they stepped inside.

They headed down the central aisle and turned right halfway down, heading for Zella's primary work area.

"Supposedly their king has a wager with some members of his council, regarding the exact words of a quote from a volume of history by Abisquedalias. A volume that has gone missing from his library. Not only do they want me to find the quote and verify it, but if we have an extra volume or two, could we gift it to their king, as a gesture of good will between the castle and the kingdom of Punctigliosi?"

'Na shook her head. "That's not a kingdom, it's a duchy, beholden to Ambramfall. What kind of game are they playing? And why do they think we're stupid?"

"And besides, Abisquedalias's works are available everywhere. He's one of the first historians to have his works produced by a printing press instead of hand-written and then multi-copied by enchanted quills." Zella stopped just a few steps away from the long, multi-level table where she spent most of her time, referencing books and copying out information and carrying on the never-ending task of organizing and re-organizing the constantly growing library. She pursed her lips and looked around, then raked her fingers through her hair, which had grown out another hand-span just in the time since 'Na left the parlor.

A sure sign of trouble, of stress, and some magic spell running around loose, perhaps even gathering its strength to act.

"By the way," Zella added, after another glance around the shadowy, blessedly quiet library. "That woman is making noises about graciously offering her services to find you a proper husband, since there are clearly no suitable men within several days' journey. I thought at first it was a cruel jab at Ambrose, but I'm of the opinion she's too self-focused to have picked up on the clues. Not even if he kissed you right in front of them."

"I wouldn't trust her to find me a comfortable pair of shoes, forget about a husband."

A soft chuckle sounded from behind her. 'Na folded her arm against her side, ready to dig into whoever had snuck up behind her. Zella glanced over her shoulder and went entirely too still.

"There's nobody there, is there?" 'Na whispered.

Books whispered and hissed and wooden covers scraped across shelves. Instinct screamed. 'Na went to her knees, yanking Zella down with her. Books leaped off the nearest shelves, into the open space directly behind her. A soft thud earned a grunt. More thuds followed: the sound of angry books hitting flesh. 'Na turned around, arms over her head, and saw the last of the stream of books hit a seeming wall in the air, about five paces away from her, and either bounce off or slide down to the floor.

The sound of bare, running feet slapping on the floor barely overcame the hissing and rustling of books settling back down. Several books flew off each shelf, marking the passage of the unseen runner, aiming for the library doors. None of them seemed to hit their mark.

"What was that?" Zella whispered.

'Na leaped to her feet and ran, but already knew she was too late. A library door swung open and light spilled in from the main entryway, then swung closed. The whispering of paper across leather and wood died away. No more footsteps.

She hit the door and ran out into the entryway. No sounds. Certainly no running feet slapping the flagstones.

"Whoever you are, you'd better show yourself now. Don't make us hunt you down. You don't want to get the castle angry with you."

"What's wrong?" Ambrose called from the hallway to the sage parlor. His words were nearly hidden by the sudden sounds of metal feet moving across flagstones and wood. He emerged a moment later and looked around, hunching his shoulders as if expecting to be struck.

Air shifted throughout the castle as all the suits of armor came to life and moved off their pedestals or stood up from where they had leaned back against stone walls for years. Some suits of armor had never moved in all of 'Na's memory. The third-floor alarm suit of armor clattered into pieces and she winced and made a mental note to apologize to him. He had deliberately been left with all his pieces unconnected, to act as an early alarm for anyone who managed to sneak in at the weak spot in the seam of the defensive magic surrounding the castle. Such as the night Prince Ruprick snuck in. Clearly, the armor wasn't aware that he wasn't knit together, and his first attempt to move had sent him scattering.

"Somebody is in here." She gestured at the two spiky suits of armor who had stepped out from behind the banners. "I hope we don't suddenly have a ghost, but I'm guessing someone with an invisibility spell."

Ambrose nodded and went down the hall again, most likely to fetch Zerocs. It was often handy to have a wizard around, even if he was the kind who did a lot of experimentation and invention, and therefore wasn't exactly familiar with standard, everyday-use magical spells. On the other hand, he might come up with something on the spot that would reveal the intruder. Preferably fasten him to one spot so he could be dealt with.

"I don't suppose any of you are able to speak?" she asked the spiky armor. One slowly shook his head with a painful amount of creaking and squeaking of the plates in his neck. "Write?"

The two suits turned their helmets to face each other. The hair on the back of her neck stood up, indicating some magic taking place, or at least something a touch spooky. She had never considered how the suits of armor communicated with each other.

"I'm going upstairs to consult Eyesallova," she told them. "Please make sure our visitors don't leave the sage parlor. And breezes, keep the library doors closed. Don't let anyone in or out except me or Zella and block the doors when we do. And could one of you bring our guests more of that awful tea, please?"

'Na thought she heard something or someone snicker as she headed up the stairs.

"Very upsetting," Eyesallova announced the moment 'Na shoved open the door to the sunny mirror room. "There is someone here. Multiple layers of spells wrapped tightly together, by someone who knows what they're doing. Try as I might, I can't see him. The breezes found him for a few seconds, when he was fleeing the books. He evaded them and got out into the entryway and to all intents and purposes vanished."

"How, when breezes don't have eyes?"

"Well, he has to move, for one thing. And they do have an incredible sense of smell and taste."

"So what are you saying? They can't smell or taste him?" 'Na thought she felt a little sick to her stomach at that mental image. She didn't know if she should feel sorry for the breezes who had tended her all her life, or a little uneasy on her and her parents' behalf, being tasted all this time.

A low, disgruntled sort of hum came from the mirror. "In essence. All this tells me whoever created the spell knows about the breezes, how they function, their limitations, and what sort of magic will work against them. Rather dastardly."

'Na agreed. They settled down to try to come up with a quick plan to deal with their visitors and the invisible intruder. Add in what Friar Ipswich had told her, and it only made sense that these visitors came with their ridiculous, time-wasting errand to serve as a distraction for the invisible intruder, to get him inside. Eyesallova agreed that the breezes would have been so busy with the unpleasant couple, they could have missed the entrance of an invisible member of the party. Especially if he moved slowly, didn't make any noise, and used spells to hide his scent.

Hazel interrupted then, giving a view into the sage parlor. Arris and Josefa huddled together in a conference. Their posture indicated a third member of the discussion, between them in an otherwise open space. Hazel quickly explained. The pair had tripled their snooty unpleasantness to Zerocs and Ambrose, muttering about the rudeness of the lower classes and servants who didn't know their place, and the rights of the superior ranks to privacy. Then they had ordered the men out of the parlor entirely. Ambrose turned his back to them to hide his actions, taking Hazel out of the saddlebag he still carried, and setting her down in an advantageous spot to keep watch on them. He offered to refresh their tea, which both refused, looking a little green. Then the two men took up positions in the hallway just outside of the view of the door. Not five seconds later, Arris came to the door and scowled when he saw them waiting. He went to close the door, but the woman snarled at him that "he can't leave if the door's closed, can he, imbecile?"

Hazel couldn't record everything they said because they spoke too softly, but clearly a third person was in the room. She caught two different men's voices. She heard fragments of sentences, such as "the book," "go to the primary plan," "love potion," "stupid girl," and "control the castle."

"Well, that's clear enough," Eyesallova said, when Hazel showed them the conversation again. When they separated, it was clear the woman shooed the invisible man out of the room. "I recommend you don't eat or drink anything until we're sure the intruder is gone."

"He's back," Zella reported, through her mirror, Primp, who kept her company when she was working in the library. "I thought it wise to lock up the newer books, especially the ones that are still rather skittish after being kept in the dark for so many years. They're too eager to get outside and might manage to escape if books start flying around again and hitting people. I was just turning around from locking the room when the library door opened, but I saw nobody come through."

"Oh, that isn't good," Eyesallova said, before 'Na could. "How did he get around the breezes holding the doors closed?"

"Those people are too well-prepared. Who gave them all that information about the castle?" 'Na said.

"I've been watching the door, and he hasn't tried to go out yet," Zella said. "Primp is set up at a good angle to watch quite a lot of the library, but the problem is we have so many shelves and so much —" She stopped, eyes going wide, and lunged forward, straight into the mirror.

"She was pushed," Eyesallova cried.

"Breezes!" 'Na jumped to her feet and headed for the door out of the mirror room. "Call the armor to help you keep all the library doors closed. Eyesallova, tell Zella I'm on my way."

She leaped down the central staircase, two and three steps at a time. As she made the turn on the landing between the first and second floor, she saw the main doors start to swing open. 'Na opened her mouth to shout for the breezes to close the doors, then saw her parents. She stumbled and seriously considered leaping over the landing railing. With the way her day was going, she would probably land crooked and break a leg. Zerocs and Ambrose appeared in the archway to the sage parlor wing, looking rather irritated.

"Froze them," Zerocs announced before 'Na could ask. He flinched and gave Lady Ashlyn and Lord Zared a guilty look. "Sorry. That probably wasn't very nice, but—"

"But they were getting demanding and it's clear they helped the intruder get in," Ambrose finished. "He was brilliant. We need to have that spell loaded in a handful of charms to use for emergencies."

"All right," Zared said slowly, looking back and forth from 'Na to Zerocs to Ambrose and back again. "What exactly has been happening?"

Something thudded hard on the doors to the library. They rattled but held fast. 'Na braced, expecting to hear Zella scream, either in fury or demanding help. Or maybe the books had managed to overwhelm the invisible intruder and he was buried?

Quickly, 'Na explained the new developments in the problem. She was pleased when Zerocs flushed dark and his expression grew stern when he learned Zella was locked into the library with the intruder.

"How long will that freeze spell last?" Ashlyn asked.

"Maybe another ten, fifteen minutes," Zerocs said, shrugging. "It's still in the development and experimentation stage. If it lasts any longer, the subjects really do start to freeze. Right now, they're just paralyzed, and getting cold."

"Can we use it on—" Zared paused for another hard thud against the library doors.

This time it sounded like the intruder tried a different set of doors. 'Na couldn't quite understand why the library needed five sets of doors leading off the entry hall. She knew better than to ask a question that could send the castle into a new series of renovations of its structure.

"—the intruder," he finished, when the echo had faded away.

"Why are the breezes able to keep the doors closed this time?" 'Na said. The suits of armor were only now arriving, meaning they weren't helping to keep the doors closed.

"My guess is that all the magic resides in Arris and Josefa, and they can't do anything while they're frozen," Ambrose said.

"Can you freeze him through the door?" Zared said. "Without hitting Zella?"

"I have to see who I'm freezing," Zerocs said. "That's another design problem to straighten out."

"Then we need a way to make the invisible visible," Ashlyn said. "If only temporarily."

"Hmm ... I'd suggest moonglow ink," Zared said, "but it's expensive, in terms of magic and ingredients, making it an extreme measure."

Ambrose grinned. A nasty sort of grin that prompted 'Na to grin back at him, because she knew he was about to make a brilliant suggestion.

Preferably messy.

"We had a problem with some visitors a few years ago," he said. "They were trying to prove a claim to the throne when a new ghost appeared in the palace."

"Ghosts don't just appear on command," Ashlyn said, and mirrored Ambrose's grin. "What did you do?"

"We set up traps in all the places where the ghost was wandering, wailing and insisting, with a very thick Grindelheim accent, that his descendants had been deprived of their heritage and he was going to haunt until Grindelheim blood sat on the throne."

"Grindelheim?" Zared said. "Six years ago? When King Ogg's daughter came here for a visit, and everyone thought she was trying to move in permanently?"

"Please tell me Ruprick got a taste of his own medicine, and someone was trying to force a marriage on him for a change," Ashlyn said, her words breaking off in muffled chuckles.

Another hard, echoing thud on the next set of library doors made the five of them flinch and killed the mirth.

"Pretty much that," Ambrose said, nodding. "She started out aiming at marrying him, but he made it very clear that he wasn't disinheriting his current heir, and he had a dozen magicians ready to bind his son to her and all the heirs of Grindelheim, so whatever harm Rathelshiffen's heir suffered would also hit them. Of course, by that time, the princess had decided she didn't want to marry the king, and —"

"Smart girl," Zared muttered. That got a grin and a snort from Ashlyn.

Ambrose muffled a chuckle. "And she set her cap toward marrying the prince. The only problem being that he was barely fifteen, and twelve years her junior. So the ghost got to work, to frighten Rathelshiffen into a marriage alliance."

"So what did you do?" 'Na glanced down the hallway to the sage parlor. "How much time is left on that freeze spell? We don't want them helping the intruder escape."

"We needed something that would mark the ghost long enough to capture him, without making a huge mess. Someone suggested ink, but the ghost was wandering the portrait hallways and the library, and King Ruprick had just spent a year's taxes on new carpeting for the throne room and audience hall and ..." He shrugged, grinning. "We filled little sacks with flour, and an entire army of servants waited in the shadows to barrage the ghost. It turned out to be Ambassador Sackwellian himself. He nearly smothered. Nearby torches ignited some of the flour—did you know flour could explode? I was one of those who managed to hit him with sacks of water from the fire-fighting measures. He was covered in paste that turned into mortar. It was quite the diplomatic scandal for nearly a year."

"Flour," Ashlyn said, nodding. "How long will it take to rig the sacks?"

"No need," Zerocs said. "Give me a good idea of where the flour is in the kitchens, and I can transport it right here, just a big cloud. I'll have it ready the moment he comes through the doors."

'Na could do that easily enough. She and Zella sometimes relaxed by spending a day in the kitchens, baking and experimenting with recipes from kingdoms on the other side of the world. With the housekeeping breezes to do all the cooking, 'Na might never have known where the kitchens were, until Zella found a recipe for ten-flavor fudge she wanted to try to make, and a new hobby was born.

The freeze spell on Arris and Josefa had two minutes remaining by the time Zerocs had a churning cloud of flour poised just above the lintel of the fourth library door. Right on time, it banged and rattled. On Zared's command, the breezes allowed the door to slam open. Zerocs dropped the cloud of flour. A man-shaped figure appeared from the midst of the cloud and headed straight for the doors out of the castle.

The breezes slammed the doors shut when he was five steps away. He ran into them, leaving a man-shaped flour imprint on the iron-bound wood panels. A cloud of flour dust exploded up into the air as the man shape fell backward, hitting the flagstones paving the entryway, and leaving a much fainter man shape on the floor.

Wailing, the intruder scrambled to his feet. Ambrose and Zared leaped at him. Sneezing explosively, he dodged sideways and skidded on the flour now covering the floor. So did they. He escaped. Both men were smeared with flour, head to toe, testament to how close they came to success. Flour trailed behind the intruder as his outline disintegrated and he headed down the hallway to the sage parlor. Everyone gave chase.

They stumbled into the sage parlor just as Arris and Josefa blinked and inhaled deeply and looked around, shivering. The curtains were still swinging, smeared with flour where the intruder had wiped it off his body. One last sneeze echoed down the hallway, proving he had escaped before they could block the doorway and keep him in the room.

~~~~~

Zared ordered all the doors and windows of the castle closed and sealed with magic, so no one could get out. Ashlyn dearly wanted to send the unpleasant couple away immediately, but she gritted her teeth and invited them to stay the night. She assigned four suits of armor to attend them at all times. 'Na found some satisfaction in seeing the uneasy glances both Arris and Josefa cast their escorts. The breezes put the unwanted guests in the sage guest quarters, all the while making little trilling sounds
~~~~~

that 'Na equated with their version of laughter

Zella and Zerocs locked themselves in the library, with clouds of flour dust hovering in the air on both sides of the library doors. They worked all afternoon and evening, trying to weave a spell that would unravel the magic protecting the intruder from detection. The best they could come up with before they went to bed, exhausted, was several clouds of mist that prowled the halls of the castle, poised to stick to anything moving and breathing that didn't wear one of the six beads Zerocs imprinted with an identification spell. They would get back to work on the unraveling spell in the morning.

No one told Arris and Josefa about the prowling mists. If they left their quarters in the middle of the night to snoop where they were not wanted and were enveloped in a nose-searing scent and a noxious shade of pink that glowed in the dark, that was their own fault.

By the time everyone retired to bed, the mists had ambushed four nests of squirrels, two beehives, and twelve families of birds that had set up housekeeping within the roofs and walls of the castle. The smell and the color precipitated quite rapid and noisy evacuations.

'Na thought she heard someone sneeze on the far side of her bedroom as she headed for the bathing room in her suite. She changed her mind about taking a long, hot bath to ease away the tension aches of the day. She closed her bathing room door, which she normally didn't do, and chose her longest nightgown, then rolled up her sleeves and the legs of her trousers, to hide under it. Not for all the magical secrets in the world was she going to confront an invisible stranger in her bedroom in nothing but a nightgown.

A giggle-snort escaped her, when she thought of Ambrose's reaction to that scenario. He had been a little touchy from the moment Josefa mentioned doing some matchmaking for 'Na. Was he a little possessive? Not that she would ever try to make him jealous. She despised tales of girls who played games with their sweethearts' perceptions and feelings. Still, it was rather nice knowing Ambrose could feel a little defensive when it came to their courtship.

She switched an atomizer from the top of the bottle of her favorite lemony perfume to a bottle of scent she only wore to discourage unmarried male royal visitors between the ages of ten and thirty-five. 'Na couldn't remember the name of the scent after all these years, but thought of it as "imperious hag, with an undertone of mothballs." She had been using it in self-defense since she was ten years old herself. It had been one of her christening gifts, from Filby, the half-Fae woman Ashlyn had met when she was younger than 'Na was now. Filby had added to the education in magic started by Cecil the seer.

'Na tucked the perfume bottle into the pocket of her trousers, split the seam of her nightgown at that spot for easy access, and stepped out into her bedroom to face down the intruder. He was going to be very sorry he had hidden in her room all this time. That was the only explanation for why the mists hadn't ambushed him by now. He had been here, sitting still and silent. Zerocs had told the mists to prowl all the hallways and public rooms, therefore since he didn't tell them specifically to prowl private quarters, they wouldn't.

The problem with magic within the enchanted castle was that it often had a mind of its own. Usually when someone depended on it to follow its current pattern of behavior, it changed. That was why she had been raised to never make a wish inside the castle. The atmosphere of wonky magic often interpreted instructions and wishes as it chose, and not quite as the person speaking the spell or wish intended. And often, that wish didn't have to be spoken, just thought, or felt intently.

Lately, the castle had been going above and beyond the limits of spoken instructions, filling in the gaps and details. 'Na supposed she and her parents, and now Zella and Zerocs and Ambrose had just expected that trend to continue. Maybe they had grown a little lazy. That was their mistake. Now, the magic that served the inhabitants of the castle decided to be excruciatingly literal in following instructions.

It simply couldn't be depended on. And the more broken, abused, wounded, tired magic came to take shelter in the enchanted castle, the more intense that field of wonky magic grew. Not that 'Na didn't enjoy living here, but sometimes it could be a little bit of a headache and inconvenience.

Like now. What was the better plan? Keep the invisible intruder imprisoned here and find a way to let someone know he was here in her room without revealing that she knew he was here? Or drive him out into the hallway, into ambush by the mists?

She crossed her room to her bed and hesitated. Was he sitting on her bed?

New, uncomfortable thought: that glimpse of him, outlined in flour, suggested he was naked.

Eww. If he was sitting on her bed, she was going to have to ask the breezes to change the sheets before she could go to sleep.

She almost giggled. Best not let Ambrose know, if she was right.

Another sneeze. Louder. Fortunately, coming from the window seat, a good ten paces from her bed. More proof he was naked? What kind of half-baked magic was he using? Couldn't he find a spell to make his clothes invisible, too?

Was he an idiot? Or was he a victim, seeking help? What if Arris and Josefa had brought this man here for help, and they were the kind of people who chose to lie and sneak around and steal the help they could have asked for? Far too many people chose to believe the enchanted castle was a menace because it was filled with wild, untamed, dangerous magic. Ashlyn had fought long and hard to be the lady of the castle and tame its magic to be useful. The castle no longer wandered the enchanted forest, and the forest had become anchored into the normal stream of time because of the risks Ashlyn and Zared had taken.

'Na wasn't going to let some distrustful, greedy, arrogant liars endanger what her parents had fought for. Maybe what she needed to do was take the unexpected tactic.

"Let's not waste any time," she said, and sat down on the bench at the end of her bed, where she had plenty of options and room to maneuver if he should suddenly leap at her. "I know you're here. What do you want?"

Silence. She tried to study the cushion of the window seat without him realizing she was doing so. Was that an indentation on the right side of the cushion? Was he still sitting there? Would he get suspicious if she asked the lamp to shine brighter, so she could see better?

Another sneeze. A sniffle.

"You're not going to scream? Or throw more of that awful powder on me?" The voice was a somewhat stuffy baritone, hinting at a blooming head cold.

"It's flour."

"What kind of flower? I must be allergic."

"No, flour as in what you make into bread."

"Oh." Another sneeze. A louder sniffle. "You just want to talk?"

"I want to know why you're here, and if those two uglies brought you here."

"Dragged me here," he said. Another sneeze. "If I'm not allergic, I must be getting a cold." He snorted, a somewhat raspy attempt at a laugh. "I've been cold all day. I do swear, I will make them pay for what they've done. To me and to my family. If anyone ever finds out how they humiliated me, making me—" He broke off with another sneeze, loud enough 'Na thought maybe her parents could hear it, down at the end of the hall in their suite.

She muffled a chuckle at the thought of Ambrose's reaction.

He would tackle the man and throw a blanket around him. And hogtie him with it, while he was at it.

Admittedly, she would feel better knowing the intruder was covered, even if he was invisible.

Another chuckle when she thought of his reaction if she called a housekeeping breeze to give him a blanket. The breezes would go on the attack, and she didn't want to risk Zerocs' mists charging into her room, spreading that nose-searing stench or that eye-bleeding shade of pink all over. He had said something about making both smell and color semi-permanent, so the intruder couldn't wipe them off as easily as the flour and go invisible again.

"If you're cold, you're welcome to wrap up in a blanket." She pointed to the wardrobe on the other side of the room.

Maybe that wasn't wise, encouraging him to move? Too late. A moment later, the wardrobe door opened, and a blanket slid down off the top shelf.

Half a minute later, he was settled back on the window seat, the blanket giving a somewhat human outline to him. Except of course, he didn't have a head, and she had a queasy moment when she could look down the opening where his neck was and see nothing.

"Thank you. I hope you never know what it's like to be caught stark … well, I shouldn't say such things in the presence of a princess, but—"

"I'm not a princess. Everyone makes that mistake. The castle tried to make my mother into a princess, and she fought long and hard to get it to compromise and let her be Lady Ashlyn. I'm not going to give in. I'm not a princess."

"Why wouldn't you want to be a princess?" He sounded genuinely interested.

"Just think of all the horrid things that happen to princesses in the fables and legends, as well as in history. If they aren't bait, to trick princes and worthy peasant boys into ridiculous quests, then they're brainless little flitterheads, covered in glitter. They're doomed to make ridiculous mistakes that bring curses down on their fathers' or their husbands' or their brothers' kingdoms. No thank you!"

He chuckled, and she thought maybe she could like him. When he became visible.

"What's your name?"

"Dolor."

"Not a very propitious name."

"Tell me about it. I swear that's why those two—very appropriate, calling them the uglies—why those two uglies chose me. They cast all sorts of curses on my family, to force me to do their bidding. They made me invisible, but could they work the spell correctly, so I can take it on and off, and just be invisible when necessary? No. I'm invisible all the time. And just me, not my clothes. It's horribly uncomfortable, going naked most of the time. It makes that nasty old hag queasy, she says, to see me riding around, just a suit of clothes on the horse, with no head, so I'm not allowed to wear anything. And the man, he just laughs at me. And being invisible does not make it easier to steal all the things they make me steal. I can't make anything invisible by touching it. If I could, then I could wear clothes, but I can't—"

Another sneeze.

"I can only steal small things, whatever I can keep between my hands. Then they're invisible."

"Why were you in the library, then? I can't think of a single book small enough to fit between a man's hands."

"I'm supposed to tear pages out of books and sneak them out, folded up between my hands, a few at a time."

"Good luck doing that." She fought nausea at the idea of the sacrilege of tearing pages out of books and the reaction of the books. Most of the books in the enchanted castle's library were aware enough to be not just outraged at having their pages torn out, but to take action to punish the one harming them. "The books won't let you get away with it."

"I got that message when they flew off the shelves and hit me today."

"You don't want to know what it's like to be buried under several hundred. I've seen it happen, and it's not pretty." She shuddered. "It can be rather... messy."

They sat in silence for several moments, while 'Na tried to think of the right words to convince him to surrender and ask for help.

This was the enchanted castle, after all. Despite the wonky, warped magic that made spells sometimes unpredictable, there were rules to follow. People or creatures or magical beings like mirrors and talking swords had to *ask* for help. It couldn't just be inflicted on them.

If her parents couldn't find the right spell to not just free Dolor but protect his family, then no one could help him. Most of the magic in the world either came here for healing, for refuge, or to protect the rest of the world from the inimical effects intended by their creators.

A loud sigh. "I was really hoping ... well, it's no use, is it, if you're not a princess?"

"Why do I need to be a princess?" A moment later, 'Na knew, and she wished she hadn't eaten quite so much éclair cake at dinner.

There were several cure-alls for complicated magic, especially of the curse variety, in legend and lore. One of them was the kiss of a princess.

"You should talk to my parents," she said.

Dolor got up from the window seat. The blanket floated closer to her.

"Please? Just give it a try? This is a castle filled with magic. Enough magic to rewrite the rules. Your parents are the rulers of the castle. That makes them the king and queen, even if they don't wear the title."

'Na gave up on dignity and trying not to alarm him. She leaped across the room and snatched the door latch. The blanket dropped to the floor. Heavy footsteps thudded on the carpet. She yanked the door open and tumbled out into the hallway.

"Mists! Get him!" She backed against the wall and pointed into her room.

The pink mist was such a violently brilliant shade, it glowed in the shadows of the hallway.

"Just one kiss! Please?" Dolor was close enough, she swore she could feel his breath.

No, she *smelled* his breath. Something sickly sweet and full of herbs. Magic-infused herbs. What did Josefa say about a love potion?

The mists hit. Dolor screamed. Violent pink filled the air. 'Na covered her eyes and backed away and regretted inhaling, because the noxious scent followed a moment later and it tasted as bad as it smelled.

Doors slammed open at either end of the hall. Zared raced to her, almost tripping over Ashlyn. Both of them were still dressed in their day clothes.

Ambrose let out a roar of fury as he flew around the corner, from the guest rooms where he and Zerocs were staying. His eyes seemed to shoot off sparks as his gaze landed on Dolor, curled up on the floor, very pink and very naked.

Even though all she saw were his huge, jiggling buttocks, 'Na was going to need a memory spell to wipe that image out of her head any time soon. Although it was rather nice to know how protective Ambrose was.

~~~~~

"Love potion," Eyesallova announced the next morning, when the six of them had gathered in the mirror room. "Of the worst, most stupefying, long-lasting kind."

It had taken all night to deal with Dolor, untangling all the spells enfolding him, many of which were designed to help him escape traps. Despite all the research Arris and Josefa might have done to prepare to invade the enchanted castle, the odds of deciphering all the defensive magic available to its residents were stacked ridiculously high against them.

Six mirrors worked until nearly dawn to interrogate the unpleasant couple. They sent queries through the mirror web to identify them, and then untangled the multiple layers of disguising spells they used.

Dolor had lied. Arris and Josefa didn't threaten his family—they were his parents. They were also the last members of one of the splinter groups that emerged when the Purple Sky magicians fragmented in disarray. They had tried for years to take control of all the magic in the world. There was no mission to steal magic books from the library. That was another lie. Dolor's entire mission was to steal a kiss from 'Na. They had used Friar Ipswich to get them through the doors of the castle, They would force him to perform the marriage ceremony while 'Na was still reeling from the effects of the love potion, thereby giving Dolor, and through him, his parents, authority over the castle.

"You have to admit, this was one of the better thought-out plans,
~~~~~

relying on the magic of the castle to give them power over it. Just not good enough. Not a single one of them studied hard enough to realize that when Ashlyn refused to be the castle's princess, she protected both it and herself. And now all of you." Eyesallova chuckled. "I am still amazed at how lucky you were, declaring yourself the lady, not the princess. You claimed authority, and yet you weakened the traditional bond of castle and princess."

"Luck, nothing," Ashlyn said, and tightened her arm around 'Na's shoulders. "A'theosius was protecting us."

"Thank you, all of you, for your help," Zared added, bowing to Zella, Zerocs and Ambrose. "We are grateful and blessed to have you as our friends."

"I don't suppose you know a spell to erase last night from my memory?" 'Na said. "The more I try to unsee what I saw when the mists attacked ..." She shuddered, trying to smile and make light of the nauseating horror of the whole nasty scheme.

"If you can do that, you can ask for anything you want from us," Ashlyn said, and laughed.

"I have an idea," Ambrose said. He was the only one not laughing or even smiling.

'Na caught her breath, when she decided he looked not just nervous, but close to terrified, and fighting hard to hide it.

"Better memories, to erase what we saw." He went down on one knee in front of the bench where she sat between her parents. "Lady Ashlyn, Lord Zared, will you allow me to protect your daughter from future nefarious schemes ... by marrying her?"

THE END

A TYPE OF WOMAN
Jim Doran

Oscar entered The Chemistry Lab nightclub, the ocean-blue and fuchsia blinking lights temporarily dazzling him. With their hands in the air, a swell of people swayed on the dance floor like cornstalks bending to breezes. Speakers the height of the dancers pounded a bass rhythm loud enough to shake the rafters of the building. Tiny pieces of cotton in Oscar's ears provided some relief from the bone-rattling beat.

Stopping at the edge of the dance floor, Oscar surveyed the patrons. The police had issued warnings about the danger of coming to nightclubs. People never listened.

Excellent.

Oscar parted closely packed people to reach the bar and ordered one of their specialty drinks, All That Ales You. The thin, frothy barm topped a golden concoction, casting a scent of soil and pleasure. Taking his drink in hand, he retreated into the shadows. Oscar might stand in the same spot for one to four hours, becoming a human lighthouse—motionless yet searching. He scanned the room for her. His woman. His type.

Tonight, Oscar spotted her within ten minutes—a record. His women had similar features. His *object d'attention* tonight had a round, baby face; dark purple lipstick; and a blonde side-swept haircut. Silver hoop earrings dangled from her ears. Her red top with string corset and black, short skirt reminded him of an anime character come to life. Fishnet stockings hugged her legs down to her stylish ankle boots.

The very picture of his type.

But Oscar would wait. Many times before, he had waited too long, and his target had escaped into the night, often on the arm of another. No matter. His type returned eventually. He was a patient man.

Sometimes the woman would come with companions. Again, his sedulousness would prevail. Often the woman's friends would leave with other partners, abandoning her. Alternately, his type would initially come with friends, but he waited for the time—her last—when she came alone. And alone, though a throng of people surrounded her, was when he'd approach.

The stars aligned for Oscar tonight as he studied his subject swing to the unending roar of the beat. She appeared to be alone, retreating not to a table but to the bar when she wanted to catch her breath. At times, she would order a drink, her hand encircling her glass with purple, manicured nails. Drink after drink splashed down her lovely throat. When others approached, his subject seemed aloof as she swished away. Alone, her mouth moved. The purple lips drew his focus.

The woman mumbled to herself. Words of encouragement, no doubt. Words inviting her to take a chance, a risk. This was good. Very good.

As a hawk watched its prey, Oscar observed her for two hours and twenty-two minutes. He noted the angle of her spine, and the sway of her hips when dancing. He imagined perfect feet encased in the boots and wondered if her toenails were purple. Oscar would find out later. The blood rushed to his head when her tongue darted over her upper lip while concentrating on the music.

Oscar patted his breast pocket. He would move in tonight.

He rarely moved this quickly, but she was too perfect. She was his type—a definition of what he was searching for. Susan had been close to the mark but strepitous. Fran was a redhead—never again. And Carri-with-no-e had been more athletic than she looked. She had nearly made it out of the grove and back to the road. Each selection was similar but lacked a little finesse. But tonight, he had found his Helen of Troy. The former ladies were Venus de Milos. His new woman came with arms, thank you very much.

Yes, at this stage, he often thought he had discovered perfection. But Oscar had been at this game long enough to know this one was special. From the way she held herself to the paint on her lips and nails, she was the saffron in his risotto. He squared his shoulders and marched in a straight line across the room.

When Oscar approached, the woman's eyes narrowed. He raised his hands to represent a mock surrender. "Ma'am, the bartender tipped me off that you might have had a few too many."

Ms. Purple Nails glared at the female bartender who was busy passing pink cocktails to a group of young women.

While she was distracted, Oscar breathed in her essence. She had a honey scent about her that pleased him. He cleared his throat to get her attention. Reaching into his breast pocket, his fingers touched the card he would lay next to her corpse. He'd put that to use later. Instead, he pulled out his identification. "I'm a licensed chauffeur with Star Motorcars. Here are my credentials and a number you may call to prove who I am."

His type never tried the number. If any of them ever called his bluff, Star Motorcars would verify his employment and assume he was being a good Samaritan. He was a model employee. Driving someone home after drinking too much was in line with Oscar's behavior at Star Motorcars. After all, he had won the highest customer satisfaction survey for the last eight months.

"I'll call an Uber."

Oscar gestured to her cell. "Then I'm going to have to ask you to call it now and wait outside to ensure you won't drink anymore."

His soon-to-be conquest's eyes went round. Yes, *outside*. The Chemistry Lab was in the section of Toledo known as Death Valley. Whenever an announcer reported on a homicide, the journalist gave the street name to tip everyone off that the city had lost another to Death Valley.

She inhaled, and her pinched nostrils enlarged. Oscar's pulse raced.

Then she did a funny thing with her left hand. She let it fall and waggled her fingers while biting her plum-colored bottom lip. Oscar waited with the patience of a birdwatcher. Perhaps this night wouldn't come off for him after all.

She released a long breath. "Are you sure?"

Odd question.

"Quite sure."

The woman hunched her shoulders, creating wrinkles in her top. "Oh, I was having fun."

Standing tall, he put his hands at his sides, conveying an impression of authority. "I have to see you make the call, or would you rather I drive you?"

She lifted her chin. "If you're a free ride, how could I say no?"

Oscar nodded toward the exit, and she advanced to the front doors. He followed her, circumventing the patrons on the dance floor by taking a circuitous route. Exiting the building, they halted on the sidewalk. Time for the next deception — act as if he didn't care if she walked away.

"I've parked around the corner." Oscar leaned in the direction of the car. "I'll pick you up here. You'll be safe near the entrance."

The woman rubbed her arms. "Yeah. Sure."

Oscar strolled around the corner and then broke into a jog to his Lincoln town car. Within a minute, he was behind the wheel and had the engine purring. He zipped around the block and parked in front of the nightclub. She was waiting there for him with no one else in sight. Abductions were almost too easy these days.

Oscar left the motor idling and eased out of the driver's seat. He dashed around the vehicle, opened the back door, and stood aside. She peered inside, remaining on the sidewalk.

"Why a barrier between the front and back seat?"

"Standard issue. Safety protocol."

His quarry frowned and lingered. Oscar's heart thumped, unsure she would enter the car. But she clambered aboard, and he shut the door after her. Pulse racing with his success, he returned to the driver's side and slid into the front seat.

Pulling away from the nightclub, Oscar turned onto a four-lane road. The locks clicked into place as he accelerated. He flipped the switch on the cell phone jammer. Everything was in place. She was as trapped as a zoo exhibit.

She viewed him in the mirror. "My name is Kitty. I live at 4462 Moss Avenue."

Oscar grunted his assent. Within ten minutes, she would realize he had no intention of taking her home. She would disappear for a while. Not invisibility, no. Invisibility was his gig, according to the police force.

The press hadn't nicknamed him The Invisible Man because of his ability to blend in with others and avoid capture. The Chameleon would've made a better moniker for a stalker who faded into the background. Instead, the media had named him after the H. G. Wells character because of the blank index card he left behind on his kills. He wrote an invisible message on the card. With lemon juice, he always scratched the words, "Ha. Ha."

Each victim he had dumped around Toledo had his missive pinned to her skin. The method lacked sophistication, to be sure, but he enjoyed teasing the police. He pictured the scene — several cops clustered together, holding his card over a Bunsen burner.

Fifteen minutes passed, and Kitty hadn't mentioned that he was heading in the wrong direction. Oscar glanced at her in the rearview mirror. She was different from the rest. They had all inquired about the route before this point. For his part, Oscar had remained silent, ignoring their demands to release them. Instead, Kitty sat still on one side of the seat in full view of his mirror.

Had he misjudged her? Was she an undercover officer? No, they would have acted too stupid or eager. He spied an intelligence behind this one's eyes, a calculating demeanor. Kitty was trapped, and she knew it. Creases on her forehead indicated she was plotting her next move.

Oh, but this *would* be fun.

Oscar sped out of the city limits to the countryside. The grove where he committed his crimes was on a farmer's abandoned field. The land bordered a lonely road without traffic. He had prepared the grove: tarp, garbage bags, extra clothes. Nobody would ever think anything brutal had happened there. He prepared for everything. Another reason the police would never catch him.

His victim broke the silence. "Will there be pain?"

Huh. Odd question. And a disturbing way to ask it. Most of them asked, "Will you hurt me?"

He responded with his stock answer.

"Not if you do what you're told."

Her last minutes on Earth would go easier if she were compliant. And he'd be merciful if she didn't fight. Their endings had all varied. For the women who had obeyed, he was efficient. Others, though...

Pulling his car off the side of the road, Oscar threw it into park. He noticed Kitty hadn't tried to open the door and make a run for it. All the others had been foolish enough to think he would let them escape. Ridiculous! Didn't they know they were dealing with a professional?

Oscar turned around and faced her. Her eyes were wide but not in a trapped, fawn-like way. Just listening. Absorbing.

He removed the revolver from his jacket pocket and knocked it against the plastic barrier. "I will leave the car and then unlock it remotely. My friend here will be aimed at you at all times. I know how to shoot to kill or to maim. Trust me when I say I won't kill you, but the bullet will incapacitate you."

Kitty didn't answer him.

Oscar flared his nostrils. "Do you understand?"

"Clearly," she murmured.

Grunting, he exited the Lincoln. Taking his time, he positioned himself a couple of meters from the back passenger door where she sat. He clicked the button on his fob, and the door unlocked.

"Out you go."

Kitty took her time extracting herself from the car. When she made her way out, she sidestepped and put her back to the front passenger side of the Lincoln with her arms raised. She had left her door open.

Who left the door open? Was this a trick?

Oscar gestured toward the back door with his gun. "Close it."

"Does it matter?"

The question made him doubt whether Kitty was his type at all. Was she as dense as concrete or brilliant as a gem? She had obeyed his orders, but her comments kept him off-kilter. He was smarter than all his abductees, but her idiosyncrasies made him twitchy.

"Yeah, it matters." He garnished the sentence with a sneer.

Kitty shifted left and shut the door with her behind, her eyes never leaving the weapon. Oscar nodded at the grove twenty meters from where they were parked.

"Now, let's go."

Sliding away from the car, Kitty walked backward. Some of his former prey had done the same, and Oscar hadn't cared. She wanted to keep her eyes on him. Fine. Her gesture didn't unnerve him. He would get what he wanted in the end.

Three dried-up leaves made a crunching noise to his left, and he halted. Nothing was there. Not even a small rodent.

"Did you hear something?"

Kitty shook her head.

"I swore I heard —"

A sharp prick on the back of Oscar's neck interrupted him. What the hell? He turned to find what had dared to hurt him, but nothing was there. A sharp intake of breath from his target reminded him he no longer had the revolver trained on her. But so what? He had the situation completely under his control. No, he dismissed the pain as just an insect with a powerful stinger.

"What got you?" Kitty asked.

The point of the stinger's contact with his neck hurt as if someone had stuck his skin with a hot shard of metal. He put his fingers on the back of his neck to touch it. The welt rose on his skin like a pimple. As his fingers brushed against the abrasion, his arm grew heavy. Why did it take so much effort to lift it?

Oscar swung around to Kitty. *She* had planned this. How, he didn't know. But he was certain it was her.

"What did you do?"

Kitty's voice was as smooth as a pane of glass. "I didn't do anything."

She lied. His arms were heavier now, and his knees started to buckle. He caught himself once. For a moment, he thought he would remain upright. Then he tumbled down. He couldn't keep his gun raised, so he leveraged it against the ground. Through gritted teeth, he repeated himself.

"What. Did. You. Do?"

A voice whispered in his ear — a voice without a body. Not Kitty's. A feminine voice, wispier than Kitty's. Someone new. Someone different.

"I did it."

Someone grabbed his wrist and took his revolver. He tried to resist, but his sluggish body wouldn't respond.

Kitty called across the field. "Are you okay?"

Why was the lady he kidnapped concerned about him? But then Oscar realized she wasn't addressing him. She spoke to the *other*.

"I'm fine. Much better than the so-called Invisible Man." She laughed.

While Oscar's body betrayed him, his mind remained clear. "Who are you?"

"You may call me Gloria. I'm a scientist and inventor. Unlike you, I've made good on my moniker."

Kitty recoiled as the gun — barrel pointed away — floated toward her. "I don't want that."

"Then throw it away," said the bodiless voice. "I've pumped him full of my serum. He'll be incapacitated for a day. At least, from the neck down. I need him to speak. Or scream, if the situation calls for it."

Oscar squinted at the air in the direction of the voice. "What do you want with me?"

"As you can't see, I'm a result of my most successful experiment. Yet, my reverse formula didn't work as I had planned. Injecting it into myself was quite painful."

Kitty laid a hand on the air as if resting it on another person's shoulder. "I warned you about experimenting on yourself, Gloria."

A hand rummaged around his pocket and grabbed his keys. "I need subjects to test my new formula. I guess you volunteered."

"Let me go," urged Oscar, "and I won't tell anyone about you."

Kitty slapped him hard on the cheek. "Don't talk to her. You only speak to me. You aren't worthy of speaking to her."

These two were intelligent, but he questioned whether they cared whether he lived or died. To them, he was nothing but a lab rat.

Gloria addressed him again. "I'm sorry to say that I don't know if the new formula will work. I may have to try over and over. But, to borrow a page from your book. Ha. Ha."

Her tone was flat and deadly when speaking the jesting words. *His* tagline.

It was time to bargain. "I have money."

The keys rattled in an invisible hand. "Please don't ruin the moment by begging. My methods are as unethical as yours." An invisible hand patted his face. "Quite frankly, I've been hoping for someone like you to come along."

Oscar gulped as Gloria's minty breath whispered in his ear.

"You're exactly my type."

THE END

THE FUNERAL CRASHER
Stoney M. Setzer

Sometimes knowing that you're dreaming doesn't help one bit. Ever since that day at Gary Cleveland's bait shop, the scene had been replaying itself in my nightmares.

In my mind's eye I kept reliving the same events, as if I was trapped in a TV rerun. Mutated frogs are overrunning the shop, and a man named Huey — who had helped engineer the mutations — is about to kill both Cleveland and me. Just as he is about to finish us off, he gets attacked by this creature that looked like a wolf but was the size of a man, with a badly maimed right arm — or front leg, depending on how you look at it. For lack of a better term, it was a werewolf, saving our lives by taking out our would-be murderer.

Even after that, there's this feeling that something else is out there, lurking. Something malevolent and destructive, something closing in…

Cold sweat drenched my skin as I sat up in bed with a gasp. As usual, it took me a minute to realize that it had just been another nightmare — or rather the same nightmare, repeated for the umpteenth time. I was at home in my bed, not at the bait shop. The digital clock on my nightstand declared that the time was 2:38 AM Sunday morning. Way too early to get up, but plenty of time to go through it all again if I went back to sleep.

Predictably, my thoughts drifted to my girlfriend, Dr. Staci Bridges. She was at her place, no doubt sleeping peacefully in her bed. If we really did get married someday, would I be condemning her to sleepless nights caused by my recurring nightmares?

Trying to take my mind off of things, I turned on the TV. An old black-and-white movie was on. I heard the distinctive voice of Vincent Price, but he wasn't on screen. I pushed the INFO button on my remote and saw that the movie was *The Invisible Man Returns*.

I didn't change the channel. Staci would probably tell me that it wasn't necessarily the best thing for a man suffering nightmares to watch, but somehow this seemed tame compared to what kept playing on the screen of my imagination.

~~~~~

I didn't get much sleep after that. Thanks to more coffee than I care to admit, I managed to make it through church without nodding off. If I had, Staci would have surely elbowed me in the ribs.

Staci and I held hands as Pastor Larry led the congregation in the
~~~~~

closing prayer. It was a typical Sunday morning service at Shiloh Baptist Church, which now included her sitting on the same pew with me and my family—Mom, my sister Carla, and my niece Michelle.

Once we were dismissed, Mom nudged me. "Are you two still coming over for Sunday dinner?"

"Yes, ma'am," Staci and I said, almost in unison. She didn't really have to ask. Our two favorite local restaurants, Leon's Barbecue and Maria's Mexican, were both closed on Sunday. Even if they were open, they couldn't hold a candle to one of Mom's homecooked meals.

"Okay, see you there," Mom replied, with a little extra smile that I could translate easily enough. She completely approved of my relationship with the veterinarian, and I'm sure that somewhere in her head she was already picturing Staci as her future daughter-in-law. Mom wasn't known for being subtle. Staci had to notice it too, but she didn't seem bothered by it. That was encouraging but also a little intimidating since my first marriage hadn't worked out so well.

As we made our way to the exit, a burly man with thick glasses stepped into our path. He was Fred Gateman, the proprietor of the local funeral home. We spoke frequently, but I could tell this was about more than socializing. He wasn't hiding his anxiety any better than Mom hid her little loaded glances.

"H-how are you doing, Sheriff?" Gateman stammered. With a nod to Staci, he added, "And you, Doc?"

"Doing good," Staci replied.

"You doing all right, Fred?" I asked pointedly.

Gateman tugged nervously at the collar of his shirt. "Uh, are you going to be on duty tomorrow?"

Thanks to a concussion and a couple of broken ribs, I had been sidelined for about a month after the incident at the bait shop, but I had been back at work for a week now. "Yes, sir, I will. What's up?"

"Well, we've got a funeral tomorrow at two o'clock, and I'd appreciate some police presence, if at all possible."

I nodded, even though I suspected that there was more to come. "Yeah, I think we've already made arrangements for a couple of deputies to escort the funeral procession to the cemetery, so..."

"Do you think there's any possible way for you to be there personally, Sheriff?"

I glanced at Staci. Her lips tightened, signaling she was thinking the same thing I was. Something was definitely wrong. "Why?" I inquired.

"The funeral is for Joey Spalding," Gateman said, speaking quickly as if he was desperate to spit the words out.

Now he had caught my attention. "You mean the same Spalding family that I think you mean?"

"One and the same."

I raised an eyebrow. "Joey wasn't all that old, was he? Early twenties, right? What happened to him?"

"Twenty-three." Gateman nodded. "He had been living in Memphis and got in a car wreck. So, with that whole family being together in one place …" His voice trailed off, but he looked at me pointedly.

I nodded solemnly. "All right, I'll be there."

After Gateman thanked me and hurried off, Staci elbowed me in the ribs. "Okay, Mr. Sheriff, you know I lived in Chattanooga for a good while there. You want to fill me in on this Spalding family?"

We stepped out into the parking lot. "Okay, do you remember a girl named Vanessa Harrison from high school? I think she would have been a senior when we were sophomores."

"Vaguely. The name rings a bell."

"Okay. She married a guy named Wendell Spalding, maybe about five years older than she was. Her family had money, but he was a rough customer. Kind of an odd couple, you wouldn't have necessarily put them together, but something must have worked because they had two kids together. Twins. This Joey is—was—one of them. Nobody has seen the other son in a long time."

"Ouch," Staci said.

"Vanessa's passing a few years back was what really put the rest of the family into the dysfunctional category, though. Now it's just a big mess, and they're all going to be together under one roof tomorrow."

"Sounds like fun," Staci cracked sardonically. "Crying shame I'll be at work. You'll have to give me all the gory details."

"Let's hope that they don't get too gory," I replied.

She raised an eyebrow at me. "Now, how about you tell me what's going on with you this morning?"

"What do you mean?"

"You had that nightmare again last night, didn't you?" She poked me lightly in the chest. "Dogs and cats aren't the only kinds of God's creatures that I can diagnose, Mr. Sheriff."

"How could you tell?" I inquired, wondering if the woman of my dreams had somehow missed her calling. Maybe she should have been a detective instead of a veterinarian.

Staci smirked. "Your eyes are red, your breath reeks of black coffee, and you've got that little overcaffeinated jitter working. That tells me you didn't sleep much, making that nightmare the most reasonable explanation."

"You've got me. And before you ask, yes, it's the same one as all the other times."

Staci's gaze darted around, making sure nobody else was within earshot. "Bait shop? Wolfman with a deformed arm?" she whispered.

I sighed. "Look, you probably think it's because of the concussion, but I promise you, I know what I saw."

Time seemed to slow down to a crawl as she studied me. I felt like I was twisting in the wind, waiting for her verdict. Finally, she nodded. "If we were anywhere else but Sardis County, I probably wouldn't believe you, but I've already figured out that you can't dismiss much of anything around these parts, no matter how strange it sounds. Besides, I was there with you that day. I may not have seen a wolfman, but I saw the frogs and everything else."

"True."

"Now whether anybody else would believe it or not, that's a different ballgame. You know that, right?"

I nodded. "Only too well."

~~~~~

I did manage to get some shut-eye Sunday afternoon. Mom had barbecued chicken in the crock pot, and I probably ate a little more than I should. Then after lunch, we sat on Mom's couch watching the Atlanta Falcons game, and Staci put a throw pillow on her lap and encouraged me to lay my head on it. As soon as I did, she started slowly running her fingers through my hair. She might as well have slipped me a sedative from her vet clinic, because it was lights out for me shortly thereafter. I have no doubt that Staci knew exactly what she was doing, and I appreciated it. Not only for the rest, but also because it saved me the pain of seeing my Falcons blow yet another fourth-quarter lead.

Naturally, I woke up to little teasing smirks from the females in my family. That was getting to be a common occurrence whenever Staci was around.

Nighttime wouldn't be nearly as restful. Yet another nightmare, and Staci was in her own house then. However, I supposed that I'd had just enough rest to deal with a funeral. I had given Gateman my word, after all.

The service wouldn't start until 2:00 PM, but I arrived just before lunchtime. With the Spalding family involved, I decided it would be a good idea to get there before they did, just in case. I even arrived before Gonzalez and Howard, the two deputies who would escort the funeral procession to the cemetery.

Slowly I poured a pack of peanuts into a bottle of Coke as I looked at Gateman and Sons Funeral Home. It sat in a big antebellum house that supposedly had once been used as a field hospital in the Civil War, which seemed fitting. One way or another, this building had long been associated with pain, misery, and death.

Fred Gateman was actually one of the sons, and now he was
~~~~~

grooming his own offspring to one day carry on the family business. For decades, the Gatemans had been very good at providing a service that they knew their clientele would rather not need. They had been in charge of funeral arrangements for both Dad and my brother-in-law, as well as countless others over the years. As usual when I found myself here, I acknowledged the memories but then once again compartmentalized them so that I could focus.

Getting out of the squad car, I stood for a minute with my bottled Coke, still fizzing softly from the addition of the salty peanuts. Thinking about what contingencies might arise, I paused to offer up a quick prayer. Under the circumstances, it seemed like an especially good idea.

Suddenly, I had the sensation that someone was standing right behind me. Quickly I turned around, but I didn't see anybody. As far as I could tell, I had the parking lot mostly to myself, the sole exception being Fred Gateman. He stood beside the entrance, smoking.

Still, I couldn't shake the feeling that somebody had been right there, looking over my shoulder. The hair on my arms stood up on end, and I felt a chill that had nothing to do with the breeze.

Gateman looked up as I approached. "Thank you so much for coming, Sheriff. As you might imagine, I'm…well, concerned."

I nodded. "Nobody wants World War III breaking out in their place of business."

"No, sir, we don't, and I can't think of a family more likely to stir something up at a funeral." He shook his head sadly, making little disapproving guttural noises.

"I understand. We'll take care of it."

Gateman looked at his cigarette and frowned. "I'm supposed to be trying to quit. Promised Becky I would, but on a day like this…"

"Well, I know you're stressed, but you're never going to get anywhere as long as you have that stuff on your person. Maybe you need to take that home for now." Gateman and his wife lived in an apartment they had built in the back of the funeral parlor, so home for him wasn't too far.

"And let Becky find it? You must want me to be my own next customer!" Gateman chuckled and shook his head. "But I reckon you're right. Do you mind if I give this to you, so I won't be too tempted?" He handed me a Zippo lighter.

Not knowing what else to do, I accepted the lighter and stuck it in my pocket. Just then, Staci's designated ringtone sounded, and I fished out my cell phone as Gateman headed back inside. "Hey, Dr. Gorgeous."

"Hey," she replied, sounding concerned. "You got a minute?"

"For you, I've got all the time you need."

Clearly, she wasn't up for playful banter at the moment. "You're going to think I'm crazy when I tell you what's gone on around here this morning."

I shifted my mood to match her tone. "This is Sardis County. Nothing surprises me too much anymore."

"Nothing, huh? What if I told you..." She paused, as if unsure whether she should continue. "What if I told you we have an invisible dog here in the clinic?"

"Say what?"

"I didn't think anything surprised you anymore," she quipped, sounding a little more like herself. Even without seeing her, I could picture the beginnings of her teasing smirk.

"Okay, so I stand corrected. So, start from the beginning."

Staci sighed. "Well, we heard barking and whimpering coming from one of the exam rooms. Only thing is, it was an overflow room we hadn't used since Thursday. Completely empty, but we all heard it. It sounded scared, and we didn't know how to approach it, not knowing if it might be hurt."

An invisible dog. Even for Sardis County, this took the cake. "So, what did you do?"

"All I could think of was to grab a blanket and throw it in the direction that the sounds came from. It landed on him and gave us an idea of size and shape. Then we put him in a kennel, until we can figure out what to do." She paused. "Are you already at the funeral home?"

"Yeah, but I'll come by there after we get out of here. Hopefully it will be uneventful and we'll get done fairly quickly."

A weak chuckle on her end. "Dane, please. With all you told me about the Spaldings, do you really think it will be uneventful?"

I grunted. "No, not really."

~~~~~

"I really wish we could renovate this old place," Gateman lamented as we stood in the lobby.

"How so?"

"For one thing, look at this old carpet," he said, kicking at the floor. "Dad got it dirt cheap years ago, but Becky swears it's an eyesore. She ain't wrong. Then all the sprinklers in the whole building are integrated. One goes off, they all go off. Not exactly ideal. And I wouldn't mind swapping out all these canvas paintings on the walls."

"Who painted them?" I asked.

He laughed. "You tell me, and then we'll both know. Thrift store specials, honestly. And then...uh-oh. Here we go."

One of his ushers opened the front door to admit Nadine Harrison, the grandmother of the deceased. As always, she carried herself with a haughty air. Wealthy was a relative term, but her late husband had left
~~~~~

her with enough money that she was used to getting her way, even if she had to pay to get it.

Maybe that was what had made her so bitter over the past few years. No amount of money she spent could have stopped the cancer that claimed her daughter Vanessa's life. All Nadine could do was pay off medical bills. Now she was confronted with the death of a grandchild, and once again the only thing her money was good for was covering the cost of something she didn't want in the first place. I could almost feel sorry for her — almost.

I was going to speak to her, but she strode past me as if I was invisible, making a beeline for the funeral director. "Are there any other expenses I need to know about, Mr. Gateman?" she demanded gruffly.

"N-n-no, ma'am, you're all p-paid up," Gateman stammered. Nadine's wealth intimidated most people, but I knew he was more unnerved that she represented half of the battle royale he dreaded.

Her stern expression softened slightly, and she lowered her voice to a whisper. "Have you seen my grandson — my other one?"

"No, ma'am, I have not. I'm sorry," Gateman answered, sympathy overriding his anxiety for a fleeting moment.

Nadine nodded, casting her gaze downward. "Very well. Let me know if you do see him." With that, she marched away toward the viewing room where Joey's closed casket rested, putting her facade back in place.

Once she was out of earshot, I leaned over. "Still holding out hope for Billy, I see."

"Yeah. Sad case."

"I remember them filing the missing person report. He didn't leave much of a trail though. Just that note saying how his life had turned to trash after his mom died."

Gateman leaned in and lowered his voice. "Rumor is he committed suicide and his body just hasn't turned up yet. Ain't nobody ever gonna see Billy again, I'm afraid."

Before I could reply, the front door was thrown open. Gateman gulped loud enough for it to be heard. The other half of his anxiety had arrived.

Wendell Spalding stood as evidence that Vanessa Harrsion Spalding must have gone through a "bad boy" phase at some point. Otherwise, there would be no explanation for how she wound up with a man better suited to a motorcycle gang than the country club living favored by Nadine. A lifetime of hard living had left its mark on him, but he still cut an intimidating figure, graying mullet and all.

He stomped through the lobby like a man on a mission, headed for the viewing room. Wendell had been known as a brawler in his younger days, and he was clearly gearing up for a confrontation. Immediately I moved, knowing that nothing good could come out of Wendell and Nadine occupying the same space.

I wove through the crowded lobby, a maze made of people. Some people moved, but others I had to dodge, slowing me down. As I rounded the corner, the crowd finally thinned. I ran like a football player breaking free to the open field.

The scene almost looked like something out of an old Western. A pair of enemies stood on opposite ends, ready to duel, while everyone else had moved off to the side to get out of their way. Instead of two gunslingers facing off in the middle of a dusty street, Wendell and Nadine were on opposite ends of the viewing room. What movement there was on the sidelines consisted of onlookers sorting themselves to one end or the other based upon their loyalties.

At least they hadn't started the fireworks without me. Maybe, just maybe, the gravity of Joey's funeral would be enough to bring them to their senses for a little while. Not a permanent truce, but just a temporary ceasefire....

"What took you so long to get here, Wendell?" Nadine snarled. Even though she was older and smaller, she showed no signs of backing down. "You have trouble slithering out from under your rock?"

So much for a ceasefire.

"Figured you'd need a little extra time to dream up a way to blame all of this on me, what with you being such a slow thinker and all!" Wendell fired back. His speech wasn't as slurred as I might have expected, but I knew better than to believe he had come here completely sober. "So what did you come up with? Make it good, now!"

"You never paid any attention to your children, not like what they needed from their father! And ever since Vanessa died, you've completely disappeared from their lives!"

"Oh, and you were any better? Traveling the world, they never even saw you for months on end! At least I provided for them!"

Lord, help me, I prayed silently as I strode toward them. The trick in situations like these was to strike the right balance between being calm and authoritative. My badge usually did the trick for the latter, freeing me up to come across as a little more cordial—my Andy Griffith style, Mom would call it. "Excuse me, what seems to be the issue?" I inquired as I stepped between them.

"Why don't you mind your own..." Wendell started. Once he turned around and saw me, he stopped cold. "Uh, hey, Sheriff."

Nadine stiffened noticeably. "Hello, Sheriff."

"Hey. Now is it absolutely necessary to carry on like this, at a funeral of all places?" I made my voice as firm as I could without raising it. Even without looking over my shoulder, I sensed that people were behind me, no doubt coming to check out the scene. At least this time there was a reason for the sensation.

Before either of them could answer, there came the sound of hands clapping together loudly, like a teacher trying to capture the attention of noisy students. I looked around, trying to figure out who had done it, only to find everyone else looking my way, as if they thought it was me.

Somebody in the crowd screamed. There was a loud thud, as if somebody had fallen on the floor. "Look! The casket!" someone else shouted.

The lid on Joey's casket was opening.

My first reaction was terror, but then all my training kicked in. Compartmentalizing my fright as best I could, I forced myself to analyze what I saw. The lid's movement was slow and deliberate, as if the lid was very heavy—or as if someone was making a huge production out of opening it, to be sure that everyone saw it.

However, I couldn't see anyone's hand on the lid. Nobody was even standing close enough to touch the casket. I even looked for the horror movie cliche of a hand from within pushing it open, but there was nothing there either. For just a moment, I wondered if this was some kind of twisted joke, if maybe somebody had put some kind of a motorized gizmo on the lid as a sick prank.

Nadine shrieked, and Wendell swore. I stood my ground, trying to make sense out of what I saw. Sure, this was Sardis County, the weirdness capital of Tennessee if not the entire Southeast, but this was something else entirely. Closed caskets weren't supposed to come open, period.

Their occupants also weren't supposed to move. Instead of abiding to such standards of funeral decorum, Joey's corpse rose to a sitting position, burns and all.

Nadine wasn't the only person screaming now, and people were sprinting for the doors. "Quiet, everybody!" I shouted, trying to restore order. It didn't work.

"The doors!" someone shrieked. "They're locked!"

"We're trapped!" another cried out.

"Everybody, quiet!" I shouted again, louder and more sternly. This time, at least some of the people listened to me.

Cautiously, I stepped toward the casket, instinctively reaching for my Glock. Seeing Joey sitting up wasn't the weirdest part of the scene. There was something strange about the *way* he had gotten into that position. It had been a slow, jerky rise, as if someone had put their arms under his shoulders and pulled him up, struggling against the resistance of dead weight. However, I couldn't see anyone there.

"That's close enough, Sheriff Carter!" a voice barked from Joey's direction. "Everyone, your attention, please! Silence!"

An eerie hush fell over the room. Everyone was still frightened, but no one dared move. My hand rested on the grip of my Glock, but deep down I wondered how much good it would actually do.

"Dad! Grandma! So good to see you both in the same place for once!" the voice mocked. "What a pity it took my death to bring you together!"

The barb led to maybe the most surreal sight of all. Wendell and Nadine, sworn enemies, were now huddled together in abject terror.

"Why are you two trying to blame each other for my death? Don't you realize that there's enough guilt to go around? You're *both* to blame here!"

Gut instinct told me that things were not as they seemed. Suddenly I thought about my earlier conversation with Staci concerning the invisible dog. As crazy as it sounded, it resonated with me now. "Who are you, really?" I demanded. "You're not really Joey Spalding, are you?"

"How dare you accuse me of.... Oh, who am I trying to fool?" the voice asked, changing slightly, as if it had given up trying to imitate someone else. I wondered if he might have been trying to sound like the deceased. A second later, Joey's body fell back into the coffin with a thud. "All right, I'll confess. I'm not really Joey, and that body is just an empty shell. The real Joey went somewhere else when he died, but I didn't come here to discuss theology. I came here to make these two people pay!"

One of the potted floral arrangements surrounding the casket floated into the air. As soon as it reached the height of a man's head, it drifted backward and hung in midair for a split second. Then it hurtled forward quickly, straight at Wendell and Nadine. He pushed her aside but was unable to dodge the projectile himself. The pot hit him in the left shoulder. It moved like somebody had picked it up and thrown it.

More panic erupted around me. I raised my voice to be heard above the ruckus. "Stop in the name of the law!" Immediately I winced, realizing how cliché that was.

The voice now laughed hysterically. "Please! How do you intend to stop the Invisible Man?"

I would have traded my big toe to wake up and find that this was just another nightmare. No such luck. Like so many other incidents I had faced since becoming the sheriff of Sardis County, the unbelievable had become real. All of those other times, however, I had been able to see what I was up against. Not today.

The maniacal laughter seemed to come out of thin air. A chilling thought crossed my mind. In the movie from the other night, invisibility had carried with it the side effect of insanity. Fiction or not, that seemed to add up here. Opening caskets and pretending to speak for the dead certainly was not the behavior of a rational man. Not exactly a reassuring thought.

All eyes were on me now, especially since they couldn't see him. No matter how rattled I might be, I had to stay strong and take control of the situation as best I could. Maybe I would have a chance if I could distract him. Thanks to Staci, I had a way to do that. "Invisible Man, huh? Did you happen to lose a dog recently?" I asked.

"So you already know about that, and you're still here?"

"My gir—uh, Dr. Bridges at the Sardis County Animal Hospital reported him this morning."

"Quite the looker, that Dr. Bridges. You have good taste. When I go there to retrieve my dog, I may just have to pay her a little surprise visit."

The insinuation in his voice made me see red. Fury rose within me, taking me to the limits of my self-control. "So help me, if you hurt her, I'll..."

"You won't do anything!" Something unseen slammed into my abdomen—a punch in the gut that I could not see to block. Before I could recover, something swept my legs out from under me, knocking me to the carpet. Worse, the impact was a painful jolt to my still-mending ribs. How was I supposed to fight an assailant that I couldn't even see?

Time to call for backup. I grabbed my radio to call Gonzalez and Howard, but all I got was static.

"Oh, please!" the Invisible Man mocked. "Come on, really? Did you think a man who could make himself invisible wouldn't think of that? Forget it! I've got a device set up outside to kill your radio and phone signals. No one from outside is coming to save you!"

Great. I had two deputies right outside but no way to let them know what was happening in here. That made me the only hope. Silently I prayed, figuring that God was *my* only hope.

"Why are you here?" I repeated, slowly pushing myself to my feet. Having no idea where he was, I needed to be careful. No sudden moves.

"Haven't you figured it out yet, Sherlock? I'm here for revenge against the people who turned my life into trash!"

"Turned your life into trash?" Nadine echoed. Her eyes widened. "Billy, is that you?"

Another torrent of deranged laughter, only this time it seemed to be coming from somewhere else in the room. He was on the move. "Finally, somebody figures it out! Took you idiots long enough! But then again, you always treated me like I was invisible, didn't you, Grandma?"

All of the color drained out of Nadine's face. "What are you talking about, Billy? I never..."

"Never paid him any attention because you were too busy seeing the world on your inheritance?" Wendell snapped. "Please! You never paid him any attention!"

"And you just proved the same thing about yourself, Dad!" Billy mocked. "I just accused both of you of ignoring me, and all you can think of is using that as ammunition against Grandma! Never mind that you were just as bad!"

Wendell scowled. "Boy, you'd better bite your tongue! I worked hard to provide for you and your brother!"

Billy's laugh could have turned a man's blood to ice. "Him again! And as for all of your hard work and provision, you spent as much time at the bars as you did at home!"

Wendell cursed. "Boy, who do you think you're talking to? I'm gonna kick your…"

His head jerked back as if he had been punched in the jaw, which I suppose was exactly what had happened. Wendell stumbled backward, but an unseen hand grabbed his shirt.

"Oh, really? How do you intend to kick something you can't even see?"

There was my chance. Ignoring the pain in my side, I slipped behind where he had to be standing. Even if I couldn't see him, I could strike in the general vicinity. Something had to be better than nothing…

"Careful, Sheriff Carter," Billy warned. "I wouldn't make any false moves if I were you. These two are toast anyway, but you've got a roomful of innocent bystanders. You wouldn't want to do something that might turn my wrath on them!"

Wendell had grabbed for the arm that held his shirt, but he immediately doubled over as if he had been punched in the gut. Before Nadine could move, an unseen hand caught her arm and snatched her closer to where Wendell stood, eliciting a shriek from her. "One wrong move, Sheriff, and you will have blood on your hands!"

I froze. Not being able to see him, I was at a serious disadvantage, and he knew it.

"Why are you doing this, Billy?" Nadine sobbed.

"Mom was the only one who ever knew I was there!" Billy accused. "The two of you were so wrapped up in Joey this, Joey that! Joey won the science fair. Joey got all A's! On and on! I was invisible to the two of you long before this ever happened to me, and it was all because of him! It makes me glad that I did it!"

"Did what, Billy?" I asked, a harrowing suspicion rising in me. "What are you glad you did?"

His deranged laughter made my blood run cold. "I put Joey in that casket! They said it was an accident, but I caused it!"

The room fell as silent as a tomb. Nadine's face went ashen, and Wendell's eyes widened in horror and disbelief. At last, I cleared my throat. "How did you cause it?"

"Mr. Hotshot had that Jeep that he was so proud of. Just left the top down while he was at work, that's how arrogant he was. He never banked on his brother turning invisible and waiting for him, right there in the passenger seat!"

Who would? I wanted to ask, but this wasn't the time for wisecracks. Not when I was trying to keep him talking. "Then what happened?"

"He got in the Jeep and started driving, but I bided my time. I waited until he got on the perfect stretch of road, one where he had a good chance of losing control. Then I started talking to him, telling him that I'm dead and now I'm a ghost, coming back to haunt him. Scared him pretty good. Only then did he realize that I had messed with his brakes before he got in the car. Didn't cut the line, mind you, because that would have left some evidence. I drained the line and then put it back in place. Then, just before he crashed, I jumped out!" Billy roared with laughter. "Not only did that get him back for making me feel invisible for all those years, but I knew his funeral would get the two of you together so I could kill two birds with one stone!"

And there it was. Sometimes I really hated it when I was right.

"You killed your own brother? Your own flesh and blood?" Nadine shrieked, her eyes bulging in horror.

"Why not? He's been killing me for years! Living in his shadow felt like being dead in your eyes!" Billy must have been trembling in anger, given how violently Nadine and Wendell shook in his grasp, meaning his hands were full.

My first impulse was to take advantage and charge forward, but I hesitated. There had to be a way to even the odds first.

Not knowing what else to do, I asked God again to help me. I didn't close my eyes, but as a matter of habit I turned my gaze upward. That was when I noticed the sprinkler heads in the ceiling.

I touched my pocket. Gateman's lighter was still in there along with my funeral program.

The idea came to me fully formed, but I knew that I had no margin for error. I was only going to get one shot at this.

"So how did you pull off this whole invisibility thing anyway?" I asked. Slowly I pulled out the program, careful not to draw attention to myself with any sudden moves. "Gotta admit, I've seen a lot of stuff—no pun intended—but that's a first for me."

"That's a secret, Sheriff. You can't expect me to..."

"If you're going to tell me that Janus Labs is involved, it wouldn't be the first time I've heard that name." Now, slowly, I pulled out the lighter.

"Ms. Owens hates them," Billy chuckled. "She wouldn't want them getting any credit for this."

Val Owens. She had her own reputation for being involved in weird events in these parts. "Funny thing is, I've heard her name before, too. So you're trying to tell me that she's the one..."

"She didn't do it herself. More like she put me in contact with somebody who did. Said they were from the Other Side."

The way he said that reminded me of my nightmares, that ominous feeling of something lurking, but I couldn't show that it unnerved me. "Don't you think you need to let your family say something for themselves before you...well, you know?"

More high-pitched, unhinged laughter. "An excellent point, Sheriff! So, what do you two have to say for yourselves?"

A look passed between Nadine and Billy. "He's right," Nadine said. "We've both been horrible people."

"What?" Billy asked, obviously surprised. Honestly, so was I, but not enough to miss my chance. Seizing the moment, I lit the paper on fire.

"One son dead, and one wanting to kill us," Wendell said. "Can't mess it up much worse than that."

I lifted the burning paper toward one of the canvases on the wall.

"Can you ever...forgive me?" Nadine asked.

"Or me?" Wendell added.

"I...I...I don't..." Billy's voice was faltering.

Seeing my chance, I swiped my burning paper up against a canvas painting on the wall near where I stood, igniting it. Somebody screamed.

I threw the burning paper down onto the aging carpet. If my plan worked, then the damage would be minimal, and Gateman might even thank me for it later. If not, then our problems were about to get worse.

The canvas burned. The carpet ignited. More screaming, shouting. An unseen hand grabbed my right arm, trying to get the lighter from me. It couldn't have been Billy's, for his father and grandmother looked like he still had them. So who was this?

The sprinklers turned on, showering the room. An outline of a man appeared in front of Nadine and Wendell. He still had his hands on them, but he was shaking like a leaf now. Moving quickly, I took Billy's left arm off of Nadine and cuffed him. Fortunately, Wendell had the presence of mind to grab the outline of his other arm with both hands. Defeated, Billy sank to his knees while I read him his rights.

Just then, one of the doors swung open.

"Where are you going?" Billy sobbed.

"Who are you talking to?" I demanded. I still had no idea who had grabbed my arm, but Billy's outline was the only one that had appeared in the downpour. That didn't sit right with me.

Billy ignored me. "You're supposed to be holding the doors shut! Why are you leaving me?"

He wasn't the only one crying. Wendell and Nadine were weeping as well and hugging each other—an unexpected sight even by Sardis County standards.

~~~~~

The sprinklers had doused the fire, and after some fumbling around Gateman had shut them off. Without the downpour, Billy was largely invisible again. Careful to keep a tight grip on him, I led Billy out to my squad car. It was easy to guess where the signal interference field ended, because my phone started blowing up with backlogged notifications, not the least of which was a text from Staci.

Dog is visible now that we got the collar off of his neck.

Armed with that bit of information, I got into Billy's face—or at least where I estimated. "All right, talk. What's making you invisible?"

For just a second, I didn't expect him to respond, but he had lost his bravado. "On my neck. That's where it is."

Carefully feeling around, I touched something that felt like a medallion. As soon as I removed it, Billy materialized. He was a young man of athletic build, with greasy long hair and a face that had seen its share of fistfights. I had seen his expression too many times in Memphis, that of a wanna-be hard case who wilted as soon as the reality of an arrest set in. He was probably going to be the best one to lean on. "How did you even do this?"

"Ms. Owens. She found me and the dog and said she could help with my situation. That was when she introduced me to the person from the Other Side. He gave us the medallions, me and the dog too."

"Why make the dog invisible?"

"Because if we were both wearing the medallions, we could see each other. It's a little like having your eyes open underwater. Dogs supposedly rely on their smell, but somehow he didn't act as spooked when he could see me too. I had actually dropped him at the vet's clinic because Ms. Owens' friend had told me about you and the vet. I was hoping that she would call you and maybe that would get you away from here."

"Tell me more about this person from the…what did you say, the Other Side?"

"He was in the room with me for a minute, but then he left…" He broke down again.

That explained the hand that had grabbed me and who he had been talking to when I had cuffed him. However, it didn't explain why the water hadn't revealed his accomplice like it had Billy. Who—or what— had he been? The question sent a chill down my spine.

~~~~~

"So what happens to Billy now?" Staci asked. We were sitting at a corner table in Maria's Mexican. I had voted for barbecue, but she had been in the mood for burritos and guacamole, a combination that I seldom rejected.

"He'll stand trial in Memphis for Joey's murder, of course, but I think he's going to be in a mental hospital instead of a prison. As soon as he starts talking about invisibility and the Other Side, his attorney shouldn't have too much trouble getting the judge and jury to buy an insanity plea."

"You don't think he's insane though, do you?" Staci asked, then took a sip of her iced water.

"I think you've seen enough now that you know the answer to that question."

"Touche, Mr. Sheriff. So…did you go by this Owens lady's place?"

I nodded as I took a bite of my burrito. "Nobody's there. All I saw were some tire tracks. One set belonging to a motorcycle that looked like it had been driven all over the property, and then a set that belongs to something bigger, like an RV or something like that. Something definitely went down, but I don't know what."

"Weird."

"Yeah."

She dipped a chip into her guacamole. "You know, it's kind of sad, really. What Billy did was horrible, but can you imagine feeling like your family doesn't even see you?"

I thought about Mom and Carla and Michelle, the way they always looked at me when Staci was around. Teasing or not, they saw me, and it was clear they cared about me and wanted me to be happy. "No, I really can't."

We talked about other things, but my mind kept wandering back to the question of what Billy meant by the Other Side. That, and the feeling of foreboding in my nightmares.

Somehow, I felt that I was in for another long night.

THE END

JUSTICE UNSEEN
Jordan Campbell

For as long as I can remember, I have known exactly what I wanted. I wanted to be *more* than others. Where some wished to learn, I desired to be learned about. I wanted more than fame and fortune. I wanted to devise scientific formulas that changed the way we understood our world. I wanted to be revered. I wanted to be immortal.

It is of little doubt that most people desire to be more than they are. Ambition is a part of human nature. And it is by that ambition that progress is obtained. Some are ambitious about accumulating wealth, while others desire power and prestige. Some are not as ambitious as they are fantastic, dreaming of possessing abilities that defy scientific explanation. They wish to fly or have superstrength or turn invisible.

Yes…invisibility is a power coveted by many. To be undetected and thus able to exploit all other secret desires. It is a dream, a fantasy, a fancy. There are comic books and television programs about individuals who can become invisible. There are video games and even children's games of make-believe.

However, I did not read the comic books or watch the television programs. I had little interest in games of make-believe when I was a child. Science and technology fascinated me far more than fantasy. Tangibility mattered to me, things that could be studied and observed.

In retrospect, such indulgences might have been wise. Had I entertained the possibility of invisibility, I might have been in a better position to handle this predicament. Certainly, my studies, however extensive, have proven insufficient. For you see, I am an Invisible Man.

Call me Griffin. It is the name on my birth certificate and my research grants, my very soul. I disliked my name in my youth, seeing it as a remnant of a world far too willing to believe in the fantastic over reality. But that does not matter now, and my name is a tie to my humanity, or what little of it remains.

I am entirely invisible to the naked eye. Flesh, bone, nails, tissue, none of it can be seen. Nor can I be observed by any image-recording device.

It is only fitting then, that I take the steps to document all that I have seen and heard, all that I have done.

I am an Invisible Man, yes, but I am a scientist first, and a true scientist makes record of his experiments. I shall start with the story of how I came to be invisible in the first place.

~~~~~

I was a prodigy. I say this without reservation or hesitation. I studied at a university level when most of my peers would have been entering junior high school. I did not limit my focus to a single field. Biology, chemistry, physics, astronomy — if it could be studied, then I would do so. I read every book on every subject and memorized every formula. While my peers memorized baseball statistics, I memorized the Periodic Table of Elements.

As I studied, I never lost sight of my goal. I wanted to be remembered, be a part of history, to rewrite our understanding of the universe. I obtained doctorates in biochemistry and molecular biology. For thirteen years, I read and researched…until it all went wrong.

I yearned to push further than any scientist had ever done in the past and in my lust for glory, I took my studies underground. I had a laboratory of my own, where I performed experiments that, while not immoral, were not sanctioned by my supervisors at the university.

I was on the verge of a breakthrough. I had developed a compound that modified the wavelengths of individual atoms, allowing me to see them with the naked eye. I had extracted the genetic code of several creatures capable of deliberately modifying their appearance to match their environment and had applied it to other organic materials. I wished to combine these two discoveries into one. It was supposedly impossible, but I possessed a superior mind. What was impossible for my inferiors, I could obtain.

The incident itself happened very quickly. One moment, I was applying my compound to the formula I used to make atomic building blocks visible and the next…I do not know how to describe it. I had taken every safety precaution and yet the beakers and vials, every single one of them, exploded at once, and my compounds and formulas pooled together in a concentration I had never imagined.

I slipped on the mixture and fell.

It was dark when I awoke. How long I was unconscious, I cannot say. Near as I can tell, the injury and contamination did not affect my mind. Given the inherent danger in traumatic brain injuries and the ease with which complications arise, some might call my relative health a miracle. I am not sure that I believe in such things as miracles.

I struggled to my feet, slipping and catching myself several times. At last, I stood, and I took stock of my body. It was then that I realized that I could not see my fingers, or my hand, or any other part of myself.

All my life, I favored my sense of sight above all others. This led to the realization that I could see the rest of my laboratory: the cabinet where I kept spare beakers and test tubes; my Bunsen burners, ruined beyond
~~~~~

repair; my emergency shower for chemical contamination. I stumbled toward the shower, wrenched open the door and slumped inside. I did not bother to remove my clothing as I twisted the knobs to turn on the water.

The water was ice-cold, but it was bracing, and it cleared my thoughts. I calmed down slowly, and I took better stock of my body. My back was sore, and I had sprained my shoulder, but my lungs and chest did not burn. But then my gaze turned to the small mirror I kept in the shower. The cold droplets bounced against the reflective surface as I seized it. The backside of the shower, the layout of my laboratory, all that was visible. But though I stared with all my might, my reflection did not stare back at me.

I was invisible, flesh and hair and bone. I screamed and tossed the mirror aside, stumbling back out of the shower.

It was a full day before I was able to grasp the full scale of what had happened to me. Everything organic that had come into contact with my formulas had become invisible. This included a significant portion of what I had been wearing. Cotton and wool are organic, of course, but the plastic tags I kept in my pocket and the silicon of my goggles maintained their visibility.

It took far longer than a day to come to terms with the scope of this experiment. The notion was entirely unscientific! Who could I tell? Who would believe me? I had desired prestige and privilege, but if I were to go forward, I would be a mockery, at best! Worst case scenario, I would be confined to a facility and studied. I refused to allow that to happen. So now, I was alone. I had never desired friends and I was estranged from my family, but now…

I was no longer in a position to be a man of science. I was bound to a horrible fate. I was less than the meanest sideshow attraction for a circus. I was an oddity among oddities. I was an Invisible Man, and I was alone in the world.

~~~~~

I was thought to have been lost in the accident that claimed my visible form. How the authorities came to this conclusion, I cannot say, as there was no body left behind. It was fortunate that I had been working on a private project, since it meant less attention was paid to my absence.

I was very much alive, but I could not prove my own existence if I wished to maintain my freedom. My life was a mockery, but it was *my* life. I would not be an experiment to be prodded and poked by lesser scientists.

Rage consumed my thoughts. I lost most of my resources after the accident and I wasn't in a position to regain them. It was unfair, given all my accomplishments—I had won numerous grants for the university— and now I was a pariah, vanished off the face of the earth. Everything I
~~~~~

had done in the name of scientific progress amounted to nothing.

Progress…what a loaded concept.

Science and technology are, by their nature, progress itself. How else could we have learned to cultivate crops if it were not for the science of agriculture and the technology of irrigation? The development of tools, from stone to bronze to iron, was tied therein as well. It is the nature of science to continually progress and advance.

None of that progress mattered to me, though. My desire to progress further than anyone else had cost me everything. I was invisible, down to the clothing I wore. I had other clothing, of course, but it was difficult to cover my face in a way that was not off-putting, so when I ventured out into the world, I tended to stick to the clothes that were rendered invisible in the experiment.

I spent a lot of time outside, desperate to find some semblance of normalcy. It was actually rather remarkable what I could experience when nobody else noticed my presence. People are fascinating in their habits and behaviors. To console myself, I called it research. To study physics, I sat outside skateparks and watched teenagers attempt to defy gravity. I walked into forests and parks to observe nature.

It was not much, and it was nothing compared to my laboratory studies, but it kept me sane. My temper, fed by dissatisfaction with my lot, flared up on occasion and research cooled it. One day, my wanderings led me to a local amusement park.

Mankind has always desired frivolity, but I appreciated amusement parks for their rides. While I did not ride them myself—could not ride them now, given my condition—the display of physics was impressive, nonetheless.

I was invisible down to the clothing I wore, and I reclined against a support beam. It was something of a vantage point and allowed me to watch the comings and goings of other park-goers. Research was research. Small children ran ahead of their parents, squealing with delight. Teenagers moved in lockstep and middle-aged adults debated over the best rides to reclaim their childhood exuberance. After almost an hour of this, it was too crowded and clustered, too noisy, for me to concentrate, so I took my leave. I moved without purpose until I found myself at a less crowded area.

The area was not off-limits, but it was worn down. There was only one ride—a tiny carousel for very small children—and it was broken down. There were a few benches, but the painted wood had faded from exposure to the elements and peeled away. It did not surprise me that there was only one park-goer here.

A girl, approximately fourteen years in age, paced back and forth, somewhat awkwardly. While most teenagers wore sneakers or flip-flops—and a few did not bother wearing shoes at all, as there were several waterslides at the far end of the park—this girl wore high-heeled sandals. The rest of her clothing was too formal for an amusement park: a halter top instead of a t-shirt, dress pants instead of jeans or shorts.

The girl clung to her cellular phone as if it were a lifeline and she was treading water, a survivor fallen overboard from a ship. I stared at her, my attention rapt. I willed myself to be as silent as possible, but then again, the girl might not have heard me anyway over the din of rushing roller coasters and screaming riders.

"Where are you? Where are you?" The girl smacked the side of her phone and bit her lip. She wore an excessive amount of makeup, and the heat of the sun caused it to run. "You said two o'clock. It's ten minutes after…"

My first impression? The fancy of a first date! How charming! An amusement park was certainly the place for a pair of young lovers and their budding romance. While I had never cared for romance, even at her age, I was not unfamiliar with the concept. If the girl and her date rode the roller coaster or the Ferris Wheel together, it would be an excellent opportunity to bond on an emotional level.

I wish that my first impression had been right.

The girl checked her phone eight times in the next five minutes, becoming increasingly anxious. She made a small noise of disappointed protest, but then her face lit up and a smile spread from ear to ear.

"You look beautiful."

I turned my head to follow her gaze. A chill went down my spine and my heart tightened. A man approached us, taller than the girl by more than a foot. He was at least a decade older than she was. I looked left and right, but there was nobody around except the three of us.

The girl's face faltered. She looked younger and younger by the second. Finally, she cleared her throat.

"You're a little older than I thought," the girl said. "Um…you are *him*, right?"

"Yes," the man said. "You're even more beautiful than your pictures. So mature too, not to judge me."

Rage curdled in my gut. Telephones and computers enable communication across vast distances—one of the greatest feats in the history of science. But technology had also allowed this man to contact this young girl. He smiled, but it was the smile of a predator. I looked left and right and left again—there were no passersby. This was not an area restricted to the public, but it was striking just how alone the girl was.

No…she was not alone. *I* was here.

The man led the girl down the path, away from the rest of the park, toward a parking lot. I followed along. I could not be seen, and I could barely be heard, but my senses hit overdrive. Every twitch of the man's arms and hands was fixed into my sight, the girl's heavy footsteps in her awkward heeled sandals were thunder to my ears.

The sun baked down on us, but I was not deterred. The man reached out and tucked a strand of the girl's hair behind her ear. Apprehension and tension lined her countenance and anxiety highlighted every flinch in her face, even if she was not consciously aware of it.

"I meant what I said before," the man said. "You're so mature. Even your fashion is mature."

Flattery…the girl's faced reddened but her smile widened. I was not in a position to intervene just yet. I needed to find a way to separate them. By now, we were in the parking lot.

"I think we should take a drive," the man said. "You're far too mature for a silly amusement park."

My heart pounded so hard against my ribcage that I struggled to keep up. The parking lot was filled with cars, but empty of people. It was surely a momentary lull in the crowd and there would be plenty of people here any minute. But a small window of opportunity was all the man needed. I scanned my surroundings again, looking for anything that might be a tool I could use to intervene. But I saw none.

I was not a tall man; even invisible, I doubted I would be successful in an ambush. The man was broad in the chest and shoulders. He stopped in front of a minivan.

It was black, as were a good fifth of the cars in the lot. There were modifications: the windows were tinted, and the frame looked thicker than it should, but I had never had much interest in machinery, however much I loved the other scientific fields.

The girl hesitated when the man opened the sliding door to the backseat. Whether it was common sense, or just survival instincts setting in, I cannot say. She took a step backward and shook her head vigorously. Her arm brushed against a trashcan that had been set up between parking spaces.

"No, thank you," she said. "It's been really great meeting you, but I…I gotta go."

"I was afraid you'd be a baby about this," the man said. He reached into his pocket and pulled out a small metal device. My first thought was that he carried a firearm, but I knew at once this conclusion was inaccurate. He pulled the trigger and the girl dropped to the ground, jittering as electricity ran through her body. A taser…fifty thousand volts coursed through her body. She was stunned, barely able to move.

He stepped forward, lifted the girl with as much care as a sack of potatoes and fairly tossed her into the backseat of the minivan. He pulled a long coil of twine from the floor of the van and tied her wrists. A moment later, he lashed her ankles together. Her shoes had fallen off when he had shoved her into the car. He tossed them into the trashcan unceremoniously.

The girl stirred a moment later and she opened her mouth to scream just as the man pulled a roll of duct tape from the floor. I slipped into the passenger's seat in the front of the car and closed it as quietly as I could. Tape tore and screams became muffled — he had gagged her. Tape tore a second time, and I spared a glance over my shoulder to see the man press the tape to the girl's eyes to blindfold her.

My hands curled into fists, and I cursed myself for not intervening yet. But I still was not in the best position to act. The girl needed to be rescued.

The driver's door slammed as the man got into the car. He thumbed the steering wheel rhythmically and the girl's muffled screams quieted to muffled sobs.

"I tried to be nice about it," he said. "But really, it's your own fault, Princess. I'm doing you a favor, aren't I? You told me yourself that you wanted to take a life-changing road trip."

He chuckled, a mirthless sound of disdain, and the girl sobbed harder into her gag. The man pulled a cellular phone from his front pocket and from where I sat in the passenger seat, I had a clear angle to see what he was looking at.

Pictures of the girl were on the man's phone. I will never tell what the pictures themselves depicted, but it was apparent that the man had been planning this for a very long time.

We drove for a long time. He got onto the freeway almost immediately and within two hours, we passed the state line. He pulled off the freeway and drove through a smaller town, then a second town smaller than the first and then he pulled back onto the freeway.

The sun was setting over the horizon when a light on the dashboard indicated that he needed to get gas. A few minutes later, he pulled into an otherwise deserted gas station. This was my chance.

As soon as the man got out of the car and closed the door, I reached forward and yanked the keys out of the ignition. As I twisted around, I saw the girl, bound and gagged, leaning on her side. The tape over her eyes had caught on the edge of the seat and torn off. Her eyes were red and puffy, her nose runny and raw.

"Do not worry, child," I said. "I will take you home."

The girl's eyes widened in shock, but the tape over her mouth muffled any question she might have had. She could not see me, but that did not matter much. I scanned the floor of the backseat in front of the girl and saw the roll of tape, what remained of the bundle of twine and a tire iron. That would do nicely.

I reached down and grabbed the tire iron, noting that the girl's eyes widened as I did so. I slipped out of the car, leaving the passenger door open. The man stood at the gas pump, fiddling with the panel. He did not notice my presence. I took two steps forward and held my breath. When the gas nozzle *clicked* to show the tank was full, I struck. I slammed the tire iron against his shoulder. He stumbled backward, cursing. I kicked him in the shin, and he flailed, yanking the nozzle out of the car's gas tank as he fell.

Gas spilled out from the hose, pouring out onto the concrete. It was all I could do to maintain my own balance. The man staggered to his feet, looking around frantically for his assailant. My footprints in the gasoline exposed my presence and he seized his chance.

I side-stepped him as he charged forward, but we both lost our footing. I landed on my hands and knees. I choked and coughed on the gasoline fumes. The man recovered and kicked vaguely in my direction. His boot connected with my thigh, and I cried out in pain.

"What are you?"

His actual words were far ruder, but I could not let myself get distracted. I had lost the tire iron, but my fingers curled around an orange traffic cone. I tightened my grip and used it to push myself back to my feet.

The man was leaning against the vehicle. In his hand, he gripped the tire iron. He took a few steps forward, his eyes manic. He swung the tire iron as if it were a club and I held out my arm to defend myself. In so doing, I took the traffic cone up with me and it deflected the blow. It did not stop the impact from traveling up my arm and I staggered backward, bumping against the gas pump.

Whether this was a deliberate attempt to fight, or merely reflex, I could not say. I grabbed hold of the tire iron and pulled forward. The man fell toward me. I was breathing very hard, which was all the more unpleasant, given the amount of spilled gasoline. I did not wish to be hurt, but I did not fear this man. I hated him and I wanted to make him pay for what he had done to the girl, what he had planned to do.

Righteous anger gave me power.

I am not particularly strong, but I made up for it in ferocity and tenacity. Being invisible had its advantages here: it is very hard to fight something you cannot see, and the wicked man was incapable of keeping pace with me. What was more, I was knowledgeable. I had studied biology extensively and, in that study, I had learned the mechanics of anatomy and physiology. In short, I knew how the body worked, and I knew how to make it *hurt*.

I knew how to break bones and tear joints. I knew how to burn and freeze flesh. By now the concrete of the gas station was slick with spilled gasoline and the man could not keep his footing. He stumbled twice, bleeding freely, as he worked his way back to the car and I let him get in. He realized too late that he did not have his car keys. I wrenched open the door and pulled him back out. I slammed him to the ground and stomped hard on his fingers.

A gas station attendant ran toward us from behind the garage, no doubt bewildered by the sounds of the scuffle. He called out a warning, but his call died off as he witnessed items apparently moving of their own accord. I swung with the tire iron and seized the gasoline nozzle. I sprayed more gasoline onto the man, aiming for his face. He spluttered and spat, desperate to get the gas out of his mouth.

I got back into the driver's seat, slammed the door shut and started the engine. The car roared to life, and I set the high beams on the kidnapper.

"Ghost car!"

The gas station attendant screamed in terror and ran back around the gas station's garage. That suited me fine. He would not interfere with our escape. I chuckled to myself. A haunted car? Such a silly superstition!

There was a dull thump as I backed the car up and I realized I had run over the girl's abductor. Glancing in the rearview mirror, I could see the man feebly stirring. I had not killed him.

The girl sobbed freely, but I could not comfort her just yet. The compassionate thing to do would be to free the girl from her restraints, but I realized that if she panicked, she might hurt herself even further. As it was, the amusement park was miles and miles away, and I had no idea where the girl lived.

I panicked momentarily, but I realized that the simplest thing to do would be to check the man's phone for messages and see if the girl had ever disclosed her address. It was repulsive, but once I pulled over and scanned his phone, I got the information I needed very quickly. I entered the address into the car's navigational system and drove on.

"It will be fine, young lady," I said. "You are safe with me. I will get you home."

The girl's response was somewhere between a scream and a sob.

It was very late, close to midnight, by the time I got to the girl's neighborhood. In the distance, I saw the flickering lights from several police cars. If she had been reported missing, surely the police would congregate at her family's home. I pulled the car over, got out, and walked to the back door. I lifted the girl up and slung her over my shoulder.

I was not a strong man, but her panicked motions were a greater hinderance than her weight. The girl screamed into her gag, protesting being handled, but as soon as she realized where she was, she quieted.

The proper thing to do would be to release her from her bindings, but it occurred to me that doing so would likely compromise my anonymity. I did not trust other scientists to rectify my condition, so if I were doomed to be invisible then I would allow myself some indulgences. Besides which, if I released her, her panicked flailing might cause me injury. I carried her to her family's home and set her gently on the welcome mat.

"I think your parents will be very happy to see you," I said, brushing a bit of the girl's hair out of her sweat-damp face. "Don't talk to strangers ever again."

"Mmmmph!"

I rang the doorbell and then vaulted myself up and over the porch, landing in the bushes. There was a commotion from inside the house and the next thing I knew, a big-bellied man yanked the door open. He shouted something indiscernible, but clearly joyful. He lifted his daughter—who was still bound at the wrists and ankles—into his arms, hugging her to his chest. The girl's mother joined him a moment later and then the family was swarmed by police officers and a man wearing a cleric's collar. My work was done.

It was a peculiar feeling that bubbled in my chest as I walked by the police cars stationed at the end of the street. For years, I had devoted myself to my studies, pursuing knowledge and practical application therein. I had sought deification for my accomplishments, but I had disregarded compassion and altruism. My self-pity over my invisibility was nearly all-consuming. But the girl…I had rescued the girl.

Two police officers sat in one of the cars. How they hadn't noticed me carrying the girl, I could not say. I crept by as quietly as I could. It was one thing to reveal my presence to a criminal or a superstitious garage worker. It would be another thing entirely to be discovered by officers of the law, given the number of laws I had broken.

But then it occurred to me…why should I bother with the law? I was invisible, and with my genius, was I not a law onto myself? Who could stop me? Petty limitations did not apply to my brilliance!

There was hardly a shortage of those who would abuse others and the officers of the law could only do so much. They punished, but they did not prevent. Their actions came after the fact. I could be the intermediary. I could bring any number of ne'er-do-wells to justice! I walked with purpose, my resolve increasing with every step. Yes, I would dispense justice!

~~~~~

Justice is not, strictly speaking, a scientific concept. In the animal kingdom, among species that form social groups, there is a sense of fairness. But fairness and social hierarchies are not the same thing as justice. There are gaps in the criminal justice system, but I would fill them with my vigilantism.
~~~~~

Had I not intervened, the girl would have been subjected to the worst of horrors, before most likely an untimely death. I had been able to put a stop to that. If I stopped it once, I could stop it again and again.

Call me Griffin. I am *the* Invisible Man, an oddity of science, and now, the terror of the criminal world. I sought immortality and accolades through scientific achievement, but now I seek it through the stories criminals tell. Let the lawbreakers beware. Justice will come to them, even if it is unseen.

No…I would be more than justice.

I would be a creature of their nightmares.

THE END

HIDDEN IN PLAIN SIGHT
D.A. Randall

Huddled in her chair, Angela smeared away the last round of tears, afraid to blink as her gaze scoured every corner of her apartment living room.

He could be watching her that very moment. Whoever he was.

She hated to stay, but she feared making any attempt to leave. So she sat in her easy chair, hugging her knees, holding the bloody knife out and ready.

A knock came on the door. Angela jerked so suddenly she nearly stabbed herself with the knife.

"Ms. Gann?" a man called from the corridor.

She scanned every area of the room again to make sure no one could spring at her from behind when she moved. "Who is it?" she called.

"Inspector Darnell Harkness, ma'am," the man answered calmly. "You called 911 about a possible intruder."

After a final glance around the room, she sprang from her chair and opened the door. She kept the door's chain in place, tightening her grip on the bloodstained knife. The man on the other side of the door was young and black, like her, which put her a little more at ease. But only a little. "Show me a badge," she said.

He produced his badge, giving her sufficient time to examine it.

Satisfied, she gave him a final scrutinizing glance before closing the door to slide off its chain and open it. "Please, come in."

The inspector stowed away his badge and stepped inside. "Thank you, Ms. Gann."

He was tall and slim, in his late twenties or early thirties, with a moustache and otherwise smooth skin. He wore a thick tan overcoat that extended below his knees, over a casual button-down shirt and gray slacks with polished leather shoes. "You can put the knife away now," he said.

She stared in horror at her kitchen knife. "I didn't! This isn't my—I mean, it's my knife, but I didn't kill anything!"

"I know."

"Oh. Okay, then, good. So … just curious. How do you know that?"

He shrugged. "I don't, for certain. But it's logical to assume you didn't call 911 after killing someone or something, only to greet the authorities with the murder weapon in hand."

"No," she said with an exhausted sigh. "I was using it to try to defend myself."

"You have me for that now," Harkness said.

She blinked, feeling a strange wave of relief. "Thank you."

His gaze was intent as it roamed about the room. He held a cellphone in his right hand, as if ready to take a call at any second. Angela moved past the kitchen island to the sink, resisting the urge to glance over her shoulder at the floor.

She opened the cabinet beneath the sink, where she had various cleaning sprays lined up. She selected the one in the middle and prepared to spray the knife with it.

"Leave that," Harkness ordered. "It will need to be examined."

"Right. Of course." She put the cleaner away and set the knife beside the sink, parallel to it.

Harkness glanced at her a moment before continuing his survey of the room. "You live alone, with your cat," he said. It wasn't a question.

"How do you know that?"

"Well-kept living space, with all of your unnecessary items put away in the cabinets. Dining table pushed against the far wall, allowing enough room for three people, at most. With a place setting for one person, across from the cat food bowl, for whenever you let the cat eat with you. No disarray of children's toys or video games. No other personal items that might belong to a man or even a roommate. Nothing to disrupt your own orderly pattern, apart from the kitty litter box, food and water dish, and cat toys on the floor. Everything is the way you arranged it, undisturbed by anyone else."

She leaned on the island and looked around, viewing her apartment in a fresh light. "You're right," she said, impressed.

"But now you believe there's someone else in the house," he said, his eyes still scanning the walls and corners of the room.

"Well ... I can't say. I think someone's *been* in the house, though. The last couple weeks, I've found some things moved around. The soap dish on the other side of the bathroom sink. The TV left on when I came home from work one day. A used candy wrapper on the floor."

"Something you wouldn't do, given your penchant for neatness," Inspector Harkness noted as he continued to turn in a slow circle, studying each area of the room. "Could you have done any of these things and forgotten it?"

"I could have. Except I don't eat candy."

He nodded, unperturbed, still methodically viewing the apartment.

"And the last few days, some of my food's gone missing. Half a bag of potato chips eaten. A lot of milk and juice got drunk. At first, I was afraid I had a mouse. Then I misplaced some earrings and a necklace, that

I know I left on my vanity. After that, money went missing from my wallet, and somebody ordered some food yesterday afternoon with my credit card. Then this morning ..." She bit her lip, fighting tears. "I found Murray."

"Murray?" he asked. Then he lifted his chin with understanding. "Your cat. He was stabbed."

She squinted at him. "How could you know that?"

"You have no other human dependents, and your cat isn't walking around the apartment. So Murray must be your cat's name. You found him, as you said, stabbed with your kitchen knife. Frightened, you took the knife, hoping to defend yourself until the police arrived."

"Yes," she said, shaking her head. "Somebody killed him and left him on the floor by his water bowl. After stabbing him five or six times! Who would *do* that?"

"Let me see it."

"He's here, in the kitchen." She folded her arms and stepped away, switching positions with him. She had no desire to see Murray's body again.

Inspector Harkness narrowed his eyes as he stood over the mutilated cat, appearing angry. Or worried. "How long ago?"

"Half an hour," she said. "I grabbed the knife, tried to pull myself together, and called 911."

Inspector Harkness continued to stare at the horrific sight on the floor. Finally, he turned back to Angela. "That will get cleaned up. Show me the rest of your apartment."

She led him to examine the bathroom, closets, storage areas, and bedroom. He lifted the corners of her bedsheets on each side but didn't lie on the floor to look underneath. He simply knelt on the floor, with his cellphone out, then stood to his feet. He trudged through each area three times, seeming more agitated each time. "I'm sorry, Ms. Gann. I can't find him."

Angela stared at him. "I'm not crazy," she insisted.

"I don't think you are. I simply can't find the intruder."

She felt her shoulders relax a little. "Then he must have gone."

The inspector shook his head. "No. He's here. But I can't find him, for some reason."

She folded her arms again, questioning the inspector. "That makes no sense. If you can't find him, why would you think he's here? Where could he even hide?"

"Anywhere he wants."

Angela squinted at him. "What do you mean, 'anywhere'? The apartment's not that big."

"Doesn't need to be."

She hugged her shoulders nervously as he paused in mid-turn and met her eyes.

"I should have explained," he continued. "I'm with Imager Investigations."

"Imager … Investigations?" she asked. "What is that?"

"You're familiar with Imagers?"

"Not really. I've heard of them, but … I thought those were just urban myths. I mean, people who make you see things that aren't there? The way some people talk about them on the news, they act like they're aliens from outer space."

"They are," Harkness said. "So you know a little more than I expected. We received your 911 call instantly and it sounded like an Imager. I was assigned to come have a look. … So to speak."

She lowered her chin, staring at him in disbelief. "You're telling me there's an alien hiding in my apartment? That's a big assumption to make."

"Merely observation. You have someone in your apartment causing problems. You can't find him, though there's no place for him to hide. Yet he's been here, undiscovered, for over a week. Eating your food. Using your shower and your television. Taking money and jewelry, little by little. You have plenty of evidence that he is here, but you can't find him. Because he has hidden himself in plain sight. Something only an Imager can do."

"You're telling me that thing is still here? Right now?"

"He's not a thing, Ms. Gann. He's alien, but he's a person, like you. And yes. He's still here."

She gaped, feeling her breath turn shallow. "Am I in danger?" she asked in a quiet voice.

"Not yet. But you may be, very soon. He's become agitated, feeling trapped and powerless. He used your credit card and now he's afraid of discovery. He's ready to lash out, unleashing his rage in any number of selfish ways. He might lash out at you someday soon, the same way he lashed out at your cat."

"What makes you think it's a man?"

"Most of the rogue Imagers are male."

"Rogue?"

"Yes. He's separated himself from the rest of his people. Either by accident or by choice. On their own, Imagers struggle to survive any way they can. Which typically results in stealing and harming others to get what they need. This Imager in your apartment is like a cornered rat, ready to attack in order to survive."

She fingered her necklace. "And you think he'll attack me next?"

"Very possible," he said. "Some Imagers are extremely dangerous.

They need to be found and contained."

"What does that mean, 'contained'?"

"Arrested," Harkness said. "Then assisted to reform, with help from some of his people. Over time, he can rejoin the group and learn to survive with them, instead of struggling on his own. Isolation is the worst thing that can happen to these Imagers. Especially here, where they can easily manipulate people for their own selfish purposes."

"You're saying I'm being manipulated?"

"I'm saying he's hidden himself, so that neither of us can find him. But we know he's here, because there's no reason for him to leave. Your apartment gives him food, drinks, a bathroom and shower, and a TV. The only reason to leave would be to avoid discovery."

Angela trembled. "You're starting to scare me, Inspector."

"I don't mean to make you uncomfortable. I just want to find the intruder and remove him. Everything will be fine after that." He stared at the wall, seeming lost in thought for a moment. "I've been here a while. I should go, but I'll be back to check again."

She blinked in alarm. "You're leaving? What if he attacks me?"

"He won't, unless he feels threatened by you. Your cat must have done something that threatened to expose where he was hiding. Whether you see him or not—and you likely won't—don't do anything to threaten his security here. If he feels safe, he won't try to leave and he won't attack you. Let me think this through. I'll return later. Until then, stay calm."

"Stay calm? How am I supposed to do that?"

"I'm sorry, Ms. Gann," he interrupted. "But I need to go. I promise I'll return."

The man glanced once more at his cell phone before pocketing it in his overcoat and striding out the front door.

Angela gaped at the entryway. Why would he tell her all that and suddenly leave? She glanced back at the knife laid beside the sink. Would she be safer with the knife in hand, posing a clear threat to the intruder, or should she remain defenseless and keep him calm like the inspector said? She continued to stare at the knife, wondering, as another knock came at the door.

She slid the chain back onto the door, then opened it carefully. A white police officer with silver hair and a pudgy face stood there, with a tall white officer standing behind him. "Ms. Gann?" he said. "I'm Officer Shrew. You called 911, said you had an intruder?"

Angela knit her brow, confused. How many times would they come back for the same call? "Yes, I called. That was half an hour ago."

"Sorry, ma'am," the officer apologized, sounding sincere. "We would have come sooner, but we had trouble finding your apartment. We kept getting off the elevator at every floor but yours. Could have sworn we were pressing for the third floor but we kept landing somewhere else. But we're here now. May I come in, ma'am?"

Angela continued to stare at him, uncertain. Then she closed the door to slide the chain away and opened it, stepping back to let the men in. She felt too confused to even know what to do. "Do I have to go through everything again? I already answered all the detective's questions."

Silver-haired Officer Shrew looked at his partner, like two people who just realized they had come to the wrong party. "What detective?" he asked.

"Inspector Harkness," Angela said. "From Imager Investigations."

Officer Shrew narrowed his eyes at her. He took out a pad and started making notes. "Inspector Harkness," he repeated. "What did he look like?"

Angela cocked her head but complied. "Tall. Thin. Black man with a moustache. Somewhat plain."

"Plain. You mean sort of ... nondescript?"

"Yeah, I guess so. Kind of a bland face. He was good looking, but there wasn't much about him that stood out."

"No scars or tattoos?" the officer pressed. "Unique hairstyle or clothes?"

Angela thought back, recalling the inspector's appearance. "No. Nothing unique about him at all, really. He looked average, like a lot of people."

"Wasn't there anything specific about him, something that would help us identify him?"

She tightened her lips. "He had a long overcoat. That seemed normal for a detective. Oh, and he had his cellphone out the whole time."

Shrew paused in his notes, staring at her. "Cellphone?"

"Yeah, he kept it in his hand. He kept holding it out."

"Holding it out?" Shrew asked.

Angela frowned, irritated at the way he kept repeating her. "He turned about the room, holding it in front of him, like this," she said, demonstrating. "But he never looked at it or made a call with it."

Shrew tapped his small pencil against his pad. "You sure it was a cellphone?"

Angela felt a strange inner chill. What on Earth was happening? "I mean, I thought it was. What else would it be?" She looked from Officer Shrew to the younger policeman. "What's going on? Doesn't he work with your department?"

"No. He doesn't," Shrew said. "And we wouldn't send an inspector out until we had something specific to investigate. This was a 911 call. I don't know who this Inspector Harkness works for, or if he even works for anybody."

"I told you," Angela said. "He works for Imager Investigations."

"Yeah, you said that," Shrew acknowledged. "Only problem is … there's no such thing as Imager Investigations."

~~~~~

The police questioned her for another forty minutes, asking her to recall any details she could about the mysterious Inspector Harkness. Meanwhile, they had taken pictures of her dead cat, Murray, before having him removed from the apartment. By the time they had cleaned the scene and left, taking the bloodstained knife with them, Angela had no idea what to think. They promised to send another officer to check on her that evening, but they dismissed the notion that anyone could still be hiding inside her apartment.

Exhausted, she pressed her palms on the counter and turned to the sink.

There, parallel to the sink, lay the bloody knife.

Exactly where she left it.

Her breath caught in her throat. The police had taken the knife as evidence. She had watched them pick it up and leave with it. How could it still be here?

She blinked.

The knife was gone.

Her nerves flared. She reached for the place where the knife had been. There was nothing there. But she had seen it only a moment ago. Either she was going crazy, or …

Or Inspector Harkness was right. There was an Imager in her apartment. He had convinced everyone that the police had taken the knife, when it never actually moved from its place.

Until just now. When the Imager took it *himself!*

Another knock rattled the door. Angela clutched her throat, releasing a squeal. She pulled out her cellphone from her slacks pocket and prepared to dial 911.

"Who is it?" she called.

"Inspector Harkness," the man answered. "I want to check your apartment again."

She hesitated, breathing heavily, wondering who she could trust. Wondering who now threatened her most.

She slid the chain across the door and opened it to see Inspector Harkness standing outside again. "Who are you? Tell me the truth."

"I told you. I'm Inspector Darnell Harkness, and I'm only trying to help you. I saw the police came after I left."

"Yes, they did. And they told me there's no such thing as Imager Investigations!"

"They don't know about it, but it still exists. And that Imager is still
~~~~~

in your apartment."

"How do you know that? How did you know to come here in the first place? You're not with the police."

"No, I'm not. We intercept various calls and sort out any hint of Imager activity, like your 911 call. Then we move quickly to investigate before someone interferes. Trust me, I'm trying to keep you safe. Has anything changed? Anything else taken?"

Angela shivered like a frightened child. "He's got the knife."

The inspector fixed her with his stare. "Please let me in. I'll help you find him."

Angela bit her lip. Then closed the door and slid the chain free to open it. She started to delete the 911 number but accidentally dialed instead. She hung up immediately.

"I'm going to check everything again," Harkness said. "We know he's here. I know how he hides from you and the police. I need to determine how he's hiding from me." He moved through the apartment, holding out his cellphone and examining it as he walked.

It was clearly not a cellphone. "What is that device you're waving around?" Angela asked.

"This is an Indicator," he said. "It analyzes distortions. Or rather, the source of them."

Angela hugged her shoulders, studying him nervously as he moved through the room. "What does that mean?"

Harkness continued to focus on the small screen of his device. "Imagers create a field, which presents an illusion to anyone looking at it. It's a form of fluid energy that interacts with a person's mental perceptions, affecting all their tangible senses. Optic nerves, olfactory senses, physical sensations, and so on. It creates an imaginary construct that looks, sounds, and smells real to anyone who encounters it. Even feels and tastes real, if necessary. So it's impossible for anyone to sense whether an Imager is present. I use the Indicator to identify those subtle distortions and vibrations of energy they create when generating their illusions."

Angela nodded slowly, believing she understood. "But didn't you use that in the whole apartment before?"

"I did. And I found nothing."

"So he wasn't here before."

"No. He's here. He has nothing to gain by leaving, and he wouldn't risk exposing himself by trying to escape while I'm nearby."

"So how can you find him?"

"I don't know. But I have to locate him before he does any more damage."

"To what?"

His cold eyes met hers. "To you," he said.

His eyes softened slightly and he turned away, seeming to grasp that Angela had already answered her own question.

"He's gonna kill me," she said in a hush. "He's gonna fly into a rage and stab me to death like he did to Murray."

"I plan to find him first."

"Well, how are you gonna *do* that? You can't see him! You don't even *know* whether you can see him. He could be breathing down our necks right now and we wouldn't know it."

Harkness held up the Indicator. "He won't risk roaming freely about the apartment while I'm here. He's hiding somewhere out of the way, taking no chances." He paused, turning to scan either side of the main room. Then he stood rigid, seeming to think through the situation. He turned to Angela. "Where would *you* hide?"

Angela blinked. "Me?"

"Yes. If you wanted to hide in your apartment, where would you do it?"

Angela puzzled over it. "I don't know. Like I said, there aren't many places. The shower, behind the curtain. Under the bed. In a—"

"Behind the curtain," he repeated dully, as if that was the answer.

"But then all a killer would need to do is pull the shower curtain back."

"True," Harkness droned, stepping to the open door of the bathroom. He stood there staring inside it for some time. "Hm."

"What? What is it?"

"Not sure yet."

He moved to the closet along the wall beside the kitchen, raising his Indicator again. "He came out here just now to take the knife. And he knew I would return soon. So he had to hide quickly."

He squinted at her closet and stepped toward it. He stared at it the same way he had fixated on the bathroom, taking special note of the closet floor. "You have a decent number of dresses. Very stylish." He continued to focus on the area below the hanging clothes. "How many pairs of shoes do you own?"

Angela folded her arms. "What I buy is none of your business. I don't need anybody judging my shoes."

"I'm not judging. I'm asking," Harkness urged. "How many pairs of shoes?"

Angela sighed, not appreciating his intrusive questions. "I've got eleven pair, plus the ones I'm wearing. It's not that many."

"No, it's not," he said, tensing and standing with his legs apart, braced.

"So what's the problem? You can count them yourself. They're right there."

"To you, yes," Harkness said. "I can't see a single pair."

Angela gaped at him. "What?"

Inspector Harkness kicked at the empty air in the center of the closet, striking something solid. A pained cry issued from within.

Angela shrieked. She saw Harkness' leather shoe pressing against a plastic curtain that had been hung from the ceiling with nails at jagged angles.

She gasped. "What in—? That's my *shower curtain!* How did that get there?"

Harkness twisted his foot, keeping the man pinned behind the plastic. "He knew an inspector might come searching for him at some point. He set this up one day while you were away, letting you think the curtain was still hanging in your bathroom. I was focused on the Indicator readings before and didn't consider the fact you have no shower curtain."

"He stole my curtain? Why?"

"The Indicator couldn't see through the curtain to see the source of the distortions, hiding behind it," Harkness explained. He shifted his foot again as the man struggled.

"You mean I've been showering with no actual curtain up? And he could *see* me?"

Harkness' eyes slid sideways at her. "He's been hidden in your apartment for two weeks. He's seen everything he wanted to see."

Angela cringed, hugging her shoulders to cover herself.

The curtain lunged in force at the inspector, knocking him backward into the kitchen island. Seated on the floor, Harkness kicked at the massive intruder, who appeared to be nearly seven feet tall with a bulky frame and shoulders. His back seemed even larger, as if deformed with a hunch, and his enlarged head looked twice the size of a normal man's.

They wrestled on the floor for a minute, as the curtain gradually pulled away from the struggling intruder's face.

It wasn't human. His eyes and head were enormous, like that of a semi-formed fetus. The arms were long and thin, resembling the limbs of an insect but meatier. The legs were meatier still, with broad hooves that gave more support, like that of a large moose.

She was witnessing the unveiled form of an *Imager!*

Rapid knocking sounded on the apartment door. "Police! Open up!"

The Imager turned at the noise. Harkness used the distraction to withdraw another device from his overcoat pocket, similar to the Indicator's design but larger. He squeezed a button and it emitted a small charge, like a taser, into the Imager's gut. The Imager groaned in pain and rage, then fell silent, his large eyes closing.

Harkness stood and adjusted a setting on the device. He pressed it again and it issued three beams of energy that encircled the Imager. As he lifted the device, the three energy rings tugged the unconscious Imager to his feet to hang in the air beside the inspector.

He turned to Angela. "Tell them it's open."

She stared at him, not wanting him to be arrested. And not seeing any other outcome for him.

Yet he nodded to her.

"It's open!" Angela called.

Harkness turned toward the door, keeping the savage Imager immobilized beside him. Then he turned to look directly at Angela as the door flew open and three uniformed officers burst through it, guns drawn. They checked either side of the apartment and rushed straight past Inspector Harkness and the Imager to Angela.

Officer Shrew moved in close to her. "Ma'am, you called 911. Did the intruder return?"

She glanced back at Inspector Harkness, as the officers ignored him completely. He nodded to her once.

"Um … yes."

"Where? Did you see him?" the officer pressed.

Harkness tossed his head toward the rear bedroom.

"Well … I heard a noise. In my bedroom. Like somebody opened a window."

"All right, stay here. We'll check it out," the officer said.

He summoned one officer to join him and they moved quickly to the rear, while the remaining officer moved about the main room, searching for anything suspicious.

He continued to ignore Inspector Harkness completely. No one bothered to question him, let alone arrest him. They had all worked their way around the inspector and his detained Imager, rushing right past them.

As if they weren't there.

She gasped and gaped at Inspector Harkness.

The third officer turned on her sharply. "Ma'am? Did you see something else?"

She continued to study the inspector, standing in the center of the room, unnoticed by the others. "No," she said. "Nothing at all."

The inspector had told her that some Imagers were dangerous. But apparently, not all of them were.

Some were only here to protect people like her.

Harkness nodded to her in silent gratitude, then moved to the open door with his prisoner in tow, floating alongside him. He stepped into the outer corridor and disappeared.

Officer Shrew returned, scanning every corner of the main room. "No sign of anyone back there, ma'am. It's empty. Nothing for you to worry

..." He paused and stared at the center of the room, where Inspector Harkness had been standing moments earlier. "Where's the pillar?"

Angela blinked. "The what?"

"The pillar," he repeated. "There was a giant round pillar here when we came in, right in the middle of the room. We almost ran straight into it. Wait. That pillar wasn't here before, was it?"

"I've never had a pillar here."

Officer Shrew ground his teeth. "*Imagers!* The reports we got weren't lying. Those things are real. One of them was here!" He issued sharp orders to the other men. "Look outside, quick! Find him before he changes into something else again!"

The other officers ran into the hall. She heard them charging down the stairwell to search for the mysterious Inspector Harkness. Officer Shrew turned back to Angela, holstering his gun as he took out his pen and pad. "Did you see the man, ma'am? Do you think you could identify him?"

She glanced at the open apartment door that Inspector Harkness had slipped through. By now, he would be disguised as something else the police would take for granted. A fire hydrant. A lamppost. A wastebasket. Even a piece of a brick wall. Somewhere right in their midst, hidden in plain sight.

"No, sir," she said, marveling as she shook her head. "I didn't see a thing."

THE END

THE EXPERIMENT
Deborah Cullins Smith

Dr. Anthony Bocchi glanced down at the open file on his desk before lifting his gaze to the middle-aged woman sitting across from him. Lacey McGerrity and her husband, Liam, fidgeted in the padded chairs, fingers tapping on the wooden curved arms like Morse code.

"Relax, Lacey," Dr. Bocchi said, infusing warmth and reassurance into his voice. "Most of your tests look very good. No signs of cancer or benign growths. And it's not MS or muscular dystrophy. We've ruled out almost all of the really serious diagnoses. Now we'll move on to the more typical culprits. Things that can be controlled with medication."

Lacey released a long-held breath in a whoosh and shook her head. Her fingers still trembled as she raised her left hand to rub her forehead and comb back her light brown hair. Liam squeezed her right hand, his eyes glistening with unshed tears.

"That's a real relief, Doc," he said for both of them. "We've been almost crazy with worry. I mean, Lacey has always had sinus headaches, but lately… well, those dizzy spells, and the nausea … We just weren't sure what to expect."

"I know, Liam," Dr. Bocchi said with a smile. "These tests always take time, which is difficult when you just want answers. But now we can get down to the brass tacks of finding some options for Lacey. Now. You asked about migraines, but the 'sinus headaches' you've described don't really rise to the level of migraines. They might indicate that something in your house is causing allergic reactions though. And of course, there is a possibility that this is fibromyalgia. That used to be the 'catch-all' diagnosis that doctors used when they couldn't find anything else wrong with a patient in pain. Now science has progressed enough that fibro is a more concrete diagnosis with specific parameters and symptoms. But then again, this could be the beginning of a migraine syndrome. There are about six different types of migraines, each with their own specific symptoms."

For the next half hour, Dr. Bocchi talked about symptoms and scientific research, until he noticed the couple had the glazed eyes that indicated he'd overloaded them with too much information.

Good, he thought. *Just what I wanted.*

"But what can you do for Lacey right now? You've given us so many options, we aren't sure which way to jump." Liam's hold on Lacey's hand looked like a death grip.

"Well, that's where it gets a little more difficult," Dr. Bocchi said, drawing out his words with a hefty sigh. "I could put you on standard narcotics for pain. Vicodin, Oxycontin, Percoset…"

"Aren't those all addictive?" Lacey asked, her voice shaking.

"Yes, they are," he said slowly. "And we really don't like to prescribe them unless we have no other choice."

"They gave me Percoset after some minor surgery a few years ago," she said, shaking her head. "I was so loopy, I couldn't get anything done for two weeks. I don't want to live like that. I mean, you're talking like this could be an ongoing condition, right? I don't want to be on drugs for the rest of my life." Her voice rose in panic.

"Okay, okay." Dr. Bocchi motioned with his hands for her to settle down. "I said that was one option I could do. There is another one —" He paused and flipped open her chart again, frowning as he pulled at his left eyebrow. He pretended to be contemplating a decision while the couple in the chairs sat with knuckles whitening on their grasping hands. *Let them ponder for a moment. I want them desperate,* he thought.

"What is it, Doc?" Liam asked impatiently. "We need answers here. You said it might be migraines? Couldn't you give her a migraine medication to see if it works?"

"Yes, I could, but that wouldn't be entirely ethical without seeing a specific set of parameters," he said, finally looking up from the papers in front of him. "There is another option. You know, my main focus is scientific discovery. I've studied pain and the brain receptors that transmit pain to specific parts of the body." He paused and studied their responses. Both sat forward in their chairs. He had their attention. "I've come up with a new serum that seems to be very promising. But it's still very experimental. I shouldn't even be considering it, however…"

"I'll try it," Lacey said quickly. "You can get me into the study, right? It *is* your project? You could fast-track me into your research."

Liam frowned. "Lace, are you sure? If this is experimental…"

"I'm tired of being in pain all the time, Liam!"

"I know, but…"

"I trust Dr. Bocchi. If he thinks it's a good serum, I've got hope for it. And I just can't take waking up in as much pain as I go to bed with every single day."

Dr. Bocchi looked at Liam, eyebrows raised. "I've got to have an unwavering yes, or I won't go forward with this. If you aren't 100 percent sure about it, I can't afford to risk the study."

"How many other people are involved, Dr. Bocchi?" Liam asked and chewed on his thumbnail.

"I can't divulge anything about the numbers or the results at this point," he said, shaking his head sadly. "I hope you understand. Ethics and science. Sometimes, they don't make it easy on us, but I do have to follow certain protocols."

Lacey tugged imploringly on Liam's hand. "I need this, Liam."

Liam exhaled sharply. "If you really think this is the best way to handle it, Lacey…"

She threw her arms around his neck and squeezed. "Thank you."

"I'll get the paperwork and your first round of medication," Dr. Bocchi said, rising from his desk. As the office door shut behind him, he breathed a sigh of relief. *Now to see if this will work like I hope it will.*

They signed off on the non-disclosure statements and waived liability for any adverse effects without even reading all the fine print in the document. Dr. Bocchi glossed over most of it, giving them just enough information to constitute informed consent. They'd already overloaded on information at this point. And he couldn't afford to taint the study by telling her all the "what ifs" that might occur.

She's perfect for this serum, he thought. *I should see some very specific results quickly. Fingers crossed.*

~~~~~

Lacey reached for her coffee cup and stopped to stare at her hands. Tremors raced up and down her fingers, shooting pain into her wrist. The coffee cup fell from her hand and shattered on the linoleum. Hot coffee splattered all over the lower cabinets as well as soaking her slippers. She jumped back with a shriek. Liam barreled into the room.

"Are you okay, Lace?" He grabbed a roll of paper towels and knelt to soak up the mess from around her feet.

Pain lanced through Lacey's eyes to the back of her skull. She pressed her palms against her eyes and fell back against the refrigerator door.

"Lacey!" Liam was on his feet and grabbed her swaying body. She leaned against him and sobbed.

"It… hurts!" she cried.

He guided her to the couch and helped her lay down, then he returned to the kitchen to clean up the coffee. "So much for experimental drugs," he muttered as he sprayed down the cabinet doors and wiped at the sticky coffee mess. He gathered the bits of ceramic and dumped it all in the trash.

Lacey had fallen asleep by the time he returned to check on her. He watched as tremors in her hands shook her fingers, even as she slept.

Returning to the kitchen, he dialed the number for Dr. Bocchi's office. Within moments, Dr. Bocchi was on the line.

"Liam, what's going on?" Dr. Bocchi's voice was sharp in Liam's ear.

"It's Lacey. She's a lot worse today. Her hands are shaking, even in
~~~~~

her sleep. What did you give her? Is this supposed to happen?" His questions tumbled out as he raked his hands through his hair.

"No, this is a new side-effect." Dr. Bocchi sighed. "You'd better bring her in right away. I'll clear some time for her without an appointment."

~~~~~

Dosage-related. It must be dosage-related, Dr. Bocchi thought as he hung up the phone. *Maybe it's too much.* He called the lab and asked to speak to his partner, Dr. Martin Faul. After informing Dr. Faul of his phone call from Liam, he ventured to say, "Maybe it's too soon. Maybe we need to test this thing a little more before trying it with a patient."

"Maybe you need to grow a pair, Bocchi," Dr. Faul said sharply. "Science has never advanced where fear is allowed free reign."

"Then let's cut the dosage back a little bit." He simmered against the insult.

"If you cut it, you'll be giving her nothing! You put her on such a low dose, it's amazing she's seeing any results right now," Faul snapped. "Raise the dosage. She needs more to control the pain. Not less."

"That's reckless," Bocchi said, gripping the phone hard enough to hear the plastic casing creak.

"That's science!" Faul snapped.

"Fine!" Bocchi retorted. "I hope you know what you're doing."

Faul slammed the handset down, cutting the connection.

~~~~~

"You want to raise the dosage?" Liam asked. He and Lacey were once again in Bocchi's office.

"She's obviously not getting enough of it into her system to stop the pain," Dr. Bocchi explained smoothly. "We've seen this a time or two before. I just didn't want to jump into this too quickly. But from Lacey's reactions, we're going to have to accelerate the process if she's going to get any relief."

He hoped that God wouldn't strike him dead for that whopper! Lacey was the first, the only, patient on this medication. But they didn't need to know that. He just hoped Martin Faul knew what he was doing this time.

Lacey nodded her acceptance. "Okay, Dr. Bocchi. I'll do it. Just make this stop."

He questioned her for the next twenty minutes about where the pain hit, how bad—on a scale of one to ten—and what she'd been doing at the time. He examined her hands and wrists, with Lacey wincing as he rotated her arms. The office lights were too bright. Photosensitivity. That was a new symptom too. When he tapped on her forehead, her cheekbones, she cried out and promptly threw up in her lap.

Dr. Bocchi sent a nurse in to help her clean up while he checked for the new dosage Dr. Faul was supposed to send over. He gritted his teeth when he read Martin's note, again chiding his hesitation. He balled up the missive, then paused.

No, this is insurance, he thought. He saved it to file with Martin's growing folder of messages.

He reentered the exam room with a bottle of pills and a syringe.

"I can't give you anything for the pain, because we don't know how it will interact with this serum. But I'm going to give you this dose in an injection. Hopefully, you'll get faster relief this way. And I did add a little Phenergan for the nausea. You will probably sleep quite a bit this afternoon, but it will kick in a little faster. Don't take another pill today, but take it first thing in the morning, then another one tomorrow night. Try to go for twelve-hour doses, just to keep the medication level on an even keel. And call me tomorrow afternoon to update me on your progress."

Liam nodded as Dr. Bocchi handed him the prescription bottle. The doctor had his nurse help with Lacey's clothing, so he could inject her left hip. Then he asked her to stay lying down for twenty minutes in case of a negative reaction.

~~~~~

After twenty minutes, Lacey said she felt much better. The pain had dissipated, and her nausea was much better. She reported that the room swam a little bit when Liam helped her off the exam table, but Dr. Bocchi assured her that was the Phenergan.

She even asked Liam to stop at the Arby's drive-through for a roast beef sandwich on the way home, which she wolfed down with a side order of potato cakes, and a cold lemonade. Feeling a little better, she sat down in the living room to watch a movie with Liam. He watched her more than he did the television, but she seemed much better for once. About halfway through the battle for Helm's Deep, Lacey's head began to droop.

"Why don't you go lay down, honey?" Liam suggested. "Doc said you might sleep a lot today."

"Yeah," she mumbled. "Good idea." She stumbled to her feet, and Liam helped her into bed. She was out almost as soon as her head hit the pillow.

Liam sighed. *So much for going into the office today. Maybe I can just work from home for now.* He made the call to arrange for files to be sent to his home computer and dug into the marketing specs for a new account. He'd told his boss, "Just until Lacey gets this new medication up and running." But he was beginning to wonder just how long this process was going to be.

~~~~~

For the next two months, Lacey's condition improved. Her pain lessened significantly, and she slowly got her appetite back. Once in a while, she'd have a dizzy spell, and twice she fell hard enough to leave bruises. But overall, the treatment was working. Dr. Bocchi seemed pleased with her progress, and they were relieved that the serum appeared to be successful.

Liam returned to his regular office hours, with the understanding that one phone call from Lacey would send him running for home. The crisis was over.

Or so they thought.

~~~~~

Liam returned home after a ten-hour day, and a very long production meeting with his client. He was exhausted emotionally and physically, and he hoped that Lacey had made something good for dinner. It had been a relief when she resumed the cooking. She had always been a great cook. Liam could grill like a champ, but when it came to the everyday meals, he had been at a loss. Hamburger Helper was about his speed, and that got old fast. He hoped it was her honey mustard pork loin. He'd seen the meat in the sink defrosting when he got his morning coffee, and Lacey had been up and cleaning the stovetop when he kissed her good-bye.

The house was darkened when he opened the front door, and the scent of cooked pork was not in the air. Why hadn't Lacey turned on some lamps? As autumn set in, it grew darker earlier now. The house was silent.

"Lacey?" he called. "Honey, where are you?"

Silence.

"Lacey?" he called again. "Are you okay?" He quickened his steps as he rounded the corner into the kitchen.

Lacey stood at the sink, staring out the window into the backyard. She didn't move or respond until he reached her side. Her eyes grew wide, and she slowly turned to look at the clock on the stove.

"Didn't you hear me calling you?" Liam asked.

"No," she said slowly. "Did you call me today?"

"Baby, I walked into the house just now, calling your name." Liam stared at her, concern rising in his chest. "You didn't feel up to cooking tonight?"

"Cooking?" Her voice was soft, almost empty. "Was I supposed to cook?"

"Lacey, what's going on? Are you in pain?" Liam's panic rose.

"No, I'm not in pain," she said, turning to stare out the window again. "I feel … odd… I feel… like I'm not really here."

"What do you mean, you're not here?"

What was this? Another bloody side-effect?

"I feel like I'm … invisible. I'm not solid—I'm losing myself." Her voice was detached, quiet, unemotional.
~~~~~

"I'm calling Dr. Bocchi," Liam exclaimed.

"Why?" she asked.

"This isn't you, Lacey! It's that medication he's got you on! It was a huge mistake."

"Was it?" Lacey asked. She sounded so detached from her surroundings, Liam's anxiety spiked. She turned to leave the room and crumpled to the floor.

"Lacey!" Liam dropped the phone and ran to her. He picked her up and gently laid her on the sofa in the living room. Then he returned to the kitchen to retrieve his phone. With shaking fingers, he dialed Dr. Bocchi's number. He got the answering service and left an urgent message that Lacey had taken a turn for the worse.

He hurried back to the living room.

"He's going to call me b—" Liam stopped cold. "Lacey?" The sofa was empty. He checked the bedroom. She wasn't there. He ran back to the kitchen, then his office in the spare bedroom, and back to the living room. He checked the bathroom. No Lacey.

She had vanished.

~~~~~

When Dr. Bocchi pulled up to the McGerrity home, police cars lined the street, their blue and red lights pulsing in the dusky remains of an overcast sunset. Liam had been borderline incoherent when he had returned the phone call, so Dr. Bocchi had packed his kit and headed to their suburban address.

"I told you, she just vanished. I don't know where she is!" Liam's raised voice was the first thing Dr. Bocchi heard when the officer at the door let him in. "Why aren't you out looking for her?"

"Mr. McGerrity, we don't usually even respond until a person has been missing for twenty-four hours. It's only because you were so hysterical on the phone that we're investigating this at all. Now did you two have a fight?" A plainclothes detective had his notebook open and his pencil ready. But he was obviously not happy with the answers Liam was giving him, and his patience was visibly wearing thin.

"I'm Dr. Bocchi. What's going on here? This man is concerned for the welfare of his wife." The doctor's tone was sharper than he had intended it to be, but he didn't like the direction this seemed to be going.

"Maybe you can fill in the blanks a little bit, Doctor." The detective's voice held more than a little sarcasm. "What type of doctor are you anyway?"

"I'm a pain specialist, with neurology as a large part of my practice." Dr. Bocchi tried to keep his voice neutral. He couldn't afford for them to look too closely at his protocol for Lacey's treatment. His stomach twisted at the thought of detectives poking around in their lab. Dr. Faul would not
~~~~~

be happy about this. "And who might you be?"

"John Lansing. Major Crimes division. And what type of treatment were you prescribing for Mrs. McGerrity?"

"It's a new drug in the trial phase. It's simply a new medication that works on pain receptors in the brain. It has been very effective in Mrs. McGerrity's case. She's come a long way in a very short time."

"Anything about this new drug that could make her suddenly leave home without telling her husband where she's going?" This time the sarcasm was thick as a trucker's tires.

"Absolutely not," Dr. Bocchi insisted testily. "There were no psychological effects whatsoever."

Detective Lansing sighed heavily. "Got a recent picture of your wife, Mr. McGerrity?"

Liam looked up, his eyes red-rimmed. "Yeah, in my office. I'll get it for you." He stood and left the room.

The detective eyed the doctor carefully, and Dr. Bocchi met his gaze as calmly as he could manage. "You do know who we usually look at first when a wife goes missing, don't you, Doctor?"

"That's ridiculous in this case," the doctor countered.

"Yep, we look at the husband. And nine times out of ten, we find a fight gone out of control, and the woman's body turns up in a ditch or a shallow grave."

"I have never seen any sign whatsoever of such behavior. Mr. McGerrity has been through every step of Lacey's—Mrs. McGerrity's—treatment. He's been one of the most attentive and caring men I've ever seen in my practice. He even worked from home for the first part of her treatment in case she needed him."

"Yeah, well… I've seen illness take a toll on marriages, sir, and I'd hazard a guess that Mr. McGerrity got tired of having a sick wife to take care of all the time."

"That is not true!" Liam exclaimed, coming into the room in time to hear that last comment. "I love my wife. I would never harm her!"

Dr. Bocchi stepped between Liam and the detective. "Easy, Liam. They'll find Lacey. They just have to ask questions—even when they cross the lines of decency." He shot a backwards glare at Lansing.

"Any relatives your wife might run to—if she felt unsafe at home, or say… had an argument that got out of hand?"

"No!" Liam shouted. "Her family retired to Arizona two years ago. It was just Lacey and me, and we've been happily married for over ten years. Happily. Married."

"Liam, you have to stay calm," Dr. Bocchi said softly. "This isn't helping."

"He's saying I hurt my wife! I never hurt her, never lifted a hand against her! I don't have to listen to these lies!" Angry tears streaked Liam's face, then he collapsed onto the sofa and buried his head in his hands.

Dr. Bocchi patted his shoulder, then turned to the detective. "I think you've asked enough to get you started. Now how about you try to find this man's wife?"

The detective snapped his notebook shut and slid it into his breast pocket. "Okay, Doc. I'll go for now, but I may be back with more questions if we don't find your wife in pristine condition, Mr. McGerrity." He stalked out of the house. They heard him shouting at the officers outside, and they dispersed to search the neighborhood. One officer remained outside on the front porch.

Liam shook his head in disgust. "They're treating me like a suspect. I just want them to find Lacey, and they act like I *made* her disappear."

"Tell me again, Liam, what exactly did Lacey say to you?"

Liam went over the conversation by the window word for word. The doctor nodded gravely, concern rising every second. *The drug shouldn't have acted this way! What went wrong? I have to meet with Marty Faul right away, but I can't leave Liam in this condition.*

Finally, Liam leaned back against the cushions and rubbed his face with both hands. "What am I going to do, Dr. Bocchi? Should I go around to all the neighbors? Drive around the neighborhood?"

"Noooo, I don't think so," the doctor said, gazing out the window at the activity in the nearby vicinity. "I think the police are already doing that. If you leave the house—which I doubt the policeman by the door would allow—they'll think you're going to move a body or try to cover up evidence. Just let them do their jobs for the moment."

"But what about Lacey? She was so... disconnected. What if she wanders into traffic? What if she hurts herself?" Liam's voice rose as if each scenario he spoke played out in his mind.

"First, I'm going to give you a little something to calm you down," said Dr. Bocchi, reaching for his medical bag. "Then I want you to rest. I'm going to do a little investigating of my own. But I'll be back to check on you. Try not to worry." He pulled up a syringe and tapped out the air bubbles. "We'll find Lacey. You'll see."

Liam was too distraught to fight off the medication in the syringe. He leaned back against the couch cushions and closed his eyes.

~~~~~

Detective Lansing met Dr. Bocchi in the street as the doctor walked to his car.

"The neighbors haven't seen or heard from your patient, Dr. Bocchi," Detective Lansing said, crossing his arms defiantly. "I think I'm going to have to talk to Mr. McGerrity again."
~~~~~

"Well, you aren't going to get much tonight," Dr. Bocchi said with a thin smile. "I've given him a sedative. He's not going to be very coherent until tomorrow morning. I'll be back to check on him then. And you need to leave your questions until tomorrow." He pointed a finger at the detective. "He's my patient now, and I won't have him disturbed any further tonight. You've almost driven him over the edge with your inuendo and suspicion."

"Your patient, huh?" The detective smirked. "Didn't do his wife much good. You think you can do better with him now?"

"I wouldn't jump to any conclusions, sir. I know my business. Do you know how to do yours?" The doctor's chest puffed out with each sentence. "I suggest you do your job and leave my job to me. Unless you carry medical degrees I'm unaware of?" The question hung in the air.

"You'd better hope we find that woman, Doctor," the detective barked. "Or your patient is going to need more than a doctor."

The doctor turned and walked to his car.

"He's going to need a damn good lawyer," Lansing added.

Bocchi's hands shook as he fished car keys from his pocket. How he had retained his calm was a question for another time. Now he needed to talk to Martin Faul.

~~~~~

"What did you add to Lacey McGerrity's medication, Marty?" Dr. Bocchi's eyes threatened to drill holes in Martin Faul.

"What's happened?" Dr. Faul sat up straight in his chair, immediately alert.

"She's disappeared from her home! Vanished into thin air. And now the police are asking her husband all kinds of terrible questions. He's about out of his mind. I had to sedate him before I could even come over here!"

"She ... vanished?" Dr. Faul whispered.

"Yes, Martin, she vanished." Dr. Bocchi's voice became acerbic. "Did I stutter? Did I use words too big to understand? *She's gone*! And the police are investigating. What have you done to this woman? Dear God! We were supposed to make her pain disappear, not her body!"

"Calm down, Tony," Dr. Faul said, a gleam in his eye and a smile playing across his face. "This is perfect. Better than I'd hoped. Now tell me everything."

"What do you mean, better than you hoped?" Dr. Bocchi stared at his lab partner in horror.

"Come on, Tony. Tell me all the details," Dr. Faul wheedled.

Dr. Bocchi told him everything from the events Liam had related through the police interrogation, to his sedating the man to keep him out of the detective's clutches, at least temporarily.
~~~~~

"Relax, Tony," Dr. Faul said, grinning widely. "We made a woman disappear! Just think of it! We've pulled off the experiment of this century! We'll be rich! Just think what we can do with a serum that makes people vanish!"

"You… you mean… *this* is what you intended all along?" Dr. Bocchi shrieked. "And you didn't tell me? I thought you were shooting for someone who would be more susceptible to suggestion!"

"But this is better, Tony!" Dr. Faul exclaimed. "When people disrespect us, when they fight against our research, poof! They vanish! How can we be blamed if someone just disappears and is never heard from again? It's the perfect crime! No body, no evidence. They just… vanish."

"This is a nightmare," mumbled Bocchi. "Like something out of an old Claude Rains movie. What am I going to tell her husband?"

"Nothing, Tony." Dr. Faul's voice became deathly quiet. "Not. A. Word. What you will do is give him the serum too."

"I will not!" Bocchi shouted. "Are you crazy? The police are looking at him far too closely. If he disappears, who do you think they'll investigate next? *Me*, that's who!"

Faul sighed. "Maybe you're right about that. We'll let the husband take the blame for this. In the meantime, we're going to try this on someone else. Who was that guy over at GCL Pharmaceuticals? The one who gave us so much grief over clinical trials?"

A chill shot up Bocchi's spine. *Faul is crazy. Gone over the deep end. What am I going to do?*

~~~~~

"Liam!"

Liam opened his eyes slowly. He dreamed he heard Lacey's voice. He fought through the haze of the sedative.

"Liam! Talk to me. What has happened to me? I can't see myself. What's going on?"

Lacey's voice. Suddenly Liam was wide awake. He jumped up from the couch. "Lacey, honey! Where are you?"

"I'm right here beside you, Liam. What happened to me? Am I dead?" Lacey's voice sounded tearful.

"Lacey, I can't see you!" Liam twisted in every direction, searching for the source of his wife's voice. "Where did you go? Why did you leave me?"

"I woke up on our bed, Liam, but I can't see myself in any mirror. I remember being on the couch, then thinking I should just go to bed. When I woke up, I went into the bathroom and couldn't see myself in the mirror. What happened to me? I'm looking down at my hands, but I can't see them. What's going on?
~~~~~

Liam tore at his hair. "I'm going insane! Now I'm hearing a ghost in my home! Lacey, you have to come back to me! They think I killed you. They'll put me in jail if you don't come back. *Where are you?*"

"Liam, I. Am. Right. Here." The voice sobbed. "I need you to help me."

"But I can't see you! Lacey, how can I help you when I can't see you?" Liam screamed in frustration. Fingers clutched his arm fiercely. "Who's there?" he shrieked. The fingers gripped his wrist and pulled him toward the couch.

"Liam, I'm here. I need you. Help me." The voice pleaded with him, but Liam could not see anyone else in the room.

"Stop it! Let go of me!" He clawed at the invisible hands clutching at him as he jumped backward. Falling over the coffee table, he landed against the side of a curio cabinet. His head broke the glass and hit the floor with a sickening thud.

Unseen fingers pulled at his collar and pushed against his neck. His eyes remained wide open and glazed. The fingers pulled away, and his head lolled limply to one side.

"Nooooooooooo!" shrieked a feminine voice.

A vase flew across the room and shattered against the television, cracking the screen into a spiderweb. The policeman posted outside opened the door, his gun drawn.

"Mr. McGerrity? Are you all right?" Wide-eyed, he took in the shattered ceramics and the busted TV screen. Then he saw Liam's body lying by the curio cabinet, covered in broken glass, his neck twisted at an ungainly angle. "Dispatch, officer needs assistance! Get me Detective Lansing quick!"

"Roger that. What's your situation?"

"I've got a DB here. But I have no idea what happened to him. I heard a commotion, but when I entered the residence, the suspect was lying dead on the floor. There's no one else in sight."

"Clear the scene, officer. I'll be right there." Lansing's voice was stern.

The officer went through every room, gun at the ready, but saw no one else in the house.

~~~~~

The investigation was short. The suspect couldn't take the guilt. The officer had heard him yelling at someone. Then the crash of glass, then… nothing.

Under the influence of the sedative, he must have fallen over the coffee table and landed head-first into the curio cabinet just awkwardly enough to break his neck. His face was bloody, but there were no knife wounds, no gunshot wounds. No signs of a struggle. Except perhaps with himself.
~~~~~

Detective Lansing was ready to file this under closed cases. Husband murdered wife, husband felt guilty, husband knew he was going to get caught, husband fell and died. End of story.

Except that they hadn't found Lacey McGerrity.

Then the coroner called Lansing to come to the morgue.

Liam McGerrity's body lay on a steel table in the first room to the left when Lansing entered.

"Ah, there you are," the coroner said, a frown creasing his forehead. "Thought you should see this. I was ready to release the body to the family until I took one last look. Don't know what made me check, but I'm glad I did."

"What's up, Doc?" Lansing asked. "How many times do I need to close this case anyway?"

"Well, that's up to you," the coroner said with a chuckle. "But I wouldn't be so quick to write this off as an accident or a suicide. Look what I found." He held up the arm of the dead man. "It sometimes takes a day or two for bruises to form, especially once the blood stops circulating."

Lansing felt a chill that had nothing to do with the temperature in the morgue.

Clearly visible on Liam McGerrity's arm were five finger impressions.

"Somebody had a tight grip on this man's arm just before he died. And from the size of these bruises, I'd say it might have been a woman."

"You... uh..." Lansing cleared his throat. "You want to shoot a few pictures for me, Doc? And ... uh... don't release the body just yet."

"Thought you might say that." The coroner reached for a file on his desk. "Already done. You never did find his wife, did you?"

"No, we didn't," Lansing mumbled. He flipped through the photos of the bruised arm.

"I also found some skin under his fingernails," the coroner added. "Don't suppose you have a DNA sample for the woman, do you?"

"Yeah, I've got a hairbrush and a toothbrush in evidence. I'll get them over to the lab right away." He turned to the body and rested his own hand on the impressions. A lot smaller than his hand.

Yeah, a woman's hand. Okay, Mr. McGerrity, you have my attention. Just where **is** *your wife?* John Lansing suddenly knew he was going to be logging in a lot of overtime.

~~~~~

Dr. Bocchi sat at his desk with his head in his hands. Liam's death hit him hard. The man had done nothing but love his wife. Now he was dead. His first instinct had been to tell Detective Lansing everything. But he had no doubt that Martin Faul would kill him if he did. Faul was insane.
~~~~~

Power-hungry, angry, bitter from years of opposition from their peers, and now — totally insane. Faul hadn't yet figured out how to use his serum on the scientists at GCL, but given time, Bocchi was sure he'd come up with something. He'd talked about putting it in the water cooler, but that could have meant widespread disappearances. That would certainly attract far too much attention if an entire company of people disappeared.

A door opened in the outer office. *Odd.* Bocchi frowned. His secretary, Janice, had already left for the day. There shouldn't be anyone else coming in.

Then the door to his office opened, seemingly by itself. Bocchi stiffened, his eyes becoming the size of saucers. The door hung open for a moment, then swung shut.

"Just what did you do to me, Dr. Bocchi?" asked a feminine voice.

"L-Lacey? Is that you?" Bocchi sat back in his chair, staring at his empty office.

"Well, I think that's who I am. But I seem to have misplaced my body since I last saw you." The voice held venom and more than a little sarcasm. "Would you like to explain to me exactly how that happened, *Doctor*? Just what type of treatment are you designing in that lab of yours?"

She hasn't vanished! She's invisible! His thoughts roiled and foamed. Martin Faul would probably be over the moon, but Bocchi could see only the ashes of his career if this ever got out. *Can an invisible woman sue her doctor in a court of law? I might be the first.* He wanted to laugh; he wanted to run screaming from the building.

"Lacey, my partner... er... a Dr. Faul, was the one mixing the serum. I had very little to do with the actual chemistry. I thought he was working on a pain treatment. But... uh... he seems to have been looking for a way to ... well.... To eliminate his opposition. I'm so sorry. Maybe if we go see him ... together... we can —"

"My husband is *dead*!" the bodyless voice shrieked.

"Did... uh, did you kill him, Lacey?" Bocchi asked, his voice rising and cracking like an adolescent.

"No! Of course not..." the voice whimpered. "Maybe I did — but I didn't mean to. He was afraid of me. He heard my voice but couldn't see me. Then he fell when I grabbed his arm. I just wanted him to know I was real! That I wasn't a ghost. But he fell... and broke his neck." Sobs shook the words. "You did this to us!" Now the voice was angry.

Bocchi pushed his chair back and stumbled to his feet. "No, Lacey, I didn't..."

"Yes, Doctor! You did! And you'll pay for it!"

His award for Scientist of the Year, given six years ago for his discovery of a new calmative, floated in the air. It was a heavy piece of crystal with a clock inset to one side and his name engraved in thick writing. Suddenly it lunged backward, then flew straight at his head. Dr. Bocchi had no time to duck. The crystal brick, hurled with great force, hit him squarely between the eyes. His head flew backward and his body crumpled against the wall. His gaze grew wide as the award rose in the air and came crashing back down on his head again and again, until his eyes glazed over and he was gone.

"Now you can disappear too, Dr. Bocchi." Hysterical laughter filled the small office, bouncing off the walls.

Dr. Bocchi's cell phone rose from the desk and hovered in the air. Filing cabinet drawers opened and slammed, opened and slammed. Then desk drawers opened and closed. Keys hovered over the last drawer. It opened and files floated out, landing on the desktop. Pages fluttered, then the file folder closed. Another file floated to the table and again, it opened, pages flipped, and then the folder closed. The files disappeared. Then the office door opened and closed. Running footsteps echoed on the marble floor in the hallway, but Dr. Bocchi was past hearing.

~~~~~

Detective Lansing paused outside Dr. Bocchi's office. It was quiet. Too quiet. He had hoped to catch the doctor still at his desk.

High time we had a little talk about this so-called treatment, he thought as he tried the door. He was in luck. It wasn't locked.

He entered the office complex and passed the reception desk. The exam rooms were numbered and lined the hallway. On the left was an ornate wooden door that bore the doctor's name on an engraved plaque.

This must be the place, Lansing thought. He knocked lightly on the door, then paused. No sounds from within. He tried the handle and it, too, was unlocked. He eased the door open. A bloody smear on the far wall behind the desk caught his immediate attention. He drew his gun and covered the room in an arc, checking behind the door as he eased around the desk. The doctor sprawled on the floor, half-sitting, and his head was a blood-soaked mass of pulp. The award lay on the floor beside him and was obviously the murder weapon.

"Well, Doc, someone didn't like your treatment plan. Wouldn't happen to be Lacey McGerrity, would it?" he muttered as he dialed his cell phone for the coroner and a forensics team.

~~~~~

"Got a few surprises for you, Detective Lansing." The lab tech was a bright kid of twenty-five with ear buds that blared rock 'n' roll as he processed evidence. Lansing expected him to be deaf before he hit thirty.

"Oh, yeah? Well, lay it on me, kid." Lansing sighed.

"First, the nail scrapings from the coroner? Yeah, those matched the toothbrush and the hairbrush you brought in. Ka-chow! Wifey did it."

"Kid, you need to cut back on the coffee," Lansing said, rubbing his forehead.

"I don't drink coffee," the tech scoffed. "But I do rock about three of these a day." He held up a forty-ounce soda cup from the gas station. "High octane Coca-Cola! *Yes!*"

"Yeah, well, that stuff'll rot your teeth as well as your brain cells, kid. Cut back to one."

The tech scoffed, but Lansing continued—just to keep him from arguing the point further. "The wife disappeared. So if she did it, where is she?"

"Dunno, but the fingerprints on that crystal brick thing?" The lab tech paused for effect. "Lacey McGerrity! Solved your case, didn't I?" He raised a hand to high-five the detective, but Lansing just glared at him.

"No, kid," Lansing hissed. "Until we *find* Lacey McGerrity, we can't *charge* her with anything! Where is Lacey McGerrity? Nobody has seen her in three weeks!"

The lab tech flushed bright red. "Look… I know you thought the chick was dead, but… well, dead people don't leave their fingerprints and handprints all over the evidence. Right? She has to be hiding somewhere."

Lansing sighed and turned to leave.

"Well, that's right, isn't it?" the kid asked as Lansing trudged down the hallway.

I need a bottle of aspirin, Lansing thought.

~~~~~

"Hey, Lansing." Police Chief Greg Iverson waved at the detective from his office. "Need a word with you on this McGerrity thing."

"What now?" Lansing murmured under his breath. "Yeah, boss?"

"I heard about Bocchi." The chief shook his head, the silver in his hair catching the light.

When did the Chief start going gray? Lansing plopped into the chair facing his boss. "Yeah, it was a real mess. And the kid in the lab says the fingerprints are Lacey McGerrity's, which makes no sense since I still think her husband offed her."

"Well, did you know that the doctor had a lab partner?" Lansing's eyebrows rose as the Chief nodded. "Yeah, some guy named Martin Faul. He got into a crapload of trouble about ten years ago over some vaccine that didn't work. Then he started delving into some hinky science experiments. Sounds like a whack-job, but if this Dr. Bocchi was connected to him, maybe they did something to the McGerrity woman. You never found her body, did you?"

"No, we didn't," Lansing said slowly. "You think he was behind this treatment Bocchi said he'd been giving Lacey McGerrity?"

The chief shrugged. "Maybe you should go ask him. Could be. Did Bocchi ever tell you any of the details about it?"
~~~~~

"No, I was going to broach that subject with him yesterday." Lansing sighed.

"And found him dead," the chief finished.

"Yep."

"Well, maybe it's time to ask this Dr. Faul what they had cookin'."

"Yeah, just as soon as I can track him down," Lansing said, rubbing his face with both hands. "He's got a better disappearing act than Lacey McGerrity. No listing in any phone directory or website that I've been able to rustle up. If he's got a lab, he's using someone else's name or company as cover. I'm going to grab some supper at the diner around the corner, then I'll work on it some more. I'm hoping some calories will shove my brain into higher gear. I feel like I'm starting to run on empty."

"Good idea." The chief nodded. "Keep me posted."

~~~~~

Lansing sat in a booth and stared at his pork chop smothered in onions and mushrooms. It smelled delicious. Lansing just didn't have the energy to eat it. This case bugged him. Lacey McGerrity's fingerprints were all over two crime scenes, but she couldn't be plugging people if she was dead. And if she wasn't dead, where *was* she? This was starting to sound like a science fiction movie script. And where was this Dr. Martin Faul? After his disastrous experiments ten years ago, he seemed to fall off the face of the earth. Did he even have anything to do with this mess? Or was it all Dr. Bocchi's doing, and someone finally got even with him?

"Hello, Detective." The voice was feminine, and it came from the bench opposite him. But no one was sitting there!

"Okay, is this some kind of gag?" Lansing looked around the diner for signs of his prankster co-workers. The place was empty except for a bleary-eyed traveler nursing a cup of coffee at the counter.

"No, sir. No gag. We need to talk."

"Well, I discuss nothing when I can't see who I'm talking to." Lansing's temper flared. Some jokes just weren't funny.

"I can't help that," the voice said. "But I can help **you**. With your case, that is."

"Oh really? And just how will you do that, Miss—you want to tell me your name?"

"I'll get to that in a minute. I have some information for you. Are you interested?"

Lansing's eyes narrowed. He still couldn't see anyone on the bench, but he did note a slight indentation, as if a body was present. He swept his hand over the table and felt an arm. He jerked back in surprise.

"I'd appreciate it if you didn't do that again." The feminine voice sounded perturbed, and the indentation in the booth seat deepened, like someone had leaned back against the cushion. File folders suddenly
~~~~~

appeared as if being drawn from a coat or sweater. "These are for you. I think you'll find it interesting reading." They slapped down on the tabletop next to his dinner.

He swiveled the folders around. The top one bore the name of Lacey McGerrity. The second one had no name on it, but when he flipped it open, he saw a stack of emails. The sender on the top one was Dr. Martin Faul. His gaze darted up to the bench again. Whoever his "guest" was, this information looked legit.

The bench squeaked as the indentations vanished. Whoever she was, she was leaving.

"Hey, are you — by chance — Lacey McGerrity?"

"What do you think?" the voice taunted him.

"If you are, you're under suspicion for two murders," he said trying to figure out where the voice was coming from now. "Did you do it?"

"Liam's death was an accident." The voice sounded sad. "He was a good man. He didn't deserve the way you treated him. I've heard the news reports. You should have never suspected him. He just… he was scared. Scared of me, when he couldn't see me anymore."

"What about Bocchi?"

"You read the notes and tell me what you think, Detective. I went to him for help and he ruined my life. I might… have over-reacted, but I can't tell you he didn't have it coming." There was a heavy sigh. "That's something I'm trying to learn to live with."

"Don't you think you should pay for the crime you've committed?" Lansing asked. He was curious about this person who couldn't be seen, but could manage to cause mayhem nonetheless.

"Well, if you can find me, maybe you'll be able to arrest me." The voice was a lot closer to the door.

"Are you Lacey McGerrity?" he asked again.

The door opened.

"Yes."

The door closed.

"So you're not dead after all," he muttered. He opened the file of emails again and read each one as he ate his supper. Appetite now back in full swing, he even ordered a big slice of cherry pie for dessert and continued to work his way through the files.

Then he noticed a cell phone sitting on the table. He had been so caught up in the files, he hadn't seen his mystery guest drop the phone. A few flecks of blood adhered to the screen, but he thumbed it open anyway. Dr. Bocchi's phone! And there was the number for Dr. Martin Faul. A little backward tracking, and he would soon have the man's address.

Time to go meet this Dr. Faul, Lansing thought as he polished off the last bite of his cherry pie.

~~~~~

The search warrant had been a little difficult to get. Judges didn't like evidence that mysteriously appeared, and they tended to suspect that the detectives were playing loose with a doctor's records when they showed up with file folders in their hands. But Lansing hadn't gone through the filing cabinets or the desk. His prints had not been on any of the furniture or the other files. There was no way he could have pulled just these two files out without leaving some evidence somewhere around them. The judge finally agreed that the emails were damning enough to warrant further investigation of the doctor's shady dealings.

When they served the warrant, Dr. Faul ranted and raved, accusing them of trying to steal his research. He denied all connection to Anthony Bocchi or to the McGerritys. But when they showed him the file of emails, he folded like an accordion.

"Those are personal! You have no right. No right. I'm being maliciously kept from my research. I only helped people with my serum. I didn't hurt anyone. It was Bocchi! He was the one who subverted my formula. He caused that McGerrity woman to die! I didn't do it! I didn't do it!"

"But you just told us you didn't have any connection to Bocchi or to the McGerritys. Now you're saying it was a form of your serum that Bocchi used on Lacey McGerrity?" Lansing's questions sent Faul into a frenzy.

They found a lab full of dead animals. In the corner, they heard the soft purring of a cat, but there was no animal in the cage to be seen.

"Leave those cages alone! Leave them alone!" Faul screamed, his face growing redder by the minute.

One of the techs shook the cage a little and jumped when a loud "Mrrrowrr" came from it. Then he yelped as tiny claw marks appeared on his hand where he had grasped the bars. He dropped the cage on the counter and leapt away.

"There has to be a cat in there! I just got scratched," he exclaimed, peering at the cage intently.

"It's evidence," Lansing said.

"I'm not touching that thing!" the lab tech squeaked, still cradling his injured hand. The claws had pierced his rubber gloves, and blood seeped from the marks on his skin.

Lansing smiled grimly at the doctor. "I think we've got a lot to discuss, Doc. How 'bout we take this downtown?"

~~~~~

Lansing had just finished typing up his notes on his interrogation of Dr. Faul, when a small army of men in suits entered the squad room. He leaned back in his chair and watched as they headed for the Chief's office.

"Oh, this does not look good," he muttered.

One of the suits slapped a thick file of paperwork on the Chief's desk. Lansing muttered several choice words. A court order. He knew without even reading it. The Chief motioned for him to come join the party. He sighed deeply.

Here we go.

"John, these folks are from GCL Laboratories. They say we're in possession of some of their classified research."

"No, sir!" Lansing said defiantly. "We have possession of Dr. Martin Faul's research, but I haven't seen the name GCL on anything yet."

"Well, Dr. Faul has committed several acts of corporate espionage, which we will be addressing in court as soon as possible." The speaker had the slicked-back hair and the seven-hundred-dollar suit of a first-class corporate attorney, if Lansing didn't miss his guess. "Those files you found in Martin Faul's lab belong to my client, Detective. This court order says you are to return them to us immediately."

"Those files are evidence!" Lansing's voice was steel.

The Chief sighed. "They've got a court order, John. Give them the files."

Lansing wilted, shaking his head. "And what if Faul walks on his part in two murders and a woman's disappearance because we don't have what's in those files?"

"Oh, we'll gladly help you nail Martin Faul, Detective. Don't you worry on that score." The attorney grinned, showing off expensive capped teeth. Lansing longed to slap that smile right off his smug face.

He watched glumly as the small army of suits walked out of his squad room with all of the doctor's lab files.

"We didn't have a choice, John," Chief Iverson said softly. "You can't fight a court order without getting a judge's dander up. And that we don't need."

"I know," Lansing said, his jaw tight. "But I don't like it. This smells like a first-rate cover up. And I don't like unresolved cases." He stomped back to his desk and geared up the computer. "Let's just see what this GCL Laboratories is up to..."

~~~~~

Donald Samuelson clapped his attorney on the back as they hit the parking lot. "Well done, Clark. You put that detective in his place."

Five flunkies staggered under the weight of boxes and boxes of files, which they loaded into a van marked GCL Laboratories.

"You'd better hope that detective doesn't turn his attention your way, Donald," Clark retorted. "You don't exactly have clean hands in this matter. And that detective looks like a pit bull. Faul was a hothead—an insane one—but a hothead. You should have dealt with him before the
~~~~~

police got their hands on him."

"We can deal with him," Samuelson said. "I predict the good doctor will manage to commit suicide in his cell long before he comes to trial."

The lawyer sighed. "Don't say things like that in front of me, Donald. How many times must I remind you?"

Samuelson laughed. "I'm the CEO of the largest pharma company in the US. No one is breaching our walls, Clark."

"Well, Faul did," the attorney snapped, his jaw clenching. "I'm going back to my office before you say something I might be forced to repeat for the authorities." Clark stomped over to his Ferrari and started the engine. Slamming it into gear, he peeled out of the parking lot.

Samuelson chuckled. "Theatrics! You gotta love lawyers—even when you don't." He turned to his head of security.

"Now—find Lacey McGerrity."

~~~~~

The cell door clanged behind Martin Faul, locking him into a six by nine space. Barely enough for the narrow bunk, a sink and toilet.

"I'm innocent! It was all Bocchi's fault. I'm just a scientist."

A bored jailer turned the key in the lock and muttered, "Yeah, that's what they all say. Save it for your trial, buddy."

He left the cell area, and the door slammed shut behind him. Martin sank onto the hard cot and raked his hands through his hair. "I'm innocent," he whispered. "Those guys at GCL must have set me up. They can't stand to see me succeed at anything."

The door opened again, but no one entered. Then it closed and footsteps echoed on the concrete. Faul's eyes widened.

"Nice to finally meet you, Dr. Faul." The feminine voice was soft and low.

"W-who's there?"

"Don't you know, Doctor? I'm Lacey McGerrity. Your most successful experiment, according to your notes."

Faul's eyes widened in terror. "That's not possible! You're dead. You can't be here!"

A low chuckle echoed against the concrete walls. Then the voice whispered right next to the bars nearest his bunk.

"Gotcha!"

Martin Faul's scream echoed off the walls of the cellblock.

THE END
~~~~~

THE HOUSE OF HIDDEN FACES
Or, The Invisible Landlord
Darlene N. Böcek

Gracie cradled her round belly, feeling a tiny foot kick against her palm. She knew a mother's stress could harm a baby in the womb, and the last thing she wanted was to pass on her despair. She closed her eyes, whispering, "Mommy's sorry, little one. We'll be okay." The words were more for herself than the baby. But was it true?

The darkening woods loomed at the end of the road, a stark reminder of approaching night. As soon as they got to the women's shelter, just ahead, they'd finally be safe from the Wind and Dusk. But for how long?

She quickened her pace, but the weight of her backpack pulled her down in more ways than one. With the baby inside and two kids in tow, the backpack brought the total weight on her life just a straw short of unbearable.

Her two boys, Josiah, five, and Franky, seven, were ready for a rest. It had been a long day, starting with a loud morning—what with her husband's fury. She shook her head, chasing away the terrible memory.

She focused on the door of the shelter as she drew closer. Soon she stood before the welcoming green portal. The small sign on the door, decorated with cherry blossoms, said *Welcome to Miss Haven's Women's Shelter*.

Relief consumed her, almost erasing Benjamin's words this afternoon. Almost.

"You never think of me," her husband had said. "You only ever think of yourself. I've never met a more selfish person in all my life."

"What did I do? I don't understand." What had she done to trigger him? Her shoulders hunched in fear of his fist to her face again. The boys were safe behind her back, but they heard every word.

"You just have to exist to irritate me," he'd sneered. "You never think about the kids and what they need. Putzing around the house all day long, doing nothing, never asking what I need."

"What do you need? Tell me, I'll do it. I'm sorry. I'm sorry."

"Why do you always have to talk back? You never take kind criticism, and you just turn it back around like this."

"What do you want me to do? I'll do it, Ben. Just say it. Tell me."

"You only care because I'm mad. You're worthless trash. I give you so much and this is what I get. You give me that face, as if what I'm saying is bad. I'm trying to help you."

It had only gotten worse, and louder — his help — until he struck her in the face. She cried, so he called her ungrateful, and gave her five minutes to pack, take the "brats," and leave his life forever. If only the boys hadn't heard him.

These confusing fights made her feel worthless for failing him at the simplest tasks. He was right, of course. She brushed away a tear and rang the bell before her.

A moment later, a short, plump woman with white hair answered the door. Gracie could see and hear a crowd of people behind the woman and the laughter of other children. She smiled at the thought of a grandma figure finally being in her boys' lives, and they'd have friends finally. Ben had never allowed for either.

"Hi." She gripped the boys' hands, hopeful. "Are you Haven?"

The woman studied the threesome, nodding. "I am," she said with a sad smile. "But if you're looking for a place, I'm sorry, my lovelies. We're full up."

Gracie drew in a sharp breath, not expecting such untimely rejection. All her hopes were in this shelter. And Dusk was almost here. "Do you know of any other place?" she asked, sweat beading on her forehead.

Haven shook her head and sighed. "As far as I know, they're all full up."

Gracie's mouth slacked and she felt panic pressing in her chest. Forget the hunger. Forget the thirst. She couldn't rent a hotel room — she'd already tried. Benjamin had canceled her credit cards and blocked access to the bank accounts. She squeezed her eyes shut, trying to find another possibility and forbidding the gathering tears.

"I could take the boys, though. The head of the foster child program will be coming in the morning, and they always have families available to care for the kids."

Gracie clutched the boys' hands, holding them protectively, reassuringly. Their gazes were on her, and she had to be strong. "No. We're staying together," she answered, a bit too snappy.

"There's been a spike of spousal abuse happening in our city," Haven added. "I feel for you, I really do. I'd suggest coming back in a couple days."

"But until then?" Gracie asked. Franky and Josiah's attention was on her every expression, as if gleaning how they should feel right now. She tugged a smile onto her face, but the lady had to know it was fake. She met the woman's empathetic look with desperation. "I can't stay outdoors."

"I know. Buses will stop soon, too. Try the E.R. I wish I could do more," she said, slightly shrugging.

Gracie turned away and heard the door snap shut behind her.

The lady could have opened her home at least for the night, at least to keep them from the Wind. Tension gripped her gut, and again she worried for the baby feeling this. They were trapped in a catastrophe. Certainly, she wasn't the only homeless woman in a city with an epidemic housing problem. What were they supposed to do?

Again, her attention drifted to the woods, and she shivered. The only place that might take her, at least overnight, was like the lady said, the emergency room at the hospital. Given her condition, perhaps they'd have mercy. Gracie's world seemed to spin around. Her blood sugar had dropped, and she needed food.

A tug on her shirt elbow brought her back.

"Mommy?"

Little Josiah looked up at her with wide eyes framed with long, dark eyelashes. She smiled through her wet eyes.

"Yes, sweetie?"

"Are we okay?" the five-year-old asked. His freckled face was etched with worry.

"Of course we are," she answered, wiping her finger along her lashes to erase her stray tears. "We'll be fine."

"Why did Daddy make us leave?"

Gracie kept a smile on her face, though her heart clenched again because it was all her fault. Ben was right. He was always right. She was a weak and incompetent person. And she deserved to be kicked out. At least he hadn't taken the kids from her.

"Your father wants us to go somewhere else," she said, hoping it was enough for now. She'd need to find a better explanation soon.

"Mommy, I'm thirsty," Franky whispered.

Gracie had no money to buy him a bottle of water, let alone food, when he realized he was hungry, too. Best hope was to find a water fountain. The baby kicked again. She'd need something in her stomach before she got nauseous. She glanced back at the green door. Maybe she should at least give her boys the chance to have a better life. As much as she hated the things she'd heard about the foster system, they would have food and shelter.

A surge of anger at the injustice of her situation ran through her as if stuck in an electric shock, not being able to take her finger off the wire. *Why, God?* she prayed.

The winds picked up and a flutter of trash hit her leg, a flyer wrapping around it on its way to the other side of the street. She pulled the paper off and was about to let it go when the words on it drew her attention.

COME TO THE WATERS
Boarding Home has space available.
Inquire within.
369 Dark Valley Road
Kantucket Township
Jeb Sheppard

There was a picture of a fountain on the front. Water. Just when she needed it—almost like a sign. Her cellphone battery was almost dead, and she'd forgotten its charger. She entered the address into the map app and found it was a ten-minute walk from the public library.

Hopefully, she had some money on her bus card. She hurried to the nearest bus stop. The map on the back of the bench shelter showed her the two buses she'd need to take to get there.

She sat down and took out her bus card, looking down at it with desperation. God willing, she had enough money on her card. At least Benjamin couldn't cancel the money she had transferred onto it. But did she have enough?

The third bus that passed by was theirs, so they loaded up. As she stood up from that rest, her backpack felt heavier than it was before. This was impossible!

The bus card reader dinged with permission as she stepped up the steep steps. Her relief was short-lived when she saw the bus driver's face plastered with concern. He wanted to be home before Dusk, surely. Everyone else had made themselves safe—the bus was practically empty. As the sun was sinking, citizens knew things were going to get very bad, very fast.

The kids ran to the back of the bus, and in a moment she sat down with relief and the bus lurched forward.

<div style="text-align: center;">~~~~~</div>

Gracie stood before the broken down place, dejected. The house at the address on the flyer looked haunted. All the window shutters hung halfway off the hinges, and deep gouges on the front door looked as if a werewolf had attacked it. Dirt caked the windowpanes, and the roof was missing half of its tiles. The weed-covered lawn was brown with sharp, dry grass. Who could live in such a place?

In a strange twist, despite the death all around it, in the middle of the dead lawn, water splashed from a giant, two-tiered fountain. The fountain bubbled up from the top tier, flowing over into a lower pool.

Without even asking permission, the boys ran to the fountain and began to drink from the overflowing water. Gracie, likewise thirsty, hesitated.

Behind her, abandoned farm fields were covered with wild hay,

178

haphazard and also dry. A path ran through the hayfields to the woods at the far end. Shadows from between the trees seemed to taunt her. She shivered. Why did this house have to be so close to the woods? She looked back at the house.

A movement upstairs drew her attention to the large window on the left side of the top floor. A curtain moved, as if going back into place after someone had pulled it aside. It was the only window that was not white with grime.

The boys' laughter brought Gracie's attention back to her sons, and she realized with horror that they had torn off their shoes and were splashing in the lower pool of the fountain, letting the water from the higher pool splash down over their shoulders and heads as they drank their fill.

The sky was beginning to turn. They needed to get indoors, not make enemies with the owner. She chastened them, "Boys! You're going to get the water all soiled. This is for drinking!"

She began to yank them out when a voice stopped her. The front door was open and the speaker, a cloaked and hooded man, stood in the doorway. She ensured the boys were out of the water, and now she felt timidly ashamed. They had trespassed, and worse, they had dirtied the man's waters.

She licked her lips nervously, and with a hand on each boy, she led them by the shoulder, directing the disgruntled children to the long stone walkway that led from the sidewalk to the front porch, where the man waited, still in the shadows.

"Excuse me, sir," Gracie said, feeling the tacky dryness of her thirst and trying to ignore the ringing in her ears from hunger. "I didn't hear what you said." To her boys, she added in a harsh whisper, "Behave yourselves, please!"

The sun at her back tipped into the woods, leaving a chill behind her. Night was coming, and she'd gambled everything on this house. She just needed a place for one night. Just one night.

Gracie pulled on a strained smile and said again, "I didn't hear you. I'm sorry for the fountain."

"Let them play in the waters anytime. It's absolutely no problem." His laughing voice was like the waters, full of refreshment and bubbly cheerfulness, which offset the hooded appearance.

Relief revived a shimmer of hope in Gracie.

"I'm Jeb Sheppard." The man pointed to the flyer in her hand. "Do you need a place to stay?"

The hope fluttered like a butterfly wanting to take flight. "Yes. Just for the night." It was an open invitation, and she hoped they weren't full. She didn't want to ask the price, though judging from the external appearance of this broken down place, he shouldn't ask for too high of rent. Maybe he would take a bus card.

"Wonderful! Come on in!"

"You have room?"

"Yes. More than enough." He lifted his arm behind him to welcome them into his scary house, and her eyes rested on his black leather gloves. "Come and dine!"

Dine? She wondered at his words. She still hadn't seen his face. Initially, she'd thought it was in the shadows, but it was as if his face was itself a shadow, invisible under the cloak. His kind voice alone persuaded her to enter the house.

The boys eagerly ran in, and in a moment, their excited voices echoed out to her, describing a table full of food, bright lights, and other wonders. Still, Gracie hesitated to step in, all of her senses on alert. Who was this man? Why was he in a haunted-looking house, and why was he wearing a hood? There was something sinister about him. But for his voice. Could she judge a man by his voice? She'd have to. *At least for one night*, she told herself. *What could happen in one night?* She prayed there were locks on the door.

A howl from the woods pushed her over the threshold. The Wind was coming.

Jeb, she guessed he was the house's owner or landlord, shut and locked the door behind her as her eyes adjusted to the light. The Wind thumped against the door as soon as it was shut, and a shiver immediately ran up her spine.

"You're here just in time," Jeb said. "Darkness is upon us."

Well did she know it. "Thank you for opening your home," she said.

She wished she could see the man's face, because a face said much about a man. But all she could see was his shape through his hooded cloak. He seemed about thirty to forty years old, judging from his stature and voice.

Before her, opposite the door, a curving staircase with a wooden banister led to the second floor. Along the walls were paintings like would be in a museum. The place had the feeling of old Victorian, and she'd expected it to be coated with dust inside, but everything was polished and clean.

He offered to take her backpack from her, so Gracie unfastened the latch at her chest. As the burden was taken off, a rush of relief and fatigue consumed her and again she felt like fainting.

He set her bag on the lowest step of the stairs before them. "Clearly, you need something to eat. Come this way." He put his hand lightly on her back, supporting her elbow with his other hand, and the touch and support revived her as he led the little family toward a well-lit room to the right of the entry.

~~~~~

He had said, "Come and dine" before he even knew her name. If she thought that strange, stranger still was the feast that was piled on the long dining room table.

He poured her a glass of cool water, which she drank gratefully. Then he pulled out a seat for her at the head of the table.

The table could seat at least twenty people, and a full service was set at each chair with bone china, real silver, and fine-cut crystal goblets. In the middle of the table was what looked like a Thanksgiving meal, the turkey still steaming. Her boys hadn't taken a seat, though they held onto the back of their chosen chairs, anxiously waiting for Gracie's permission.

The food was a puzzle. She looked at the hooded landlord again, unsure. "Are you expecting guests?"

"I am, and they have come!" he said again in his warm, cheerful voice.

Us? She wondered again at his words. How had he been expecting them when they'd just found out about the place?

"Have a seat."

The boys scrambled into their chairs and reached toward the food on the platters.

"Boys, when we all sit down," he continued, "I'll say grace and we can begin."

They pulled their hands into their laps.

"Please." The landlord still held the back of the chair at the closest end of the table, waiting for Gracie to be seated.

She settled into her place and finished her glass of water as he went to his place at the other end. Then he picked up a loaf of bread.

"Blessed be the God of the Universe who brings forth food from the earth. For what we are about to receive, we are truly thankful. Amen."

"Amen!" the boys shouted and reached again for the platters.

"One more thing," Jeb said, a chuckle in his voice. "This table is special. You have only to point at what you want, and it will serve itself onto your plates." He demonstrated by pointing to a bowl of corn. The bowl lifted itself and scooped a large spoonful of corn onto his plate.

Her boys grinned at the idea and began filling their plates with food. Gracie smiled at the luxury in front of them, but leaned forward onto her elbows and rested her head in her hands. She had no energy to understand the power behind this strange place. Since the Wind had come, even stranger things were happening in the city. *Let the boys eat and be happy.* A deep fear worried itself in her heart like a burr. She could not afford this meal for three, four if she included her little one inside. She didn't want to cheat the man by making false promises about her ability to pay for all
~~~~~

this.

She rubbed her stomach as she pondered tomorrow and tomorrow's tomorrow. What was she going to do? How were they going to make it?

Candles in the middle of the table and along the walls flickered happily over the foursome. The landlord scooped the food carefully from his plate onto his fork and carried it to his mouth. But rather than the action bringing his face into the light, the food disappeared into the shadow of his hood.

She still did not serve herself. Maybe her bus card would pay for the boys' meal. This bus card was her only hope, and she didn't even know how much was on it.

A bowl of mashed potatoes hovered in front of her. "Would you like some potatoes?" the landlord said. "The meal is on the house." He laughed as if making a joke.

On the house? She blinked away grateful tears. *Oh, God, thank You!* She nodded and then allowed him to bring the other dishes to her plate. Soon, Gracie was eagerly but politely eating of the feast. *On the house? How could he afford to offer such a meal for free?*

"I didn't catch your names," Jeb said.

"I'm Gracie. This is Franky and the little greedy one over there is Josiah." She squinted across the table, realizing how much of relationships were based on seeing a person's face. Why was he hiding his? She guessed he was severely deformed. "Thank you again for your hospitality. We hope to be here for one night."

"That will be fine," he said. "Do you have another place you are going to tomorrow?"

It was as if he knew the one question he should not ask.

When Gracie hesitated, Franky answered for the family. "We don't have a home anymore. My dad kicked us out, and the lady at the shelter had no room for Mommy, only for us boys. So we were thirsty and came here."

"You did well," Jeb said with a proud nod of his head. He turned back to Gracie. "If you have no other place to go, this is the place for you. I'm opening a boarding house, and I actually need a housekeeper, if you're looking for work. The place isn't hard to care for, not really. Before I tell you more, are you interested?"

Gracie processed the words he'd said. He had just offered her a job and, she assumed, a place to live indefinitely. She could work. Work had never been a problem for her. But there had to be a catch.

"What exactly is the job?" It was a silly thing to say. Whatever the job was, it was her only option in life. And with a magic table like this, it would be hard to tear the boys away in the meantime.

"The housekeeper will be primarily in charge of the upkeep of the house, making sure everything stays in order, caring for the needs of the tenants."

He paused just enough for her to ask, "You have tenants?"

"Not yet. They'll come sure enough. You and the boys are the first. More will come soon. I've sent my flyers out all over the city. What with the increase of crime and the problems we have coming out of the woods, there will be people enough. But I hope you'll stay." He took a breath, as if thinking. "Of course, in your condition, you'll have every convenience. I'm sure you can do it. And the boys will have chores, naturally."

"Oh, rats!" the boys groaned.

"I'll take it," she said. First of all, because it was a once-in-a-lifetime opportunity. And second, the boys' response disappointed her, so she needed to model the value of a work ethic.

They finished their meal, mostly with Jeb asking the boys about their lives and likes. When everyone was finished, they stood up.

As housekeeper, she knew she'd have to clean up from this meal. With a full stomach and after such a long, painful day, this would be the test of her stamina, of being able to do this job. But maybe the boys would help.

She reached for a plate, but Jeb held out his gloved hand. "One moment, Gracie. That's not how we do it around here. Everyone, take two steps back from the table." They did. Then he clapped his hands twice. "Clean up," he said.

The items on the table immediately rose up and hovered. The unused plates and silverware stacked themselves with like items, and returned to the large wooden hutch on the wall.

Their four dirty plates scraped themselves off into the trash, and then everything arranged themselves, like with like—as if in army units— plates with plates and glasses with glasses, in a hovering display of dishes.

"Whoa!" Josiah gasped. "That's so cool."

The silverware lined up like little soldiers, mid-air. Then, following the food platters, everything floated in a quiet, orderly line out of the dining room and through a doorway leading, Gracie guessed, to the kitchen. Finally, the tablecloth folded itself up and, gathering the napkins like little chicks, floated, presumedly, toward the laundry room.

Gracie was flummoxed. She did not know how her cellphone worked. Because the tech worked, she had to believe in it. This magical table was just as miraculous. Clearly, something other than tech made this happen. The dishes had a sort of sentience to be able to act like this.

As if the wonder all around was commonplace, Jeb took the boys by the hand and asked, "Would you like to see your bedrooms?"

Josiah's wide smile as he looked back at Gracie warmed her heart. His worry was gone. This might be a good place for them.

But then her attention rested on the hood of the landlord and she frowned as the foreboding thought entered her mind: Not all was as it seemed.

~~~~~

The house was two floors, with a beautiful wooden bannister running along a curving staircase from the entryway to the upstairs. At the very top of the stairs, to the left, was Jeb's room, which looked out over the fountain. There were eight bedrooms upstairs and eight downstairs. To the right of the entryway was the dining room, and the kitchen beyond, and to the left of the front door was the warm parlor with a lovely piano in it. The downstairs hall passed by the bedrooms and ended at the back door, which led out to the vast orchards. The upstairs was similar, with a hall along the bedrooms, though at the end of the upstairs hall there was a locked room. This door was off-limits. She didn't ask what was in there, and it didn't matter because it was one less room to take care of.

The house was a pleasure to clean. Jeb hadn't been exaggerating when he said it practically cleaned itself. It really did. The cleaning cloths merely needed to be directed where to go. She would point to the area and her thoughts, it seemed, were enough for the cloth to understand where to go and what to do. The cleaning sprays hovered in mid-air and joined in when needed.

She wondered why Jeb needed a housekeeper at all. It was a breeze to clean, and the boys likewise had the easy job of picking a basket of oranges every morning, and the less glamorous job of weeding for an hour each afternoon.

They had food, water, shelter, and a place of rest, finally. And best of all, here there was no disapproval from Benjamin. She was free from the strain of second-guessing her every word and every action, free from apologizing unceasingly for unintentional crimes against her suffering husband.

Jeb Sheppard kept to himself up in his bedroom. What he was doing in there, she didn't know, but he was always with them at mealtimes with his easy conversation and mysteriously hidden face.

The routine brought its own kind of peace. Gracie would be up with the chickens, literally. She'd gather the eggs—for the eggs were not magical. She'd bring the eggs into the kitchen, as would the boys bring their fruit. They'd deposit the food at the kitchen door, where the magic would take over. They'd quickly back out as the kitchen itself prepared the meal. They had to keep their distance from the eager pots, pans, and knives. Chopping and peeling and sautéeing and boiling. The foods made in this kitchen were finger-licking delicious. And since she was not the cook, or the dishwasher, it was easy to manage.

In the afternoons, she'd refresh the bedrooms, opening the curtains
~~~~~

and airing out the beds, then dust and sweep—of course, with the help of the happy, lively tools. She'd dust the stairway, hallways, and bedrooms, always enjoying her time looking at the hundreds of paintings on the walls in every hall and room. Such variety of images, none the same. One man featured in many of the paintings. She wondered if it was either his father or if it was Jeb himself. If it was Jeb, he had a pleasant face. She honestly hoped it was him—before his accident or whatever had caused him to hide from people.

In the evenings, she'd tell the kitchen to get started on a meal, and sometimes would give meal plans, if Jeb had made a special request. After dinner, as the kitchen washed up, they would sit in the parlor and chat, or Jeb would play his piano for them.

It was a merry life. She'd never seen the boys so animated. After she got the boys in bed, she'd come back down for a cup of peppermint tea before bed. Jeb sat with his feet on a cushion, smoking a pipe.

~~~~~

On the fourth night after they'd arrived, as they sat in the parlor, Gracie watched as the smoke swirled out from his hood and up and around his head. She didn't know how old he was. He seemed to have an ageless voice, at once young and old.

Outside, the winds roared and spun around like a monster, because inside the Wind was some kind of hungry beast, an invisible power that stole away anyone who remained outside at night.

Gracie sat with Jeb as the winds pummeled the windows.

Jeb's pipe smoke swirled around his head in beautiful patterns. She contrasted the orderly smoke over his head with the raging elements outside.

She couldn't believe that Benjamin had sent her into that. He had kicked her out—her and their kids—thrown her to the Wind, as far as he was concerned. How terrible she was to have earned that, to have deserved that from him.

But he was right. She should have listened more. She should have been more thoughtful of his wants and needs. Should have done more to remember it all.

Jeb interrupted her thoughts, and she got the uncanny feeling that he had heard them, for he said, "Tell me about your husband."

She looked at him, a brow raised nervously. How did he know what she'd been thinking? "He was my greatest critic," she said. That word perfectly described Ben. "He showed me who I was and who I should have been, but wasn't."

"Is that so?" said Jeb.

This time, Jeb's words touched deeper, as if challenging her greatest beliefs. But she knew she was right about Ben's analysis of her. "He was
~~~~~

not happy with me. I'm glad you didn't ask for references for housekeeping, because if you were to ask him, he would tell you I was a terrible housekeeper. Never ironed his shirts correctly, never washed the laundry right, always put things in the wrong place and certainly not where he wanted them to be."

"He sounds hard to please," said Jeb.

She thought about this, but quickly disagreed. "No. Maybe I was just not living up to his expectations. I wanted him to be happy, but never quite managed."

"Why did he kick you out?"

"My failure to meet his expectations. You see, I wasn't a very good wife or mother or . . . anything, for that matter."

Jeb shook his head. "Oh, I doubt that. You're a fine mother. I've seen it. You do a very good job around the house."

"Your house practically cleans itself," she replied with a wry smile.

"Certainly the problem is inside him. What work does he do?"

"He is a brilliant scientist." She smiled, remembering her husband. She loved him so much. Or she *had* loved him. "He created a Perpetuator device that's used everywhere now. You know, it creates renewable energy, a continual energy source that doesn't need batteries or electricity. Have you heard of it?"

"I have. But didn't Winslow and Mehta create the Perpetuator?"

"Carter Winslow and Arjun Mehta got the credit, you're right. But Benjamin made it. All by himself. He's so smart. He deserved all sorts of awards. But Winslow and Mehta got all the attention. I really don't understand why they didn't give him any credit. He's brilliant. He's the brains behind everything, and Cosmic Corp wouldn't exist today without that invention."

She paused and thought again about how her husband had practically thrown her to the Wind. Her shoulders sank, recalling that betrayal. She wanted to be proud of him, of what he had done, but couldn't love a man who'd so easily throw her away. She shook off the thoughts, at once trying to defend him and to uphold her own integrity. But it was an impossible balance.

"So what happened when your husband didn't get his credit? Did he change at all?"

"Oh, he changed. He lost his patience with me. I've always been a little forgetful and get lost in my thoughts, I guess. He couldn't stand that anymore. He started to point out all my failures, so I'd see them. The thing is, he never would see all the positive things I was doing. Just what I failed to do. He always reminded me of what I should have done. Always should, should, should. And I admit, I don't get it all done. I admit, I sometimes do things halfway, because I get distracted in the middle. But he would not fail to point that out, and he would tell me how I needed to fix myself. To be what he needed me to be. What I wanted myself to be, I guess."

Jeb hummed thoughtfully. "Did he want to know the you inside, Gracie?"

She shrugged. "I think when we were first married, he did. But then he got consumed with his project."

"I wonder if he saw you at all."

She jerked back at the idea, as if struck. Had Ben ever seen "the her inside"? The Gracie she was, really and truly? "Maybe that's what the problem was," she said at last.

"What's not to love about you?"

Gracie stared at the landlord, the word "love" hovering in the air between them. For a second, she wondered if he was flirting. If he was, this was an unsafe place. She'd been here for four days and had never got even an inkling of any impropriety in their relationship. She shook off that idea, feeling drawn to him as a fatherly figure, or even a grandfatherly figure. In the large scheme of things, he meant something more meaningful, something beyond physical attraction.

"Honestly, I loved him. He is so smart, and he was so good with the boys. And then he kind of lost his joy when he didn't get credit for his amazing invention, and everything fell apart for us."

The Wind shook the front door, making a scratching sound. Gracie wondered if that was why the door had been so deeply scarred. "Where in the world did that Monster Wind come from?" she asked, pulled from the discussion. "One day, the ghouls just appeared and started tearing people away from dusk to dawn. Do you know?" The magic of his home and his own invisibility made her think there was a connection.

Jeb sighed. "This world is filled with things we don't understand, isn't it? The important thing is that we stay indoors at night."

"That's easy for many people," Gracie said. "But the shelters are full. They told me people are fleeing from abusive homes, but there's no place for anyone anymore. They can't stay on the streets, or the Wind will take them. What happens if they get taken?"

"The Wind is strong and hungry. That's why I wanted to open this boarding house," said Jeb. "I want a place where people can always be safe from those powers that rage. We've got plenty of room for whoever comes."

He got thoughtful for a while, and Gracie watched him. She was sure he was invisible. She'd never seen even a peek of his face, even when he put his pipe into his mouth. The entire pipe she could see clearly, but not his mouth. When he blew out, she saw smoke, but never his lips. The shape of his hands and feet, but only hidden within gloves and slippers.

Given the magic nature of his house, it wasn't terribly surprising to think that maybe he was invisible, too. And since the house felt safe, she hoped he was safe. But then again, the Wind was invisible.

"Where'd this house come from?" she asked.

"I got it from my father," Jeb said.

"When did you come here?"

"Not too long ago, actually. It took a lot for me to be able to get this place ready. But I'm hoping that we'll have some more people finding the flyers. That's why I called for you, and I'm anxious for everyone who will come. And we'll get tenants very soon. Then they'll be free from that Great Wind."

"What do you mean, you called for me? I came on my own."

"Yes, Gracie. It's the same thing. But you're here. And I'm glad you are."

Confused at the dichotomy, she stood up. The window rattled, and she moved aside the curtain to peek out.

Without warning, a ghastly face manifested on the other side of the glass, its translucent white appearance sending waves of fear through her. Its stretched-out face and perpetually open mouth, frozen in a scream, intensified her horror. Then a deafening screech erupted from the face, piercing her eardrums. She threw the curtain back over the windows, and the sound grew distant.

Jeb chuckled, almost to make light of the Wind. "Yeah, those ghouls outside are not very friendly, are they?"

"I don't know why I looked. I know better." She laughed as fear and relief mixed inside her, still reeling from the apparition. "I've seen it drag people away." She thought again of its open mouth, wondering what happened to people it took.

"It's a horrible sight," agreed Jeb.

"When Benjamin kicked me out, he was sending me into that. I had until sunset to find a place. What if I hadn't found you? He knew I'd be taken. How could a husband ever do such a thing? What kind of guy ...?"

She stopped talking, asking herself what it was that had drawn her to Benjamin in the first place. It was his brilliant mind, his dreams for science. But he wasn't very thoughtful. Like Jeb said, the real Gracie was invisible to him. And he made her feel like she didn't deserve to be seen.

"I wish you'd forget what Benjamin thought of you," Jeb said into the silence. "You are altogether beautiful."

She flicked her attention back to him, her heart tightening. Again, his words were deep, calling to deep, but spoken kindly and like a father. No, more than a father. Not being able to judge from his expression, she had to evaluate him solely from the gentle words and kind tone of voice. Both hinted that he was not trying to take advantage of her. God knew this world had enough people like that. Jeb was different. He had to be.

"Thank you," she answered at last. "But wait till you know me better."

He raised his pipe in her direction as if saluting her, or raising a cup in a toast.

Her heart clenched at the salute. What did he mean? It felt like he meant he was agreeing to disagree. Or accepting her right to disagree with his assessment.

She wished she were what Jeb said she was. To be altogether beautiful was a lifetime goal, but Benjamin had proved it was far beyond her ability to attain. And Jeb didn't know her yet.

Why would Jeb say such a thing? What was his angle? This very question brought to mind the locked room at the end of the hall and all the other secrets he kept.

~~~~~

The next morning, at the crack of dawn, the doorbell rang. Still in bed, Gracie opened her eyes and immediately fear struck her heart. Dawn was a gray time, where the Wind sometimes came and sometimes didn't. Someone had to be in trouble to be here so early.

She hurried into her robe and then down the stairs as quickly as she could maneuver. She unlocked the door and yanked it open to find a haggard, bearded man standing there, eyes wide with fear, and hat pressed against his chest. He looked like a miner, dirty clothes and all. In his fist was a flyer like the one she'd found. The Wind howled, and the old house groaned as if in reply. This could quickly go south. She took him by the arm to pull him in, but suddenly his legs were pulled out from under him. He hung horizontally, mid-air as the Wind tugged him by the feet. Gracie's strength alone kept him from being torn away, and she was quickly weakening.

"Help!" Gracie yelled into the house for Jeb. If she couldn't hold her ground, the Wind would pull her outside as well.

Her boys ran down the stairs, their footsteps like thunder, and together grabbed onto the man's belt, pulling back with all their strength.

"Don't step outside," she warned them, "but don't let go." Gracie tightened her grip on the man and leaned backward, throwing her weight against the Wind's strength.

"Please don't let it get me," the man cried, his own hands clenching her wrists.

Gracie's side began to cramp. Certainly Number Three didn't appreciate the strain inside. Still, she kept holding on. The Wind surged, its power trying to wrench the man away, but the three of them held fast.

Out of nowhere, the apparition she'd seen in the window loomed menacingly, nose to nose with her own face, wide eyes glaring as a shrill
~~~~~

voice screeched in her head, *Why must you interfere? You meddler.*

The sun's rays struck the door. With a twist to avoid the light, the Wind's face swerved away from her and disappeared swiftly toward the shrinking shadows. The man dropped in a heap on the floor. Gracie and the boys pulled him indoors and slammed the door behind him.

Jeb, in his hooded bathrobe, ran down the stairs.

Gracie stood against the door, catching her breath. Josiah leaned against her, crying, and she held him close. Franky's eyes were wide with fright, and he looked into Gracie's face for support.

The man knelt, gasping for breath. "It's terrible out there. What is that Wind?"

"I have no idea. I'm surprised we won against it," she said, trying to regain her composure, to know what to do next.

"I got stuck in the woods last night. Idiot me. Found a cabin. There were broken windows, but I boarded them off and stayed there. Thank God, the Wind didn't get in. I thought I was safe when I left this morning."

Jeb took him by the elbow and helped him to stand. "Dusk and dawn are the worst. Very unpredictable," he said, with an understanding voice. "I'm Jeb Sheppard." His gloved hand was still on the man's arm as they shook hands.

The man lifted a surprised expression from Jeb's hand to his face. But this look morphed into terror when he saw a shadow where Jeb's face should have been. He yanked his hand away with a yelp.

Jeb stepped back with a pat on Gracie's shoulder, passing off the hospitality duties to her.

"You're welcome to stay here," Gracie said, trying to distract him by pointing at his flyer. "We have a room just for you. Are you hungry? Or would you like to get freshened up first?" This was their first tenant, and she hoped she was doing this right.

"I really could use a shower," he said, glancing nervously at Jeb.

"We have lots of room. All you can eat food and drink. A safe roof over your head." With a smile, she took him up the stairs and to the first room on the right. He glanced at the pictures on his way up.

"What's your name?" she asked just before opening the door.

"My name is Smith."

She wasn't sure if that was his first or his last name, so she said, "Welcome, Mr. Smith."

"No, it's just Smith." He leaned in to whisper, "Can I ask about that man?"

"That is the owner of this home, Jeb Sheppard," she said matter-of-factly, hoping to instill confidence. "He makes all this possible for us." She waved her arm to display the home.

Smith remained close. "What's wrong with his face?"

Gracie took affront at the question. "I don't know," she answered, a bit too sharply. "That's the way he is."

"I didn't mean no disrespect. I just wanted to know. Was it an accident? An experiment gone wrong?"

She shrugged, because she'd never been brave enough to ask him. It seemed impertinent, especially given his great generosity with these accommodations and benefits for all tenants.

"Here's your room." She pushed open the door and let Smith go inside.

His eyes widened, as hers had when she'd seen her own room. Everything—from the poster bed to the heavy wood dressers to the white desk in front of the window—seemed to meet his pleasure.

But he hesitated. "How much is this place going to cost? It didn't say on the flyer."

"The landlord will give you all the details at dinner, but we function by compact here," she explained. "Everybody works for their keep, and each person gives what they're able to give from their time and their efforts. I assure you, it will not be beyond your ability."

"So it's a work-stay program."

"Yes. In a way." She opened a door in the hall that led to one of the home's large bathrooms. "Whenever you're ready, come on downstairs," she said. "We've got some food for you."

"Oh, food would be nice," he said.

She showed him the towels and then left him to get refreshed.

When he closed the door, Franky came over for a hug. "Mommy, why did the Wind stop? I thought it was going to get us."

Goosebumps ran up her arms at the thought. She'd also thought they were done for. "I don't know. It gave up for some reason."

A while later, when she heard Smith coming down the stairs, she pulled her boys over and introduced them. "Smith, these are my sons, Josiah and Franky." The boys shook his hands politely, and he thanked them for helping to save him.

He looked much nicer as a clean person. He had apparently found the razor, and he cleaned up pretty well.

"Is that man going to be coming?" Smith looked at the doorway nervously.

"He'll be down for dinner. That man, the owner of this house, is named Jeb Sheppard. You know, there are things we don't understand about him, but he is safe. And he is good." She led Smith to the dining room. "I'm sure you're hungry. There might be some startling things about the meal. Please prepare yourself for our interesting boarding house."

He looked at her from the side of his eye, his expression questioning what she meant. He would find out soon enough. His question about why Jeb hid himself still bothered her. She had no answer for him, and more than that, she had no answer for herself. What kind of landlord was this, and was he really safe? All she wanted was a safe place for her and her boys.

They sat down at the table and Josiah prayed a very simple prayer. As Smith looked at her for permission to start, she said, "This is the fun part. Watch." She pointed at a dish in the middle of the table, and she sent it toward him. "Would you like some apple-cinnamon oatmeal?"

His eyes widened as much as hers had when she had first seen this amazing magic. "Yes, ma'am," he said. She gave him some thick oatmeal with stewed apples and a cup of coffee with cream.

"How does that work?" Smith asked.

Franky answered for her, "You just point to what you want and it comes to you."

Smith tried it and succeeded in bringing the cream pitcher over to himself, and covered his oatmeal with the warm cream. He looked over at Gracie, his eyebrows pinched with concern. "What is this place?"

"It's just a boarding house for people who are thirsty," she replied.

"Well, I'll be," he said, accepting the rather weak answer.

She also wondered what kind of place it was.

After Smith had eaten about half his oatmeal, he looked up at Gracie and said, "So, what work do I have to do around here?"

"There's a lot that needs to be done," she said. "The boys are in charge of picking fruit out back, and we gather the eggs and do some other chores like that. But it all depends on what you're good at. What are your gifts? What are you able to do?"

"I was a carpenter in my past job."

"Oh, wonderful. That surely will help. Tonight at dinner, Jeb will explain to you what your job will be, and he'll probably want to use your carpentry skills."

Smith looked at her again with a puzzled expression. "What's the rent here again?"

"The rent is your work," she said. "It includes breakfast, lunch, and dinner, and a place to stay. And if you'd like to join us in the evenings, we enjoy talking as we relax in the parlor."

"That sounds pretty nice, ma'am," he said. "Like a downright family home."

"Yes, it is," Gracie answered.

She'd been here for almost a week and it indeed already felt like home. But she wasn't sure it would last long. Jeb would soon enough find out she was the wrong person for this job, and she'd be homeless again, forced to face that Wind alone. *No.* She pulled her thoughts into check. *I have to make this work.*

Later in the morning, another tenant came to the door, a tall, lanky redhead whose haunted eyes reflected the desperation she knew so well. He pulled out a flyer from his pocket and unfolded it. "Is this the place?"

"It is!" she said cheerily. "Did you get some water?"

"Absolutely. It was the best water I've ever had. I was very thirsty."

"What's your name?"

"My name's Dwight. Can I see the accommodations?"

She welcomed him in, feeling a growing sense of purpose and strength, and took him to the room next to Smith's. He immediately approved, dropped off his backpack, and followed her back down the stairs. He stopped halfway, a quizzical look on his face. "Did you see that?"

She turned around. "See what?"

He faced one of the paintings on the wall.

"Looks real, doesn't it?" Gracie said. "They're painted so perfectly, sometimes I think they're actually moving."

Dwight shook his head incredulously. "No. It *is* moving. Look."

She had dusted these pictures, from a distance of course, and had never really taken the time to study them.

The picture he stood in front of was of a boat on the sea in a storm. But as she stood with Dwight, Gracie saw that the boat seemed to actually move. Why hadn't she noticed this before? The boat rose and sank with the waves.

"How does it do that?" Dwight asked. "Is it some kind of tech?" He studied the frame. "Is it a monitor?"

"It's not the strangest thing you'll see here." Gracie chuckled, turning away from the animated painting. She was anxious to show him the self-filling dining table. "There are many things you'll find out about this place that don't quite make sense. Don't quite fit our presumptions about the way we're used to things being."

He followed her down the stairs. "Like the Monster Wind?" he said with a sigh. "Moving pictures are nothing in a world with a Monster Wind. My poor Sally got taken."

Gracie gasped and pulled her hand to her chest. "I'm so sorry!"

He stopped at the bottom of the stairs, his eyes tearing up.

"What happened?"

"We couldn't pay our rent, and couldn't find a new rental in time. So we were sitting in our car at night, and . . ." His voice caught in his throat. "The Wind came through the crack in the windshield."

Gracie held the wall for support. The poor man. "I hope you find comfort here," she said, trying to bring solace with her voice and a soft touch on his back. "Let me know if you need anything."

For some reason, that day the doorbell rang continually. By the time the sun went down, there were eight more tenants, five more adults and three children. It thrilled Grace to be able to offer a home to them all. Everybody had their stories and everybody had their skills. At dinner that night, they sat around the table waiting for the landlord.

When Jeb walked in, hooded and gloved and almost hidden inside his dark cloak, the excitement stilled to a terrified silence. The tenants looked from one to another. The three children slid under the table to avoid the darkness that was his face, but Franky and Josiah showed no signs of fear.

Gracie was sure now that he was invisible. How he'd become invisible was anybody's guess. Dwight had asked if it was an experiment gone wrong, and for some reason—perhaps because of her husband being a scientist—that made the most sense. But that was one of Jeb's secrets, and she'd learned to accept it along with the other unexpected things about this house.

But how could she explain it, especially with him in the room? She decided to just wait and see what would happen.

Jeb welcomed everybody. "It is wonderful to have you at my table." She heard the kind smile in his voice, though his face was hidden in the shadow. "As I'm sure Gracie has explained to you, my home is offered to you free of charge. All you would like to eat and drink is yours. You can stay as long as you want. Forever, as far as I'm concerned. The only rule is that you need to help out around the place." His gloved fingers drummed the table. "We want to make this place into a strong home for all of us, and we want it to function as a place to help others in need. As you can see from the outside, there are a lot of repairs needed. So if you're willing to help me, then I'm willing to provide a place for you, without limits."

Gracie smiled at this promise, "without limits." She'd never known anyone so generous. The faces of the other tenants showed that they also were eager to stay in a forever home where all they had to do was help out. With the dangers outside, only a fool would ignore the offer.

Jeb stood and said grace, then showed them how the table worked. They were awed enough to dismiss—for now—the shadow that was his face. Soon, it seemed that the tenants had accepted both the strange landlord and his generous hospitality, eating the feast with great relish. Serving bowls magically replenished, and no one went hungry.

Over the course of the meal, Jeb surveyed the men and women, asking them about their abilities. Soon, all the tasks to fix up the home were divided among them. Some were carpenters and could work on the roof. Others could help in the yard with the weeding, planting, and watering, and others would help around the house and with interior design. One of them was a musician, and she was thrilled to be able to play music during the rest times. With everyone feeling a part of a bigger project, the gathering grew to have a warm, family feel.

Finally, after the children went to bed, the adults sat in the parlor together and conversed of their former lives out in the city, and what had brought them to Jeb's place. And all of them spoke with such hope and joy about finally being in a safe place. It warmed Gracie's heart to know she had a role in this. All thoughts of her former life drifted into a far forgotten memory.

By the end of the week, there were twenty tenants, each one with their own unique story, needs, and talents.

After Gracie had welcomed each one in, Jeb would show up at the next meal, and they would have to accept him as he was. Only one man had refused to stay after meeting Jeb, and it had been horrifying to see him flee into the Wind rather than live with an invisible landlord.

The home itself seemed to grow to accommodate every person who moved in. The first week, eight bedrooms on each floor turned into twelve bedrooms on each floor, as the home expanded with the need. The dining room would likewise grow with the additional need. Never would any be turned away. But that locked room remained at the end of the upstairs hallway and it remained locked.

~~~~~

It was bound to happen. Jeb's absence, except for meals, gave the tenants time to talk. And as they talked, the murmurs grew louder, until Gracie heard them.

The tenants cornered Gracie in the parlor one morning after Jeb had returned to his room.

They wanted to know his story. "You're the only one who can do it," a tenant named Luke said. He had come with his wife and son.

Smith and Dwight stepped in, in defense of the landlord. "Jeb will tell us if he wants us to know. We should just wait."

"He locked the room for a reason. He's hiding something that he thinks we might want."

Almost everyone agreed with Luke.

"But he's so good to us," Gracie said. "Why should we deny him the one thing he asks of us?"

"I think he's connected to the Wind," Luke interjected. "I heard him speak to it once. You were bringing someone in at dusk." He pointed to two in the crowd, Cho and Kimi. "It was you. I was standing next to his door. I heard him tell it to go away. Don't you remember how strange it was?"

Gracie remembered. "I do remember when they came. I heard the Wind coming, but it never arrived."
~~~~~

"He can control it. It's connected with him, somehow. And it's related to that locked room. If you don't find out, how can we stay here? If he is controlling the Wind, that means we are in danger. Maybe he's saving us—plumping us up—for something."

It had to be a mistake. Gracie couldn't imagine Jeb having any nefarious reason for opening his home to them. But the crowd voted, and Gracie was chosen to be the one to open the locked door. She would do it at night, alone, and report the next morning what she found.

Going to bed, she felt a terrible pain in her heart. She didn't want to betray Jeb like this. But keeping the tenants happy was also her job, so she was caught between two duties.

Though, truth be told, she knew what was right, and it wasn't this. It wasn't right—but she was just as curious about his invisibility, his secret room, his power over the Wind, and the magic of this house.

~~~~~

She lay in bed, unable to sleep. The Wind was powerful that night, beating against the windowpanes and tearing at the door. It was the same turmoil inside her. Betrayal. Hurt. He had been nothing but kind. His voice told her all she needed to know of his character. The time they'd had together before the tenants had come had proven to her that he was good-hearted.

But a little part of her, a very loud little part, also wanted the answer to the mystery.

Moonlight filtered through the window, painting the floor with shadows and light. A cloud passed over the moon, darkening the floor of her room ominously. This was a bad idea. But she'd made a promise.

She heard a sound in the hall, almost imperceptible, a little click, and she sat up, heart pounding. She prayed it wasn't Jeb. What would he do if he found out? Would he kick her and the boys out?

Probably. She knew it was likely—highly likely—that this was her last day of working here. But the pressure the tenants had put on her was an ultimatum. Either she would do this for them, or they would leave. And in a sense, she was doing what Jeb wanted—keeping the tenants happy by compromising one little rule.

She hoped her skeleton key would work, and she slipped it into the pocket of her robe.

Silently, she slid her feet over the edge of the bed and, hoisting herself up, pushed her feet into her slippers. She tied her robe around her large belly and walked quietly to the door. The boys' room was next to hers, with a doorway between. She moved slowly so as to not awaken them.

She pressed her ear against the door to the hall and listened. There was no more sound. She turned the knob as slowly as possible until the door unlatched. She slipped out and then closed it again behind her.
~~~~~

The hallway was quiet, the almost realistic action in the wall paintings the only movement. Gracie drew in her breath and exhaled silently. Jeb's door at the stairway end of the hall was closed. She walked in the other direction, a joint feeling of power and of shame wrapping her as tightly as her robe.

She pulled the skeleton key out of her pocket and held it. By the light of the moon, the metal glistened. This was her last chance to change her mind. She only needed to look inside and then to close the door and return to her room. *Simply find out what's in there. That's the only request of the tenants.*

Gracie tried to excuse away her crime by putting the blame on Jeb himself. If he didn't have a locked room so prominently at the end of the hall, nobody would have put this pressure on her in the first place.

The skeleton key slid smoothly into the keyhole. To her left and right, the upper floor tenants slept peacefully. She heard no sound from any room, and that was good. If anyone should be kicked out, it should be Gracie — she was the one who had been hired — hired with no valid credentials, too. The others were guests. Firing her would be better than losing all the others.

She pressed her lips together tightly as she held the knob and turned the key slowly, slowly, to unlock it without making a sound.

She stopped. On the other side of the door, there was a sort of humming or a whirring. She pressed her ear against the door and listened for Jeb. She didn't hear sounds of a person moving around in there, and she prayed he wasn't inside, sleeping.

Gracie swallowed the lump in her throat. She hoped he was forgiving. He would know. He'd certainly know. Maybe even his magical furniture would tell him — she didn't know if it could talk, but this house had secrets she still knew nothing about.

She turned the key the rest of the way until she heard the telltale click. She tried the handle, but it was still locked. She pivoted the key again in its slot and it clicked again. This time, she felt the release of the handle and the door was free.

Moonlight shone out of the now unlocked room, leaving a long white line on the floor of the hall behind her. Gracie stepped through the door, quickly turning to shut it quietly before looking at the room. She dropped the key in her pocket again.

Then she turned on her heel and surveyed the room. Straight across from the door was the window through which the moon was shining. But to her left there was a strange apparatus. This was the source of those strange sounds! She stepped over to it and tried to understand what it was. It was tall and wide and — she touched it — made of glass. And warm. It pulsed. She stepped behind it to see its shape. It was not quite rectangular, but rather heart-shaped. Yes, it was a glass heart with something inside. Something liquid, but red, but like glitter.

From the edges and sides, the top and bottom of the glass heart, tubes that looked almost like electric wires led to the four walls of the room. Strange. What was this thing? Stepping over these wires carefully, she walked around the glass heart to look at the other side of it.

There was a chair, high-backed and upholstered. The tubes led to the chair, or perhaps from the chair to the heart. She moved two steps forward and froze.

Jeb Sheppard was sitting on the chair, apparently asleep. His hands and feet were uncovered and flesh! And the tubes were connected . . . into him. She was at his side and could see his real hair and a glimpse of his real nose. Tubes came out of his bare chest and stomach as well, all leading into the heart behind him.

Shame consumed Gracie. She shouldn't have come in here. She shouldn't have let them manipulate her like this. No matter what questions she had, intruding on Jeb—in his sickness, or whatever this was—was the greatest treachery.

Gracie backed toward the door, hating herself and her weakness more now than ever before. It was wrong because he had said not to come in here. And more than that, it was wrong because he was so kind.

She turned away and tiptoed toward the door. Reaching out for the handle, she was about to open the door when Jeb spoke.

"Don't leave." The words were weak, like of a man half asleep.

He knew she was here! Ice cold rushed to her face. She'd have to face the consequences. As would her boys.

But at least the tenants would stay, she reassured herself. She lifted her chin, tightened her jaw, and stepped back toward Jeb.

His hood was over his face now, but the cables were still connected.

"You might as well know, Gracie," he said. "It's not for the weak at heart."

"I'm so sorry, master." The title was natural, and now, here, calling him by his name seemed so brazen. She had done him such a wrong. "I..." What could she say? She had no excuse.

"I know what they did to you. You were weak, Gracie. I told you not to come in here, and you did."

She dropped to her knees, her head bowed. "It was wrong."

"And yet, I gave you the key. It was time for you to come. Gracie, you now must be strong by not telling them what you saw."

That would indeed be hard, but she gave her word.

"Then I'm glad you came. By knowing, you can bear my burden with me."

"What is all this?" she asked, her gaze lifting to him again. His hood was up, but his hands and feet were visible, but half opaque.

"This is where the magic comes from." His voice was low.

Her eyes followed the tubes from him into the heart and from the heart into the house. She kept her voice low as well. "Is it your blood?"

"It is more than my blood. It is my life. My soul. My everything."

"Where is it going?"

"Into the nooks and crannies of the house."

"The magic? But why? We don't need all that. We could be a normal house and survive without all those magical things. Don't you think it makes us a bit lazy — ."

"No," he stopped her. "It is my gift. This house is alive through my life. What I give, I give from me. All the necessities: the rooms and the roof and the safety. All the conveniences: the food and the drink and leisure — that is me giving it to you and doing it for you. Do you understand? I want my tenants to have peace, to not labor for what does not satisfy."

"But it can't be just this. Why? Why are you invisible? Why are you giving your life to this house?"

When he didn't answer, she moved closer. "The people think you can control the Wind. Your home is magical and your ways are unknown and they don't know if they can trust you. What can I tell them about the Wind? They say you control it."

"The Wind feeds on the pain and suffering of this world. It hates my house, because I give of myself to rescue hurting and suffering people. I give; it takes. I am quiet; it is loud. I am weak; it is strong. But I am stronger."

"Can we stop the Wind?"

"You will see when you look. Follow the wires, Gracie. It will all make sense." He sighed a tired, weary sigh. "Go back to bed, please."

She stood and hurried to the door. Just before leaving, she whispered, "I'm sorry." But he did not answer. She slipped back to her room, wondering how she'd ever face him tomorrow.

~~~~~

The next day, around the breakfast table, the tenants assaulted Gracie with questions left and right.

"Did you go in?"

"What's in there?"

"Is he the mastermind behind the Wind?"

"What is he hiding?"

All night, she'd tossed back and forth, wondering how to answer. She was forbidden from telling what she saw. But what he was doing there was for everyone. She was overwhelmed.

His love. His forgiveness. His kindness to these people. He was giving his entire essence for their upkeep, and yet the people assumed the
~~~~~

worst. The lone voices of the few faithful, Smith, Dwight, Cho, and Kimi, were overwhelmed by the doubt and blame of the others.

When Jeb did not come down, she started the breakfast and still hadn't answered. What could she say? He didn't want them to know the extent of his love.

An inkling in the back of her mind made her turn around. The pictures on the wall, she thought. They were snapshots of him. But maybe they were more.

As the tenants became focused on their meal, she left the dining room for the entryway. Someone had brought their luggage to the front door. Were they planning on leaving? Was their trust so weak? If only they knew what Jeb was doing in that room!

She took a few steps up the stairway to the picture of the boat that always drew her. *It really looks like the boat's moving in the water*, she thought.

The longer she stood there looking at it, she was sure the boat was actually sailing, as Dwight had said.

Suddenly, she felt a whipping wind blowing against her, tugging her hair left and right. She heard a voice, and she looked up and around.

There was talking in the dining room, but the voice was coming from closer.

She listened. And she looked closer.

Could it be? It was! The wind and the voices were coming from the picture.

Gracie studied the boat. It was a fishing boat, and men stood on the deck, throwing nets into the water.

The clear skies darkened, the wind picked up, and heavy clouds gathered into a storm. Her eyes riveted onto the picture. It was like a movie, but not. Because it was almost as if this event was really happening. She couldn't understand why it felt like that. She kept watching as the fishermen shouted at one another to get the boat under control. But it tossed and turned on the waves.

The storm shook the painting, and the frame tilted a bit on the wall. The boat rose and sank on the huge waves. The movement made her feel as if she were there, too.

The terrified fishermen panicked. "We're gonna die. We're gonna die," they shouted. "This is too much for us." Suddenly, one of the sails tore and fluttered toward Gracie. She caught it in her hand.

She looked from her hand to the little boat. She couldn't believe she'd caught the sail! It was a small fragment that looked like a cloth, except for the stringlike ropes and tiny metal pulleys of the mast.

"Master, master." The frantic men ran to someone who was asleep at the stern of the boat and they shook him. "Lord, we're going to die."

The sleeping man awakened. With a brief frown, he focused on the men, then he glanced around at the storm. Stretching his legs out, he stood and braced himself against the ship's railing. She noted he had a body and build similar to Jeb's.

"Why do you doubt?" the man said. "Where is your faith?" His voice! She knew that voice. It had to be Jeb!

The man raised his chin. He lifted his hands out toward the storm and said, "Peace. Be still."

With that, the painting went back to the beginning, where it was a boat on the sea and the men were safely fishing.

The sail that had been in her hand was gone.

A chill rushed through Gracie.

The man in the picture—most likely Jeb in his earlier days—had stilled the winds with his word.

She suddenly made the connection. Luke had said Jeb had spoken to the Wind.

Behind the door at the top of the stairs, Jeb's window looked out at the fountain, out at the garden, out at the Wind. He wasn't simply resting in there. He was holding back the Wind.

Last night, Jeb had said the Wind fed on the pain and suffering of this world. That it hated his house. She looked again at the frame. Along the edges, a hairline thread ran all the way around the frame. She moved closer, her nose almost touching the frame. That thread was a pulsing, prismatic red—with the same glittery phosphorescence of the liquid in the glass heart upstairs!

She stroked her chin thoughtfully and went to the next picture. Along its edge as well were these small wires, the veins of the house, and they spread all throughout the house. As she looked, she saw more of these hairline veins. As Jeb had said, she'd see them if she looked. Her heart beat fast within her.

These images were coming out of his life. They were his life—or connected to him somehow. They showed who he was, what he was, why he was—though his own face in this boarding house was invisible under his hood.

She ran up the stairs to another picture, a picture of a fig tree. How was she supposed to get it to start, she wondered. At that thought, the tree leaves began to flutter in the breeze. She reached in and pulled off a leaf. It was tiny in her fingers, but real.

A man approached the tree, and she forgot the leaf. The man—Jeb— reached into the tree, looking for fruit on one branch after another. Not finding fruit, he turned away, sad. And she saw he had a very kind face. Was that what Jeb looked like? Lifting his hands—the hands that had stilled the storm—he said, "Let no one ever eat fruit from you again."

Immediately, the fig tree shriveled up. She reached into the picture, and she could actually feel the rough bark of the tree. One of the dry leaves came off on her finger and crumpled as it touched her hand. A moment later, the frame reset, and the fig tree was healthy again. She studied this. What did this tell her about Jeb?

It showed expectations. Consequences. He expected so little for how much he gave. It showed opportunity. The reset was a promise that they had time to prove themselves.

She looked at the dining room. *Proving yourself. Doing your duty.*

These paintings were thrilling! How could she get it to start over? She looked at it. She dusted the top, thinking maybe dusting it would work. It didn't.

She hurried back down the stairs to the dining room. On the wall next to the diningroom door, there was a painting of a mountain pass.

She dusted the sides and the frame, but it didn't start. She'd need to find the power switch for the action. Her finger touched the small magic vein that led, almost imperceptibly, into the wall. *This was where he was giving his life*, she mused. It hurt her to think she wasn't allowed to talk about that.

Gracie did not know what this mountain pass would say about Jeb, but it didn't matter. She wanted everyone to know about this.

Stepping into the doorway of the dining room, she called for everyone's attention.

"If you are all finished with your breakfast, I'd like to talk with you about the locked door." The silence in the room was heavy.

"Our master—our landlord, Jeb—is not nefariously connected with the Wind. He is very actively fighting the Wind. Most significantly, by protecting us in this house. Jeb is good. You can trust me in that."

"But what was in the room?" Luke asked.

His question disappointed her. It was as if he was the fig tree with no fruit. But that didn't matter. The reset of the picture showed everyone had a chance to improve. She needed to do what she could to help him to be a faithful tenant. What could she say?

"It's like a control panel for something. I need to show you. This should help you to feel safer here. Come, please." She welcomed everyone into the entryway. Calling it a control panel seemed innocuous enough. Her finger brushed the hair-thin vein running along the edges of the picture, feeling Jeb's sacrifice so deeply. She hoped these people would understand.

There were thirty tenants now, and they all squeezed into the entryway behind her. The little ones came to the front.

"I learned from that 'control room,' that every picture in our home tells us about our invisible landlord. They are about him. They show him, or something about him. And this will reassure us about Jeb Sheppard. Watch," she said. Gracie stood in front of the picture, but did not know how to ensure it moved. She hoped Jeb would make it start, because now was when it mattered. "What do you see?" she asked. She dusted it, not sure if dusting made it start or if just standing in front of it made it start, but she touched it. It didn't start.

"A mountain," someone said.

"What is this about?" another asked.

"You think it's just a mountainous scene," she says. "But it's more. So much more."

As they watched, the glass dissolved away, and the sound of wind in the mountains blew out from the image.

Hope, she thought with a smile. Hope made it start. Wonder.

"Do you smell the scent of wet earth?" she asked the kids at the front.

They inhaled and nodded eagerly when they noticed.

"What's gonna happen?" a little boy named Aiden asked.

She stroked his cheek. "Let's see." Glancing around, she saw looks of boredom and confusion on most of the adult faces. This had better work.

All at once, baaing of sheep came from within the image. The children froze, staring with jaws agape. Suddenly, from the center front of the painting, the white heads of sheep appeared.

The adults noisily shoved forward, trying to get into an advantageous position to see the painting. Gracie stepped to the side to make more room.

The crowd began to understand.

"What in all tarnation?"

"Is it a movie?"

"How is that happening?"

In the image, the sheep ran forward, entering the dark valley. Looking up and around, they stopped before the valley, huddling closer to one another and refusing to move into the shadows. The crowd of sheep turned toward the open frame while more sheep walked forward along the path to join them.

The smell of sheep and the sound of distressed baaing came out of the display.

Then a man stepped forward, wearing a robe and holding a shepherd's staff in his hand. Over his shoulders, he carried a little lamb. He passed through his large herd of sheep, boldly walking into the valley, clicking a signal for them to come behind him.

With that sound, their bleating decreased in volume, as one by one, the sheep followed their shepherd into the valley.

On the cliffs of the mountains all around the sheep, lions and wolves watched hungrily. The shepherd threw rocks at them to chase them away, opening the way for his sheep to eat the fresh grass and to drink from the mountain stream. Finally, the shepherd walked them out of the valley and into the bright sunshine.

The panorama stopped, and the glass returned to its place, and Gracie immediately knew what she needed to say.

She stepped in front of the image. "This picture is a message to us about our landlord. Do you see? We are the sheep. He is taking us through a frightening place and taking care of us. We don't need to be afraid because he's here."

"How does this picture say all that?" asked Luke skeptically.

"I see it," one of the older tenants, Mrs. Plumquest, said. "It's amazing that his last name is Sheppard, because he's like that for us. And the picture is right here in the entryway, next to the dining room where we are always passing by."

Kimi spoke up. "Are you saying all the pictures and portraits do this kind of action?"

Gracie nodded confidently. She hadn't checked them all, but she knew it had to be true. "They all have a message about Jeb. It's like a puzzle we have to decode."

The tenants murmured in excitement. "How do we get them to work?"

"I am not positive, but I think we need to *hope* for it to work. We need to *wonder* and *hope* at the same time. Then it starts."

Most of the tenants ran off to test the paintings until just Luke and his wife remained standing with her.

"I am fed up with this crazy place and its invisible landlord," Luke said. He called his son back, away from the painting. "All this magic. It's evil, and it's way too much to expect of us." His voice was loud, as if he wanted everyone to hear his announcement and join him in his revolt. "I'm not staying any longer."

Gracie remembered the fig tree. She didn't want Luke's family to leave, because that would be like the terrible end of the tree.

"It's not a great burden. We merely have to allow it."

"I'm a man, not a puppet," Luke said. "You can't make me do things I don't want to do."

"But isn't it all amazing?" she said. "This house. This magic. The stories. You don't want to face the Wind outside."

Her words had no effect. "What is the Wind? I've been in wind before. The Wind is more predictable and easier to live with than a strange invisible wizard in a magical house. I'm taking my chances with the Wind."

"But it will sweep you away!" Gracie looked at his son, Aiden. The boy had seemed enchanted by the pictures. Even now, his brows were pinched in worry.

Luke pulled his son and his wife to himself. "We would rather risk the mysteries of the Wind than the controlling power of the master of this house."

Aiden didn't seem persuaded, but his mother turned him toward the exit. They picked up their luggage, which was by the door, and in a moment they were outside. They were ready to leave. It was almost as if nothing would have persuaded them to stay.

When the door closed behind them, she sensed silence all around. Jeb stood at the top of the stairs, watching. From their various places in the hallways, the others looked on, horrified. They had until dusk to find a new place. God help them.

"I feel sorry for Aiden," Josiah said, coming over to his mother.

Gracie pulled him against herself. "I hope he makes it." She glanced at Jeb again. Would the boy be a victim of his father's obstinance?

Jeb walked down the stairs, and as he descended, the tenants looked upon him differently. From their awed expressions, Gracie knew the images they had seen had deepened their awareness of who he was and what he could do. Jeb came over to Gracie and patted her on the shoulder.

"Well done," he said softly.

She smiled, and goosebumps ran up her arms. She had done something good. She had made him happy! He went into the parlor and soon the room was filled with tenants wanting time with him. The happy chatter of tenants softened as people went about their morning chores, a lightness in their step and a joy in their laughter.

~~~~~

It was late afternoon days later when Gracie hurried to the door. She hoped — as she did whenever she heard the bell these days — that Aiden and his mother, maybe even Luke, had returned.

But it was someone altogether abhorrent to her.

If it had been the face of the Wind again, this man wouldn't have been more unwelcome. Gracie stood at the door, speechless.

The tall, slouching man who waited on the porch should not be here at all. Of all the people who would have wanted to come, he was the very last person she would ever have imagined.

Here stood Benjamin, her husband.

Like a wildfire spreading with a whipping wind, his presence reignited all her old feelings of inadequacy, all her fears, in every part of her body.

But just as this old sense of identity began to awaken, she remembered — he had thrown her and the kids to the Wind.

What kind of man did that?

"Hi, Grace," Benjamin said, looking her up and down, as if she was
~~~~~

a sack of flour he had purchased from the mill. Property to use. Once again, she was nothing special.

In the far recesses of her mind, she heard Jeb's words. "You are altogether beautiful." Those words grew inside her, turning her attitude indignant. She was a person, not property. She was lovely inside, Jeb had said so.

Having been with Jeb and the tenants, she knew what it meant to be appreciated, to be valued.

But then she again knew the truth. She'd been a failure as Benjamin's wife. That was the real her. The one Jeb didn't know about. Yet.

Gracie's shoulders slouched with the burden of it, and she almost sensed Benjamin's chin lift in triumph at the defeat filling her. She hated feeling this way. Why did he have to find her? *God, if only the Wind took him.*

"Yes?" she asked, making no effort to allow him inside.

"Looks like I found you," he said, waving the boarding house flyer. "You didn't think you could hide for long, did you?"

Gracie was torn. She wanted to do what pleased Jeb, but her whole being hated Ben.

Little fingers slipped into her waistband. It was Josiah. Then Franky firmly slid his hand into hers. Then the baby kicked. Was it her stress that made the baby respond like that? Or was it solidarity? The whole family, against Ben.

Having her boys next to her gave her courage. He should leave. *Leave,* she thought. But the words would not come. The door was supposed to be open to anyone who came. He had a flyer. He was to be welcomed in.

She swallowed away the bile in her throat. "Have you had any of the water?" she asked, pointing at the fountain outside. If he went to the fountain, she could lock the door behind him.

Benjamin turned to survey the lawn. It was green now, a result of all the tenants caring for the grass and flowers, the watering and weeding. No longer were there broken shutters and grimy windows. Everyone had pitched together, working faithfully to make the place look its very best. Hard work had turned a broken down place into a lush home. Their boarding house was beautiful. She knew it.

Benjamin sneered, and his face told her all she needed to know. He didn't want the water, and he didn't like her new home. He didn't belong. He turned back to her and rolled his eyes in condescension.

She knew, if he would but drink some of the water, he would make a significant choice. He'd either flee to the woods or begin to change.

Truth be told, she didn't want him to change. She didn't want him around her or the boys. Why did he have to come? She had been free!

"Aren't you going to invite me in? What's wrong with you?"

"Oh, right." She stepped back so he could cross the threshold. He entered and dropped his coat by the door, stomping his muddy shoes in the entryway. She didn't close the door yet, in case he wanted to leave.

Ben's criticism hurt, awakening all the other moments he demeaned her in her past life with him. Practically all of their moments together. And now, here he was, making a mess in Jeb's house. She was supposed to ask him if he was hungry. She was supposed to ask him if he needed a place to stay. But she didn't want to offer it. He couldn't stay.

The tips of the trees of the woods beyond trembled, and the dead hay field swayed with a breeze. The Wind was awakening. She couldn't kick him out now, what with it being almost dusk and all, but it was a long time till tomorrow and the burden of his presence stole all her stamina. And her joy.

Benjamin tore Josiah's hand from Gracie's waistband and drew the child toward himself. "Aren't you gonna welcome your daddy?"

Fear widened the boy's eyes. "Welcome, Daddy," he whispered, and he glanced up the stairway, his gaze resting on the door at the top of the stairs. She willed the door to open. Jeb would see he was a dangerous man, might even chase him away. Ben couldn't stay more than tonight. He couldn't stay. But he acted as if he owned the place.

Just then, Smith came in from the back door at the end of the downstairs hall, his arms full of a large basket of oranges. He walked toward them down the hall, a smile spreading across his face when he saw the guest.

"Welcome!" he said cheerily. "So glad to have you here." His smile weakened as he looked at Gracie, and his eyebrows pinched a bit in the middle. "Everything okay, Gracie?"

Her tension was evident, no doubt about that. Trying to shake off her tumultuous feeling, she was simultaneously on the verge of tears and on the brink of a scream. "Yeah," she said. *No, it wasn't okay*. That was clear. Her beautiful life was ruined. That man had found her. He'd take her away. Again, she glanced at Jeb's door. Why wasn't he coming down?

Smith set the basket of oranges on the floor by the diningroom door, then pointing at the basket, directed it to its place. It rose into the air and floated off through the dining room and into the kitchen.

Gracie watched Benjamin's face morph from greasy arrogance to stunned puzzlement to sheer horror. His eyes met hers, seeking an explanation.

She wouldn't do him the favor.

"Are you here to stay?" She prayed he wasn't.

He blinked away the confusion, focusing on her again. "No, I got here just in time. You need to be rescued from your own bad choices. Again! We're going home." He glanced at the doorway to the dining room where the basket had floated, then back at her with a self-satisfied look, as if he would rescue her from this terrible place where she lived.

Gracie checked the sky behind him. The sun had begun to sink behind the trees and it would soon be dusk. She wasn't going anywhere. The Wind was about to hunt!

"We are home." She braced herself for his reaction. Josiah had pulled away from his father and hid behind her now, his warmth giving her strength.

"That so?" Benjamin snarled. "You've never been good at making a home. I guess they have low standards here."

Smith made a gasping sound and took a step forward. "Watch it, mister. Gracie here is our house mother. It wouldn't have been a home without her. So keep your words civil, or else."

"What are you gonna do about it?" Benjamin took a stalking step toward Smith, his chin raised in challenge, but wisely not touching him. She saw a cruel light come to life in Benjamin's eyes — the one that always meant she was in for it. She prayed he wouldn't hurt Smith.

"Then I'll take the boys." He lunged for Josiah. "They belong to me, and the law is on my side." But before he could grasp the boy, Josiah and Franky scurried halfway up the staircase, out of reach.

Gracie needed to keep the peace here. The boys trusted her to keep them safe, and keeping Benjamin happy was the only way to do that. Until morning.

She wasn't leaving, and she wasn't letting the boys go anywhere at this time of day. And she could hardly let Ben go out into the Wind. She'd have to keep Ben inside, at least for now. If only Jeb would come. Jeb would scare him away, she was sure of it.

The idea came suddenly. Dessert was the answer. He was a sucker for sweets.

"Benjamin, would you like something to eat?" she asked, pointing the way to the dining room. It wasn't a meal time, but she could get coffee and cake for him, if only to keep him calm. Though the food sometimes changed people, she was willing to take any gamble, if only to keep the peace.

She led the way into the dining room. Again, she felt a hard kick vibrate along her belly. Was the baby telling her something? As she glanced back toward Benjamin, her gaze was drawn past him and up the curving staircase to the image of the storm-cast ship.

She felt like she was on that ship right now. *We are going to die! Where are you?* She needed Jeb to calm the Wind that she had welcomed into the boarding house — almost as if Benjamin was an extension of that Wind outside.

Why do you doubt? The words from the story seemed to answer her, prodding her to keep positive.

They passed by the painting of the dark valley, and she knew how frightened those sheep were. But they were safe, because the shepherd kept them safe. She could do this.

She waved her hand at the table, directing the tablecloth and dishes to arrange themselves for the five of them. Benjamin frowned as he looked from her to the floating tablecloth. She did her best to ignore him as she attempted to faithfully offer Jeb's hospitality. For Jeb, not for herself.

Steaming coffee and a freshly made carrot cake came floating in on a tray, and she directed them to the center of the table.

Benjamin yelped and jumped up as the tray settled closer to his seat. "What is this voodoo?" He scrambled back toward the wall, as far as he could get from the table. "What are you doing, Grace? What's wrong with you?"

Gracie ignored his words with a forcefully calm blink and directed the cake knife to slice a triangle of carrot cake and place it on his dish. She knew where she wanted to put this knife, and it shamed her to even think it. But this man was no good. He shouldn't be here.

With tight lips, she poured some warm cream cheese frosting over the top of the cake piece. This was Benjamin's favorite dessert, the way he liked it, and she hoped he would at least taste Jeb's food. It might make him nice for a couple of hours. She sliced pieces for herself and the others.

"Come, Benjamin. It's a delicious carrot cake." She took a bite of her cake and tried with difficulty to swallow. It was delicious, but her stomach was queasy from Benjamin's unwelcome presence.

Her husband nervously returned to the table and waved his hand over the top of the cake and coffee tray. "No strings," he said. "How are you doing this?"

There were no strings, but those hairline veins had to be working in this room somehow. And that meant this was all coming from Jeb's life-force.

"It's one of the cool things about this place," Smith said, trying to ease the tension. "A kinda magic that makes life easy." He took a bite of the cake. "Wow, Gracie. This is fantastic."

The boys likewise settled down to the cake on their plates.

She clenched her jaw as she directed the coffee pot to fill the adults' cups and then gave milk to the boys.

Benjamin had to decide whether to leave or accept the terms of this dining room. She'd seen others flee at this point and honestly expected he would leave her for good. Near dusk or not. But instead, he surprised her by sitting down.

If I had really wanted him to leave, I wouldn't have given him carrot cake, she thought, hoping her hospitality hadn't deserted her completely. She couldn't understand the feeling inside of her. Panic mixed with calm, as if a wild lion was sleeping and if she was quiet enough, she could survive.

Benjamin ate some more of the cake, and the slight pleasurable murmur that came from him softened her heart a little more toward him. She recalled, there were some days when he had been good to her. A long time ago, before his co-workers had deleted his name from his life's work. He had been whole once, and that trauma had taken the life from him. He'd just shriveled up inside.

That was why she'd stayed as long as she had. She pitied him for that and wanted him to not feel so unseen.

When he was just about done with his cake, he looked at her and must have seen the pity on her face. He set his fork down and said, "I really miss you, Grace. I miss this cake. I came here to get ya. Please come home." His words were civil, echoes of the love they'd had once upon a time.

But then the civility mixed with all the incivility she'd endured, instantaneously causing a storm inside, anxiety and disgust and guilt and pity. She was his wife. She belonged to him. Maybe she should go with him.

But her heart feared leaving this home. He was as bad as the storm. She'd let the Wind take her before she'd go home with Benjamin.

Jeb had not come down, and she so needed him. *Where are you, Jeb? Oh, Jeb.* She remembered a painting of barrels of water turning to wine. Jeb would do that. Jeb could turn something base into something miraculous. That was what she needed now. She needed Jeb to come and save her before Ben got his way. Because he always got his way.

Benjamin reached for a second piece of cake, and she breathed out in relief. She still had time.

Smith directed the serving utensil to serve him a large piece. "So tell me about yourself," he said, redirecting Ben's attention. Smith glanced at Gracie, and she knew he was attempting to help her out of her distress. Thank God for Smith.

She leaned back in her chair, the stress and relief playing havok on her mind, both fighting for control. *Calm down, just eat.* Each step was purposeful. Just as she sliced her fork into the cake for a second bite, a cramp radiated throughout her lower abdomen. Gracie bent inward to endure the pain. She pressed her hands over and under her distended stomach.

Oh, no. Not now. She cringed, hoping they were false contractions. It was still two weeks too early for the baby. Certainly the little one was feeling her tension here. *Calm down, Gracie. Calm down.*

Benjamin did not notice her discomfort. He took another bite of cake and answered Smith's question. "I'm a scientist," he said proudly. "Pretty good one. I've created all sorts of famous inventions." He smiled, but she saw the strain at the edge of his eyes.

She tensed even more, because this was Benjamin's point of greatest anger, and once he started talking about it, she'd end up being assaulted physically or, worse, verbally.

She leaned back in her chair, trying to appear as inconspicuous as possible as the men spoke about his discoveries. Smith was genuinely interested in the details of the invention. Next to Smith on the table was his phone. Thank God he didn't fact-check search for Benjamin's achievements, because he would immediately find that those inventions were credited to others. Ben's name was nowhere on the patents, as if he hadn't invested his whole life into that research and development but rather had disappeared from history. Most of the time, people called him a liar for even claiming credit. That was why he hid that fact like a contagious disease. Whenever anyone discovered the truth, Benjamin would become a monster, lashing out with words and hands. Trembling raced through her as she remembered.

Again, the question surfaced: *Why did he have to come?* She had been so happy here, without him. Free, loved, seen, valuable. She'd given him the due hospitality. It was time for him to leave. There was time before dusk. He could get . . . somewhere safe, if he left now.

Another cramp grabbed her middle, and this time it was so painful that she gripped the edge of the table, her knuckles whitening.

"Mommy, are you okay?" Franky said, deep concern etched on his face.

She bit her bottom lip and endured through the pain. Franky dropped his spoon and hurried over.

"I'll be fine," she whispered to her son when it was over.

But the men in their intense conversation still hadn't noticed. Her pain had kept her from being able to follow the topic. That was when she saw tears in Benjamin's eyes. What was going on? She focused on their conversation again.

"Can you sue them?"

"Not the way they wrote the confidentiality agreement," Benjamin explained. He slammed his hand onto the table. "They erased me from all my work!"

Her breath caught. *It had begun.* How had Smith gotten Benjamin to share his secret? She watched her husband nervously. Now what would he do? Who would he hit? "I couldn't take them to court because of my signature. I had no idea what I was signing. In all that legal mumbo jumbo, they stole it from me." He wiped his cheek. Was he crying? "Honestly, it was over before it began. As if I was invisible to them. Never there. Did nothing. But it was my baby. My life project." Ben's voice broke again and her pity awakened into compassion for a moment.

Smith stretched his arm around the back of Benjamin's chair. "Look, man, if there's anything I've learned from Jeb Sheppard, it's this. I am seen. I am known. I am valued. It's a shame what they did to you out there, but here at this boarding house, we try to be more." Smith nodded, as if deciding how to proceed. "So, how do you deal with such great disappointment? I don't know what I'd do."

"I take it okay," Benjamin said, glancing at Gracie.

At that look, all the abuse came into the space between them and she cringed. Benjamin always took it out on her.

Benjamin's attention dropped to his lap, and he spoke again. "That's not exactly true," he said. "I admit, it makes me mad. Every day I walk past the plaque that those men got for my work, and it infuriates me. I can't get rid of my fury."

His gaze rested on Gracie, eyebrows pinched in pain, as if he wanted to say something but couldn't find the words. What was it about Smith that got Benjamin to be so honest? She felt strange inside.

Then she looked at the air above them. She saw it. The life-force. That same multi-hued phosphorescent substance that ran out of the glass heart, throughout the house, and within the hairline veins around the pictures was in the dust particles above them! Jeb's lifeblood was even in the air! Benjamin was inhaling it.

Oh, glory. What did this mean? Pins and needles prickled up her back, and she focused on what was happening with Ben.

"People out there are all takers," Smith said. "We try to be different in this boarding house. Take Gracie here. From day one, she treated me respectful-like — as if I mattered. She sees me."

Both men looked over at her, and a flicker of concern crossed their faces. But she pulled on a smile to hide her discomfort, and their attention turned back to the conversation.

"What she did meant so much to me," Smith continued. "In spite of being pregnant, she fought the Wind for my life. She physically pulled me from the power of the Wind that first day. Then she loved me as if I wasn't the broken down person I was when I came to the door. She's a wonderful woman. She sees beyond who I am here on the surface."

Benjamin looked down at his hands again as he folded and unfolded them on his lap.

Smith kept talking. "Gracie sees deeper into me. Because Jeb does. I think that's why I want to give the same to you."

Her husband lifted his head to Smith, his eyebrows twisted in confusion. "What do you mean?"

"Benjamin, I want you to know what it's like to be here. I think you should hang around. I think you should stay. I think you should get to know Jeb."

The words startled Gracie. Guilt mixed with horror. It should have been her inviting him to stay, but from the beginning she'd wanted him to turn back around and leave her life forever. Did she want Benjamin to be here? She'd felt so free with him gone from her life. But then again, the air was filled with Jeb.

Smith pushed his chair back. "I want to show you something," he said, and welcomed Benjamin to join him at the stairway where he drew him to look at a small picture at the lowest step.

Gracie clapped for the room to reset itself, but as she followed them out, another cramp struck her. The windows told her it was dusk already. She couldn't get to the hospital until morning, and she prayed she'd make it till then. These had to be false cramps. It was still too early. But what if the baby wanted to come now? Her boys stood faithfully by her side. By their troubled expressions, she could see they recognized her trouble and didn't know how to help. She braced herself on Franky's shoulder.

"Josiah, please go and find Mrs. Plumquest. I need her fast," she whispered.

Josiah nodded and ran up the stairs, passing Benjamin and Smith at the lower step.

Gracie held onto the edge of the banister behind Smith, focusing on their words to chase away the pain, and watched the little portrait as it morphed. It was a portrait montage, and she knew it well, loved it dearly.

The image was a close-up of a man with his head hanging low, so only the top of his head and his cheekbones were visible at first, showing other glimpses of his face as the story progressed. No other people would appear, and only their voices were audible. The focus was only the man.

At the beginning of the moving tableau, he was a child, and he grew to be a man, always with his head hanging low and tears on his cheeks.

At the start of the story, words of children all about him could be heard mocking him about his parentage.

"You don't even know who your father is."

"Your mother is a prostitute."

"You always were unwanted."

"You were an accident your mother couldn't hide."

The boy grew older, and as his physique changed, the taunts grew, with teen voices telling him he was a freak, a misfit, unloved, unwelcome. He grew older to words calling him a nutcase, a loony, a deviant, a nonconformist, a better-than-thou.

In the final stage of the tableau, he was a man. His head jerked left and right as the sounds of physical beatings echoed forth. At the telltale sound of a sharp whip, his face began to bleed. He spoke not—only grunted as he was struck and taunted.

"He saved others, but he can't even save himself." The words struck as hard as the abuse.

"See if his God will save him." Their laughter was full of hatred.

And then there was silence, and the bleeding face became the face of a dead man.

When the picture stilled, Benjamin brushed tears away with his hands and wiped his palms on his jeans. "Who is that man?" he asked.

"A Man of Sorrows," Smith said. "He knows what it's like to be misunderstood, unappreciated, unseen. And when I see this, I feel . . ."

"Seen," Benjamin answered for him.

Smith nodded. "Precisely."

As Benjamin sighed loudly, he glanced at Gracie, then spun toward her. "Are you okay?" He wiped his tears again and his voice was edged with fear. He drew near and put his arm around her back to support her. "You don't look right. Is it the baby?"

The sensation of his arm around her, in honest concern, overwhelmed Gracie and tears she'd been suppressing made their way down her cheeks. She nodded just as another labor pain struck her.

She wanted to pull away from his touch. These were the hands that had struck her. His was the tongue that had lashed her to no end. But she could do nothing but lean into his arm right now.

Mrs. Plumquest ran down the stairs toward Gracie. "Sorry I took so long," she said. She gasped and pointed to the puddle under Gracie. "Looks like Baby's on its way. Can you gentlemen help me bring this dear one up to her room?"

She ran up the stairs ahead of them, and as she passed by Jeb's room, she called out, "Master, we'll be needing you." She hurried to the closet and pulled out extra sheets and bedding, which she had spread over the bed by the time Gracie arrived, carried by Smith and Benjamin.

Gracie collapsed onto the bed and her knees flexed up. Mrs. Plumquest shut the door behind the men as she prepared Gracie for the birth. "Ye might have been planning for a hospital birth, dearie, but time says it's a home birth for this'un."

Gracie didn't care. The pain of labor was nothing to the confused anger she felt inside at Benjamin being here. It was his fault the baby was coming early. He shouldn't have come. It was his fault she had a broken home. His fault everything bad had happened in her life. And yet, the dust particles in the air and the pictures on the wall and the glass heart down the hall told her there was more going on than met the eye . . .

With that thought, she passed out.

~~~~~

Gracie awoke to a darker room. Jeb sat in a chair next to her, holding her hand, and Mrs. Plumquest was gone, as were Benjamin and Smith. It
~~~~~

was just her and Jeb.

Her heart lurched. Had she given birth? Was the baby dead? She cradled her stomach, relieved to find the baby was still there. But something was wrong. She felt it between her and the landlord.

Jeb stroked her hand. "I met Benjamin," he said in a gentle voice.

His words made her sad. She'd missed their introduction. If she had been there, she could have encouraged Jeb to send the man packing. Clearly, he hadn't.

She pulled her hand out of his in disappointment. She didn't want him to know Benjamin. Her two lives were supposed to stay as far apart as the moon from Earth. "Where were you? I wanted you to send him away."

He took her hand again. "I was with you."

No. He hadn't been there.

But then she remembered the dust in the air. That was him. He had been there—the whole time. She glanced apologetically back at him, into the void of his hood, and she startled at what she saw. For a moment, the darkness under his hood was not a shadow. The sparkly dust in the air gathered into that space, showing a man's face, a concerned face.

More startling was that she recognized him! His was the face of that Man of Sorrows image downstairs. The man in the boat, the shepherd, the man at the tree.

Now he had no tears. A kind, gentle, concerned face studied hers. Jeb's warm, loving human face gave her the revitalizing feeling of being seen for who she was, of being known, of being cherished.

Oh, how she loved his face. Her glimpse was momentary, and too soon it was a shadow again.

"Jeb," she said, squeezing his hand tighter. She wasn't sure if she should tell him she saw his face. More pressing was Benjamin and his cruelty. "I don't want him here. Will you make him leave?"

"Dear one," said Jeb. His other hand brushed her sweaty hair away from her forehead, then he wet a facecloth with some water and wiped her face. "None will be turned away."

It wasn't fair. Tears trickled down her cheeks. She would lose her peace here. "But he didn't drink the water. Let the Wind take him. He was so wicked to me and the boys. He threw us out to the Wind. Is it right for him to be here? He should go."

"Whosoever wills, let them come. He desires to be here. I desire for him to be here."

Her strength left her. Jeb wanted it. Weeping took over. That meant she would have to leave then. Just when she'd found a new home for her and her boys, and just as this new one was about to be born. Again, she'd be homeless. Again, they'd face the Wind.

"But I don't want to leave you," she said. "Jeb, I want to be here. But not with him. He has to go, not me."

"I know."

His words meant something else. She thought about what she knew of Jeb. The Man of Sorrows tableau came to mind and the abuse that man had endured. Jeb knew. He didn't agree, but he understood her feelings. And more than that, he had felt her pain.

"Are they all you?" she asked, her suspicion finding words. "In those pictures? Are they you?"

He nodded. She searched for his face again in the shadow of his hood and glimpsed a smile.

Oh, she loved Jeb's smile. She wanted more of that smile. She'd do anything to have that smile shining down on her all the time. Jeb had his own secrets, his own reasons for keeping his face hidden. But he showed them in the portraits. He wasn't invisible. He was very much seen.

A labor pain struck her again, and she gripped his hand for strength, counting all the way to forty. Jeb held her firmly, giving her strength to endure.

Gracie caught her breath. "So, you know what it's like," she said, panting. "All the things he did to me. You've felt it."

"Yes," he said, and his thumb caressed her hand. "None of my tenants come in here with perfect resumés."

"You're right." She chuckled at the irony, thinking of all the ragtag tenants they housed. Moreso, he'd taken a chance on a lousy housewife and her little boys and given her the chance to run his home. "I think this baby's coming soon," she said, feeling her body changing. "Where's Mrs. Plumquest?"

"She's getting dinner ready."

That was important. She thought through all her evening duties. Everyone would be hungry, and there was so much to be done. Thank God for Mrs. Plumquest. But very soon she would have a baby in her arms and work would have to wait indefinitely. But she needed Mrs. Plumquest here!

"So, let's talk about Benjamin," he said with a tender squeeze of her hand.

All around her, the glittery dust circled the air, almost strengthening her for this unpleasant conversation.

Tears flowed again. "It's too much," Gracie said. "The baby. Benjamin. His words." She looked into his hood, hoping for another glimpse of his kind face.

"I understand," Jeb said. And she knew from the tone of his voice that he had lived through the same, or worse. People had been bad to him, too.

"Why are people so mean?" she said, scratching the edge of her eye. The Wind was like people, and people like the Wind.

"Not everyone is," he said.

She turned to him and this time saw a clear, full view of his lovely eyes. With that vision, she knew that people in this boarding house had been freed from the fear of the Wind. She'd been freed from it, too. And that fear was what made people selfish and cruel. What had he said? The Wind fed on the pain and suffering of this world. It was almost as if Benjamin's fury — and everyone else's — caused the Wind.

"My people are kind, generous, and hospitable," Jeb reminded her.

She nodded, understanding what she needed to do. "Do you want Benjamin to be a tenant?" she asked.

"Do you?" he replied.

The question was deeper than anything she'd ever heard. In it, she saw herself being thrown out with her boys in late afternoon with no money to her name. She saw no room in the women's shelter and the one-night plan to stay in the ER. She saw that nameless man being sucked away by the Wind, and she recalled the face of the Wind telling her not to meddle.

"You see Benjamin as he was. And I understand you've suffered much." As he said this, under the hood she saw him, sad, much as he'd been in the weeping man tableau. "But I see him as he can be. As he will be." With this, he sat closer to her, and his eyes, brown and passionate, met hers.

The top of his hood slipped back slightly, and she saw it. Perhaps even the reason he hid his face. His cheeks were scarred, and she recalled the blood in the same tableau. Then she realized why the image had struck her so deeply. He had remained true to himself, even from his youth. He had not given in to the words hurled at him. The words had struck him as much as the weapons. He was a Man of Sorrows and understood suffering well.

"Jeb, do you know I can see your face?" she risked asking.

"Can you, now?"

"I see your scars."

He sighed then and pressed her hand to his lips. "Yes, you see me, don't you?"

"I'm sorry they hurt you. All your life you've been attacked."

"But Gracie, this makes me able to feel your hurt. I know you. I can be here for you."

A labor pain struck right then, and Gracie's back arched in response. Counting helped her endure, and she got to fifty seconds. The child would be coming soon. Jeb held her hand firmly, stroking her arm with his other hand. "Now we'll call Mrs. Plumquest," he said, his brown eyes still on her.

"Hurry," she said, catching her breath, looking at him with a prayer to always see his face. It made life easier to live. Oh, that she could always see his eyes!

"Shall I also call Benjamin?" he asked.

This time, she remembered his kindness in their first years together, until his tragedy at work. Memories she thought she'd forgotten. Was it true he had truly cared?

Jeb wanted her to separate herself from the pain, as he had in the picture. She had to let go. To . . . forget. If not forget, to start again. To give it to the dust. Let the dust change her and Benjamin.

It was a big ask.

She acknowledged that this home could be a haven for Ben, too. If she was willing to risk it.

"It's not easy, master," she said. What would she have to put up with? Would he even change? What if he continually accused her? What if he lied about her to her again, making her wonder what was true? What if he did it in front of her friends here? She'd die of shame.

"We must endure many trials to run this boarding house," Jeb replied. He wiped her forehead with the damp cloth again. "And I assure you, he will not be harsh with you."

He assures me. She held to this promise as tightly as her hand clenched the sheet.

In the end, Jeb was the landlord. And he had never failed her. If he thought it was right, it would be right. "Please bring Benjamin in . . . I need him," she added, as an afterthought that she realized was true. She needed the other Benjamin. The one who hadn't been stomped out by injustice at work. The one he was inside and not the one he'd become. *Bring Benjamin,* she prayed inside.

Jeb lifted his hand toward the door and the latch opened. "Benjamin, come on in," he said.

Benjamin was waiting just outside. He rushed in and hurried to her side.

She reached out to him. What could she say? She didn't want to give him any stipulations. She wanted him to live here with Jeb. To be safe, free, seen with Jeb. To inhale the air. "Ben, please stay with us at this boarding house." Her body was signaling that cramps would intensify very soon. Once the birthing started, she wouldn't be in her right mind. She needed to take care of this now.

"Drink the water. Eat the food. Become a tenant," she said. "Get to know Jeb."

"I saw some of the paintings on the wall," Ben said, looking at Jeb rather than at Gracie. His whole posture and voice seemed different. "I do want to stay, if you'll have me, sir."

"By all means."

Benjamin smiled and turned his attention to Gracie as Jeb left the room. Mrs. Plumquest came in with some hot water and towels. She checked the progress of the birth and then patted Gracie's leg. "Little one is on the way, dearie."

Benjamin scooted closer and took her hand, and with her husband at her side, Gracie moved through the exciting and painful process of bringing a child into the world.

~~~~~

Benjamin held their daughter and a warm, hopeful feeling pulsed inside of Gracie. The baby was perfect, and they'd named her Faith. The little girl looked up at Ben in trust and he gazed into her eyes, visibly smitten.

Gracie smiled. It could work. Under Jeb's supervision, with the tenants all around, she had allies to keep Ben accountable. It had to work.

What was the option? Send him out, hopeless, into the Wind? She'd never do such a thing. She'd seen the other tenants soften, just by being with Jeb, living in his home, breathing the air, and remembering who he was by the tableaus on the wall.

Ben hadn't apologized, and to be honest, his apologies had never meant anything. Instead of an apology, he was different. She held to Jeb's promise that Ben would not be harsh with her.

This was a safe house. Her boys were safe, she was safe, Ben was safe, and — she hoped — her marriage would soon be safe.

Benjamin handed Faith to Gracie, and as she took the baby into her arms, her husband pulled his arms around her and held her in a warm embrace. "You are amazing," he whispered into her ear. Goosebumps ran up and down her arm at these words. They were almost magical.

The boys ran over and threw their arms around them, making a unified whole. Gracie sighed and a little tear dripped down her cheek.

It was beautiful to have a home with those she loved.

A knock on the bedroom door startled them from their reverie. Not wishing to leave this bond, she called the door to open on its own. Jeb Sheppard stepped in, carrying a tray of crystal glasses with a pitcher of water.

Behind him, the other tenants peeked into the room, trying to catch a glimpse of the new baby. She welcomed them all in, handing Faith to Mrs. Plumquest and embracing everyone. She gave an extra big hug to Smith. "Thank you," she whispered in his ear.

The room was full of excitement and joy, a testament to the success of this boarding house. Everyone here had been freed of their fear of the Wind. This was what the city needed.
~~~~~

If this home could grow to fit anyone who had no home, if it could bring restoration like the one she'd lived through. If it could make the unseen people seen and loved, they should increase their efforts at distributing those flyers. She was determined to motivate everyone to bring in as many people as they could.

"Anyone thirsty?" Jeb asked, pouring a cup of water. He smiled at her from under his hood, and she was not surprised by her new ability to clearly see his full, beautiful, scarred face.

THE END

MEET THE AUTHORS

Darlene N. Böcek is an award-winning author of YA Sci-fi. She is a pastor's wife living on a farm in Izmir, Turkey. She and her husband have a plethora of pets named after pop culture heroes, a son named after a sci-fi hero, two daughters practicing science-fact (dentistry), and a daughter studying to be an author. Her well-acclaimed first book, YA historical *Trunk of Scrolls,* was re-released this year. See her books and join her club at *darlenenbocek.com.* (Editor's Note: Darlene also published stories in *Moonlight and Claws* and *Don't Go in the Water* by Ye Olde Dragon Books!)

H.L. Burke has written more books than she can count—because she's written a lot of books, not just because she can't count very high. Her current focus is the *Supervillain Rehabilitation Project* superhero series, starting with *Reformed.* She's also written multiple fantasy novels including the *Spellsmith & Carver Steampunk* series and *Ashen.* She is an admirer of the whimsical, a follower of the Light, and a believer in happily ever after. Find her at: *www.hlburkeauthor.com*

Jordan Campbell was born in California and moved to Maine when he was eleven. All through his childhood, Jordan had a book in his hand nearly continuously. Educated at the University of Maine, majoring in English, Jordan has had almost a dozen short stories published in the last two years. He is excited to bring his stories to the world. Jordan's first story for Ye Olde Dragon Books was "Neher, Demon of the River," which was published in the third Classic Monsters Anthology, *Don't Go in the Water.*

Rosemarie DiCristo loves co-writing Ye Olde Dragon stories with Pam Halter, and since they both love the beach, the setting of "The First" was a no-brainer. Rosemarie dedicates this story to her parents, who weren't aliens (but to her adolescent brain, they sometimes seemed to be). She also gives a shout-out to the real

Claudia-the-she-guard, who wouldn't let Rosemarie stray one inch off public property when scouting story locations in the gated community of Breezy Point, The Rockaways, Queens. (Editor's Note: Rosemarie has also written for several of our other anthologies: *Tales from the Forest, Don't Go in the Water* and *Perchance to Dream*.)

Jim Doran is a genre writer who enjoys transporting his readers into worlds of wonder, mystery, and danger. Whether it's the fairytale hijinks in the five novels of his *Kingdom Fantasy* series or his multi-genre short stories, Jim has been published *in Havok, Every Day Fiction*, Ye Olde Dragon's *Moonlight and Claws* and *Who's the Monster?* and *Havok's Casting Call* anthologies. When he's not writing, he's usually enjoying the seasons in Michigan or playing a board game.

Pam Halter is a children's/middle grade/YA Author and a picture book editor who lives in Southern New Jersey. Her answer to the social media question, "If you could have a superpower, what would it be?" is almost always, "The ability to turn invisible!" In her and Rosemarie DiCristo's story, "The First," they call it "veiling". Fortunately, Pam is not invisible on the web. Read more about her at www.pamhalter.com. (Editor's note: Pam has been published in all of our anthologies except the first one!)

Michelle Levigne fell into fantastical fiction writing in college and has yet to escape. She has a bunch of useless degrees in theater, English, film/communication, and writing. She writes in science fiction and fantasy, YA, suspense, women's fiction, and sub-genres of romance. Her stories for Ye Olde Dragon anthologies are part of *The Enchanted Castle Archives* series. The heroine of the shorts, 'Na (short for Belladonna) is the daughter of the heroes of the novels. Her training includes the Institute for Children's Literature, proofreading at an advertising agency, and working at a community newspaper. She is a tea snob and freelance edits for a living, but only enough to give her time to write. Her newest crime against the literary world is the storytelling podcast, *Ye Olde Dragon's Library*, which features audio of new books, as well as chats with authors of fantastical fiction. Be afraid… be very afraid.

Despite that, please visit her websites: *Mlevigne.com* and *YeOldeDragonBooks.com*, or her blog, *MichelleLevigne.blogspot.com*.

D.A. Randall is the fantasy and paranormal thriller pen name of Randall Allen Dunn, who was raised on a steady diet of *Star Trek* and *The Twilight Zone* before pursuing his studies of *Buffy, the Vampire Slayer, Harry Potter, The Lunar Chronicles*, Richard Matheson, H.G Wells, Edgar Allan Poe, and *Doctor Who*. He has taught writing, acting, and storytelling techniques to teens and adults. He now writes fantasy and paranormal thrillers that read like blockbuster movies. Action-packed, fast-paced, and fun, with larger-than-life heroes wrestling with moral dilemmas and diabolical villains. He publishes Character Entertainment stories that build character through fiction, demonstrating courage, friendship, acceptance, faith, and self-sacrifice. You can find his books online, and subscribe to his newsletter for upcoming releases at *www.RandallAllenDunn.com*

Samantha Seidel devotes her time to discovering unique vocabulary, designing whimsical websites, and writing thought-provoking fantasies. Based in Tampa, FL, she's working with an agent to get her first book published. She spends time daydreaming new stories, crocheting adorable critters, and developing a green thumb. Here's a blurb from her upcoming book, *Foresight*, coming soon. "Stacy Marang wasn't supposed to live. One mad scientist later, and she can see the future. A future riddled with mysteries and military raids." To contact Samantha, visit her website at *www.srsinkfeather.com*.

Stoney M. Setzer lives south of Atlanta, GA. He has a beautiful wife, three wonderful children, and one crazy dog, and his is also a diehard Atlanta Braves fan. He has written a trilogy of novels about small-town amateur sleuth Wesley Winter (*Dead of Winter, Valley of the Shadow*, and *Day of Reckoning*). He has also written a short story anthology *Zero Hour*, featuring Twilight Zone-like stories with Christian themes. Several of his stories are set in the fictional community of Sardis County, Tennessee, including his story in this anthology. He has also had some of his short stories featured in such publications as *Residential Aliens* and *Havok*. Learn more at www.tinniepress.blogspot.com or on Facebook *@stoneymsetzerofficial*. (Editor's note: Stoney Setzer is our hero! He has been in every anthology we've published! That's a record.)

Deborah Cullins Smith has been writing stories ever since she could hold a pencil, but she came to her actual career in writing rather late in life. In 2019, she published the trilogy, **The Last of the Long-Haired Hippies,** in a rapid-release timed for the 50th anniversary of Woodstock, which she covered in great detail in the second volume. *CWG Press* released *Shroud of Darkness, The Birth of the Storm,* and *Victoria's War* over a four-month period, a culmination of almost twenty years in development. Deborah's first Mina Harker adventure, *Mina: Warrior in the Shadows,* won the 2022 Realm Award for Best Horror Novel. Her next novel will continue the saga of Billy the Kid and Mina Harker, which she began in the anthology *Moonlight and Claws* with the story "Habitations of Violence" and continued in *Who's the Monster?* with the story "Phillippe." Her love of historical research makes these books challenging, as she is devoted to maintaining as much historical accuracy as possible while sliding things sideways to suggest that a few characters might be more than we gave them credit for! (No disrespect intended.)

When **Jessica A. Tanner** isn't writing stories full of vivid characters and creatures, she enjoys a view of the Rocky Mountains, takes long walks, and hangs with her many critters. She is a member of the American Christian Fiction Writers (ACFW), Realm Makers, and Wolf Creek Christian Writers Network (WCCWN). Jessica has a short story published in *Looking at Life,* a collection by WCCWN, a testimony in *Twenty-Three Journeys to Christ,* compiled by Gregg Heid, three stories in *A Book of Remembrance: A Collection of Everyday Miracles,* compiled by Lynn Moffett, and several pieces published under the Matter of Faith column of the *Pagosa Sun's Preview.* Her first novel, *Sonji,* is a YA fantasy about a girl and her magical horse. To connect or learn more, please visit *www.jessicaatannerauthor.com*.

So ... WHAT'S NEXT?

Get ready for the next fairytale anthology, coming May 1, 2025.

Brace yourselves ... the Big Bad Wolf is back ... only this time he's not after Red Riding Hood. His mouth is watering for the **THREE LITTLE PIGS.**

So, start brainstorming. Give us your best, your wackiest, your scariest, your funniest, your twistiest (it's a word because we *say so!*) piggy story.

Are they good guys? Bad guys?
Victims? Troublemakers?
Idiots? Role models?
Heroes? Innocent bystanders?
In desperate need of a life coach?
In the wrong place at the wrong time?
Totally oblivious?

Lunch?

Submissions open November 1.
Publication: May 1.

Ready?
Set?
GO!